PART I

THE PAST

Cavaleri Brothers
Book One

THE DEVIL'S DEAL

LILIAN HARRIS

This is a work of fiction. Names, characters, organizations, places, events, and incidences are either products of the author's imagination or used fictitiously.

© 2021 by Lilian Harris. All rights reserved.

No part of this book may be reproduced, or stored in a retrieval system, or transmitted in any form or by any means, electronic, mechanical, photocopying, recording, or otherwise, without the express written permission of the publisher.

Editor/Interior Formatting: CPR Editing

Proofreader: Judy's Proofreading

Cover Design: Black Widow Designs

GOODNESS LIES EVEN IN THE DARKEST OF SHADOWS.

CHIARA
AGE 10

ONE

Dear Diary,
I hate my life.
I hate it here, in this house. In this body. In this world I'm stuck in.
The rooms are big, but the walls squeeze me tight. I can't breathe. It really hurts. All of me hurts. I wish I didn't have to hurt anymore.
Every day, I fight the bad feelings away, wishing I could run away. But I can't. I'm stuck living in this stupid house with my stupid dad.
I'm scared of him and his bad moods. I never know what will make him yell at me and Mom or hit us. He gets mad about everything! What music I like, what shows I want to watch, who I want to be friends with.
I don't even have friends. Not really. No one except Dominic, the

boy I have been friends with since third grade. But I call him Dom. I think I told you that already. That's what his family calls him, so I do too. I don't have any nicknames, but that's because I like my name the way it is.

The other kids at school all suck. They only pretend to like me, but they don't invite me anywhere when they make plans. I know because I hear about the stuff they do together. And when I invite them to my house, they're always busy. I'm not stupid.

I don't know what I did to make them hate me, but I can't make people like me. It's their loss. I want to ask why they never include me, but I chicken out. One time, I heard Caitlin say to another girl that her mom said my dad was dangerous. They stopped talking once they saw me walking by.

Why is my dad dangerous? Do they know he hits me? Hits my mom? No, they can't know. No one does.

Whatever. I don't care. I have Dom. He's a real friend. My best friend in the whole world. We haven't been apart since we first met in class.

But Dad hates Dom and his family. He won't let me be friends with him at all. I couldn't even invite him for any of my birthdays. My stupid dad says they're losers, but that's dumb. He's the loser.

I really don't get why he hates them so much. So what if they don't have as much money as we do? How could my dad hate someone who's so nice to me?

Dominic's family is also much better than ours. His parents really love each other, like for real. I don't remember the last time Dad was nice to Mom.

Dom's parents are so kind to me every time I stop by their bakery. They make the best chocolate chip cupcakes ever.

I'm glad I have Dom. I'd be so alone without him.

My phone buzzes on the nightstand and I pick it up, finding a text message from Dom.

> **Dom:** Hope you're not bored at home. Text me if you are.

Holding my cell phone with one hand, I finish my latest diary entry.

I have to go now, Diary. Dom is calling, and I want to talk to him before my father gets home. Bye!

I decide to call him instead of texting because texting on this stupid Razr phone with the number pad sucks.

When I dial his number, the phone rings for a second before he answers.

"Hey, Chiara," he says cheerfully. "How's your day going? I would invite you over for dinner, but I know your dad hates me, so..."

He laughs, but in a sad way. I feel so bad.

"He doesn't hate you," I lie, trying to sound honest.

But it's no use. He's heard my father tell me to stop being friends with "that boy." But I never listen. He can't control who

I'm friends with while I'm in school. I'm not going to let my dad ruin my entire life. He's already done a great job at it.

"It's okay, Chiara. I don't care what he thinks about me. As long as…" He takes a pause.

"As long as what?"

"As long as you don't agree with him."

"Of course I don't! You're like the best ever. Okay?" My exhale jumps out of me angrily. "Don't let my douchey dad make you think anything else. He hates everyone, anyway. He doesn't even like *me*."

"Douchey dad," he laughs, making me giggle too. "I like that."

"Dominic! Respect!" I hear his mom, Carmella's scolding voice.

"Sorry, Ma," he grumbles. "But it's true."

He lowers his tone to a whisper with that last part, causing us both to let out a giggle.

"Tell Chiara I said hello," his mom continues. "And I miss her coming to the bakery."

"I think she heard you, Ma," he says in a joking way. "You're kind of loud."

"Hey, you'd better behave over there or you're not getting any of that chocolate cake your papa promised to bring home from work."

"Okay, okay. I'm sorry," he mutters. "But I want two slices."

"Dream on. You're barely getting one as it is." I can tell she's kidding, though.

"Tell your mom I miss her too," I jump in between their teasing conversation.

"She misses you too," he tells her.

"Give me the phone," I hear her say, and the next thing I know is her voice coming through the line. "Hey, honey. Is everything okay at home? I haven't seen your mom or you in weeks. I miss you girls stopping by."

"We're okay. The same, you know."

But I don't know. I have no idea how much she knows about my family.

"Yeah, I know, honey. Listen, you're always welcome here. I told your mom the same last time we spoke. You guys are like family to us."

I huff out a defeated breath. My mom loves their bakery. It's the best one in town. She started to go because I'd beg, and the only reason my dad allowed it was because he liked the chocolate cake she'd bring home for him.

Whenever we stop by, my mom and Carmella always have their chats. But my dad hasn't been letting us go lately, saying we go too much, and I'm too embarrassed to tell them that. My dad doesn't let us do anything without his permission.

"You there?" Carmella asks with concern.

"Yeah. I guess."

"You can talk to me, you know? I would never betray your trust, Chiara."

My stomach does this twisty thing and my heart jumps with nerves. I wish I could tell her everything, but I tell no one but my diary.

I clear my throat. "Can I ask you something?"

"Anything."

"Why do you like us? My mom and me? No one seems to. At least no one likes me at school and no one lets me come over. I think it's because…"

I don't finish the sentence. I can't. She'll ask more questions and I won't be able to give her the answers. If my dad finds out I talk bad about him or the family, he'll hurt me.

"Because why?" She sounds genuinely curious about what I have to say.

I gulp down the nerves, the fear. My heart beats loudly in my chest. I can almost hear it. Feel it in my throat.

"I...umm." My voice shakes with dread.

"Whatever you tell me, it stays with us," she reassures me. "You have my word."

I nod on instinct, as though she can see it. "Because of...um... my dad." I let the words tumble out quickly, and they don't stop. "No one likes him, so no one likes me. That's probably why I have no friends other than Dom. He's great, so I don't need anyone else, but it still sucks not to be liked. To be talked about. Please don't tell my mom what I told you! She'll be so sad to know I'm sad."

"Oh, sweetie..." Her voice drifts low and sympathetically. "I won't say anything, but you listen here. You're not your father. No one has a right to judge you for someone else's actions. And those kids at school? Screw 'em."

A teary laugh bubbles out of me. "You just cursed."

"I know," she whispers. "Don't tell Dom."

"I won't," I giggle, wiping under my eye.

"I'm so happy to hear that laugh. Now we both have a little secret between us."

"Thank you for always being nice to me."

"I love you, Chiara. You're like one of my kids. I've got four little knucklehead sons. I need a daughter."

"They're not so bad," I add with a laugh.

"You kidding? They drive me up the wall, especially Enzo and Dante. Those two are the reason I have gray hair."

"Ma!" I hear Dante's voice call out. "When will Dad be home so we can have dinner? I'm starving!"

"You see what I mean?" she asks me. "I just gave them a snack thirty minutes ago. Oy, these boys. Let me go finish cooking before they revolt. Tell your mom I said hello and to call when she can."

"Okay. Tell Dom I said bye."

"I will. Bye, honey."

Long after she hangs up, I lie in my bed, hoping I didn't say more than I should've. More than what can get me hurt.

DOMINIC
AGE 10

As soon as my mom grabbed the phone away, she went into the kitchen to talk to Chiara alone. I hope she didn't say anything embarrassing about me. My mom is definitely good at that. She still expects me to kiss her goodbye when she drops me off at school.

I'm ten now. Not five like Matteo, the baby in the family. I'm the oldest, so I don't know why Mom treats me like a kid.

The kids at school already look at me weird. I don't need to give them another reason not to like me. Kissing my mom is not going to win me any friends.

Whatever.

I don't need them. I have Chiara, and she'll always have me. I don't even know how not to be friends with her. We kind of always were.

I hate that her dad doesn't like me. I'm kind of afraid she'll start hating me too. That maybe he'll make her stop being my friend. I don't want that to ever happen. It's one of my biggest fears, and she has no idea.

For the next hour, I continue doing my homework until Dad gets home from work, and then my brothers and I get to setting the table while he takes a shower.

"Take this," I tell Dante, handing him two plates while taking the other four.

My mom is busy putting some baked ziti and grilled chicken on one of those big oval plates.

"Why do you get so many?" Dante asks, looking annoyed. "I can carry more."

"I'm older. Duh!" I roll my eyes. "And stronger."

"Nuh-uh. You're not strong. I can jump higher than you, and I bet I can pick you up and carry you around."

"Wanna bet?" I ask, putting down the plates on the counter as he does the same.

"Oh, no, you don't!" Mom yells. "You'd better pick those plates up and put them on the table. You get three each, and that's the last I want to hear about it."

"Ugh!" I groan.

"Yeah! In your face," Dante brags as he carries the plates out to the dining room.

"Shut up," I fire back in a whisper so Mom doesn't hear as I follow him out. Dante is a year younger than me and forgets that.

Enzo is placing all the forks around the table as we walk out.

"You two are so slow. I'm already done. See?" He gestures with his hand as he sets the last fork down.

"Shut up, Enzo," Dante and I say simultaneously. He's seven, and just as annoying as Dante.

"What can I do?" Matteo asks as he hops off the sofa, running over to me, excitement filling his big brown eyes. "I want to help too!"

I rub the top of his head, his dark chestnut hair as thick and soft as the rest of ours. "Go get the napkins from Ma."

"Okay!"

He runs off to do just that and is back seconds later, a bunch of white napkins crunched up in his hand. I shake my head with a laugh. He's just so cute.

"How's your *girlfriend?*" Dante teases.

"She's not my—"

"Stop torturing your brother, Dante," my dad says, coming down the stairs.

"Yes, Dad," Dante mumbles, puffing out his cheeks.

"How is Chiara, though, son? We've missed her at the bakery."

"She's okay. It's her dad." I grimace, rolling my eyes. "As usual."

"Poor kid." He shakes his head, his lips turning downward. "Such a nice girl to have a crazy father like that. What a shame."

"Francesco!" Ma says as she walks out with the large plate of food.

Dad smiles, going over to her. "I'm sorry, beautiful wife. I shouldn't have called him crazy in front of the kids." He winks at me before kissing Mom on the cheek. "Let me get that for you."

He takes the food from her hands and places it on the table.

"Finally!" Dante exclaims. "I thought we'd starve to death."

Mom shakes her head. "God help you if you leave one thing on your plate after all that complaining."

Mom and Dad start filling our plates, and once we're all eating, I look around at everyone, knowing how lucky I am to have a normal family and wishing Chiara were part of it.

CHIARA
THREE DAYS LATER

TWO

"Mom! Mom!" I shout, running into the living room where she's wiping the coffee table while Dad watches TV. "Dominic is on the phone, and—"

"Are you fucking kidding me with that stupid boy again?" my dad hollers, running his hand through his black hair, not noticing the tears streaming down my face. Or maybe he notices, but doesn't care.

"But, Dad, he—" I try to explain but he stops me with a sharp rise of his palm.

"I fucking told you about that family! How many damn times? Huh?" His cheeks grow red from the way he shouts. "They're trash! You hear me?" His eyes grow wide, his cheeks getting redder. "And you tarnish our name by associating with them? My own fucking daughter?"

They're not trash! I scream inside my head. *They're better than you! I hate you!*

"Faro! She's crying. Don't you see something's wrong?"

"Was I talkin' to you?" He lifts a hand like he's about to hit her, and I gasp. "Finish cleaning and shut your damn mouth when I'm talkin' to my daughter."

"His mom died, Dad. Can't you be nice for a minute?!" I half-shout, half-sob with a pant. "He can hear everything you're saying." I lift the phone in the air. "Don't you care?"

Mom's body stills. The rag stops moving on the table.

"Wha-what did you say?" She turns to me, straightening up, her brows tightening.

"He said it was a car accident. He said she—"

My chin trembles, tears sting my nose, and my throat grows achy.

"Oh, Mom," I cry, running toward her, phone still in my hand as she holds me tight.

She then takes the phone from me. "Dom, baby, I'm so sorry."

She's crying now, her tears falling faster than mine. There's a brief pause.

"Oh, God. We're coming by the house. Okay? You stay put. We'll be there soon."

She hangs up, holding me with both arms again.

"Go put on your shoes," she tells me.

"You better not think about going there," my dad spits out. "Send some goddamn flowers, but that's it."

She glares at him.

"We're going. Those boys just lost their mother. I don't care what you do to me," she says with her chin high. "But I'm going, because I'm a fucking human being."

My father's face grows madder by the second, his thick brows dipping and his thin lips bending like an evil scientist. "One of my guys will take you. You'll have one hour."

Then he storms out, his footsteps heavy.

Mom exhales out a sigh of relief, wrapping the warmth of her arms around me, her hands gliding up and down my back.

"Why couldn't it be him?" I ask, speaking so low into her ear, I don't know if she even heard me.

"Don't say that, baby," she whispers. "I know he's awful, but I don't want you to think that way."

"Well, I am." I pull back, peering at her glazed eyes. "Why couldn't he die?!" I whisper-shout. "Why do good people like Dom's mom have to die?"

Oh, Dom.

New tears fill my eyes, the hurt building.

"I don't have the answers to that, baby. I wish I knew." She wipes her own tears away as she sniffles. "But right now, we have to focus on your friend and his family. They need us."

DOMINIC
THREE DAYS LATER

I keep punching my arm, thinking this is a dream and Mom isn't dead. That the officers never came to the house three days ago to tell us she is gone forever. A car accident, they said. That's all anyone will tell me.

"I just saw her," Dad had cried while I hugged him. "She told me she was going to go and pick up Matteo from kindergarten so he didn't have to take a school bus. She can't be dead."

He wasn't really talking to me. It was like he was talking to himself or something and I was just there to hear it.

My belly wobbles as I remember the two officers showing up at our house after my brothers and I got home from school. They didn't want to tell me anything, asking for my dad. They came inside while I called him.

After Dad got home, I called Chiara because I needed her. I'm glad she stopped by with her mom. They stayed with us until after the cops left. Her mom helped put Enzo and Matteo to bed while Dante and I stayed up to take care of Dad.

Tears drip down my eyes and I hate them. I practically knock them away. How can she be gone?

"Mommy. Please come back. Please." I cover my face with my hands, sobbing into them. My entire body shakes with all the hurt.

Once my father got home, he knew something awful happened to Mom. He yelled at the cops for answers, and then he got them, wishing he hadn't.

How can she be gone? How is it possible we buried her today? Why my mom? What did she ever do to anyone? She was the best.

My heart races while I hold on to my chest. I can't breathe. My throat hurts from all the crying.

I miss you.

The tears continue, and I don't stop them. I don't think they'd go anywhere even if I asked nicely. I grab a pillow from my bed and put it over my face, screaming and crying all at once.

There's a small knock on my door before the handle turns. I quickly put the pillow back and swipe under my eyes.

"Dom?" Chiara's voice calls out from the crack in the door.

I clear my throat. "Yeah, I'm in here."

Everyone is downstairs at the house after Mom's funeral, and I couldn't take being there with them all. They're crying like she was their mother.

She was ours. *We* lost her, not them.

I escaped to my room, wanting to be alone. But not from Chiara. She's the only person I'd never want to run from.

The door swings open a little at a time until I see her face.

"Is it okay if I'm here?" she asks, sounding unsure.

"Yeah, of course. I just couldn't be down there."

She nods, clasping her hands in front of her as she walks toward my bed.

"I got you something." She opens her hand, revealing a silver necklace with a heart.

I stare curiously at it, peeking up to find her biting her lip as she takes a seat beside me.

"It's a friendship necklace," she explains, cracking it in half and handing me one half of her heart. "That way, no matter where we are, we're always together."

I glance down at my half, then up at her.

"Is it stupid?" she asks, crinkling her nose. "Yeah, it's stupid." She waves her hand in the air, answering her own question.

But it's not stupid at all.

I like it. A lot.

I grip her hand, keeping it steady. "I love it, Chiara."

"Really?" She smiles a little, her face slanting to the side. "You mean that?"

She's so pretty.

"Yeah." I nod, lifting it up and placing it around my neck. "It's kind of cool." I grin for the first time in days.

"It has our names on the back." She turns her half and shows me her name on it, while I glance down at mine.

"Wow, that's neat."

"Yeah." She scoots closer. "It kind of is."

"I'll never take it off," I promise.

She smiles, then both of us stare at the wall in front. I scoot even closer, and when I do, her hand slowly creeps toward mine, her fingers slicing in between my clammy ones.

I lay my head over hers, and we stay that way for a long time. I let her hold my hand tighter, hoping it makes me feel just a little bit better, just a little bit safer.

But it doesn't.

My mom's gone, and I'll always be broken.

CHIARA
AGE 13

THREE

For the past three years, my friendship with Dom has only gotten stronger. We hang out either at school or at their bakery when Mom and I stop by.

Mom likes keeping tabs on the boys and spends time talking to Dom's father while Dom, his brothers, and I eat way too many cupcakes.

We never stay too long—maybe thirty minutes—thanks to my father. He has his driver take us and bring us back. I'm still not allowed to go to Dom's house, and neither is Mom.

The day his mom died and the day of her funeral were the only exceptions. But at least we have a little time to goof around and be ourselves at the bakery. That's something.

Sometimes, when I'm allowed to go, I get to see Dom at the library.

I feel bad for my mom, though. She has no friends since Carmella died. She only has my aunt Kirsten, who we don't see much of because Dad forbids it. I don't know why.

But at least Mom has Dom's father to talk to. I'm sure she's lonely. Everyone needs friends.

Whenever Dom and I aren't together, we're chatting on the phone any time my father isn't home, which is a lot lately. He runs a ton of different businesses and is always busy. Thank goodness. I hate it when he's home.

But unlucky for me, he's home today, and all I want is to see Dom.

I miss him.

I'm hoping I can sneak out undetected while he's still watching TV and return less than an hour later. Will he even notice if I leave? He didn't say anything when I tiptoed down the stairs. It's like I'm invisible sometimes, until he needs something.

I tread slowly toward the door, right past the back of the couch he's sitting on. I'll just text Mom after I leave.

My palm lands on the door handle.

Almost there.

"Where you goin'?" my father clips out, the sharp edge of his tone coming through across the room.

My hand trembles as I twist my neck toward his voice, the side of his head greeting me, his eyes still glued to the football game.

My skin comes alive with fear, prickling with dread. "I'm just going to the library."

I attempt with all my might to keep my voice even. If he smells fear, he'll know I'm lying. Well, sort of. I am going there, but for reasons he won't approve of.

"I have to work on a science project with kids from class."

He's quiet for a second, and I bathe in relief, hoping his silence means he'll let me go. Sometimes I'm lucky and catch him in a good mood. And though it doesn't happen a lot, those are the very best days because those days Dom and I get to spend hours together at the library. They have a snack area where we can hang out as long as we want. It's the only place I can hide out and be a kid without anyone my father knows watching. His driver always stays parked in the front. Never once has he come inside.

"No."

One word, and my hope dashes away.

"That's not fair!" I scream. "You always do this! I'm never allowed to go anywhere. I'm in school. I have things I have to do! Don't you get it?"

The TV goes silent, and I know instantly I've overstepped. But I'm so sick of him controlling me and not letting me have a life.

Who wants to be friends with a girl who's never allowed to do anything? A few kids have tried to hang out with me, but it was always a no from my father. I may just be thirteen, but I'm old enough to do stuff instead of sitting at home in my room. It's not like I can do anything after school, either. He has his driver pick me up and drop me at home.

He gets off the couch, his round belly bobbing as he approaches me, the short-sleeved white t-shirt wet with a beer stain on his chest from the bottle still clutched in his fist.

Once he's in front of me, he stares blankly into my eyes. Then suddenly, his other hand flies out and lands hard against my cheek.

"Who the fuck do you think you are, talking to your father like that?" his voice bellows, scratching up the walls, filled with memories I'd love to rip away and bury somewhere they can't touch me.

Tears sting my eyes as I hold a palm over my cheek, a whimper bubbling out of me.

"Faro!" Mom's voice comes through, her long, black hair coiled on the top of her head. We look so much alike, even with me being a lot younger. "Don't you put your hands on her!"

He marches over to her, his face twisting with disgust. "What the fuck you gonna do, you fucking puttana schifosa?" *Filthy whore.*

He spits in her face.

I pant, my eyes widened, my heart hammering so loudly it hurts to breathe.

Don't hurt her!

But I can't seem to speak. Terror is all I know.

She shuts her eyes, wiping it away, not shocked at all. This is a common occurrence, but every time it happens, I'm scared like it's the first time.

His hands jump out, grabbing her around the neck, his face pressing into hers before he lifts her off the floor.

I rush toward him, hitting his back with my fists.

"Let her go!" I shout as I land another punch. "Let her go!"

Mom's face turns red as she tries to breathe, her hands jumping out to claw his shoulders with her long French-manicured nails.

I continue to scream, to beg him to leave her alone, but it's as though I'm not even there. His rage sees nothing but what it wants to consume, and right now, that's my mother.

Running to the corner of the foyer, I grab the broom my mother had been using earlier and whack him on the head.

That's when he finally drops her, holding the back of his head as he glares at me.

"You hit me?!" he growls with a thin slit of his gaze. "I'll fucking break your hands!"

My eyes bulge, breaths flying out of me, fear plunging into the pit of my stomach.

"You hear me, Chiara? I'll kill you!"

My mother runs over to me, standing between the two of us. "Don't worry, baby. Mama's here."

He laughs cruelly, taking another step while we take one backward.

I'm almost against the wall when someone knocks on the door.

"Not a damn word!" he warns with a pointed finger in Mom's face.

She clutches me in her arms, both of us trembling.

"Shhh," she calms softly while I try to take normal breaths.

In and out.

In and out.

But I can't calm the beating of my heart. It's about to explode from my chest.

My father faces the door, nearing the peephole. And as he looks outside, he smirks, opening the door.

In walks my uncle Salvatore, his short brown hair spiked at the front.

"I've been calling you," he tells my father, looking from us to him, his brows tugging curiously. "We have to get some business taken care of. Did you forget while you were scratching your ass all day?"

He glances at me with a smile, but I don't return it. My arms curl tighter around my mother's hips.

His lips form a thin line as his eyes return to my tormentor. "Get a jacket and let's go, Faro. They won't like us being late."

"You think I give a fuck, Sal? Who the hell are they, that I should care?"

My uncle shakes his head as my dad heads for the walk-in closet in the hallway.

Crazy, Uncle Sal mouths to me, leaning over a little, gesturing with a finger around his temple, a suppressed smile on his mouth.

This time, I giggle.

My father whips around sharply toward the noise. But my uncle straightens, pretending nothing is going on.

Between my three uncles, Uncle Sal is the most normal one. He can be funny, unlike my dad. And his daughter, Raquel, and I get along as well as sisters.

My uncle Benvolio is okay too, but he doesn't really talk to me much other than to say hello whenever I see him for family events or holidays, or when he comes over to do work stuff with Dad.

My other uncle, Agnelo, seems just as crazy as my own father. When I see him with my other cousin, Aida, he's always yelling at her. She's so timid around us. I hope he doesn't hit her like my dad does me. But I think she's scared of him. I really do. She barely ever talks when we have the family over. When she tries to, she keeps glancing at her dad like she's scared he'll hear.

Once my dad has his jacket on, he leads Uncle Sal out the door. As soon as they're out, Mom runs, locking the door, then her arms are holding me again.

"Listen to me," she says in a whisper, crouching down as she tucks my face within her palms. "I have enough money to get us out of here. My friend is setting up a place for us far away."

"What? Where?"

"Shh!" she warns before telling me more in my ear. "You'll find out soon. In one week from Monday, we'll be gone. I'll get you early from school while your father has a meeting scheduled, and we'll run away before he can find us. Don't say a word to anyone. Not Dom. Not your teacher. Not a soul. He has eyes and ears everywhere. We can't risk him finding out."

She draws back as I nod, my heart pumping like crazy in my chest. Her eyes scatter over my face, her brows squeezing as tears flow over the edges of her eyes.

Swallowing the lump in my throat, I cram my trembling hands together, hoping that will stop the tremors. But that only makes it worse. My mom notices as she peers down between my eyes and my hands.

"It'll be okay, my baby." She takes both my hands within hers and brings them to her mouth, kissing my fingers. "We'll both be okay. You'll see."

I nod more frantically this time, my voice lost to the fear.

I hope she's right. I hope there's a way we can run without him finding out.

But not everyone gets what they wish for.

On Monday at school, all I can think about is what happened with my father over the weekend. When he got home later that night, he stayed away from my mom and me. I remained in my room, shaking with the fear that he might hurt us, but he didn't.

"What's wrong, Chiara?" Dom asks as he turns to me, taking the book from my hands and closing it on his lap. "I can tell you're upset."

I shrug, twisting my pursed lips to the right, ignoring that look he gives me, like he can read whatever is in my head.

He takes my hand and gives it a squeeze. "You can tell me anything. I wouldn't tell anyone. You know that by now, don't you?"

I glance back at him. "I do. I trust you. You're the only one who knows me at all."

I'm afraid to tell him what happened a couple of days ago, when my father slapped me for wanting to go to the library. When he hurt Mom.

"Is it your dad? Did he flip about something again? Is that why you bailed on Saturday?"

I huff out an exasperated breath. He knows that whenever I'm in a crappy mood, it's always my father's fault.

"Yeah. He wouldn't let me go. He started an argument. All my parents do is fight. Everything is his fault. I don't even want to be there."

I want to tell him about Mom's plan, but I know I can't. Not yet. I can't risk putting my mom in danger, not even for Dom.

"How bad is it at home?" He tightens his hand over mine.

I sigh deeply, letting out more than my breath. Letting out the truth.

"I can't take the screaming. Him hitting my mom all the time."

"Does he hit you?" he asks with a hushed breath.

I've never told anyone. Not a soul. But I've known him long enough to trust him not to tell. He knows what could happen if he does.

"Sometimes," I answer coolly, shrugging as I stare at my hand clasped in his. I can't manage to look at him.

He plants his palms on my shoulders, and my hand still tingles, wanting his back.

"Why the hell didn't you tell me?"

I peer up at him shyly, embarrassment flinging through me. "What could you do? No one can stop him."

His teeth clench, his bright green eyes narrowing. I've never seen him look this angry.

"One day I will," he promises. "One day, when I'm bigger, I'll be stronger than him, and I will hurt him for what he did to you. I swear, Chiara."

And I believe him.

"Oh, Dom." I toss my arms around him in a tight hug. "I love you so much. I'm so happy you're my best friend."

Tears sting behind my eyes, but I push them down. I don't like to cry, especially in front of people.

"I...I love you, Chiara. You're my best friend too. You always will be." He hugs me tighter. "Promise me...no matter what happens, we'll always be friends."

"Of course we will be!"

We separate, and as he looks at me, his lips turn into a frown. "Sometimes I get scared you won't like me anymore, like your father."

"That'll never happen. And if you ever try to stop being friends with me, you'd better watch out. I know you're afraid of me."

"Oh, yeah?" he laughs, the worry now gone. "What can you do to me?"

I roll my eyes playfully, swatting him on the chest. "I'll figure it out. Give me a second."

"Uh-huh. You figure it out while you read. We have a book report due in two days, or did you forget?" he whispers.

"Stop changing the subject." I fold my arms over my chest. "Just admit you're afraid of me."

"Fine." He raises his hands like he really is. "I am afraid. You can be crazy."

He smiles, and those dimples I love make an appearance.

"Hey!" I giggle softly, pushing at his chest with a hand.

But I am crazy, because one of these days, I plan to find the courage to tell my best friend in the whole world that I think I like him as more than a friend. I don't know what it means to have a boyfriend, but I want him to be mine.

If he doesn't agree, I'll probably cry. I can't risk making things weird. But I also can't keep my feelings to myself either, especially with Mom and I leaving in a week. I need him to know.

"Together forever," he says as he lifts his pinky.

"Together forever," I promise, hooking mine into his, rubbing the half of the heart at my neck, the one I gave him three years ago. His is still on him too.

I have every intention of keeping my promise. Because no matter where I go, Dom will always be with me.

CHIARA
FIVE DAYS LATER

FOUR

Something is happening this morning. I don't know what it is, but my dad seems way too on edge. He's been talking to someone in his office, and there have been men in dark suits coming in and out. Men I've never seen before.

Mom's not home, and she hasn't been home since I woke up. She's always here to make me pancakes. I've called her multiple times, but she won't pick up. I left her a few voicemails just an hour ago.

She knows we have plans to meet Dom at the bakery this afternoon. She knows how important that is to me since we're leaving in two days.

Why isn't she picking up? I hope she makes it home soon.

I twirl the spoon in my hand, flipping around the Cheerios in the bowl.

I hear Dad's office door slam, and then he's whispering with one of his men right outside the kitchen. But as soon as they quiet, his heavy footsteps pound across the tiles, coming closer.

I keep staring into my bowl, hoping I'm somehow invisible. My stomach rolls around like I'm on a roller coaster.

"Your phone," he snaps harshly. "Now."

Glancing up, all I find is the look of anger on his face.

"Why do you need my phone?" I ask quietly, scared he'll flip out on me if I don't act timid.

"Are you questioning me?!" he yells so loudly his cheeks turn into red tomatoes.

I want to giggle, but that will only make him angrier.

"Your phone is *mine*! Everything here is mine. I fucking pay for it." His face glistens with sweat. "Don't ever question me again." He grits his teeth like a savage animal. "You do what I fucking say."

I reach into the pocket of my jeans and pull it out, and as soon as he sees it, he yanks it from me. My pulse beats heavily in my throat while my eyes go round with terror.

"Now you won't get it until I decide to give it back." His nostrils flare. "The next time I ask for something, you make sure you do it."

He gives me one more intense scowl, then turns around, storming out.

Suddenly I realize that without a phone, I won't be able to talk to Dom! What if he texts and my dad sees it, knowing I went against him? He'll never give me my phone back then.

And what if my mom calls? What if she's hurt somewhere and there's no one to help her? My pulses races, and I can't stomach any more food.

Standing up, I empty the bowl into the trash and rinse it out, along with the spoon, before placing both in the dishwasher.

Not sure what else to do, I head for the couch, flipping on the TV. But a few minutes later, I'm no longer alone.

My father is there with one of his employees. At least that's who I think he is. I don't ever ask my father about what he does. I don't think any of it is good. My skin crawls every time I see him.

"Stay here and watch her," Douchey Dad tells the man. "Make sure she doesn't go anywhere. And don't allow her to use your phone or the house phone either."

"Yes, boss." The man with the black hair and muddy eyes nods.

"I'll be back later. Call me if there's trouble." That's all my father adds before he walks out, leaving me alone with a man I've never seen before.

DOMINIC
TWO DAYS LATER

FIVE

"Watch Enzo," I tell Dante. "I've gotta go check on Dad. He isn't picking up his phone, and he knows we're supposed to head to the bakery in thirty to meet Chiara."

"Why do I have to babysit?" he groans.

"Who the hell else can do it?"

"I can stay by myself!" Enzo grumbles. "I'm ten! I'm not a baby."

I roll my eyes and glare at Dante. "You're watching him. Stay by the phone in case I call."

"Whatever." Dante turns around and heads for the kitchen.

"I'll be back soon. I'm sure Dad's fine."

They both ignore me, Enzo following Dante while I head out the door.

It isn't like my dad not to answer the bakery phone. And why would his cell phone be turned off? It's very weird. Matteo is with him, so it's not like they can go far.

With everything that happened to Mom, I'm always waiting for something else to go wrong in our life.

The bakery is only a few blocks away from home, so I can always go back and get my brothers and come back with them.

Once I arrive at the shop, I find the closed sign on the door.

What the hell?

This makes no sense.

"Dad?" I knock on the door. "It's Dom, where are you?"

I knock harder, but there's no answer and the lights are off.

"Hey, buddy," Gerard calls as he walks out of the candy shop he owns next door.

"Have you seen my dad?" I ask, my voice strained.

"No, I…ah…" He scratches his gray hair. "I actually haven't seen him all day."

"Okay, thanks." I start walking away, unsure where else to go, before the panic sets in. "If you see him, tell him I'm looking for him."

"Is everything okay?"

"I don't know. I hope so."

Then I run out of there, looking for him at the bank, the grocery store, the supermarket. But he's nowhere. I dial Chiara's mom's phone, but she doesn't answer either.

Deciding to walk back home and wait there a while, I take the long way, hoping to run into them. I make it a block before I pass an abandoned warehouse some kids from school sometimes hang out in.

There's a single black car parked outside. It's so shiny, I decide to check it out. When I pass the entrance to the warehouse, I hear voices coming from inside. They seem a little distant, so I don't know what the man is saying.

My pulse speeds up, and instead of running away, my feet start moving inside.

Who can that be?

I sneak in, passing a dripping pipe, my sneakers not making any noise as I hide behind a partial wall beside the entrance. It's a little dark in here and hard to make out faces, but when I peer around, I find four men.

A whimpering sound comes out of nowhere, like that of a kid.

I peek my head out a bit more and that's when I see them: a little boy and a man, both on their knees. I can make out their shape and size from where I am.

My legs grow stiff, my body trembling.

What kind of weird shit is happening here?

A man lights a flashlight, illuminating his face, and when I see it clearly, I gasp.

Out loud.

Chiara's dad's head jerks in my direction.

"You hear something?" he asks the others.

My heart beats so loud, my chest and throat hurt, the panic taking over my entire body. If he finds me here, he'll kill me.

He's dangerous. That's what Dad always says. My chest flies up and down, and even the hand resting against my beating heart can't quiet the noise in my head.

"It's that damn pipe, I'm tellin' you," another man says. "Fuckin' annoyin'."

Her dad nods and turns back to the two people on the ground, their arms tied behind their backs.

And once he flashes the light on their faces, my eyes go round, my lungs frozen inside my chest. My hands shake, and warm liquid trickles down the inside of my leg.

That's my father and brother on the floor with a gun pointing at them.

My pulse pounds so hard, I'm afraid the bad men will hear it.

Chiara's dad stands over them, holding the weapon at his thigh. Walking closer to my father, he rips the tape from his mouth.

Dad cries openly, turning to his right. "It's okay, Matteo. Daddy's here."

"Daddy won't be able to do shit for you, kid," Faro says with a humorless laugh.

My heart beats in my throat. This can't be real. It's a dream. I close my eyes, counting to three. But when I open them again, I'm still here, about to see my father and brother die.

I want to run, to help them, but I'm frozen here like a coward, pissing my pants as Faro points that same gun at my brother.

"Please, Faro. Please don't hurt the boy. He did nothing wrong," my father whimpers, his voice breaking. "You can do what you want to me, but leave him out of it. He's innocent."

Faro snickers cruelly. "The mistakes of the father always come back on the son, Francesco. You should know that."

I pant heavily, terrified.

"Say goodbye to your son before it's too late."

My eyes hurt from the tears that fall. The middle of my chest is heavy as I put both palms over my mouth, wanting to throw up.

"N-no. No. Please no," Dad wails, leaning into my brother as they both cry. "It's okay, Matteo. It's okay. Shh."

My brother only cries louder, the whimpers cutting into my heart.

"Want me to do it?" another man, who looks like one of Chiara's uncles, asks.

They all look like her uncles, I think. I've seen pictures of them.

"What the hell, Agnelo?" Faro yells. "You think I don't fucking have what it takes to off some kid?"

"What the fuck are you playin' games for, then?" Agnelo asks. "It's the middle of the fucking day. You should've waited until tonight."

"The cops here are in our pocket. Who the hell are you afraid of?"

"It's not the cops," another man says. "The kids from the school come to this shithole. You want to kill multiple kids today?"

"Don't look, okay, son?" Dad tells Matteo. "Ju-just look at me and close your eyes." His voice cracks with a sob. "I love you, my boy. You hear me? Papa's sorry. I love—"

Pop.

I gasp as the bullet hits my brother, my mouth and my eyes widening from the horror. My lips tremble, my body shakes, near crumpling to the floor.

"Matteo!" my father screams as he drops over Matteo's body. I have never heard him scream that hard in my life.

My brother's body falls, his boyish face planted on the floor looking at me, blood oozing out from around his body. I silently cry, my shoulders rocking. I weep into my hands as Faro kneels in front of my brother's dead body, grabbing my father by the shirt.

"Get back on your knees, you motherfucker."

But my father refuses, sobbing, pushing his way back down to my brother.

I want to kill Faro and his brothers. Rip all of their hearts out of their chests. If only I had a gun, I could shoot them from here.

"You think I'm done?!" Faro asks. "You think this is it?"

That gets my father to face Faro, letting go of my brother.

"I'll kill you, then take every one of your sons and kill them too. The Cavaleri bloodline will die with you."

"Please," my dad pleads. "Don't kill my boys. You killed one. Let the others go."

Faro chuckles. "You should've been smarter than to get involved with my wife."

Pop.

My eyes go round, tears flooding them, as the bullet enters my father's forehead. And when he falls, that's when I snap out of it. I've failed them, but I can't fail my other brothers.

With my pulse beating in my throat, I creep back down the wall I was hiding behind, quietly taking each step backwards until I'm back outside.

As I run, my feet are doused with adrenaline, needing to save my brothers before we all die. Taking out the cell from my pocket, I call home, and Dante immediately answers.

"Hell—"

"Listen, go get that black duffle bag from Dad's closet and pack some clothes for us three. We've gotta go."

"Why?" Dante sounds worried.

"Just do it! Unless you wanna die."

Click.

The line goes silent as I continue to run. My feet are moving so fast, I didn't even know I could run this quickly.

Once I'm at the front door, I put the key in the lock and run inside.

"Dante! Enzo!" I call out upstairs. "Let's go!"

"Why? Where's Dad?" Enzo asks as he comes down the stairs, his brows pinched over his green eyes.

"I don't have any time to explain. Do what I say for once! It's life and death."

"Help me with the bag," Dante calls from upstairs.

I'm running up, grabbing the handle, the wheels on the bottom slamming harshly over the wooden steps.

"Wait here," I tell them, rushing into the kitchen, hitting the cookie jar and taking out the two grand my dad had stashed inside for emergencies.

That's all we'll have until I can find a job wherever we end up.

"Ready," I say, grabbing the duffle and hoisting it over my shoulder.

As I'm about to lock the door, my phone buzzes with a text.

I release a big sigh when I find Chiara's name, hoping I can tell her what happened after we get to wherever we go. I hope she forgives me for leaving her behind.

But when I read the text she sent, when I scan over the ugly words, I feel colder and even more alone. How could she say that to me?

"Come on!" Dante shouts as I read the message for the second time.

> **Chiara:** I talked to my dad today and I decided I don't want to be your friend anymore. I don't want to see any of you.
>
> **Dom:** What? You don't mean that.
>
> **Chiara:** I never actually liked you, Dom. I never liked your family either. I was only pretending because I felt sorry for all of you. You're all losers like my dad always said you were. I had a lot of fun laughing at you all behind your back.
>
> **Dom:** How could you say that? What about the necklace?

Chiara: Get the hint and stop texting or I'll have my daddy call the police.

Dom: I hate you. I hope I never see you again.

  My chin trembles and the hurt pools into my gut.
  She was never my friend. She's as horrible as her father. How did I not know?
  With one last look at the door, I toss my cell behind the tree and run like hell.

CHIARA

SIX

Today was supposed to be the day my mother and I ran away. But I haven't seen her for two days now. I've been unable to eat or sleep, constantly crying, sick to my stomach, wondering where she is.

The only person with answers won't give me any. Whenever he's home, my father only brushes away my questions about Mom, ignoring me as though I'm a fly. Annoying. Irrelevant.

He didn't return my cell either. If only he'd give it to me, I could check if Mom called. I don't even have anyone to ask about her, which sucks even more.

Where could she be? She'd never go away without me, would she? No way. She'd never leave me with my stupid father.

And to make things worse, Dom didn't show up at school today. Is he sick? Did something happen to him? I don't even have my stupid phone to ask! I need someone to talk so badly, but instead I'm all alone in my room.

My lower lip trembles, then my chin, and the tears come rushing out. I cry, sobbing into my pillow, knowing no one will hear me anyway.

I need my mom. If something happened to her, I'll die.

My foot bounces across the floor while I sit in my bed, face in my hands, tears leaking into them.

"Ahhh!" A muffled shout escapes from my damp lips.

I wish I'd never been born. I wish I wasn't his daughter.

Grabbing a chunk of my hair, I yank it in frustration, unable to take another minute without finding out where Mom is. I know my father knows. He just won't tell me.

But he will. I won't give him another choice. He won't ignore me this time.

Wiping the tears away and taking a minute to calm down, I get up and head downstairs to get answers.

Once I'm in front of his office, my pulse beats in my ears.

Thump.

Thump.

Faster and faster, my heart pounds. And the air falls out so quickly from my mouth, it becomes harder to catch my breath.

I swallow against a lump that's suddenly jammed in my throat. My hand jitters as I form a fist and knock against the closed door.

It's quiet inside, but I know he's in there.

I knock louder this time. Then again.

You won't ignore me. Not anymore.

When I knock again, the door swings open.

"Why are you botherin' me?" he asks, his tone so agitated it hurts somewhere deep inside where I crave a father who loves me.

"I...I," I stammer, my voice as broken as my heart.

"Spit it out already." He glares at me. "I have things to do."

I bite down, my teeth aching, stifling the need to cry.

"Where's Mom?" I'm surprised at how steady my voice is with the amount of fear I have inside me. "It's been days, and you won't tell me. I'm worried, and I know you always know where she is. Did she go on a trip?"

He drags a sharp breath through his nose like a dragon, his eyes narrowing.

"Something like that," he snickers darkly. "Get inside. I'll tell you exactly where she is."

He opens the door fully, allowing me to come in.

I move into his large office with a big dark brown desk in the middle. It's the first time I've been in here. He's never allowed me inside.

I take a seat on the end of the brown couch, furthest from his desk, while he plops down on top of the black office chair.

He pulls himself closer to the desk, his elbows on it. "I didn't wanna tell you shit, but you insisted, so I'll tell you the truth."

I scoot to the edge of the sofa, anticipating his words.

He clears his throat. "Your mother…she's gone."

It sounds like he just gave me the weather report, but in reality, he's destroyed my entire world.

My chest jumps hard with every breath. And inside, it hurts like I've been cut open with a knife. The loud noise that sounds like my heart invades my ears and the room spins from sheer panic.

"Wha…?" I can barely form a word. Vomit sits at the pit of my stomach, slowly slithering up.

"She's not dead," he continues with a laugh, his shoulders rocking at my torment, the sinister tone sliding up my body like roaches.

My eyes pop out. "What?"

My ears are ringing, so maybe I misheard.

"I meant she's gone. She left us."

My face twists with confusion. "What do you mean?"

Nothing is making sense. This is like torture. First, I think she's dead, and now he says she left me?

"No." I shake my head. "She'd never do that."

To me, I want to add. *She'd leave you, but never me.*

"Well, she did." His brows twist up. "She don't want you anymore. She ran off with another man and didn't take you. What's that shit say to you, huh? Your mom's nothing but a whore."

"Stop it!" I jump to my feet. "Don't call her that!"

"She is what she is."

"You're a liar! I don't believe you," I whimper, my lower lip quivering, tears slipping from my eyes with every lie he tells.

"I know you loved her, but she don't love you as much as you thought she did," he adds.

"You're lying!" I accuse, not caring what he'll do in return. "She'd never go without me."

"Think what you want." An evil chuckle falls out of his wicked mouth. "But I'm not lyin'."

My chin trembles as I back away slowly, shaking my head as tears continue to fall.

"You've only got me now, Chiara," he snickers while digging into the top drawer of his desk. "Here."

He reaches out a hand, my phone clutched in his grasp. I go back to retrieve it, even though I don't want to be anywhere near him.

He's a liar. I know he is.

He hurt Mom. He had to have.

He's evil.

A monster.

Yanking the phone from him, I turn, beginning to leave.

"Close the door on your way out," he demands. "And don't bother me anymore. You got your answers."

I rush out, leaving the door the way it is. He can close it himself. He can get mad, do whatever he wants to me. It doesn't matter anymore.

Reaching my room, I lock the door, panting with a whimper, my pulse hitting me hard with a thick web of agony. I can't handle this. It's too much.

A sob tears its way out, and then another, until I'm crumbling against the wall, wailing for her.

Needing her.

Mom.

Come back.

CHIARA
TWO DAYS LATER

SEVEN

Mom is gone, but I'm still here. Dom is gone too. Everyone is gone but me. And I want to be where they are, but I'm not and I can't be.

It's been two days since my father's lie: that my mother abandoned me. Four full days without her. I could barely go to school yesterday. My eyes have been puffy and red since the day I realized I'll probably never see her again.

All the kids stared at me as I passed the halls. But none have bothered to ask if I'm okay. No one cares. Even the girls who'd be a little friendly with me in class, didn't bother with me.

I've called Mom every hour since I got my phone back, and hers goes to voicemail now. I've left so many messages, the robot voice says her voicemail is now full.

And to make things even worse, I don't know where Dom is

either. He didn't show up at school for a third day now. How could they both abandon me? I've called his cell, leaving messages, begging for him to call me, but it's dead like my mother's.

I decide to skip school today as soon as I saw he wasn't here. Our lockers are right next to each other's, and we always head to class together.

Worrying my father's goons will spot me while they stalk me at his command, I make my escape from the back of the building and head for the bakery, a quick walk from school. I know that the one place Dom would be is there, and if he isn't, someone from his family will be.

But as I get there, a chill rolls down my spine.

I'm wrong. So wrong.

My heartbeats echo in my ears while I stare into the dark emptiness, no longer a place filled with so much life.

They're all gone.

Silent tears spring into my eyes, falling, drifting into nothing.

Why is everyone I love disappearing?

Where can Dom be? Why would he leave without telling me? He'd never do that. He'd never hurt me like this.

"Hey, Chiara," says a man behind me.

I turn around, finding a short, older man with gray hair. I recognize him as Gerard, the one who owns the candy shop next door.

"You speak to Dom today?" He scratches his thick, gray hair. "I've started to worry."

"No." I shake my head with a tremble. "When were they here last?"

His brows tug gently, and he places a finger on his temple, staring absently.

"Well, Friday, I saw Francesco all day, but then Dom stopped by Saturday afternoon looking for him, but the shop was closed. The boy seemed as concerned as you do right now." He squints, looking inquisitively at me. "What's going on?"

The weekend is their busiest time. I remember Dom telling me that. Unless there's an emergency, his father would never close.

Wait...

My heart races while I freak out.

Saturday is when Mom disappeared, the day my dad took my phone. Did he do something to Dom's dad?

A shiver runs down both my arms, leaving thick prickles.

No. It can't be.

But, I wouldn't put it past him. He hated Mom, and he hated Dom's family. What if he decided to hurt them all? What if...

I can't even think those thoughts. I can't imagine a world where Mom and Dom are not in it.

"Did you speak to them the last few days at all?" Gerard interrupts my thoughts.

"No," I speak over the ball of anxiety in my throat. "Dom won't answer his phone." The words shudder from my lips. "It doesn't seem to be...on."

"Oh, goodness." He exhales sharply. "I don't have Francesco's number. I'll have to call the police."

Police? Oh my God.

"Okay," I mouth with a barely there whisper as he walks away.

Glancing back at the bakery one last time, I run out of there with tears raining down my face, unable to handle another second of staring at my own reflection.

PART II

THE PRESENT

DOMINIC
AGE 28

EIGHT

"Where the fuck is he?" I demand, twisting the collar of his shirt tight in my fist, gritting my teeth as I stare at a man who looks terrified. He should be.

He's the only one currently alive in this warehouse, but not for long. When we get what we need, he'll be dead, and just as pretty as the rest of them.

"I swear I don't know," he cries.

Actual fucking tears. Pathetic.

My brother Dante is holding a gasoline canister behind me, opening and closing the top, taunting him. "Maybe if we pour this over his head and light him on fire, he'll talk faster."

"Please!" Greg begs. "He and his brothers are in hiding! No one knows where they are. He didn't tell us."

Smart. I didn't expect Faro to tell anyone where he is.

It makes no difference to me. I plan to kill every soldier, every capo, in the Palermo crime family if I have to. Until I kill the don himself, Faro Bianchi, along with his three brothers.

If anyone in their organization stands in our way, they'll pay the price.

But before we kill the Bianchi men, we'll burn every legitimate business they own and enjoy watching it go up in flames.

I look Greg up and down, the blood of his soldiers smeared across his white t-shirt. It looks much better now. Adds a little character.

"It's unfortunate that you don't know where they are," Enzo says from beside me. "Without that information, you're damn useless. Kinda like them."

He gestures toward the twelve dead bodies with the gun in his hand.

"What else can I do? Please. Come on," he openly sobs. "I don't wanna die. I didn't do shit to no one."

"That isn't true," I spit out, clenching his shirt in my fist, the anger for anyone who associates with Faro spiraling through me. "We know who you are. You work for that piece of shit. You kill for him. You sell guns for him. You're as bad as he is."

Greg here isn't some low-on-the-totem-pole moron. He's a captain in the organization. A capo, as they call them.

He leads the crew of the now-dead group of soldiers and works directly under Benvolio and Agnelo, two of Faro's brothers. It's not common to have two underbosses, but I guess good old Faro couldn't choose just one. His other brother, Salvatore, is his consigliere, the right-hand man, the one who's supposed to be giving him advice.

"My family's gotta eat, man."

The tears shining in his eyes have no effect on me. I only tighten my fist around his shirt.

"He's my boss," the sorry son of a bitch continues. "I don't know what he did to you, but I'm sorry, man. Please, let me go. I'll do whatever the hell you want."

Dante chuckles, walking around me, his shoulders shuddering as though someone's just told him the funniest joke he's ever heard.

He reaches to the back of Greg's head and yanks on his long, brown hair until their eyes meet.

"Do we look like we'll let you come out of this breathing, my man? Have you not been here when we were slaughtering your pals over there?" He twists Greg's face toward the dead bodies.

Greg sobs worse than a kid who's lost all his Halloween candy. But soon, his fear will be gone. He'll be nothing more than rotting flesh.

I don't pity him or any of the dead men here. That's what they get for working for a man like Faro. The one who destroyed my family fifteen years ago when he pulled the trigger on my eight-year-old brother, Matteo, and my father. And for that, he must pay with every ounce of his blood.

They all must.

His brothers were there and did nothing to stop him.

I vowed to get revenge, and every day of the last fifteen years has been building up to their deaths.

When he took our dad and brother from us, he killed my brothers and me in the same moment. We turned numb, and any values our parents instilled in us, like "thou shalt not kill," vanished.

And when I helplessly watched them die at only thirteen, I suddenly grew into a man within a boy's body. My mind became filled with nothing beyond their blood, their cries, their screams for mercy.

We were my father's everything. The only reason he was slaving in the bakery he's owned since before we were born. He and my mother put every penny they had into that place, and it became really successful.

My parents both loved to bake. It was something they did together all the time. Oftentimes, my brothers and I would help, and it would be this family thing we did.

Then, one day, my mother's car was hit by a drunk driver. She was dead on impact. And nothing was the same. Not for my brothers, and definitely not for my father. The love of his life was gone.

Some piece of shit was drunk at two in the fucking afternoon and smashed right into her. My father didn't give me the details then because I was so young, but the boys and I found out years later.

Our home was broken from that day on, but my father did his best to raise us without her, continuing to work hard, to bring us up into the men he knew my mother would want us to be.

But if she saw us now, she wouldn't be proud. She'd hate everything we've become. The crimes we've committed, the lives we've taken, all in the name of retribution.

It's worth it, though.

I hope she can understand that. They took her baby boy. That has to matter.

After my brothers and I ran from Faro, hitchhiking our way across state lines, I swore one day I'd find a way to kill them all.

We spent a year living on the streets before going to shelters, keeping faith we'd somehow become rich as fuck so we could find some guns, hire some people, and kill every motherfucker who had a hand in our brother's and father's death.

We dreamed big. We had to. It was all we had left. We didn't see any other way. And after two years in a crummy shelter and working side jobs, I hit a lucky break, changing our entire life.

I was only sixteen when I met the man who helped secure our future. I was working at a small coffee shop, mopping floors every damn day, when he saw me. Powerful gray suit, coffee in his hand. When he tapped me on the shoulder, I thought I did something wrong at first. Worry over getting fired ran through me. I couldn't lose my job. We needed the money. I was saving everything to make a life for us. Being the oldest, I was their protector, and I took that job very seriously.

Tomás Smith was his name. The man who saved us. He asked me why I wasn't in school. I lied, saying I was homeschooled, and that was partly true. I used books from the shelter we were at and taught my brothers what I knew.

Contemplating my answer, Tomás then asked if I wanted a better job. At first, I wasn't sure what the fuck he wanted. Some creepy-ass dude talking to me, asking if I wanted work…it felt slimy.

He must've seen my hesitation, so he pulled out a card and handed it to me. *Royal Onyx Resort & Spa,* it read. I looked back up at him, not understanding what a kid like me could do there.

He told me he liked hiring young kids to work for him, to give them a path to something more. I assumed it was the cheap labor, but I was wrong. He paid everyone well.

He explained that he ran a hotel chain, five locations in total, and was looking to expand his cleaning crew. I would've been stupid not to try it out. The money was way more than I was getting at any job I had.

I told him I didn't drive and would have to figure out how to get there by bus. He waved off the idea, offering a driver to take me back and forth.

I didn't know what the hell to say. I had no home. I had brothers to take care of. It wasn't going to work out, and I told him why. Instead of leaving, he made me get our stuff from the shithole, as he put it, and offered us a room at one of his hotels free of charge, plus a teacher for all three of us.

I couldn't believe it. I even asked if it was a joke. He laughed, saying he was just a man who had a rough start at life and wanted to repay the good that someone had done for him when he was young. It was his way of giving back.

After my brothers and I moved to the hotel, we realized he was telling the truth. Some of his staff had been with him since they were our age, telling us how much he helped them.

Tomás had everything: money, power, women. But he was lonely as hell. I could see it. He lost his daughter and his wife five years before we met. They both died in a house fire while he was on a business trip. He never forgave himself for it, he told me one night while we drank a little too much whiskey.

Maybe that was why he treated me more like a son than a stranger. Maybe it was the loneliness. And maybe that was why he left his CEO position to me when he died a year ago, and ensured my brothers had a seat on the board as well. He believed that his legacy would live on with me, and I haven't disappointed him yet.

Tomás knew everything about our past and helped shape our future. Within a year of working for him, we became very close, and I confessed about what happened back home.

In a week, we had new identities created. This allowed us to have a life.

Finally.

Then, a year after that, he asked to adopt us.

We were no longer the Cavaleri brothers. We were the Smiths. I was Brian, Dante was Chris, and Enzo was Patrick.

We have our true identities back now. Tomás ensured a way for that to happen through his lawyers if we ever needed it, and he secured our positions within his company, no matter which names we decided to use.

When he was diagnosed with stage four rectal cancer a year before he died, I confessed of my plans for revenge. He wasn't an evil man. I never thought he'd bless my decision, but he did. All he asked was my promise I wouldn't get myself or the boys killed.

Of course I promised him that, even though we both knew I might break it.

Once his condition worsened and the chemo stopped working, I swore I'd not only continue his legacy, but make my own like he taught me. He wanted us to have something of our own one day.

So, my brothers and I opened three nightclubs right before he died, under our own newly formed company, Vendetta Corporation, which we set up using our real names.

Tomás was proud. It was the last thing we were able to give him before he was gone.

And the name of the company? Well, we're not very creative, and we were done hiding from the Bianchis.

When we lost him, it felt as though we had lost another parent. He was family to us in every sense of the word. We were indebted to him for everything.

We wanted Faro to know we were back in case he was still looking. I have no doubt he spent years tracking us down, and being bested by some kids is probably not something he's chosen to forget.

Dante tosses Greg onto the floor.

"Your time's up," I tell him. "Time to meet your maker, or the other one."

He raises both hands, wailing like a drowning cat, begging for mercy that'll never come. "Please! I can help you. I can work for you! Whatever you want."

"Can we just fucking do this already?" Enzo urges. "I've got shit to do in an hour, and I still have to wash this blood off of me."

I know what kind of shit he has to do. It's more like *who* he has to do. I don't know her name, because they change every week, but it's definitely a woman. My brother's always either drowning in pussy or liquor, and usually at the same time. The clubs made that much easier. Dante is just as bad as he is, but Enzo's worse.

Enzo peers down at his bloodied hands for a mere second, clenching them into a tight fist, the knuckles stained with dark crimson.

I glance at his navy pants and gray button-down, blood spattered all over him. All over each of us, as though someone has thrown paint on us, like in one of those weird-ass paintings people call art.

"Let's kill him already," Enzo insists.

I remove the gun from the holster at my waistband, and at the sight, Greg prays through the tears in his eyes.

"No God is gonna help you," Dante mocks.

I lift the weapon, point it at Greg's leg, and pull the trigger.

"Ahh!" he screams as the bullet rips apart the flesh of his thigh.

Then I do it to his other one.

No hesitation.

But we're not done yet. Not even close. By the time we're through, this place won't be recognizable.

Greg continues to scream through the pain, holding on to one leg, covering the bullet hole with blood seeping out between the slices of his fingers.

Dante opens the canister of gasoline still in his possession.

"Wha-what are you gonna do with that?" Greg asks, eyes widening in sheer terror, the tears drowned out by fear accosting him.

"What the fuck you think I'm gonna do?" Dante tosses the cap somewhere onto the ground. "Fry you up nice and crispy. Then we're going to blow this whole place up so your boss has a nice mess to clean up."

"Oh my God! You're all crazy! What the fuck, man? Just shoot me!"

"That's too easy, my friend," I add. "And a lot less fun."

I look to Dante, with Enzo now beside him, both with matching sinister smiles. Dante flips the canister over Greg's head, the smell of gasoline permeating my nostrils as it spills down his body, pooling around him.

Greg struggles to get up, forgetting about his legs, before giving up, crying heavily, knowing the end is near.

A torturous end.

Enzo takes out a matchbox from his pocket and lights it up, staring at the dancing flame. "It was nice not knowing you."

Then the match falls on top of Greg's lap just as we jump back.

A fire roars to life, blending with the howling of Greg's screams. We all move further away, watching the blaze eat away at him, melting and destroying, the way he's destroyed so many innocent families at Faro's request.

How many of those people begged him for mercy he never gave?

Fuck him.

We pick up some more canisters, pouring gasoline all over this place. I retrieve a t-shirt we took off one of the men, light it on fire, then throw it on the ground.

The fire starts slow, growing, getting fiercer as it continues to combine with the gasoline.

I know we have to get out of here before the whole place blows into an inferno.

I look around at our handiwork. Twelve men, all dead, all shot in their legs, then finally their head. We would've burned them too, but we saved the best for last. Greg is one of their best hitmen. Those crocodile tears didn't put a dent in our hatred for him.

"All right, let's get the fuck out of here," I say, heading toward the exit, taking a quick look at the spot where my father once begged for our lives. For Matteo's life.

Now, this entire place will burn to the ground, burying that memory with the ashes of Faro's mistake. One he'll regret once he realizes our plans for him are only just beginning.

Once outside, we stand side by side, watching the flames rise, painting the walls with its golden-orange heat, connecting with ferocious power no man can destroy. Not in time at least.

Revenge is beautiful.

And it'll be a lot better once we destroy everything Faro ever cares about.

CHIARA
ONE WEEK LATER

NINE

I'm being watched.
 I can feel it in the marrow of my bones.
 That sixth sense, causing the hairs on the back of my neck to stand up, knowing someone is there in the shadows.
 Waiting.
 For what, I don't know.
 Every time I'm out to work or with a friend, my skin prickles, that deep sense of awareness causing the knot in my stomach to tighten.
 I may sound crazy, but knowing the type of life I live, I'm probably not. I have a feeling I know who's watching me: my father. Or more likely his men. It's not like I can go and ask him. We still don't have that kind of relationship.
 After Mom died, he didn't magically become nicer. He got

worse. With the years, my disdain for him only grew with his wrath.

The teenage years were awful. He hurled degrading words seeped with so much venom, it tore me apart from the inside out. But he only dug the blade in deeper, wanting every little bit of my agony, like he did with my mother.

He reveled in our pain.

He made me feel worthless.

I thought foolishly that after she was gone, he'd finally love me like I deserved. But as he chucked hurtful word after hurtful word, I knew it was time to bury that dream where I could no longer taste it.

To this day, I'm nothing more than a chess piece he uses whenever it suits him. That revelation doesn't cause me grief anymore, and I guess that's sad.

Each time he calls or forces me to see him for a business meeting, I want to pick up one of the large vases in his home and bash him on the head until every bit of oxygen leaves his lungs, until every ounce of blood flows out of his battered body.

I'm so grateful to whoever is after him, causing him to go into hiding. Who knows who he's started a war with or how long it'll last? It's not the first time he's done something to piss someone off, and I'm sure it won't be the last. My father has a problem with anyone telling him what to do, which doesn't always work out to his benefit.

Oh, well.

Maybe they'll kill him and save me the trouble. There are so many times I've thought about doing it myself, but never had the guts to go through with it.

Whenever I show up to a meeting with him, I have my gun from work on me. Sometimes, while he's talking, I imagine that split second of shock on his face before my bullet hits him right between the eyes.

I only ever had one parent. My mother. Mom was everything he wasn't. And I still don't know what happened to her.

I'm afraid of the ultimate truth: that she's gone forever.

That he killed her.

But I do think he did.

He must have.

A rotting ache builds in the middle of my chest, stabbing the very core of me, engulfing me in the memory of the day he told me she was gone.

Eyes drifting to a close, I take deep breaths, quieting the pain. I need to be strong, even when it's far more difficult to mask the pain. But living with it day in and day out is unbearable.

I've tried to dig into my mom's disappearance, but it's led nowhere. Any useful information he may have on where she may be is locked in his study, the one no one's allowed to step foot in. The one he locks every time he isn't home. I'll find out what happened to her. I won't rest until I do. Even if it means finding her remains.

When my mother disappeared, I told myself I'd eventually find a way to leave. I had no choice. I had no one in my corner anymore. It was just me and him in that house. Him and his cruelty, his need to control me in every aspect, including who I marry.

Yeah, that's right. When I was sixteen, he told me he had picked a guy for me, someone a little older. A son of a boss in another family.

At twenty-one, I was to marry him. It didn't matter whether I agreed, who this guy was, whether he'd treat me right. All my father cared about was uniting the two families to make himself stronger.

I knew then that it wasn't happening. No one was going to tell me who to marry, especially my father.

I'd wanted to run away from home as soon as my mother was gone. So, from the time I was fourteen, I saved every penny I received from birthdays and side jobs, like working at his friend's wife's beauty salon.

By the time I was eighteen, I had over fifty thousand. Let's just say my dad's friends were extra generous at parties, and my father was too drunk when they handed me the envelopes. Luckily, he never looked under my mattress or in my closet. I slowly began to put the money into a secret bank account.

One day, I was ready to go. I had my plan all mapped out. My father was away on business, and I figured it was now or never. Except I didn't realize that never was the only option I had.

When I arrived at the airport, he and a dozen of his men were waiting for me.

I thought he'd kill me—or worse, make me marry that man sooner. But he didn't. He silently drove me home and locked me in my room for weeks, only coming in to give me food once a day.

I was slowly shattering into infinite fragments, but I didn't show it, even when all I wanted was to be free for once in my life. I remained strong, keeping the agony within my heart where it always remained.

Then one day, after two weeks, he came and sat down on the bed beside me. He told me I could either marry Michael or get my degree and run his strip club.

Girls in my position don't have many options. Our families are old-fashioned, expecting marriage at a young age and kids not long after. We're supposed to be good, well-mannered Sicilian ladies, who do what Daddy tells us. Like marry a man we don't love.

Michael is the son of the don of the Messina family. He's

handsome, sure, but I'll never marry a man who's part of the lifestyle I grew up in. Living with Michael would be everything I have spent my entire life trying to avoid.

So my father's offer wasn't much of an offer, and he knew it. I accepted his deal to run the club.

It's not just any club, either. Tips & Tricks is one of the most lucrative strip clubs on the East Coast, about a one-hour drive from New York City. Celebrities and politicians frequent this place, and I do a hell of a job of making sure it's run smoothly.

My father owns a few other businesses, but it's all for show. He uses every single one as a means to launder money, including the one he put me in charge of.

I hired someone in secret who regularly checks the club, my car, and my home for bugs. He even scans the employees' cars. Between the law and my own father, I can't be too careful. He's yet to find anything.

I have no desire to end up in prison or be forced to snitch on my father and get killed for it. He wouldn't even hesitate. He might even pull the trigger himself.

Pushing a button, I turn on my laptop to look over the club's finances for the month. We're in the black, just how dear old Dad likes it. If he thought for one second that I couldn't handle running his place, I'd be in a white dress already, exchanging vows with a man I don't know.

Tapping a few more keys, I check on my current liquor order, making sure all the shipments are on time. If they weren't, they'd lose my business quickly. I pay them enough to ensure prompt service.

Finally done, I shut my laptop and lean against the back of my chair, stretching out my feet beneath the high-heeled black over-the-knee boots I'm wearing.

Knowing I have some free time, I decide to call my aunt Kirsten, my mom's sister. She lives alone, and I know she'll be up at midnight, being that she's an author who prefers to write in the solitude of the night.

I feel awful knowing she has no one in that house of hers. She was married once, a long time ago, to a man who preferred to beat her instead of love her, causing severe damage to her ovaries when he kicked her one too many times. She can't have kids as a result.

It took her years to leave him, and she never found anyone again. I think it was my mother's disappearance that gave her the courage to finally pack her bags and go. As sad as that is, knowing what my mom was going through and fearing her sister's death at the hand of an abusive man gave my aunt a glimpse into a future she could have.

At least that's what I think. She never outright told me any of this when she shared stories about the horror she'd endured.

Picking up my cell off the desk, I dial her number, and she answers on the second ring.

"Hey, Chiara," she yawns.

"Hey, Auntie. Up writing?"

"You know it," she laughs with another yawn.

"I don't know how you manage to write your scary stuff in the middle of the night. I still have nightmares after your last book. I can't step foot into a bank without wondering if one of the tellers will look me up and murder me. Thanks for that."

"Hey, it was a bestseller for a reason," she tosses out with a smile in her voice.

She's so talented. I can't believe we're related. If I tried to write a book, I probably couldn't even put two exciting sentences together.

"Enough about me," she throws in. "How are you? Are you at

the club?"

My office is soundproof, which is great, since I don't actually want to hear what's happening out there. Unless a customer gets handsy with my girls, then it's a bad day for Mr. Asshole.

I could let my bouncers handle it, but I like to show my face. I want those dickheads to know a woman runs this place, and she won't allow any of them to shit on any woman who works here.

"Yep. Just another day in the office." I lift my feet, placing them on top of my desk, ankles crossed.

"I really wish that asshole father of yours would leave you the hell alone. And if he's fucking listening, fuck you, Faro. I know you can't see it, but I've got a middle finger with your name on it."

I choke on a laugh. The kind you feel in your soul. The kind that brings you warmth.

"I love you," I tell her.

"I wish you could come see me soon. I really miss you, Chiara. It's been months."

She's right, it has. I'm so glad we're close now. As a child, I never saw her, but that's because my father wouldn't let Mom and me visit her. He dictated everything Mom did. Every friend she had. She couldn't go anywhere without one of his men chauffeuring her around. She wasn't even allowed to drive. He controlled everything, from what she ate to what she wore.

My father despises my aunt all due to her hatred of him. But who in the hell would *like* him?

I had her number saved back from when Mom gave it to me in case of emergencies.

"Your aunt is the only one you can trust. Remember that, baby," she'd say.

Even at a young age, I knew that number was important, so I kept it hidden.

My aunt and I got pretty close after Mom disappeared, and we now speak at least once a week behind my father's back. I'm glad I have her in my life. She makes me feel a little closer to my mom. When I was younger, I'd find a way to meet her whenever I had a break between my classes in high school. Dad had no idea. At least I don't think he did, since he never mentioned it. It's unlike him not to gloat when he's caught someone doing something they shouldn't. When I couldn't see her, we'd talk via email. I was afraid if I called her, he'd find out.

"I miss you too, Aunt Kirsten." I release a weighty sigh. "I'll figure out a way to make it out to you on the one day a week I have off, unless he forces me into a meeting with him, which kills most of my day."

"I know we shouldn't wish bad things on people, but I hope he gets his."

"Yeah, you and me both."

We laugh simultaneously, but she sounds exhausted.

"Go to sleep," I tell her.

"I will, I promise. Right after I get some more words in."

I shake my head with a grin. "Okay. Go write. I'll speak to you soon."

"Good night, honey. Love you."

"Night. Love you too."

I end the call, dropping the cell back on the desk. Hopefully, the men are behaving tonight. I don't feel like dealing with the occasional dickhead.

The ladies at my club are all special to me. It's my job to watch out for their well-being. They all have stories to tell. They're all trying to earn a paycheck to feed themselves or their families. They deserve respect.

And here, they get it.

I make sure of it.

One of them, Joelle, who's my age, has been my work friend since I've started. We don't hang out when we aren't at the club or anything, but before the clock starts, we sit back and enjoy a drink and girl talk.

Not that I have much to share in that department. Sex isn't even on my radar. It's been almost a year since I've had a good bang. All the men I meet are sleazeballs, and they're not coming anywhere near me.

The last guy I slept with was a quickie in the bathroom of a bar I went to alone on my day off. He was in a suit and hot as hell, with his honey-brown eyes and lips made for kissing.

I won't even blame it on the alcohol. This girl wanted him.

Badly.

The sex was pretty hot for a bathroom stall. And since then, it's been crickets.

I have no desire to marry anyone. I'm not pulling any poor sucker into this life of mine. Nor will I have kids who may be forced to carry my father's legacy and bad name. Not to mention, kids deserve a sweet grandpa, not an evil son of a bitch.

If I ever manage to escape his leash, which is crazy unlikely, maybe then there's hope for a future.

But I'll work here as long as I need to, just so I don't have to marry anyone having anything to do with my father or the likes of him.

I'm about to rest my eyes when my door pounds with a loud knock.

Great.

CHIARA
ONE WEEK LATER

TEN

"Come in," I say before the door opens.

Marco, one of my bodyguards, towers over the doorframe. The man's six-eight and two hundred eighty pounds of muscle. The customers here know not to fuck with anyone when they see him come through, and the resting man-bitch face he has going only helps me.

But Marco is a big softie. The sweetest, kindest man I have yet to meet. And I don't meet many of them.

Scratch that. I know none.

"What's wrong?" I ask him, noticing the look of alarm in his eyes.

"Ma'am, there's an issue with a customer. I know you wanted to be made aware."

"Just when I thought I could have a quiet night." A grin wraps around my lips. "What's going on?"

I sit up straighter. If anyone hurt a girl, they're going to fucking pay.

"I can take care of it so you don't have to be around that shit."

"You're too kind to me, Marco. But it's my job. Plus, I have you to beat the crap out of them if it comes to it."

His mouth twitches as he cracks a fist. "You know I will."

"Oh, I know." I arch a brow. "Now, let's go and take care of the problem."

I get to my feet and walk out alongside him, the blast of a hypnotizing melody greeting me while we rush down a long, dimly lit corridor. The music gets rowdier as we make it onto the main floor. The club is huge. There are three stages, and the girls rotate every half hour, with ten girls in total.

As he leads me near the cause of the problem, Marco informs me there was an unruly man in one of the sections who grabbed one of the girls by her hips and threw her onto his lap, after which, he tried to fondle her breasts. Marco and Antonio, my other bouncer, pulled her off of him.

As we get closer, I find Antonio next to a table in the corner, holding a man by the back of his neck. Antonio may not be as big as Marco, but he sure as hell can be a lot crazier.

"Hello, gentlemen," I greet them.

As Antonio turns around, I notice the man's shirt is in quite a disarray. It probably used to have buttons on it, but almost all have been ripped off. Oh, and there's a nice shiner around his eye. Looks like Antonio's handiwork.

"I like what you did there." I grin, drawing a circle around the man's face.

"Thanks, boss." Antonio shrugs, his head glistening beneath the pink and purple lights. "I try."

The man winces, gritting his teeth as Antonio tightens his grasp around him.

I finally take a better look at the asshole. He's about an inch shorter than me with my heels on. I'm five-seven without them, and a good five-eleven with.

"You're the one who decided to ruin my night?" I eye the man who looks at me as though I'm a joke.

"Who the fuck are you?" he asks, his lips twisting in disgust.

Antonio's other hand forms a fist under the man's chin, roughly shoving his head back. I can see in his glare that he's close to landing another punch.

But I hold out a hand, stopping him, my eyes never leaving the man's.

"I'm Chiara. Chiara Bianchi. This is my club, and these are my girls. And I heard you put your hands on one of them."

A small laugh bursts out of him. "That's what they're here for, aren't they? To make me happy. What else are whores good for?"

I narrow my eyes, edging closer to him until my face is less than an inch away from his. "My girls aren't whores. Call them that one more time and see what happens."

He grins, and I have the urge to wipe it off his face.

"You're so feisty. Are you sure you're not a stripper too? I'd love to see those big tits bounce up on that stage. I think I'd like to put my hands on them next."

"Please, ma'am, let me do it," Marco practically begs behind me.

Even with the music, I can hear the huffing of Marco's breath on my neck. Both men are very protective of me.

I spin his way, donning a big smile. "You have to let me have some fun too. It's boring otherwise."

When I turn back to the asshole, I clench a tight fist and throw it square at his nose.

He screams, blood gushing out like a fountain as he palms his nose, hyperventilating. There may or may not have been a possible crack. It's kind of hard to say. He'll have some good memories to look back on. He starts to stumble, but Antonio keeps him upright.

The men at the table to our right mutter something with a chuckle.

"Do you still want to feel my tits?" I ask with a bitter laugh.

All those boxing classes I took for a year have come in handy.

"You stupid bitch!" he cries. "I'm going to sue you for this."

I roll my eyes. "You're either stupid or have a death wish. I can't quite figure out which one." I release a bored sigh. "I suggest we pretend you didn't just say that."

I near his face again, practically smelling the blood still spouting out.

"I'll break a lot more than your nose if I ever see you near me, my club, or anyone I know. You'll wish we've never met." I shove at his chest. "Now, you're gonna scatter like the bug you are and go crawl into whatever hole you came from before I call the cops. And believe me, you'll stay in prison for a very long time if I do. I'll make sure of it."

I back away.

"Get this trash out of here," I tell Antonio and Marco.

Antonio nods. "With pleasure."

He drags the scumbag by his hair, the man practically falling over his feet. I rake my fingers through my long black hair that cascades down to the small of my back. This is my life. I didn't ask for it. I didn't want it. But here I am anyway, kicking ass and taking names.

I wanted to be a teacher. Crazy, right? I intended to make a difference in the world, I guess to counteract the bad my father was doing. It'll never happen now.

I'm twenty-eight, stuck here working for my father for however long he makes me. I couldn't even pick my own major in college. My father instructed I choose business so he could use me when he needed me.

This was his plan for me all along: force me into a marriage he knew I'd refuse, so I'd have no choice but to do his bidding.

Walking up to the bar, I order a drink. I need it after that incident.

"Hey, Tina," I call to the bartender. "Could you get me a Short Southern Screw?"

I love ordering that one, makes me laugh every damn time. And I could definitely use a screw. Not a short one, though. Preferably a long, thick one that knows what it's doing.

I drag in a long, deep breath. I guess it'll be another lonely night with me and my friend Pat, a.k.a. my dildo.

Tina places the shot before me, and I immediately let it pour down my throat. It's got a hint of peach and orange mixed with vodka and Southern Comfort. I wanted something to burn and hit me fast, and that sure as hell did the trick.

As I'm about to head back to the silence of my office, someone taps me on the shoulder from behind. I peer around, finding Joelle standing there.

"Are you okay?" she asks, her brows bending. "I saw what happened with that shitbag. I can't believe he did that to Sienna."

She shakes her head, pursing her lips with worry, her long, wavy strawberry-blonde hair flirting along the curves of her face.

The woman's gorgeous, and I don't even swing that way. She's the favorite in the club. Every guy who can afford her wants a private dance. Not only does she look like a 1920s pinup, but she also knows how to move her body well.

I wouldn't know what to do with a pole if my life depended on it. The one time I tried for fun, I looked ridiculous. Sometimes, it sucks being a boss of a bunch of strippers who know how to wrap around a pole better than you could ever dream of, especially when they ask you to join them.

I don't know why I agreed. The girls were practicing their routines one day and invited me to try it. I was the only embarrassment. I never did it again. These ladies make it look so easy.

It's not.

"I'm fine," I tell her. "You should've seen the other guy."

"I did," she laughs, shaking her head. "Remind me never to mess with you."

Her lips curl in amusement.

"A girl should always know how to stand up for herself," I tell her.

"You're right." She flips her hair past her shoulder with the back of her hand. "I'm going to start taking self-defense classes with this trainer at my gym. He's an ex-MMA fighter. And he's cute! You should join me. He may love throwing you around a little." She wags her eyes deviously.

"I'm not looking for that."

"Oh, please! You're talking to me here." She gestures at herself with a thumb. "I know how long it's been."

"Why do I tell you things?" I roll my eyes playfully, letting out an exaggerated sigh.

"Because you love me?"

"Yeah, yeah. Get back to work. I think you're up next."

"Fine." She backs away, the crystals from her lime-green bra sparkling underneath the colorful overhead LED lights. "But just in case you change your mind, his name is Frank, and his arms aren't the only big thing about him." She winks with a curve of her red lips. "Come to the gym and see for yourself."

I narrow an icy stare her way, shaking my head with a smile pulling at the corner of my mouth. She turns from me, and before she heads up on the stage, I call out her name.

She looks back, popping a brow.

"Text me the number." I don't have to marry the man to have a little bit of fun.

She grins. "You got it."

The emcee introduces her just as she seductively climbs up the steps, grabbing the pole and spinning around it once, before her legs hold on tight and don't let go.

I whirl back around, intending to head for my office, but instead I walk straight into a brick wall.

Well, not a wall, exactly. More like a man with a chest that feels harder than rock.

His hazel eyes flick to mine, connecting in an extreme stare. Why the hell is he staring at me like I killed his favorite puppy? Maybe if I were someone else, I'd even be a little afraid of him, but I'm not. I've known men far worse than he could possibly be.

But just as quickly as his harsh expression came, it vanishes, replaced with a flirty jerk of his full, dangerously sexy lips.

"Excuse me," I blurt out in irritation, staring at his chiseled face and the soft brown hues of his eyes.

The corded muscle of his bicep flinches just slightly, straining from within his light blue short-sleeved t-shirt. An intricate tattoo is wrapped around the length of his right arm, stretching up from his knuckles. I try to coyly make it out, but it's hard to see anything beyond the thorny vines, black roses, and a skull.

He doesn't bother moving out of the way, not that I really want him to. I bite the inside of my cheek. Desire to run my nails over his buzz cut while riding his face has my core in a state of frenzy.

The man is hot.

Sorry, Pat. This girl may be riding a different joystick tonight.

"You handled that well back there," he finally says, over the wave of thundering music, the tone of his voice draped in a sensual rasp as he gestures with his chin toward where the incident from earlier took place.

I prop a hand on my hip, lifting a brow. "You sound surprised. What? Never seen a woman handle her shit before?"

He chuckles low and deep, his gaze slipping to my lips before crawling back up to my eyes. "Never that well."

Warmth pools at my core from the way he gazes at me, from the way the words fall from his lips as though he's reading a poem rather than just speaking simple words.

I let my eyes roam down the length of him, letting him know he wasn't subtle when he took an obvious peek at my lips, and I'm not about to be either. Maybe I really should fuck him. He looks like he'd know just what to do.

I clear my throat. "Maybe you haven't been around the right women, then."

I'm met with the most awfully handsome lopsided grin. And he even has a fucking dimple like Dom once did, except his were on both sides.

I pull in a small breath, swallowing down the tightening throb in my throat. As I raise my chin and straighten my spine, my attention reverts back to the sexy stranger.

"You're right. Maybe I haven't been around the right type of woman yet." His gaze slinks over my breasts, his deep, gravelly voice slicing through all of my clothes, landing right in between my thighs. "So how about I start now?"

Time for me to get out of here before I really do invite him to my office. Did I mention it's soundproof?

"I should really be going," I mutter under my breath but loud enough for him to hear, too turned on to get my legs to move.

His tongue darts out, swiping over his lower lip as his eyes tangle with mine. I can't look away. His carnal prowess over my body is a magnetism I can't shake.

He leans in, his breath warm over my lips.

Intoxicating.

"Stay." The word is silkier than his gaze, caressing me with a burst of flames, heating me from the inside. "I know you want to."

I scoff at his advances, not wanting him to see a bend in my armor.

"I'm gonna go now. I have a club to run, in case you haven't noticed. Make sure you're a good little boy and don't do what the other one did. I wouldn't want to mess up that pretty face."

He chuckles in response. "You think I'm pretty, huh?"

His eyes zero in on my mouth and he clenches his jaw, enhancing the hollows beneath his cheekbones. And that jawline? Sharp and etched to perfection. I want to run the tip of my finger over the stubble there.

"Please. Like you don't know you're attractive." My eyes roll teasingly.

He smirks. "It's nice to hear it from a beautiful woman."

I pop a brow like I'm bored, but I'm smiling internally. "Is there anything else I can do for you?"

"May I buy you a drink?"

"Nope. I'm on the clock and I don't drink."

"I just saw you down a shot." He grins. "You're not as good at lying as you are at punching men, are you?"

I shrug a shoulder, the corner of my mouth curling up with a barely there smile.

"Come on, one drink." He runs his large hand over the back

of his neck, his silver watch—which I suspect is a Rolex—on full display. "I won't take too much of your time. I'll even make it a virgin."

"I'm not much of a virgin...drinker."

A smile tugs on his lips before he leans in, so close I can hear his breaths and feel them wisping over that sensitive spot below my ear. "Well, then I *promise* to make it extra dirty."

I suck in a breath. His words reach inside me, filling me with all kinds of terribly inappropriate, yet equally delicious thoughts.

Did I just pant? Oh, fuck me. I just panted like a damn virgin, didn't I?

My toes curl within the confines of my boots. The idea of sleeping with him doesn't sound so bad now.

He pulls back, his lids hooded with the same desire coursing through me. "So, about that drink..."

My pulse races while he continues to stare, as though he's thinking about just how dirty we could be together. As though we're alone and he's already undressing me.

A frazzled exhale slips out from my lips. "Fine. One drink. That's it."

He chuckles dryly. "We'll see."

What the hell does that mean?

But I don't ask. I'll survive for one drink with my sexy stranger, and then I'll never see him again. Unless he becomes a regular, and in that case, we're definitely fucking. I can only behave for so long.

I take a step back to the bar, taking a seat on a swivel chair, while he takes the one next to me. He pulls it really close, leaning his thigh into mine, causing my inner ones to tighten into one another.

I stare at the liquor bottles, the TVs above, anywhere but at him. Every time his eyes hold mine, it's like I'm held in place by an invisible pull, one that refuses to let go until we do something about it.

He waves for the bartender while I internally scold myself for being so pathetic. So what if the hot guy with the muscles in all the right places is flirting with me?

I'm Chiara fucking Bianchi. I don't cower to any man. They cower to me.

But as I pivot my head slightly, I find those captivating eyes already pinning mine, paralyzing me, and every breath of mine seizes in my chest, burning through my lungs.

His gaze drops to my lips, his eyes telling me just what he wants to do with them.

My stomach bottoms out, the knots already there tightening. His thick fingers drag over the bar, nearing mine as he raises his other hand to get the bartender's attention.

"What can I get ya?" Tina asks, breaking our intense lust-filled connection.

"Martini for her. Whiskey neat for me."

"Who the hell told you I wanted a martini?" I ask firmly as Tina strolls away.

He rotates in the swivel chair, quirking up a brow. "Was I wrong?"

"No," I grumble, threading my fingers through my hair. "But that's not the point. Ask next time."

Who does he think he is, ordering for me like he knows me or something? I mean, it is one of my favorite drinks, but that's not the point.

"There's going to be a next time?"

"I didn't mean…"

The tantalizing way his gaze fills mine with want has me

stammering. Those eyes glow like skin warmed by the sun, radiating down my body in waves of heat.

There's a touch of a smile on his face, a genuine one. "Uh-uh, you can't take it back now."

I breathe out an unintentional snicker.

"Wow, she finally laughs," he says.

"Barely." I roll my eyes.

He angles his head to the left. "It's a start."

The drinks arrive and I quickly pick mine up, taking sip after sip, needing the lull of alcohol.

He doesn't touch his drink yet, watching me enjoy mine. A quiet moment passes as he stares deep into my eyes like he's trying to figure out a Rubik's Cube.

It makes my heart beat faster.

"Would you stop looking at me like that?" I say. "It's kind of creepy."

And also a little hot. No, scratch that lie. A lot hot.

"I apologize. I'm only trying to figure out how someone could be this beautiful."

I roll my eyes, shaking my head. "What's your name, Casanova?"

"Brian Smith. What's yours?"

"Chiara."

"No last name?"

"Nope. Just Chiara." I don't know if he's heard of my father, but I think it's better if I don't give him that part of me. I haven't enjoyed a conversation with a man in too long, and I don't want it to stop just yet.

My dad's reputation has done a number on this city. Sometimes I wish I could change my name, but I'm stuck with the one I have.

He reaches for my hand, the one on my lap. Picking it up, he kisses the top of it, gazing at me from below a full set of dark brows.

"Nice to meet you," he says, lifting his mouth away. "I have a feeling we'll become fast friends."

The corners of his lips tip up wickedly with a slant of his gaze.

I have a feeling he may be right. It may be the alcohol, but I'm looking forward to it.

Minutes turn to two hours, and we're still talking, lost in each other, lost in the words and the attraction building with every moment that passes by.

I haven't felt this way before. This sense of want for another person. Not this badly. I want him even more now than I did when I first saw him.

Every time he talks, all I want is to know even more about him, to know his lies and the truths behind them.

He's given me bits of himself, and I've given him crumbs in return. Little tiny fragments of our real selves, but it's been enough to keep us both interested.

It's not like I can share anything too personal, and he seems the same way too…guarded, keeping his deck of cards close to his chest. I get that more than anyone, and it makes him even more intriguing.

I intend to figure him out. Maybe not today, but I will know him.

"How come some man hasn't swept you off your feet yet?" he asks, seemingly curious, as he picks up his whiskey, downing it without even a grimace as though he just drank some water. He pushes the glass away.

"Maybe I don't want to be swept?" I cock a brow. "Maybe I want to be pushed. Hard. Fast."

What the fuck am I doing?

But I can't stop myself, especially with this liquor pooling into my empty stomach.

As I take another sip of my drink, he's suddenly off his seat, spinning me in my chair until I'm facing him. His palms land hard on the bar, caging me in as he lowers his face close enough to mine, capturing me.

Excitement shivers, running down my spine as my lungs battle for air.

"Say one more dirty thing, Chiara," he warns, holding my gaze with his heavily-lidded one. "And I'll push you harder than you've ever been pushed before."

My lips shudder. My stomach flips and bends from the power of his words, the close proximity of his hard body, the woodsy smell of his cologne.

His mouth lowers closer to mine and I inhale a breath, anticipating the feel of him, but instead, his teeth graze over the corner of my lower lip, sending a sharp tingle to my core.

My pussy clenches, feeling hollow, needing more. I think I may have whimpered. I hope he didn't catch it with the beating of the music clouding over us.

He pulls away, gazing at my mouth like he's about to make a full meal out of it. My breaths fall shallow and shaky, the center of my chest aching from the tattered beats of my heart.

Then he moves back, finding his seat again.

And I'm left trying to figure out what the fuck just happened.

DOMINIC

ELEVEN

Sitting across from me is the girl I once loved, and I keep having to stare at all of her to believe I'm really beside her after all this time.

Her long, wavy raven-black hair spills over one side past her shoulder as she takes sips of her drink.

My gaze devours her, from those round, deep brown eyes to her insanely curvy body. She's all grown up and has only gotten more beautiful. Her shirt can barely contain her tits. They're not massive, but they're huge for her frame.

If she wasn't his daughter and the girl who ripped my heart out, she'd be up against the wall already with my cock buried inside her. Wouldn't be hard at all. She's practically begging for it.

But that'll never happen. Not with her. I shouldn't have even done what I just did, but I couldn't deny our chemistry.

Why the hell does she have to be so beautiful? And why the hell can't I stop thinking about those lips sucking on my cock here in this club?

Fuck.

My dick throbs. I bet I could have her bouncing on my lap right on this stool if I wanted to.

Getting women to spread their thighs has never been my problem. It's making them leave after I'm through with them that is. But I have a feeling that won't be a problem with her.

Clenching a fist, I force all thoughts of the mafia princess out of my head. I'll never fuck her.

Not even if she begs.

Not even if it's all I can think about.

I don't fuck the enemy. I ruin her.

This pretty little thing may want me now, but soon, when she realizes what I'm about to do to her, she'll want nothing to do with me.

Chiara Bianchi may be the devil's daughter, but she'll soon be mine, and not in the way she wants.

I didn't intend for it to happen this way. It fell into my lap when I least expected it. But now, I can't wait.

"How long have you run this place?" I ask, though I already know almost everything about her.

I don't even know why I came here. I didn't need to see her before tonight. But the sick piece of shit that I am, I want her to see me like this before I cause her entire life to fall apart like she did mine. I have lots of plans for Faro's only child, and none of them will make him happy.

"Since I graduated college seven years ago," she answers.

I knew that too. Between gathering information and following her for about two years, I know more than she can imagine.

I didn't just follow her because of her father. It was deeper than that. Our past—the history I still haven't been able to free myself from—haunted me.

I've never stopped thinking about her.

Not once.

And every time I remember how badly she hurt me, I only want to hurt her more.

My brothers and I have been making plans for the Bianchi brothers for years now, but in the last year, our plan became concrete. We've organized everything to perfection, making sure nothing was overlooked.

"Was it something you've always wanted to do?" I wonder.

I'm curious why she works here. I haven't been able to learn that information. Yet.

She laughs humorlessly. "Run a strip club?" Her brow flies up. "Definitely not."

"Why are you doing it, then?"

"Let's just say I had to."

"I'm sorry you were forced into something you didn't want," I add, picking up another whiskey I ordered and downing it fast, letting the amber liquid burn a path down my throat.

"Things could always be worse," she says nonchalantly.

And for you, baby girl, they're about to be.

If she only knew how much her life is about to change and how much her father had to do with it, she'd run. Or maybe she wouldn't. I haven't quite figured her out yet. But running wouldn't help. I'll always find her.

I wonder if she ever thinks about the boy I once was. Whether she regrets what she said.

Did our friendship mean anything? Did I ever matter?

I steel my jaw, waving to the bartender to order another drink, needing to burn away the scars of our past.

As I watch her watching me, I can't help but smile. I look forward to the moment when she realizes who I really am. When everything she thinks she knows is ripped apart.

"You really don't have a boyfriend?" I ask, even though I already know she doesn't.

She shakes her head. Her expression is kind of broken, and my stupid heart feels it too.

"Would I be here flirting with you if I had one?" Her face is easygoing again, traces of unhappiness now gone.

"*That* was flirting?" I tease with a smirk.

Her lips twitch as she shoves her boot into my calf, and my hand snaps for her ankle, clutching it hard as our eyes connect.

Her narrowed gaze squeezes every ounce of my desire to feel her writhing under me while I give her the kind of punishment I've been aching to give her for years.

"You must be lonely," I say, letting go of her foot, needing to calm the savagery lurking in the dark.

She circles her finger around the edge of her glass, looking absently into her drink as though it holds the answer to whatever is on her mind.

"You don't have to worry about me, Brian Smith." She grins as she looks up at me with a hint of straight, white teeth. "Is that a real name, by the way? It sounds fake as hell."

I chuckle low. She doesn't realize how right she is.

Don't worry, Chiara Bianchi. You'll know my name soon enough, and you'll wish you hadn't.

"Do you always insult people you just met, or am I just lucky?"

"Don't be so sensitive." Her mouth pulls into a teasing smile. "It doesn't suit you."

I grab the side of her chair and pull her harshly close to me until her knees hit mine. Her eyes tangle with my gaze as I lean into her neck, inhaling the scent of her floral perfume. My nose traces up the column of her neck until I get to her ear.

"How would you know what suits me, Chiara? Hmm?" I question with a low growl as my other hand lands on her thigh, my fingers wrapping tightly as she pants, her breathing intensifying.

She may be in charge at the club, but not with me.

I own her, and she doesn't even know it.

This is all part of my plan, I convince myself. *Make her want me until she realizes what I'm about to do to her.*

I pull back, scanning her parted lips and heavy-lidded eyes. She's so damn sexy, and even more so now that she's turned on.

Fuck, I want this woman. I want the sound of her voice, broken and bruised, just as much as my heart was all those years ago when she threw away our friendship like it meant nothing.

"You...ah..." she stammers, rising to her feet. "I...I need to get back to work now." Her eyes turn to slits as she assesses me. "It was nice meeting you, Mr. *Smith*."

I get up too, lifting her hand to my mouth. "The pleasure has been all mine."

She begins strutting away, her hand drifting away from mine while she peers back at me over her shoulder.

"Chiara, one more thing," I call.

She cranes her neck, giving me the "what the fuck do you want?" face. That feisty woman is back, and my cock hardens, wanting a taste.

"Make sure you're careful when you leave tonight. There are lots of crazy men out there."

Like me.

"Thanks for your concern, Smith, but I've managed to handle myself just fine in the last seven years." Her gaze cruises from my eyes down to my chest before she finally goes, her round ass bouncing out of view.

I wonder how her daddy would feel knowing his daughter wants to fuck the trash. My brothers and I may have been trash to him then, but these days, we're nothing short of a weapon with his name on it.

We're ready for vengeance. Ready for his blood to spill onto the streets he runs like a tyrant.

The shit we did to his warehouse a week ago is only the tip of the iceberg that will be his hell. They probably didn't suspect it would happen so soon after the laundromat attack two days before that.

Faro runs two legitimate businesses, one of which we've torched. But the laundromat was just a shell, a farce of a business, one where they run guns from. No one other than their people ever used it. More than half the time, they were closed to run their illegal operations. We had our men watching them. We knew everything they did.

Once we killed everyone inside, we took all the weapons, then torched the place. It's become our signature calling card—destroying everything he owns until it's nothing but ashes caught in the wind.

That was the first crew of his that we took out, and we left a note, smeared in blood.

Morte.
- C

It's the event that set everything in motion. He and his brothers hid like the sacks of shit they are. They *should* fear us. That's smart. They can hide all they want. We're patient. We've had to be.

We'll annihilate every one of their men who dares stand in our way until we find them and kill them.

If we need a little help, we'll have that soon enough, in the form of Chiara's cousin, Raquel.

Before Faro ruined our life, I was a normal kid. I wanted to become a lawyer. Yeah. Me, a fucking lawyer. It's funny now.

I wonder if our father is ashamed of us, or proud. He was a simple man who didn't have a mean bone in his body. I don't know why Faro killed him, or why he killed my brother too.

But I will find out. The devil himself will tell me the truth before I take his life, and he'll be begging for a bullet when I'm through with him.

No mercy.

When they killed our father, we were nothing but little boys. Bugs they could squash in a blink of an eye. Up until we blew up their laundromat, the Bianchi men didn't realize we were even alive.

But now they do.

They don't yet know the full extent of our strength, the number of hired guns on our payroll. We have so much fucking money now, we don't know what to do with it. The days of living in squalor are long behind us.

After we watched the warehouse burn, we cut the head off of one of his soldiers, the one we didn't let burn with the rest, and had it specially delivered with a big, red bow.

Dante's idea.

He's got a sick sense of humor and an even sicker mind. If he wasn't good at running our businesses, he'd be the perfect assassin. He kills with zero apprehension.

Faro thinks he's above retaliation from anyone. He thinks wrong. Inside the box was not only his pal's head, but a bloody note that read:

Hope you enjoyed the show. There's more to come.
- C

We also left him the number for one of my burner phones, just in case he wanted to chat and catch up on old times. I wanted to hear the son of a bitch beg for this to stop.

He did call a day later. But he wasn't begging. He had a proposition for me, one I made him think I'd consider, but one I never will.

I don't make deals with the devil. I burn him to the ground.

I thought about saving him for last so he could see his brothers die, but I realized he doesn't care about anything but money, so waiting to take him out would only torture me.

Fifteen years is a long time to wait for retribution.

The time has come. And the time is now.

CHIARA

TWELVE

I'm finally alone at the club. It's peaceful with the music off, the lights dimmed. The place looks so different now. I like to stay here all alone for a little while before going home. Marco and Antonio hate that I close the club by myself, but I'm a big girl.

I'm sure Daddy has his eyes on me anyway. His goons are probably watching from some obscure hole, making sure his commodity is secure.

That's all I am: an insurance policy for his business.

When he's done using me, he'll toss me aside like everyone else in his life. No one means anything to him. I think he lacks a soul. Maybe he's one of those psychopaths. Or sociopaths. I always confuse the difference.

Even my uncles have more heart than he does, or at least I

think so. They're all crazy sons of bitches, though. No, really, my grandma was a bitch. She was mean, cold, and never offered any of her grandkids a nice word. Maybe that's why my dad is the way he is. Or maybe he was born with it like Maybelline, just uglier.

I'm not close to anyone from my dad's side of the family except my cousin, Raquel. We were born weeks apart and are pretty inseparable. Her father, Salvatore, is my father's advisor. He's basically the man who wipes my dad's ass if he asks. Raquel hates him, but not because he's abusive like mine. Her parents are forcing her into a marriage she wants no part of.

She's been promised to marry Carlito, one of the soldiers in the family, who's fourteen years her senior. She has no one to help her out of this predicament.

My cousin is smart, currently a resident at a very prestigious hospital in New York City, and insanely beautiful with long, black hair and deep brown eyes. She constantly talks of running from this life and away from the grabby asshole she's supposed to marry in six months.

I see Carlito here a lot, with a new girl grinding on his dick every week. Sometimes he pays for two at once. He definitely doesn't look like a man who wants to get married. I bet he's even cheating on her, and I doubt that'll stop after the wedding.

My heart hurts for Raquel. I wish I had money to help her. At least I got away from a future with a man I didn't want. Not to say this life is any better, with no choices to make of my own. But I'd rather work here and be alone for the rest of my life than marry into the family.

Running this club is the only thing I have, and maybe that's why I take it so seriously. But even that's an illusion. It's not *my* club. It's my father's.

I decide to call Raquel to check in on her. She's been working crazy long hours, but is actually off today because she had a party to attend for Carlito's family. I wonder if she's home yet. The parties in our circle run really late.

Reaching into my red handbag, I take out my cell and dial her number. She answers on the first ring.

"Hey," she whispers, her voice sounding alarmed.

There's a male and female voice in the background, and worry gnaws at the forefront of my chest.

"Raquel? What's going on?" I ask with a low tone, my pulse racing in my ears.

"Carlito and my mom are talking about moving the wedding up by three months!" I can hear the tears in her voice. "I can't marry him, Chiara. I'd rather die."

"Don't say that! We'll find a way. I promise."

But that's a lie. There's nothing I haven't tried, between speaking to her parents and even my father. He told me to mind my fucking business, while her parents just patted my hand and assured me this is for the best.

Whose best? I'd asked them. *Your daughter would rather end her life than marry a man she doesn't want, but you think that's what's best for her?*

I'd never spoken to my aunt and uncle that way. But I had to try and get through to them. Unfortunately, it didn't work. I'm afraid of what Raquel will do if she's shoved into a corner with no way out.

"I mean it, Chiara. I don't want to live this way. I'd rather die."

An ache builds behind my eyes. She's fucked. We both know it. There's nothing she can do to get out of this. Her mom wants this even more than her dad.

And Carlito? He's obsessed with the thought of marrying her. He won't give her up, even if her parents put a stop to it.

"There has to be something we can do!" I urge. "Maybe you can join a monastery and swear yourself to God or some crap."

"Yeah, okay. Be serious. My parents wouldn't allow that. They'd drag me out of there kicking and screaming. I wish there was someone else I could marry, even if I had to pay him to pretend. Someone more powerful than my father. Someone who can take him on. Take them all on."

She sighs, the credence in her voice that I know and love no longer there. She sounds…lost. Defeated beyond measure.

We don't know anyone who could help her by faking a marriage. She has no other viable options. No men out there would take on the mafia for her. Definitely not another doctor at her hospital. They'd run the hell away at the first sign of trouble.

"Oh, my God!" she exclaims in a hushed tone. "My mom just said she'll take care of moving all the arrangements. She thinks I'm old and that there's no reason to wait. She said I need to have children soon. I can't believe she's doing this to me!"

My face grimaces with disgust. Raquel pregnant with that animal's kids? I can't even think about it without hurling.

She sniffles, her composure breaking down. The pitiful whimpers coming from her mouth cause my own tears to run past my cheeks.

I know how she feels. When I thought I'd have to marry Michael, I thought my life was over. I even considered jumping off a bridge, as awful as it sounds. But when you're stuck with no way out, you create one.

I hear her shuffling around, heavy static coming through the phone. "I have to go. I think she's about to come to my room."

"Bye," I mutter. But she's long gone.

I let out a harsh breath. This is insane. We're grown women, yet we have people telling us what the hell to do, planning out our entire life as though we're inept to handle our own shit.

Stuffing the phone back into my handbag, I get to my feet, needing to lock up the place and go home to a nice, warm bed.

I head for the exit, opening the door to a muted street, except for the crickets breaking up the silence. There are a few other businesses in this area, including a cigar and sex toy shop that's long closed. My car is the only one in the parking lot, which is the nightly occurrence since it's already past three a.m.

Taking out my keys, I start to close the place down when the loud screeching of multiple sets of tires coming from around the corner has my heart racing like a stampede of wild horses. It must be some teenagers out for a joy ride.

I fumble with the keys, the cars getting closer, my heart now beating in my throat.

Shit. I have to get the hell out of here. What if they see me and stop? What if they hurt me?

My hand trembles with the keys still attached to the door.

Close the damn thing and run to your car!

Suddenly, the noise stops as though it never was. The cars must've left. The relief comes like a grenade.

Crunch.

Crunch.

Loud thuds of someone's feet crash against the pavement, and my eyes widen with the rapid pacing of my breathing.

My stomach dips, diving with the fear taking over all my thoughts. My mind says to go, but my body won't budge.

Multiple footsteps now.

My knees buckle. An icy cold tremor runs down my body.

Don't turn around.

This is a dream.

They're not here for you.

A shiver runs down the entire length of my body, and I tremble out a breath just as a hard body presses into my back from behind. A man's bulky chest shoves into me until my cheek lands flat against the cold door.

He takes deep, calm breaths, the feel of them running up my neck, bathing me in more fear than I've ever known.

"If you scream—if you so much as *flinch*—I'll kill you," says a deep, husky voice.

Wait.

I've heard that voice before.

It can't be...

Before I have a chance to discern if the voice really belongs to the man I spent hours flirting with, a strong, masculine hand is on my mouth, covering my lips with sticky tape.

"Fire! Fire!" I scream, trying to fight him off, the adrenaline within me battling for control, remembering my boxing coach telling us to scream "fire" when faced with trouble, because people tend to ignore the word "help."

He grabs my hair and pulls hard until I'm met with a pair of hazel eyes staring from within a black ski mask.

Now there's no doubt. It's him. The man who called himself Brian Smith.

Here I thought he actually liked me, but it was just a game he was playing.

As though wanting me to know it's really him, he pulls up the mask and smiles, lips twisting viciously.

I narrow my gaze, and his smirk only deepens.

"Nice to see you again, Chiara Bianchi. We're gonna have a lot of fun together. I promise." His other hand lands over my mouth and nose, covering it with something white.

I grumble, struggling against him even as I start to drift away.

Before everything turns hazy and black, I hear his deep, throaty voice.

"Don't fight me, baby. You'll lose."

My eyelids dangle between sleep and wakefulness. It's hard to open them. I'm so groggy and lightheaded, like I'm just waking up from a nap cut too short. There's a slight headache at my temples too.

Light filters through my lids, and I groan, fighting against it, hoping to keep my eyes closed forever. My body feels liquified. I can barely move my limbs.

Where am I? What happened?

I pull my right arm up, but something tight holds it hostage, straining against my wrist. I try moving the other hand, but the same thing happens.

What the fuck?

And that's when I remember the events that led me here.

Brian fucking Smith.

I recall everything now. The cars. The fear.

Now I'm bound, gagged, and tied up.

"Help!" I scream, but it sounds more like a whimper with the damn tape he put on me.

I yank at my arms harder, shouting with all my might. The muffled sounds that come out only make me angrier.

No, no, no. I can't be locked away again.

Memories of when my father confined me in a room for weeks pummel into my mind, and panic sets in. My chest heaves from rapid breaths.

This isn't happening again.

My stomach churns with deep-seated dread and every breath

ns faster, until all I want is to claw at my lungs for relief.

My eyes start getting used to the light, and I manage to pry them open all the way.

"Good morning, princess," Brian says with a condescending undercurrent.

I lift up my head, zeroing in on him, my blood boiling with fury as I grind my teeth with a roar. My hands squeeze, despite the bindings on my wrists.

"I hope your nap was satisfactory."

My cloudy vision clears enough for me to register that smirk of his. I find him leaning back in a black leather armchair parked against the wall to my left. He crosses his leg over his other knee, black loafers covering his feet.

Getting a burst of energy, I push up with my back, pulling my hands hard against what looks like rope. My eyes glare into his in an intense battle as I growl like a barbaric animal.

He chuckles. "Where do you think you're going? You're kind of at a disadvantage."

I pant, the anger and horror simmering from within me.

He'd better tell me what the hell I'm doing here, and he'd better take this fucking tape off of me.

He gets off the chair and makes his way to me. His light pink button-down shirt strains against his muscular form as he moves. He looks like a hot businessman, but he's anything but that.

Once he's on my side of the bed, he reaches a hand down, stroking my cheek with the rough touch of his knuckles. Bile rises in my throat, entangled with sheer terror.

"This doesn't have to be bad for you." The corners of his lips deepen into a smile, and that dimple makes an appearance as he draws his hand away. "If you behave and keep those tiny claws to yourself, I'll remove the tape. If you do decide to scream, no one will help you, so you'll only be hurting yourself. Understood?"

If I want to get out of these binds and this room, I can't act like a crazy person. I have to think of a plan while pretending to be a good little girl. I nod, giving him the indication that I'll be on my best behavior.

Everything's going to be fine.

Yeah, right. Who am I fooling? This is bad.

"This is gonna hurt," he warns with satisfaction before ripping off the tape.

I groan, suppressing the scream wanting to get out.

He crunches up the tape and places it on the black nightstand next to the bed.

"Why the hell am I here?" My voice comes out smaller than I intended.

He doesn't answer, staring down at me, his brows knitting tightly as he runs the back of his hand over the edge of my jaw, his gaze filled with an emotion I can't name. It's as though he's not looking at me, but through me. Like his mind is somewhere else entirely.

"Hello? I'm talking to you, asshole!"

His jaw clenches, and the trance is broken. He lifts a brow in challenge. And before I can say any more, his hand reaches for my neck, his thick fingers wrapping around and squeezing just the right amount.

"Watch your fucking mouth." His exhales roll out of him like a dragon breathing fire.

"What are you gonna do, huh?"

My heart pounds faster against my rib cage, to the point that I'm afraid it'll rip right through my chest.

"You wanna fuck me? Is that it? Poor little man." My tone turns pestering. "What happened? You can't get it up any other way?"

He squeezes harder, and my lungs burn enough to know he'll kill me if he wants to. I won't underrate my fear. This man before me is dangerous, and if he's anything like my father, he won't hesitate to end me.

I'm a commodity yet again. It's as though I was born with a sticker that says: *Use me and abuse me.*

His fingers land on my mouth.

"Say one more goddamn thing, and I'll slap another piece of tape over those pretty lips." His face nears, close enough for his mouth to brush over mine, but it doesn't. "And if I wanted to fuck you, I would have done it already. Nothing you could do to stop me."

I squirm uncomfortably at the thought of being fucked by him while tied to his bed. It's sick that the imagery even crosses my mind.

He notices my discomfort, his eyes leisurely scanning my body, leaving a scorching path of pure flames.

Gritting my teeth, I stare down at him, needing this attraction between us to burn out. I despise him and his chiseled jaw with that five o'clock shadow, making him even sexier.

"What happened, princess?" His gaze slams into mine, his finger running down in between my breasts, stopping at my belly button. "You look a little flushed."

My body heats up again, my core clenching inadvertently.

"Don't call me that!" I roar.

The word "princess" makes my skin crawl. My father used to call me that when he'd pretend I meant something to him. But it was all for show when his friends were around. To this day, I can't even hear that word, let alone be referred to by it.

He laughs. "Why not? Did your ex-boyfriend call you that?"

My brows pinch tightly.

"Just don't, okay?" My voice falls with the painful memories, scratching at the wounds I want to keep closed forever.

"Fine. I won't call you a princess anymore." He grins, knowing he just said the word again.

I shake my head. "You're such an asshole."

"Which part from today gave that away?"

I scowl. "Do you even know who my father is? Do you realize what he'll do if he finds out what you've done?"

My father may not give a shit about me, but this stranger doesn't have to know that. Then again, my father is very possessive of his name, and he won't let anyone think he's weak by allowing his daughter to be kidnapped without starting a war first.

For appearance's sake, he'll get every ally to join in a war that'll have Brian—and whoever he has working for him—look like little children.

"Your father is the reason you're here, Chiara."

I narrow my eyes. "What has he done for me to deserve this?"

"You'll find out soon, but now isn't the time. Go rest. I'll be back a little later. You'll eat and take a shower then."

"Wait a second!" I widen my stare. "You expect me to sleep like this?" I pull at the rope.

"What did you think? That I'd let you roam around my house?"

"Why can't you just take this shit off and stop treating me like an animal? I didn't ask for any of this. I didn't choose my father. I'm nothing like him."

He snickers. "Right. Of course you're not."

Then he whirls away from me, his footsteps batting across the wood floors. He reaches for the door, but before he goes, he looks over at me, his gaze turning soft, like that of the man I met at the club. I feel the weight of his eyes on mine.

"Close your eyes and go to sleep. No one will hurt you here,

Chiara. I promise."

"No one but you," I retort softly.

He gives me a lingering look before he's gone, the door clicking to a close behind him.

CHIARA

THIRTEEN

I haven't slept at all. My eyelids ache, and my body feels as though I need a pound of caffeine just to function. When I do end up sleeping, I know I'm going to crash.

I glance around the expansive bedroom, looking for a clock, but there is none. The room is more like three bedrooms in a regular house. I wonder how huge this place is. By the looks of this room, I'm sure it's massive.

There's nothing in here besides a nightstand, a flat-screen TV that takes up three-quarters of the wall, and the armchair he was on. Oh, and the bed holding me hostage, of course. Can't forget that.

I wish he'd tell me what this is about. I need to know so I can somehow convince him I'm on his side.

That won't be much of a stretch. Under normal circumstances,

I'd never consider helping my captor, but we're not in normal circumstances. My father is a scumbag who hurts people whenever it benefits him. I'm sure he did something awful to this man. If helping him means I can get out of here alive, then I'll do whatever the hell he wants.

The door jolts, and my body goes into alert, my pulse racing within my neck. I try to sit up, but I keep sliding down.

With a creak, the door parts, and in walks the man of my dreams and nightmares, carrying a tray. He's changed, now wearing a dark blue button-down rolled up one side, exposing a tanned arm without tattoos, unlike his other.

A gray tie sits obediently over his neck, matching his gray slacks. He exudes powerful masculinity and all the things I crave in a man. Too bad that man decided to be a psycho. Figures those are the types I'd be most attracted to.

He lays the tray down on the nightstand beside me. "Slept well?"

"No. I didn't," I say with a glare, the words rushing out from behind gritted teeth.

"I'm sorry my hotel is unsatisfactory. I hope we don't get a bad Yelp review."

"You're enjoying this, aren't you?"

He chuckles. "So much. You have *no* idea."

"You live here alone?" I dive right into getting more information.

"Why? Want to move in?" He bathes my body with a smoldering gaze. "You do look good on my bed."

"Not even if you paid me." After a few seconds of silence, I speak up again. "You're as bad as him. Do you realize that?"

His brow wrinkles in question. "Who?"

"My father. Who else?"

His nostrils flare, and his breaths fall harshly out of his lungs.

"I'm *nothing* like him."

"No? Could've fooled me. You kidnap me, tie me up, treat me like a savage."

"We could look at it that way. But I haven't actually hurt you, have I?" He lifts the top off the tray, and the whiff of sweet goodness hits my nostrils. "And as you can see, I've brought you a cappuccino and a tray full of berry-filled crepes and some bagels. I know for a fact that your father doesn't treat *you* that way, let alone his victims."

That part stings. Knowing that a stranger knows my father treats me badly is more embarrassing than I'll ever admit out loud.

"Bringing me food doesn't make you a good guy. You're still holding me against my will."

"I am, and I could say I'm sorry, but I'm not. And like I said earlier, you won't be harmed. Not unless you don't behave." His lips wind into a sneer, causing my insides to twist right along with them.

"Children are told to behave," I fight back. "I'm a grown woman."

He lets out a deep laugh. "I like that little fire inside you, but it's useless here, I'm afraid."

My gaze lands on his, and the comeback I had planned in response vanishes from the ravenous way he looks at me. It's like he does one thing, but his eyes say another.

I swallow down the weighty lump in my throat, finding it hard to tear my gaze away.

He grips the back of his neck, his lids drifting to a close for such a quick second, I'm not sure if he actually did it.

Picking up the tray, he sits beside me and cuts off a piece of crepe with a fork.

"Open your mouth," he demands as the hand holding the fork

nears my mouth.

I shake my head, refusing to eat this way, being fed while tied up. Hell no.

"Eat. Now." His eyes flare with anger.

"No." I glare right back.

He pushes the fork in a little. "I wasn't asking. I said eat."

"And I said no," I mutter as bits of crepe land in my mouth, and I spit them out. "Not when you still have me bound like this!" I yank my wrist. "Untie me."

He roughly drops the fork onto the tray, and it clatters loudly while his hand simultaneously lands on the back of my head, his palm harshly fisting my hair.

"This is not some fucking negotiation, Chiara. Stop fighting me. It will go a lot better for you if you do."

I clench my jaw, my gaze battling with his. "I've been around men far scarier than you. You're nothing."

He drops his hand. "Fine." He stands, picking up the tray. "You want to kill yourself? Go ahead. Starve."

"If I'm dead, so is your bargaining chip," I say. "It's why you have me here, isn't it?"

"If you're dead, I'll serve your head on a silver platter to your daddy. You have no idea why you're here, and believe me, you don't want to know. So go ahead, baby, make it harder on yourself."

"I'm *not* your baby."

"Okay, not baby." His shoulders rock with a small laugh. "You have ten seconds to decide if you want me to feed you or I'm leaving. There will be no food until later."

"Fuck you!" I spit out.

"Suit yourself."

Then he strolls back out of the room.

His words play over and over in my head, making me wonder

why I'm actually here to begin with.

The sound of the door opening jars me out of sleep.

Wait? I fell asleep? Shit.

I should've tried harder to stay awake. I can't trust my safety to that man who's walking back in with the same damn tray in his hands.

I refuse to accept anything from him. He can shove that food up his tight, round ass.

"I've come to see if you're hungry enough that you've lost that stubbornness." His voice drifts closer.

My stomach growls, as though on cue.

Damn traitor.

I turn my face away, staring off to the side.

He groans, lowering himself onto the bed beside me. "You're going to make me damn crazy the whole time you're here, aren't you?"

I peer over at him again, popping a brow, the corner of my mouth twisting upward. "Pretty much."

He sucks in a breath. "You're a fucking pain in my ass."

I shrug my shoulders, pursing my lips.

He shakes his head. "Don't make me regret this."

Then his hands are on my wrists as he sets both of them free.

"Shit," I mutter as I massage each one, sitting up against the bed.

"Let me." He takes one of my hands in his, his calloused fingers working my skin, easing the raw pain radiating there.

But I don't let myself enjoy the feel of a man's hand on me. Not this man. I snatch my hand away.

"You don't get to play the hero, or whatever the hell this is!

You're the one who caused me pain!" I shout, lifting up my wrist for his viewing pleasure so he can see the red ring around it. "You don't get to take it away!"

His jaw pulses. He doesn't say anything as he picks up a steaming cup of what smells like coffee and sets it on the nightstand before handing me the tray.

"Make sure you eat."

"How about you stop telling me what to do?"

"How about you stop fighting for just a second?"

"I can't do that. I've been fighting my whole life. I'm not about to stop now. If anything, being with you is even more reason to keep on fighting."

A deep sigh leaves his body. "I get that. More than you know."

This man has me confused. He's hard, yet soft. He's like a jigsaw puzzle with so many undiscovered parts. My father would never have set his captive free, nor feed her. Brian wasn't wrong about that.

I pick up the fork and slice away a piece of the crepe, and when it hits my mouth, I fucking moan.

Holy shit, this is delicious.

I don't even care that he heard whatever noise just came out of me.

"That good, huh?" He laughs genuinely for the first time.

"Mm-hmm," I mumble with my mouth full, my eyes widening. I take another bite, ready to eat the plate too.

"My cook, Sonia, is the best. She can make whatever you want. If there's anything you'd like to request, let me know."

I nod. Maybe I could get used to this new life. No one cooks for me. I survive on pre-made food. If I tried cooking, I'd probably burn my house down.

"After you're done, I'll show you the bathroom. I had all your essentials packed up and brought here last night, so you have all your things."

"You were in my damn house?" I question with shock, my eyelids blinking rapidly.

"I was. I really enjoyed your panty collection, especially the crotchless ones."

My mouth opens wide. "You're gross."

The taunting gleam in his eyes is the only response he gives.

"How the hell would you feel if someone invaded your privacy like that?" I ask.

"I'd probably kill 'em," he answers casually.

"Exactly," I mutter as I pop another bite into my mouth.

My stomach growls again. Man, I'm hungry.

I continue eating my breakfast in silence while he sits in that armchair I found him on when I first woke up here.

Picking up the coffee, I proceed to drink it all in a few sips, then set the cup back down. I go to work on the second crepe, devouring it in a few bites, finally feeling full.

Brian rises to his feet, taking the tray from me.

"Come on, stand up. The shower is right through the door." He points to the one in front of me. "Don't think about escaping through the window, though. I have men outside, and they can be a little trigger-happy."

I look at the door, then at him. "Are you going to kill me? Just tell me so I can be prepared. It's the least you can do."

"Whether you die depends on you. But I have no intentions of killing you. Let's keep it that way."

Great. So I'm pretty much dead, no matter what.

If I do something he doesn't like, he'll kill me. If I help him take down my father, dear old Daddy will kill me. Seems like a great situation to be stuck in.

I still have to figure out a plan to get out of here. Then I'll worry about finding a place to hide. I have some money stashed away, just enough for a plane ticket somewhere close, which wouldn't do me any good.

I don't get a salary from work. My father refuses to pay me. He knows all of my expenses and provides me a weekly stipend, with which I can pay bills and buy groceries. I only have a few dollars left over after that. If I want to buy myself anything, he'll give me the money as long as he approves of the purchase and sees the receipt.

I don't have a mortgage. My house has been completely paid for…by him. He's in charge of everything. I'm not living my own life. I'm only visiting.

"Go inside and shower." Brian disrupts my thoughts. "I'll be out here waiting." He takes a seat on the bed. "Don't take too long. I have to be at work. But I'll be back to check on you during my lunch break and bring you more food."

"Wow. I'm so lucky."

"Come on, Chiara. I don't have time for your bullshit. Go inside and start stripping, or I'll do it for you."

My body heats up from the images of him forcefully yanking my clothes off.

Would he touch me?

"Will I still be tied up the entire time you're gone?" I purposely make my voice sound small and needy, hoping for his pity.

He considers my question, his brows furrowing. I can see the battle raging in his wavering gaze. His tongue darts out, taking a quick swipe of his full lower lip as he peers from my face down to my wrists, etched with rope marks.

"*Please*, Brian." I hate begging anyone for anything, but I'll say whatever he wants to hear not to be bound. "My wrists really hurt."

I can tell that somewhere deep inside, he has a savior complex. Considering what he did to me, it makes no sense, but it's there. I know it. If I can pick at it a little, make it bleed, maybe he'll budge.

"I promise I won't do anything stupid," I continue. "I do believe you won't hurt me. I'll just sit here and watch something on that giant TV." I scoot back against the cream-tufted headboard. "I can't remember the last time I had a day where I had to do nothing at all."

Shit. The club.

I haven't even thought about what will happen tonight. My dad will be more pissed about that than my well-being.

"Fine," he agrees sternly.

I internally do a happy dance.

"But if you try anything you're not supposed to, I'll know about it." His body gets too close to mine. "And the next time, I won't care how hurt your wrists are. You'll stay tied up."

His hand inches toward me, a finger smoothly landing under my chin. "Do we understand each other?"

He lifts my face up to meet his, his voice lacking the malice I'd expect.

I nod, somehow lost in his gaze.

Tell me why I'm here. I search his eyes for answers that he may never give me.

His hooded gaze is as lost as mine as he peers down at my lips. He sighs, and his minty breath skates over my mouth just as his hand falls.

"Go." He points a finger to the door to my left, leading to the bathroom. "There's a towel and robe there already. Your suitcase is in the closet over there." He gestures toward another door, further down from the bathroom.

"Thanks."

I feel strange thanking him for anything. But how does that saying go? You catch more flies with honey than you do with vinegar. I have to do better at controlling my temper. My attitude will not work with him.

He sits back on the bed while I head inside, finding an all-white, luxurious bathroom, straight out of one of those "homes for celebrities" shows. The flooring is shiny marble with a spray of gray. There's a jacuzzi in one corner and a standup shower in another.

I turn on the spray of the scalding hot water, hoping to melt away this awful day. I still can't believe this is happening to me. I need to figure out what to do. I can't rely on my so-called father. If it comes down to his life or mine, he'd sacrifice me to save himself.

I remove my clothes, leaving them on the countertop beside the double sink, and walk into the shower. When I look for something to wash my hair with, I find all of my things already there. He wasn't kidding when he said he'd been to my house.

I spend my time lathering my hair, enjoying the feel of the hot water running down my body. After I'm done, I wrap a gray towel over my head and use the other to dry my body before throwing on the robe, tightly securing the belt around my waist.

I exit the bathroom, and the cool air hits my legs, causing my shoulders to shiver.

Brian stands, heading for the closet and pulling out my luggage.

"How was the shower?" he asks, his gaze zigzagging from my face down to my tits, trying hard not to stare at them through the robe, but failing.

I don't blame him. They're nice. My nipples are hard from the chill. I hope he's enjoying the barely there view, because he'll never get to see them without my clothes on.

"It was fine," I answer, grabbing the handle of my luggage from him.

While I do, my finger grazes his. I gasp as my skin ignites with electrifying heat and my entire body comes alive with tingles shooting up every inch.

He doesn't so much as flinch, but I can tell from the way his eyes bore into mine, he felt the impact of our touch.

"I have to go," he informs me dryly, whatever connection we just shared now gone. "I'm locking the door from the outside. The remote is in the drawer of the TV stand. I'll see you later."

He gives me his back and leaves. I wonder what mood he'll be in when he returns.

DOMINIC

FOURTEEN

I'm supposed to hate this woman, not be tempted by her beauty. And she *is* beautiful. Not just sexy or hot, or one of those poorly constructed adjectives. She's stunning, with the power to bring me to my knees if I allow her to get close enough. If I allow her to remind me of the past.

But I won't.

She'll never get under my skin. Chiara will always be kept at an arm's length.

She's nothing more than a means to an end. When I get what I want, she'll be free to go.

And I always get what I want.

I should've tied her back up, but I can't deny somewhere inside this broken man is a boy who'd turn the world upside down to see the girl he once loved love him back. No matter how much hurt I carry for what she did, there's no way I'd ever hurt her, no matter what I want her to believe.

Seeing her bruised wrists hurt me enough. I hated what I did to her, and I don't want to do it again. She's a part of my past, sewn into the very depths of my soul, and there's no way to erase her. No way to pretend we never were.

Reaching into my pocket, I retrieve my cell and press a few keys to access the cams I have set up at my home, including the ones in her room. It's merely for her protection and mine. I have to keep an eye on my most valuable possession.

She's lying in bed, her body barely covered at all, her long, tanned legs on full display. Tiny gray shorts ride up the insides of her thighs, a place I bet she's warm and soft. Too soft for a man like me, even if I did allow myself to have a taste.

She's in a loose-fitted tank top, the tops of her breasts pushed up. The desire to run my tongue over those perky tits has my cock throbbing.

When I saw her in the robe earlier, those hard beads of her breasts pushing against the soft fabric, I wanted nothing more than to tear open that flimsy piece of material and have every inch of her. I can't stop thinking of her that way, even while knowing I shouldn't.

Chiara Bianchi is more of an enemy to me than her own father. The way she destroyed our friendship is unforgivable. We may have been young back then, but not young enough for her not to know what she was doing.

I trusted her.

I *loved* her.

But she was nothing but a liar.

My focus right now is on her father though. I'll worry about his precious daughter after I'm done with him.

There's a light knock on my door before Dante walks into my office at work, with Enzo on his tail. They both take a seat on one of the black leather chairs before my desk.

"How's your wife doing?" I ask Dante with an amused tone.

"Good." He nods with a curve of a brow. "Considering Raquel has no idea what she's gotten herself into."

"Poor thing," Enzo adds. "She could've had me but she gets you instead."

"You may have the looks, baby bro." Dante winks. "But I've got *all* the charm."

Enzo scoffs. "Shit, I've got that in the bag too. She would've had a much better time with me."

Dante clasps his shoulder. "Believe me, I know just how to keep my girl entertained. And how would you have made that work, with all the women you have coming and going from your place? Or did you think you could do both?"

Enzo narrows his eyes, thinking for a moment, and shrugs. "You're right. I'd rather get all the pussy instead of one."

Both of these morons have women flocking to them, but Enzo is the pretty boy with those green eyes and brown hair. If he wasn't running the company with us, he could've been a model or some shit.

Dante got our father's looks, dark brown hair, and equally brown eyes. His smile has women eating from the palm of his hand. You'd never know how dangerous he can be from looking at him.

Neither of my brothers are ever starving for company, but Enzo is a different breed. At twenty-five and with more money than he knows what to do with, there are women going in and out of his house on a loop, usually together. Threesomes, or even foursomes, are very much his thing. He once fucked triplets at once. He's very proud of himself.

Dante is only twenty-seven, but a lot more in control of his dick than Enzo.

I, too, supply my appetite. But I'm the oldest at twenty-eight, and the CEO of two brands, ours and Tomás's, so I'm not about to get anyone pregnant. I can just see the tabloids.

"Are you even fucking her?" Enzo asks Dante, his voice saying *if you're not, you're a pussy.*

"We'll get there." A cocky smile appears on his face.

Just like I've been keeping tabs on Chiara, Dante has been doing the same with Raquel. She's the perfect bargaining chip if we need to use one. Unlike Chiara's father, Salvatore actually loves his daughter.

That's been part of our plan: I take Chiara and he takes Raquel. He's been on her trail for a year now and has gotten to know everything he can possibly know, like the bar she likes to go to alone, especially when she's upset. And when he saw her storm out of her parents' house after intercepting a call with Chiara, he knew just where she'd go and beat her to it.

Dante didn't have to take her against her will. She agreed to his arrangement, which included a lot of money and a new identity, so she can run off without the man her parents want her to marry. The only condition is she must stay married to him for three months to help him with a business deal.

But he lied. He has no plans to divorce her. With the amount of hatred the Bianchis have for us, I'm sure there's nothing worse to them than for their flesh and blood to breed with one of us. It's a fate worse than death. Salvatore would never allow her to marry my brother.

But marrying off his daughter to the likes of Carlito? Well, I guess that's okay. Dante took great pleasure in knowing he'll have the daughter of a man who thought so low of our family once upon a time.

My, how the tables have turned.

We knew Raquel was supposed to marry someone she hated. It wasn't a well-kept secret, even if Dante hadn't been tailing her every move.

People talked, especially at strip clubs. And Carlito wasn't shy about telling Dante how he's going to make her suffer for not wanting him while he had a stripper grinding on his dick. The man would tell you his whole life story while he was drunk.

Dante became his friend at the club, making sure he was there when Carlito was. Sharing strippers, paying for his bill, anything to get close enough to learn everything we may not know.

My brothers turn to me.

"How's your girl doing?" Dante asks. "I can't believe she doesn't remember you."

Clenching my jaw, I pick up the decanter filled with whiskey and pour some into the glass beside it.

"Why would she?" I fire back, hating any talk of her. "I barely look anything like before."

Like Enzo, I have green eyes. If she saw them, she'd know me instantly. That's why I wear contacts. I can't have her realize who I am yet. I need her scared, so she doesn't run. If she does, she has no idea what she'll be running into.

"I hope you're making up for lost time," Enzo says.

I grind my teeth. "You know that's not what this is about."

"It doesn't mean you can't have a little fun." He wags his brows.

"Enough!" I bang my fist on the desk, causing the decanter to rattle.

They drop the conversation immediately, knowing me well.

I take a swig of my drink. "Be ready at three a.m. We hit the strip club, and we do what we did to the other places. Don't forget your bulletproof vests. They'll be expecting us."

Enzo rubs his palms together and tilts forward, his elbows on his knees. "I can't fucking wait."

"Did Chiara do her part yet?" Dante asks, leaning back, cracking his knuckles.

A smile forms at the edge of my lips. "She will."

The plan for the club has been carefully constructed like everything else, and she's part of the key.

I arrive back home in time to feed her lunch, as promised. Balancing a tray on one hand, I unlock the door with the other.

As soon as she sees me walk in, Chiara sits up on the bed, her legs crossed at the ankles. She's still in the same clothes I saw her in during the livestream on my phone. But the view up close is so much better. Hardly anything is left for my imagination, except her ass parked on the bed, which I bet looks even better without those shorts on.

"Finally," she huffs out, irritation simmering in her glare. "I've been starving. You didn't even leave me water, you asshole!"

Shit. She's right. I am an asshole.

If I were a better man, I'd apologize. But I'm not.

I pick up the breakfast tray, putting it on the floor, and place the new one on the nightstand.

"Drink." I hand her a water bottle.

She opens it quickly and guzzles the entire thing. "Make sure you leave enough before you go. Maybe you'd like to get me a bowl too, so I can get on my hands and knees and drink like a dog, since that's how you treat me."

Her on her hands and knees...

I suck in a breath. There are so many things I could do to that curvy body.

I crack my neck, needing to curb the thought of grabbing her by that delicate throat and pinning her against the wall while I fuck her mercilessly.

"I'll make sure you have water from now on. Anything else you'd like? Maybe some steak and lobster?"

She swings her feet off the bed and comes around to my side, swaying her hips until her tight little body is pressed against mine.

"How about fuck you?" she bites out as her gaze finds mine, her finger digging into the center of my chest.

I love a woman who fights back. And this right here would have any other woman tied to my bed and fucked so hard she'd remember who's in charge.

I cup her chin roughly in the span of my palm and lean into her mouth, my lips hovering over hers. "You have a very big mouth on you, Chiara. If you're not careful, I may find better ways to fill it."

She gasps, not expecting the vulgarity. Her cheeks flush, and the temptation to mark her ass cheeks has my palm aching.

I narrow my eyes, leaning closer until her lips graze mine.

Her mouth falls into a quiet moan, one I know she didn't mean to give me.

Fuck.

My dick hardens, wanting her.

What the hell am I doing?

I drop my hand, stepping back and creating an arm's length of space between us. Why can't I resist this temptation? I need her out of my mind for good.

I run a quick hand past my face, clenching my jaw.

"Do you have the phone numbers of all your employees at the club?" I ask, my voice harsh and cold now as I finally get to the real reason why I came.

She lifts a brow. "Why? Are you going to kidnap them too?"

I take out her cell from my pocket. "Tell me the code."

"Excuse me?" Her brows bend with disbelief.

"You heard me. I wasn't asking, Chiara. Code. Now."

She crosses her arms over her chest and gives me her tough-girl face. "Swear you won't hurt them, and I'll give it to you."

"They're lucky you care so much," I say, meaning it.

"Yeah, well, they're my people."

"I'm not out to hurt them. The opposite."

She exhales a sigh. "Fine. I'm going to believe you. Zero, two, zero, two." I can tell by her voice how hard that was for her. "What are you going to do to them?"

"Tell me all the names of your employees."

"You didn't answer my question."

"I know. Now, tell me."

She groans. "Fine! Go to my contacts. They're all under the name 'club.' Happy?"

"Very," I answer without looking up, finding the list of people and preparing the mass text I'm about to send.

Glancing up at her, I find the daggers in her eyes pointing right at me.

"How do you word a text when you send them one?"

Her features tighten with irritation. "What do you mean?"

"What the fuck do you write in it? You know, shit like, 'Hey, it's Chiara. I'm a shitty boss...'" I smile.

"Oh my God!" She throws her hands in the air. "You're gonna pretend to be me? You'd better not hurt them! They're good people."

"I told you I won't. I don't like to repeat myself."

"Just say, 'Hey.'" She sits back on the bed, shaking her head as she stares ahead, not really looking at anything specific.

I write the text. They'd better fucking listen, or we'll have a huge mess to clean up. None of us want anyone who doesn't deserve it to die tonight.

> **Chiara:** Hey. Stay home tonight. The club will be closed. I found a rat. You'll be paid. Don't worry.

Before sending it, I walk over to her and hold the phone before her face. "How's this?"

She scans the text and looks up with confusion marring her features. Then suddenly, her eyes widen.

"Fuck. You're the reason my father and uncles are in hiding, aren't you?"

"I am." I grin. Not a kind one, either. One that says I'm the monster behind the destruction and damn proud of it.

Today's attack will inform Faro Bianchi that I reject the deal he offered me the day after we burned his warehouse. He thought he could stop the war, but I have no intention of ever taking the devil's deal, no matter what I led him to believe.

The Bianchi men will pay with their blood. The battle will rage on until every last one of them is dead.

CHIARA

FIFTEEN

I can't believe I didn't put two and two together. He's the one that has my father scared. I have never seen him hide from anyone…until now.

Brian Smith must be different somehow, and I have to figure out why. I know my father is planning a war behind closed doors. He may have disappeared, but he's never truly gone. He's always there. Watching, waiting for his chance to strike. He's never been the type to sit behind a desk and have his soldiers do all the fighting. He's been the one leading them.

I hope Brian and his army are strong enough to win. A daughter shouldn't want the death of her own parent, but this one does.

Knowing my father is scared of Brian should have me scared too, but I'm holding on to the hope that he needs me enough to let me live.

Lord knows he could've easily killed me already, especially when I talked back to him, but he didn't. He didn't even hit me. The men in my life would slap a woman around for ever talking to them that way. He just took it. And I liked giving it to him.

I know what I told myself about keeping my attitude in check around him, but every time he walks into the room, I can't help myself. I can't stop the need to bite and claw until I see that inferno burning in his gaze, the one that tells me exactly what he wants to do with me.

He excites and unnerves me all at once. I'm a fool for playing this dangerous game, but I don't think I could stop it even if I tried.

Grabbing a pillow adjacent to my head, I hold it close against my chest, worry carved onto every beat of my heart, not for myself, but for the people I employ. I really hope none of them show up at the club tonight. I'll never forgive myself if any one of them gets hurt. It'd be my fault. By virtue of being a Bianchi, I could lead them to their death without lifting a finger.

I don't care about the club itself. I never have. I only care about the people in it. I'm grateful that Brian is going to torch it, even if that means all of them lose their jobs. They shouldn't work there anyway, not when my father is the boss.

And as an added bonus, I won't have to work for him. Well, until he finds another purpose for me or another man for me to marry. I love my cousin to death, but I don't want to be her.

Standing up from the bed, I walk around aimlessly before turning on the TV. I flip through channel after channel, not finding jack shit to watch. I hate being locked away in this room, like a mouse on a wheel. But unlike the mouse, I'm fully aware of my surroundings. Unlike the mouse, I know there's more out there, and I'm digging aimlessly with no way to escape.

There has to be something I can do to get out of here. First, out of this room. Then, out of this house. I need to get him to trust me.

Maybe I can offer him something he may not know about my father. Show him that the man whose blood I share means absolutely nothing to me.

But there's something else I can try on top of that.

Something riskier.

Bolder.

But something that may work.

I can use his attraction for me to my benefit.

I can tell he's fighting it. I can see the flares of caution warning him away, as though I'm the sun and he's a mere mortal who'll burn from a single touch.

But if I can find a way to extinguish his trepidation, if I can make myself seem like I'm not unattainable, maybe I can find myself in *his* bed instead of this one.

And once I'm there—once he has my body and I have his heart—I'll crush it as I make my escape.

A set of keys jangles at the door. He must be back. At least I hope it's him. I never hear anyone else here, but then again, I'm sure that's because the house is huge. Too many places for someone to hide.

The door flies open as Brian marches in, carrying a mini fridge.

I slant my head to the side from the bed, brows rising.

"What are you doing?" My voice is as curious as my face probably appears.

"What does it look like? I brought you a fridge so you won't bitch about thirst and hunger. I've bought stuff to fill it. Give me a second, and I'll hook it up."

"Thank you," I say in the most gracious voice I can muster.

He carries the fridge to the corner. Even through his black hoodie, I can see his biceps straining, wanting to break free. I'd pay to see him without those clothes on, doing whatever he's doing.

My body tingles at the thought, making my plan much easier to accomplish. Being attracted to the man you need to fuck is a lot better than being physically repulsed by him.

Setting the fridge down, he plugs it in. I stand there biting the corner of my thumbnail, watching him like a voyeur as he squats in black sweats, his ass as muscular as the rest of him.

I'm suddenly warm everywhere, slipping into the trap of our mutual attraction. I run my fingers down my neck, the pulse beneath my skin biting into my flesh. The desire for those rough, masculine hands all over my body is overwhelming.

The need to fuck him, yet hurt him, battles for space in my head, both weaving through my heart. And I do have every intention to hurt him. Just because I want to sleep with him doesn't change that.

Once he has the fridge situated, he walks back to the door, carrying in a couple of paper bags. Crouching down, he begins emptying them, stocking the fridge with bottles. Rising to my feet, I head toward him with every intention of setting my plan in motion.

When I'm right beside him, I lower myself, reaching into a bag and taking out a few containers of Greek yogurt while he places a carton of mixed berries in the fridge.

He side-eyes me. "I've got this."

My mouth tilts up at the corner. "By the looks of you, I'm sure you can handle plenty." I reach out a hand, a finger landing on his shoulder. "But I wanted to help."

His jaw pulses as our eyes connect, and my heart plummets into the pit of my stomach. I let my nail slowly trail down his arm, our mutual gaze drifting into a state of vulnerability neither one of us wants to surrender to.

His unrelenting gaze is so powerful, it has the force to shatter my resolve, forgetting the plan I want so badly to work.

His hooded eyes caress a path from my lips down to the top of my breasts, hidden under a thin scrap of fabric. I suddenly feel claustrophobic in my tank top. The hunger in his eyes robs me of all my breaths, my finger still glued to his thick muscles.

He releases a low, sharp exhale before his palm snaps around my wrist, yanking it away.

"Don't ever touch me again," he growls deep in his chest.

But I don't think he means it. Not with the way he's still gripping my hand. Not with the way his eyes can't seem to stop drinking me in, savoring every bit of my face.

It's okay to be attracted to your kidnapper, right? Is there a handbook on this? I mean, I was into him before I knew what he was capable of, so this isn't some kind of Stockholm syndrome thing, right?

But it still feels dirty. A good kind of dirty. Like I want to shower with him instead of wash his filth off me. And he's filthy, all right.

"I'm sorry if my touch somehow offended you." My voice grows weak as my eyes fall downcast, hoping he believes the show. "I'm sorry if I'm not the type of woman you'd normally go for." I start getting up, trying to pull myself out of his fastened grip. "I'll, ah…" I tug at my lower lip. "Go back to…"

Before I can attempt to walk away, his arm curls around the small of my back, pulling me flush to his side, one of my legs falling into his lap. Our gazes meet, raging through my well-constructed wall.

His heavy breaths mingle with mine, our lips falling closer, barely anything between them, both of our chests rising and falling with every frazzled exhale.

"Where do you think you're going?" he stamps out, his erotic growl pulsating over my trembling lips.

I pull in a quick, sharp inhale, the rhythm of my quaking heartbeats slicing through my rib cage. A heavy ball of anxiety forms in the emptiness of my stomach, diving deeper.

I can't seem to turn down the fire he's an expert at setting. He's an aphrodisiac and the whole fucking meal. But this is purely sexual, and that's all it'll ever be.

He drops my wrist, his hand falling to my hip, grazing up as his eyes stay fastened on mine.

"If you weren't his daughter…" His fingers climb higher, reaching my arm, trailing up, biting into my skin until he finds the back of my neck. "I'd have you naked and thoroughly fucked multiple times. I can tell how badly you need it."

My core aches, needing the emptiness to be filled with his all-consuming power. Needing to end this persistent desire for a man I should never want.

He draws even nearer until his lips skim over mine.

"But, baby…" he says, his gravelly tone dripping with masculine husk. "I know you more than you realize."

He smiles against my mouth, and I let out a whimper just as his tongue snakes out, the tip dipping in between my lips.

"And this little act of yours…" he continues, "…is never gonna work on me."

His hand spreads over the back of my head, his fingers sinking gradually into my long hair, like a serpent before an attack. He fists my strands in his palm, winding it around his wrist, pulling my head backward with brutal force.

A moan falls from my lips, one that tells him how much I enjoy a little pain with a little pleasure.

"Whatever this is, Chiara…"

He yanks harder, and I hiss.

"It'll never work. I'll never touch you," he promises, his intense gaze piercing through mine. "Not even if you were naked and spread open for me like an offering, your fingers inside you, begging for my cock."

He tilts his lips over my jaw, his nose creeping up my neck, sending goose bumps erupting throughout my body.

His mouth lands over the soft spot below my ear, his breaths feathering softly over my skin there until the need to come overwhelms all my thoughts.

He pulls in a quick inhale. "Save that energy on surviving. You'll need it."

Dropping both hands away from me, he gets to his feet, turning toward the door, as though walking away from me and whatever just happened is the easiest thing in the world.

I sit there with some of the groceries still on the floor for me to put away, my breaths tormenting me with every pull.

I have my work cut out for me. He's not as easily manipulated as I thought he'd be. That's okay, though. He doesn't realize how much more I can push him. When I'm through, I won't need to beg for anything. He'll be the one doing all the begging.

"Wait!" I call out as his hand lands on the doorknob.

He pivots, snapping his glare at me. "Make it fast. I have to go."

"What did my father do? I need to know."

His teeth clench and a fist forms at his side. At first, I don't think he'll tell me, but after long, dragged-out seconds, he begins to answer.

"He killed two people who were very important to me."

Even though he said the words with an edge, I feel the raw ache in every syllable. I close my eyes, my heart breaking for the two people I didn't know.

Whoever he lost meant a lot to him. That much is clear. I'm sure they were innocent. It wouldn't surprise me if my father used the murders as some kind of leverage. My father's such a fucking asshole. He deserves what's coming to him.

Brian turns for the door.

"Hey, before you go," I say. "You should know something."

He releases an annoyed exhale, facing me. "What is it now?"

I bite on the inside of my cheek, sealing a new course in my life, one I should be afraid of. But I no longer care. I can offer him something he wants, something that could get me killed. But if it gets me out of this room to start with, it'll be worth it.

"I think I know where he is. Where they all are."

He tilts up his chin, his brow rising an inch.

"I'll tell you," I go on. "But I need one thing in exchange."

He chuckles deep in his chest. "Do I look like the kind of man who makes deals with little girls?"

I grind my teeth. "Fine. Good luck finding him. You never will."

The only reason I even know is because I overhead my father and my uncle Sal talking in hushed voices in my father's study right after the laundromat fire. I took a risk eavesdropping while waiting for him after being summoned for a meeting. But right now, knowing how useful that information is, I'm glad I did.

Brian stalks over to me until he's only a finger apart from my body.

"What do you want?" he growls, his jaw twitching in the wake of his frustration.

"I thought you don't make deals with little girls?" I grin salaciously.

An arm curls behind me, gripping my back firmly, thrusting me into the hardened weight of his body.

"I can find other ways to get this information out of you, Chiara." His other hand journeys up my side until his palm reaches my face, cupping my jaw roughly. "And if you don't hurry up and tell me what you want in exchange for your father, that little sliver of gentlemanly behavior my mother raised me with will wear thin."

"You, a gentleman?" I scoff. "Where?"

His tongue darts out, seductively swiping over his lower lip, the wicked hunger sweeping through his gaze. "Goodbye, Chiara."

He swings his body to the door, making his way across the room once more.

"I want out of this room!" I call out.

He freezes for a second before spinning around. "Why would I ever do that?"

"Because I have something you want." I pause, inhaling deeply. "And you can give me something I want. I call that a fair exchange." My lips tip up into a triumphant smile.

"Go on. We'll see how useful your information is."

"No," I say harshly. "I need your word that once I tell you, you'll let me out."

A pain settles behind my eyes and nose. I fight through the incoming tears, blinking them away.

"Why are you so desperate to leave here? Is the room not up to your princess standards?"

I narrow a glare.

He smirks.

I'd really enjoy hate-fucking him, then blowing his brains out. A girl can dream.

An exhausted breath jolts out of me, not wanting to tell him why it's so hard being locked away in a room. Not wanting to give him a piece of myself that's real. Something no one knows, not even Raquel.

"Many years ago..." I reveal, my eyes on his. "I tried to run away from my father, but it didn't quite work out."

My eyelids shutter closed for a mere second before I draw up the courage to dig up the scarred memories of my past.

TEN YEARS AGO

I'd always dreamed of running away from home as a child. It took many years to get here, but now, at eighteen, I'm finally there.

Handing the cab driver some money, I grab my small suitcase and fling the car door open. It takes me a moment to get out as I clutch my airline ticket in my hand.

Paris, France. That'll be my new home.

Staring at it, the back of my nose aches, wishing my mom was coming with me like we always talked about. But I'll be doing this for the both of us. My heart lurches in my chest, practically spiraling down into my stomach.

If my father finds out, he'll kill me. But I'll be long gone by then, hoping he never finds where I'm going.

Finally slipping my feet out of the car, I grab the suitcase and roll it down onto the pavement, closing the car door behind me.

The cab speeds away as I make it to the door leading into the airport. Stepping inside, I scan the screen above my head, finding my gate, but as I begin to head that way, I gasp.

Fear like I have never known before swarms every inch of me until I lose all sense of control. Until my body shudders with despair and dread.

My father is here with a dozen men.

He found out.

How did he find out?

No. No. I can't go with him. He can't take me.

I back up a step until I hit someone. *"I'm sorry. I..."*

I turn around apologetically, but I don't find a stranger. I find one of his men. The man grips me by my elbow, cementing me in place until my father draws toward me.

Feet turn to inches until his menacing smile is before me.

My heart drops into the pit of my stomach, my inhales freezing within my lungs at the sight of his victorious grin.

I'm dead. He's going to kill me. Or force me into a marriage with Michael.

What have I done?!

"Don't make a scene," he warns, his tone low. Deadly.

His arm goes around my shoulders as he walks me back out of the airport and into one of his black SUVs.

He shoves me into the backseat, taking his place on the other side of me. The driver gets us onto the road. My father doesn't say a word. Doesn't so much as look at me.

I want to beg for forgiveness, for a second chance, but I don't have it in me. I will never beg this man for anything.

Once we arrive home, he steps out first, coming around to my side and opening the door.

"Let's go," he barks out.

An icy shudder skates up my spine when I step out, following him into the house where hell will be waiting for me.

Once the door bangs to a close, his fingers wrap tightly around my upper arm and drag me up the stairs. I practically jog to keep pace with him. When we reach my room, he opens the door and throws me inside as I fall onto the cold, hard floor.

But the sound of the door locking, the key turning...that's a sound I'll never erase from my memory.

My pants grow heavy as I right myself, trying the door, knowing he locked me in, but hoping I imagined it.

But I didn't.

I'm his real-life prisoner now. Like I've always been, but worse this time.

I've always tried to be strong. To show him that what he's done to me—what he keeps doing—doesn't affect me. But with each passing night that I'm locked in here, my resolve, that tough exterior I've spent years building, begins to crack, like an egg hit in just the right way.

But every time he walks into the room once a day to give me food, I don't show it.

I don't cry.

I don't beg.

I lie on the bed, staring at the ceiling, pretending not to give a shit.

But I want out.

I hate being caged like an animal. If it weren't for the window, I'd lose all sense of time.

I count the days.

One.

Five.

Ten.

Fourteen.

That's the day he finally talks to me. My hope is that I've served my punishment, but with my father, I doubt it.

"We need to talk about my expectations of you. You're my daughter, and you're going to act like it. You have two options, and that's the only choice you'll ever be given, so choose smart."

I cross my arms, staring daggers into his round face. Those dark brown eyes of his would never appear malicious to anyone who didn't know him, but beneath that warmth lies the heart of a killer. A brutal one.

I've heard the stories. I knew what he was. And I know what he still is.

"You can either marry Michael or you get your business degree," he continues. "Then I want you running my club. The feds are sniffing, and Pauly isn't cut out to run his ass let alone that place. He's as good as I've got right now, but you've got the brain. I want you to do it."

That's the only compliment my father has ever given me.

I have the brain. Well, I guess it's better than the alternative.

I know there's no negotiating with him. It's either I pick one of these so-called choices or he does it for me. So I choose the one I can live with.

I choose the club.

When I'm finally done re-living the trauma, I peer up at Brian, finding his knuckles white at his sides, his features contorted with fury. His brows dip with his own emotion, too great for a man whose harshness overpowers him.

I look down at the floor, not wanting to see the softening of his eyes, or the pity.

"I hate him. I always have," I go on, glancing up at Brian.

His jaw flexes, his eyes growing teeth strong enough to tear my father apart.

"I'd help you take him down for nothing, but being stuck inside this room only reminds me of the pain of being locked away before." I evade his eyes again. "I can't handle it."

Tears sprinkle within my eyes. I can sense their heaviness encroaching.

THE DEVIL'S DEAL

"I know I appear like I have my shit together…" I gaze up at him, letting the tears fall. "But I don't. I have cracks like everyone else does. I just try very hard to disguise them."

Swiping at my eyes, I erase the outer evidence of pain. Weakness isn't something I'm proud of, but sometimes it's the only way to survive.

"So, please," I implore. "Don't lock me away. I'll stay in your house for as long as you want, and I'll do what I can to help you destroy him, but I need out of this room."

He cuts the distance between us, cradling my cheek possessively in his palm, his brows gathering. "Why didn't you tell me?"

I roll my eyes with a smile, tears filling my eyes as I inadvertently lean into the comfort of his touch. "When was I supposed to do that? When you came up from behind and drugged me? Or maybe when you had me tied to your bed?"

His lips curve up. "If you'd told me all this earlier, I wouldn't have had to lug that fridge up two flights of stairs."

"I'm sorry for being such a constant disappointment." I nuzzle into the roughness of his palm.

"Do you want me to move you to another room?" he rasps, his thumb hovering beside my mouth, as though fighting within himself to touch it.

"No," I whisper. "This room is fine. Just don't lock the door when you leave."

He nods, his finger brushing the corner of my mouth.

My heartbeats quake from his feathery touch. I shut my eyes for a brief moment, enjoying the feel of a man and pretending he truly cares. I've never had a man care about me before. I don't think I ever will.

"You have a deal." He drops his hand. "Now tell me where the bastard is." His voice loses its softness at the mention of my father.

"Then I'll show you around the house and introduce you to Sonia."

This is good. He's trusting me. Step one of getting out of this cage is complete. But I'm not done yet. I will do whatever I have to do to get out of this house and find a way to hide from all of them.

My heart beats louder against my rib cage, fighting for space in my chest, the air in my lungs frozen with paralyzing fear.

I'm about to betray my father. He can never find out. If he does...

But I have to fight the enemy I know, and right now, that's Brian.

"My mother got a house in an inheritance from my grandparents," I tell him. "My father and uncles use it as a stash house for drugs and weapons. I overheard him say that's where he'll be after the incident with the laundromat. You know, when you set it on fire."

"What can I say?" He shrugs. "I like a good show."

"I would've loved to watch," I throw in, knowing how much I'd enjoy seeing my father's place go up in smoke.

"You like to watch, huh?" There's a naughty gleam in his eyes, and his dimple deepens with a tug of a smile.

"I'm talking about the fire." I shake my head with a teasing grin.

"Me too." He smirks. "Just a different kind."

I bite the edge of my lower lip, the blend of intoxicating lust and hunger seeping through my pores, winding through my brain, filling it with images of him and me.

"I need the address, Chiara," he says, ripping me away from the fog of my fantasies.

I give him the location as he types it into his cell.

"You did good." He nods.

"Don't tell him it came from me."

"I wouldn't."

I run a hand through my hair. "Be careful."

"You're worried about me?" His brows knit tightly.

"Is that so bad?"

He pulls in a rough breath.

"I'm sorry," he says, his voice pressed with sincerity.

"For what?"

Our gazes tangle in something unspoken, a connection building between us.

"That your father is a piece of shit. Every kid deserves a good one."

I shrug with a feigned smile. "I wouldn't know any different."

CHIARA

SIXTEEN

He leads me out of the room and into a long, all-white hallway. There are so many doors, I can barely count them all. I continue to stare, learning my surroundings while he's already heading down.

My feet hit the black wooden steps, my hand gliding over the shiny black banister of the spiral staircase as I make my way down.

While I hit the foyer, my eyes immediately notice the cathedral ceiling with a large silver chandelier hanging in the center. I follow him deeper into what clearly looks like a mansion, and into the den.

"Wow," I say. "The ceiling is extraordinary."

The dark gray of the roof is framed with white overhead beams crossing at different angles, creating an illusion of a checkerboard. It's ornate and beautiful.

"Don't get too comfortable," he throws over his shoulder as I continue to take in everything.

"I'm hoping I can kick you out and move in," I tease as my hand runs over the cream suede L-shaped sofa on one side with two dark gray armchairs on the other and a rectangular glass table in the center. The sofa is facing a fireplace with light gray bricks surrounding it.

"Stop staring and keep moving," he orders.

But I ignore him, looking at the pale gray walls and the floor-to-ceiling windows, revealing a large white gazebo with a matching bed plus an oval-shaped pool surrounded by a bunch of lounge chairs.

It's pretty obvious he's filthy rich. We definitely had money growing up, and lots of it, but this is a whole other level of wealth.

A set of footsteps approach from behind, then another. I freeze, turning to find two tall men wearing head-to-toe black coming toward us. I gasp, causing Brian to turn around.

Who the hell are they and why are they here?

My eyes widen and a chill creeps up my back as I take slow steps backward, landing hard into Brian. His hand reaches around to my hips, holding me against his body.

"They're not gonna hurt you." His voice caresses against the shell of my ear. "They work for me."

He squeezes my hip possessively, then sets me free.

"Miles. Kevin," he says by way of greeting. "This is Chiara, and she'll be staying here for a while."

The men give me a cool, collective nod before walking away, standing on each side of the door that leads out into the yard. They must be bodyguards.

"Come on, Chiara," Brian prompts, striding past me toward the doorway. "Let's go meet Sonia."

I pick up the pace, following him into the kitchen. There's a short woman with black hair mixed with silver, chopping something on the counter with her back to us.

"Sonia, I want to introduce you to a guest of mine."

She whirls her neck and places a knife down.

"Oh, hello there, dear." She wipes her hands on her black apron as she treads over to us.

I give her my hand. "I'm Chiara. It's nice to meet you."

She takes it in a warm embrace, the sides of her eyes crinkling with a tender smile.

"Always happy to meet friends of the boys," she says fondly, peering up at Brian.

What boys? I wonder to myself. *Does she mean the guards?*

"I won't be home tonight for dinner," he tells her, his voice growing softer. "Just throw the food in the fridge when you're done."

Where will he be? It's only six p.m. It's hours until he has to be at the strip club. I'd imagine he doesn't plan on destroying it before most of the world is asleep.

I was hoping to spend some one-on-one time with him before he left, giving me a chance to reinforce my plan and get him to want me enough to let his guard down. Only then will I have the opportunity to escape his well-fortified fortress. But getting there will prove to be a much harder task. He fights me at every step.

"No problem. But make sure you eat." Her hand reaches for his face, patting him gently on the cheek. "A growing boy needs to eat."

She's like a sweet grandma figure. It's actually adorable seeing them together.

"I'm not sure if you noticed, Sonia." His tone is set with slight playfulness. "But I haven't been a boy in a long time."

She drops her hand and waves it dismissively. "Eh, to me, you boys will always be babies. I don't care how strong and tough you are. You hear?"

"Yes, ma'am," Brian chuckles, complete adoration for this woman stamped on his features.

Sonia's dark brown eyes are on me now. "Maybe you'd like some nice hot dinner before I put it away?"

"She would," he answers for me.

I tilt my head toward him, lifting a brow, giving him the "I can answer for myself" look.

Sonia purses her lips as she takes a gander between Brian and me. "Okay, I'll make you a plate."

"Thank you," Brian and I say in unison, our gazes narrowed at one another for a brief second.

"We will go," he tells her. "I don't want to take away from your time."

"It was nice to meet you, Chiara, dear."

"You too," I say.

"She'll be staying a while," he adds, his eyes peeking knowingly at me. "Isn't that right?"

I glare, twisting my lips at him with an aggravated smile. "Not that you've given me a choice."

From the corner of my vision, I catch Sonia bunching her brows, glancing from Brian to me.

His jaw clamps, his eyes brimming with a layer of well-contained ire.

"I'll see you tomorrow, Sonia," he barks out gently. "We're leaving, Chiara. Let's go."

Sonia notices the change in mood.

"Behave." She lifts a finger at him, then gives me a small wave before returning to her workstation.

Brian storms out of the other side of the kitchen, not the way we came, making a right and disappearing from my view. I keep up with him as best I can, finding him pacing in a narrow hallway.

As soon as he sees me, he rushes forward, grabbing my wrist and pulling me further down, away from Sonia's earshot.

"What the hell are you doing?" I snap, attempting to yank my hand away, but his grip is solid.

He doesn't answer, pulling me until we reach the end of the hall, until my back hits the wall with a light thud. He plants his palms beside my face, spearing me with a venomous look.

"What the fuck was that?" he whisper-shouts, leaning his face into mine, his snarl drifting over my lips.

"What are you talking about, you psycho?" My voice is hushed, but anger swells in my gut.

Who does he think he is, manhandling me like this? And why do I want him to pin me to the wall and fuck me ruthlessly?

"Chiara, I swear to God." He grits his teeth, his gaze wandering between my lips and my eyes. "I'll lock you back in that fucking room if you try that shit again. Sonia knows nothing about this side of me, and I want it kept that way."

I slant my head to the side. "So she doesn't know you kidnap women and lock them in your big, bad room?"

"I don't kidnap women." His lips curve, so close to mine that if I moved a fraction, I'd taste his. "Just one in particular."

"Maybe next time you should give me a heads-up regarding who you've told about me being your hostage," I spit out through clenched teeth. "I prefer an Excel spreadsheet."

"I'll think about it." He smirks, his breath licking up my mouth.

"How can she not realize anything?" I whisper, the roar of desire warming me from the inside. "Isn't she suspicious with these men around?"

"No," he stamps out low and deep, his eyes narrowed. "Who does she think they are? Your friends?" I let out a small laugh.

"Guards. She knows I have businesses and competitors. One can never be too careful."

"She really has no idea you brought me here against my will?"

"Not a clue." A hand finds my jaw, his fingers roughly delving into it. "And if I were you, I'd keep my mouth shut, princess."

"Stop calling me that!" I say with a soft shout, my fingers landing on his back, my nails clawing down the length of it, enough to make it hurt.

He lets out a small growl as one of his legs slices in between my thighs, his body pressing roughly into mine as the hand on my jaw slithers to my neck.

I exhale a quiet moan when I feel his hardness pushing into my lower belly from beneath his clothes. The span of his large palm envelops the column of my neck, his fingers gradually closing in, pushing into my throat until I fight for every one of my breaths.

"I think you've forgotten who's in charge here." He leans in further, his lips brushing over my jaw. "I hope this is a good reminder." He squeezes harder. "Don't fuck with me, Chiara. You won't like what you find."

"You don't scare me," I choke out the words with a snarl, finding it harder to inhale, my nails piercing deeper into his back.

A spark ignites within his stormy gaze, pulsing through me, the desire for what we could be together so evident in his eyes. If only we were different people, born into a different life.

"I guess we'll have to remedy that." The words are meant as a threat.

My nails slowly trace up his spine, to the back of his neck until I reach his head, biting into his skin.

"Bring it on," I challenge with a stuttered tone while my nails sink deeper into the hardness of his muscles.

He hisses with a wild growl, clearly enjoying my hands on him. I like knowing he does. It helps further my cause. The more we touch, the better chance he lets me walk right into his bed, and after that, I'll slip right into his heart when he doesn't even see it coming.

Once I'm there, there will be nothing he wouldn't do for me, like allow me to leave his house whenever I want, giving me the opportunity to disappear before he ever has a chance to take my heart in return.

I know men like him: powerful in all aspects, guarding everything, even their hearts. But it only takes one single crack to crumble every wall they've so carefully built.

"Don't provoke me, baby," he asserts. "I could snap you like a twig, and there'll be no one here to stop me."

My pulse thumps in my neck.

I can hear it.

Feel it.

It pummels within me like a hammer, over and over, until it hurts.

"Do it, then," I push. "What are you waiting for?"

I can taste my fear mingled with desire. He excites me, yet terrifies me. And I like it. This game we're playing may hurt us both in the end, but sometimes the burn is worth the scars.

"I'm not here to make my captivity easy for you," I continue when he refuses to utter a word, his piercing gaze doing all the talking for him.

"That's too bad." His mouth falls to mine, just barely. "For you."

His long, deep breaths skate across my lips while his thigh

thrusts into my core, eliciting a low moan from deep in my throat. A grin spreads over my mouth even as my lungs burn, even as my chest rises up and down rapidly, scratching for every breath he allows me to have.

"You're lucky I like looking at you," he rasps, his eyes holding mine, his lips dipping toward the shell of my ear. "Or else you'd be dead already."

That smoky voice brushes over my sensitive earlobe, the husk within it rubbing against the achiness between my thighs. I hurt there, wanting this bastard to finish what he started. But instead, his hands fall and he backs away from me as his breathing returns to a normal pace while I try to steady mine.

Our unrelenting gazes align, staring into one another, fighting a battle we can't name with words. His eyes darken with a ball of frustration.

"I'm leaving now." He casually slips his hands in his hoodie. "There are cameras everywhere, and my men will be watching. Don't try anything."

"What do you mean everywhere?" My eyes pop wide. "My room too?"

My pulse slams into my throat, trying to recall if I did anything embarrassing or if I walked around naked.

Oh, God! I don't think so.

"You mean *my* room," he chuckles as his lips curve into a wicked grin.

"You asshole!" I bellow, not giving a shit if Sonia or anyone else hears. "You've been watching me this whole time?"

"That's right, baby."

He strides up, his body meeting mine in a tantalizing touch. A finger slides under my chin, the back of it lifting up my face to his.

"But you're kinda boring." The words hum over my lips to a

perfect beat, my body heating up from both fury and lust.

Boring, huh? I'll give you boring.

"Stay in your room, and don't go wandering into mine. It's the one next to yours. I'll know if you've been there."

He begins to go, stopping mid-stride, halting in place. His back flexes as he inhales, turning to me, his features less harsh now. He searches my gaze so intently, I'm almost lost within his.

"Sleep well, Chiara." The sensual cadence of his voice wafts through the air, bathing me with carnal need.

I pull in a long inhale, fighting the nonsensical urge to run into his arms and kiss him.

"I meant what I said earlier," I admit. "Be careful tonight."

He releases a harsh sigh, cutting his gaze to the wall above my head, then storms out of the hallway, leaving me there in tattered ruins, wondering why I'm here worried about my kidnapper when the only one I should be concerned with is me.

DOMINIC

SEVENTEEN

Even back when I was a kid, I knew what sort of animal her father was, but hearing her tell me what he did to her, locking her away like that, it did something to me. I couldn't do what he did to her. I couldn't hurt her that way, no matter what happened in our past. She deserves better. She always has.

But I have to be careful around her. I can't let her get to me. I won't allow her to ruin the plan my brothers and I have carefully set into motion by tempting me with her body and ruining me with her tears.

I know she wants out of here. I know what she's trying to do. But I can't let her leave. She has no idea what's waiting for her beyond the comfort of my home and she doesn't want to know.

Once I'm done with her, she'll be gone. Far enough where I

can't be tempted to get a taste of those luscious lips and every other place in between.

I have to get the aftertaste of Chiara off my tongue before I bury myself deep inside her the way I've been tempted to. She makes me crazy. There's a fire within her that ignites my very soul, making me want her with sheer depravity.

No woman has ever spoken to me the way she does. She's different than the rest. I want to kill that fiery spirit while cultivating it and helping it grow. I like her fighting back, but I fight harder and a lot dirtier.

Rubbing the back of my head, I keep the focus away from Chiara and on the mission at hand.

"How long?" I ask Miles, our head of security and the driver of the van my brothers and I are in. He's the only one of my men I truly trust.

"Five minutes out, sir," he says over his shoulder.

Miles is excellent at his job, an ex-sniper who was once a Navy SEAL. All the men who work for me have high-level military backgrounds. For the kind of shit we're involved in, only the best will do.

He makes a quick left as I scan the faces of the other two guys here. Another eight men are in the van behind us, heading for the strip club, not knowing what awaits, but ready for anything.

After I left the house, I prepared for tonight with my brothers and our men at Enzo's. I can't do shit at my place with Chiara there, and Dante can't either, with Raquel at his place.

The van stops, arriving a quarter of a block away from the club with nothing but trees and lanterns lining up the quiet street. The crickets are the only ones awake, and we want to keep it that way.

One of my tech guys in the other van was in charge of killing the camera frequencies within a three-mile radius. Every Ring cam, dash cam, every fucking cam you can think of has been dead for hours.

"Sir, we're positioned," Roger alerts me through my walkie-talkie. "We see some movement inside. Two men so far. Both armed."

Roger is one of my most lethal guys, probably from his days as an Army sniper. He also runs a mixed martial arts school by day, but no one knows exactly what he does for me at night.

"Stand by," I say.

"Ten-four."

"We're going through the back," I tell my guys. "Keep your masks and gloves on at all times. Kill any man inside."

My brothers and the rest of the guys pull down their black face masks, semi-automatic pistols in hand, and another two strapped to each of their bodies. I like these weapons. I remove mine from the duffle bag on the floor. Faro has good taste. The irony of using his own guns on his people doesn't escape me.

We exit the van, taking slow, measured steps to the back of the club. A few men from the other van wait inside on standby, watching for possible threats.

Our boots crunch over the gravel, and as we near the door, I peek inside through the glass window on the door, finding two men pacing back and forth, nine-millimeters in hand. But they don't see us yet. They're not close enough. They're positioned around the middle, by the bar where I first spoke to Chiara. I gesture with two fingers, alerting everyone of what I see.

Faro must've seen me grab her from the camera footage at the club and sent his people here. I wanted him to know. There must be more men hiding inside.

I take out the keys I stole from her and carefully place one in the door, turning until I hear a click. And in the silence of the night, it sounds louder.

Ominous.

Dante and Enzo are on the other side of the door, with the rest of the guys spread out behind us.

I nod once, giving them the signal to be ready. Shoving the door open, we rush inside as the men shout in alarm.

Pop.

Pop.

Pop.

We start shooting, bullets flying past my head. Three more men run out from the doors leading to the back of the club, firing round after round.

One bullet flies past my ear as I duck and kneel, firing at one son of a bitch right in the calf as I go down.

He screams in agony.

"You piece of shit. You're all dead," the capo I now recognize as Mikey threatens. "Faro will have all your heads."

Still on my knees, I point my gun at his torso. "Good night, motherfucker. I'll make sure Faro pays you a visit."

I pop him in the chest. He finally shuts up.

One down.

My eyes fly around the room, the pulse in my neck pounding with fury, matching the rage inside my heart. I want all of them dead. Everyone who's ever worked for that family will die.

Dante shoots another one dead, while Enzo's punching some soon-to-be sorry son of a bitch off of him, the man's gun on the floor.

I rush for it, picking it up. Enzo makes eye contact, and as he slightly shoves the guy off to the side, I fire at the asshole on the back of his skull. He falls on top of my brother.

"Fuck, man," Enzo mutters, pushing the dead weight off

completely. "Did you have to kill him right on top of me?"

I give him my hand and pull him up. "Maybe I should've left you there and had him rearrange your face."

"On your left," Enzo warns with a head gesture, as another four men come for an attack.

How many fucking people do they have back there?

Boom.

Boom.

I shoot one in his eye, ducking as the other fires at me, while Enzo takes care of the other two.

My shoulder burns, but I ignore the pain, firing two more rounds at the one who just tried to take me out.

He drops to the floor, blood gushing out in spurts from his neck. Standing over him, I fire another bullet into the center of his chest.

He's definitely dead now. And as I watch the blood seeping out of him, I realize the bullets have stopped.

It's quiet now.

"Fuck!" Dante growls behind me.

I rush over, finding two men dead beside him.

He clutches his left arm, his lips peeled back, teeth gritted, face twisted in pain. "I'm hit."

"Let me see," I tell him as I start to gently pull at the sleeve of his hoodie until his arm is free.

Blood leaks from the top of his arm, right below the shoulder.

"Shit, we have to get you to Raquel. She's the closest."

She'll know how to treat this shit. I remove my hoodie, wrapping it tightly around the wound, applying enough pressure to stop the bleeding.

"Let's load up and get the fuck out of here!" I shout to my men.

Looking around, I find they're all still in one piece. Relief washes over me.

As Enzo and I grab Dante, we hear whimpering. A woman's voice.

What the fuck?

"Did you hear that?" Enzo asks, his eyes narrowing, voice low.

I nod, pointing toward the bar with my head.

Go, I mouth.

He nods back in understanding, and as another of our men takes over holding Dante steady, Enzo makes his way toward the sound.

He takes a few slow steps, and then he leaps over the bar. That idiot is reckless. If I didn't have Dante, I'd kill him. She could have a fucking gun back there.

"Get away from me!" the woman yells, tears evident in her tone.

He holds out his palms as he peers down. I can't see her from my view.

"We're not going to hurt you," he promises. "Come on out." He reaches a hand for hers. "I've got my brothers out there, plus a bunch of the men who work for us. We swear we won't do anything to you."

"I don't care! You need to leave now before I blow your fucking brains out."

So she does have a weapon. He's lucky she hasn't used it yet. Or, she's lucky, I should say. I'd shoot her dead if she killed my brother.

"As much as I love a hot woman with a weapon, especially when that woman is you, you need to stop pointing that thing at me, Joelle." He smirks.

He knows her?

"Fuck you, Enzo."

Well, that cleared up any confusion.

He casually leans against the bar, his arms now crossed over his chest like they're having a friendly chat. "You should know by now the main reason I come here is for you. The way you own that pole…" He grunts like he's picturing it. "Damn, girl. You're like a snake on that thing."

I knew he came here with Dante, but I didn't know he was making friends with strippers. Not that I'm surprised.

I'd pay to see that kid settle down. I'm not even talking marriage. I mean like a girlfriend. But with the life we've been dealt, none of us can have that. Not yet. Not until all the blood of our enemies spills across our feet. Not until we can leave the past and live in the present.

"How about you put that gun down and come out with us?" Enzo tells her. "I'll drive you home."

"I'm good here," she counters. "You can go."

"Okay, sure, babe, you stay." He backs off the bar. "But it'd be a real goddamn shame to see all that beautiful skin turn to a crisp when we burn the place down. Wouldn't want all that talent to go to waste."

"Fuck you!" she yells.

He shakes his head in mock disappointment. "Such a pretty mouth saying such dirty things."

And before she can say another word, the sound of what I think is the gun landing on the floor splits the air.

He quickly leans down and out of view.

"Don't fucking touch me, you asshole!" she screams.

Enzo groans, and there's the sound of shuffling and movement. Finally standing back up, he clutches the arm of a woman, about our age, with wavy blonde hair and light blue eyes.

"Asshole?" he asks accusatorily, with his other hand flat against his chest as he faces her. "That was me being a gentleman. If I were an asshole…" He fists her hair, pulling her face close to his.

"I'd drag you out by your throat."

She narrows her eyes with venom, steeling her chin as they both glare at one another.

"Come on, man. Dante needs help!" I shout.

He finally looks at me. "Yeah, shit. My bad."

He yanks her by the arm and brings her around from the bar, finally joining us. When he's next to me, he bends over to my ear.

"Do you realize who we have?" he whispers.

"What are you talking about?"

"She's the Bianchi brothers' favorite toy. And she makes them a crap ton of dough." I can see the gears turning in his brain.

"What do you wanna do with her?"

I already know the answer to my question.

"I wanna keep her. What better way to fuck with them? We burn their club and take their favorite girl."

"Fine. She stays with you."

"Wouldn't have it any other way. I have a feeling she and I will have *lots* of fun together." The smile on his face is deadly as he yanks her closer to his side.

She groans with displeasure, refusing to look at him, staring straight ahead at my men.

Once I get Dante into the van. I return to the club with a few of the men and burn every inch of that place until it goes...

Boom.

CHIARA

EIGHTEEN

I gasp, instantly jumping to a sitting position from the thunderous bang somewhere close, waking me from the dead of sleep.

I clutch my chest with both hands, my heart racing with quick beats, ricocheting within my body. Glancing out the window, I find the thick cloud of darkness still covering the night sky.

My breaths leave in rapid bursts as my trembling hands lift the comforter off my body.

Who could that be? Is it Brian? My father? Maybe he found out I gave up his location and sent someone to kill me.

Thud.

A footstep causes the floor to creak.

My eyes bulge, my body running with an icy chill while my heart slams with every breath, almost exploding from within.

I slowly swing my feet out of the bed and just sit there. Unable to move. Frozen in time.

Ice cold.

Shivering.

Thud.

Thud.

Thud.

The stomping footsteps get closer. I find the courage to get up, tiptoe across the floor, and lock the door, leaning my ear against it to see if I can hear any voices.

Nothing.

Whoever it is has stopped moving. The wooden floor creaks again.

I hear my exhales. Louder in the echo of the room.

The floor squeaks right outside my room, and my stomach flips, my pants getting louder. I have to find a place to hide. I swallow the heavy fear weighing me down into the floor, my legs refusing to move.

Please be Brian. I don't want to die.

The footsteps return, heading away from me, and I hear a door close.

"Brian?" I whisper, almost to myself.

I have to know if it's him. I have to know what happened tonight. If my staff is okay. My hand nears the doorknob, then backs away. I hate being afraid. It makes me feel weak and pathetic.

The amount of fear I lived in while I was growing up was overwhelming, and it's kind of sad that I'm still living those days, in one way or another. My father has always been at the center of it all, and not much has changed.

Returning my palm to the doorknob, I attempt to turn it, but fear accosts me from every angle of this room. I give myself a few more seconds to stabilize my racing pulse and erratic heartbeats.

With massive apprehension, I turn the handle.

Slowly.

A little at a time.

Turn.

Turn.

The door squeaks as it parts.

Fuck.

I can practically taste the bile rising in my throat.

I wish I had a gun. My father taught me how to use one in case I needed to protect the club.

I know where Brian's bedroom is. If I can run there and get inside, I'll be safe. At least I hope so.

Okay. On three, I tell myself.

One. I part the door a little more and find the hallway covered in total darkness.

Two. I take a step out as my eyes adjust to the lack of light.

Three. I run like hell toward his room and open the door. I don't even knock.

"Who the fuck is that?" he barks, and I hear what sounds like metal clanking.

"It's Chiara. Don't kill me," I quickly say.

The lamp on his nightstand turns on, and he's there sitting up, slouching, with a pistol in his hand, smears of blood marring the tattoo on his arm.

He doesn't look right. Something's wrong.

The strong, confident man is shadowed with a layer of pain.

"What's wrong?" I ask. "Are you okay?"

I move forward with a single step.

He glares up, his chest inching up and down with ragged pants.

"Why'd you come in here?" He lifts the gun inadvertently as

he speaks.

"I heard a loud noise. I thought it was my father."

He snickers. "Your father wouldn't dare show his face here."

He leans forward, placing the gun on the nightstand.

"Fuck!" he growls, landing a palm on his shoulder.

I tilt my head to the side. "Are you hurt?"

A groan is his only answer.

"Did you get shot?" My eyes widen as my heart slams into my throat.

"Let me see!" I hurry toward him, kneeling to a sitting position as I grab his wrist.

"I'm fine." His eyes delve into mine, and there's pain within them.

"You're not," I say in a low tone, afraid he'll stop looking at me if I speak any louder.

I tug on his hoodie. "Take it off."

"What the fuck can you do?" he questions.

"Depending on the severity, I can remove the bullet, clean it, wrap it. Do you have a doctor?"

Not the first time I've done it, I want to say. When my father got shot a few years back, Raquel walked me through what to do in case I ever needed to.

He smirks. "I have someone if I need it."

"Great. But since they're not here, you've got me. So stop being all macho and shit and take that damn thing off so I can see the wound."

He rises to his feet, and so do I.

"Damn, princess," he chuckles, all sure of himself. "If you wanted to see me naked that badly, all you had to do was ask."

"Not interested," I grumble. "And what did I tell you about that word?"

He laughs, taking off the hoodie and throwing it on the floor by my feet. There's a white shirt, now stained with too much blood, wrapped around his arm.

"Why didn't anyone take you to the doctor?"

He snickers with a groan. "They would've if they knew."

I shake my head at his stubbornness.

He sits back down on the edge of the bed. "It's just a graze. I'll live."

"You're an idiot. This isn't the movies. You know how dangerous a gunshot wound on the arm can be if you hit a damn artery?"

"Are you a doctor too now?"

"No, but my cousin is. I know some shit."

He sighs deeply. "I didn't hemorrhage out. Still breathing. So I think my arteries are good, baby. Don't worry." The last few words are said facetiously.

"I'm not worried."

I grimace as I unwrap the shirt and find a long fleshy wound. The blood seems to have stopped, for the most part.

"I need to clean this and re-wrap it." I twist my lips with worry. "Where do you keep your 'in case I get shot' stuff?"

"Why the hell do you care enough to help me?"

"Maybe because I have a heart and you don't. Now, where is it?"

He points to the left, at one of the doors. "Bathroom. Left bottom cabinet, under the sink."

I run in, finding myself in a bathroom that's a bigger version of the one he designated for me.

I open the cabinet, finding everything I need. Grabbing the saline, a roll of gauze, a pad, and cotton balls, I'm ready to go back out, but when I look up, he's standing over the doorframe.

My heart stops as our gazes fall into one another's. My stomach flips again, but this time it isn't fear.

"Um, I—"

"I'll sit here." His mouth curves up at the corner. "Don't want you dirtying my sheets."

My breath falters, my body going instantly hot with images of us tangled in his bed.

He moves past me, lowering himself on the toilet lid.

"Let's get this over with," he says, extending his arm for me.

Making my way to him, I open the bottle of saline and pour a little right over his wound.

"Shit," he winces. "You trying to kill me or something?"

"That's for calling me princess." I grin, pouring some more into his marred flesh.

He slants his head sideways with a taunting glare behind his gaze. "You'd better stop hurting me."

He grabs my wrist, and my other hand with the saline in it, rattles.

"Why do I get the feeling you like it," I taunt with an arch of my brow and a tip of my lips.

He clenches his jaw, his eyes boring into mine, confirming what I had already known. Relieving the grip from my hand, he lets me finish. And I don't push my limits anymore. I clean him with care, then wrap his arm.

"Get to bed," I demand.

"You're telling me what to do now?"

"Someone has to."

He laughs. "You're a crazy woman. Not that I'm surprised."

"What the hell does that mean?" I close the saline and put all the supplies away.

He treads over to his bed, with me close behind, and lowers

himself into it, the uninjured arm tucked under the back of his head.

He peers up at me, his gaze soft. "Thanks. You didn't have to."

I ignore the gratefulness. "Did anyone else get hurt tonight?"

"None of your people got hurt. Everyone's safe."

I close my eyes and sigh with relief. "Sleep well, Brian. I'll see you tomorrow."

As I exit his room and shut the door behind me, I lean against it, overwhelmed with my unexplained feelings for him. I care about his well-being while I shouldn't. It's crazy even to me.

But my goal remains the same: getting the fuck out of here one way or another. I hope this incident between us was the turning point and that he learns to trust me. Maybe him getting shot was the best thing that could've happened.

CHIARA

NINETEEN

My eyes fly open as though someone has dragged me out from the clutches of sleep. Gripping my comforter, I hold it close, refusing to give away the last few minutes of shut-eye.

It took me a long time to drift off after I left his room. Between losing control of my feelings for him, coupled with the fear of the unknown, I was a wreck.

I keep wondering who my father and uncles killed for Brian to hate them so much. Will I really pay the price for their sins? Will I be dead when this is all over?

And who the hell is Brian Smith? He has to have ties to some sort of organized criminal faction. He's probably cut from the same cloth my father is, running legitimate businesses combined with the not-so-legal kind.

I sit up, my feet swinging off the bed as I rub the tiredness away from my eyes. Glancing at the clock, I can't believe it's noon. It feels like I've barely slept. I'm not one of those people who needs a lot of hours of sleep to function.

I quickly change into a black tank top and tight black leggings. Black is my favorite color. On a rare day, I'll add in some color.

I wonder how Brian is feeling today.

And why the hell do I care?

He doesn't give a shit about you, so stop worrying about him.

My stomach growls. I hope there's something to eat. Maybe Sonia made those crepes again.

Reaching for the door, I pull it open, heading for the stairs, but before I do, I tiptoe a few feet toward Brian's room. It's still closed. I lean closer, edging my ear nearer.

Silence.

He's probably still asleep. Who wouldn't be, after the night I'm sure he had?

I walk toward the stairs, going down very quietly so as not to wake him. Once I'm downstairs, I forget where the kitchen is for a moment, but then I remember. Why does a single man need a home this big?

Stepping into the kitchen, I find Sonia washing tomatoes by the sink.

"Good morning, dear. Would you like some breakfast, or would you prefer to wait for lunch?"

"Breakfast would be great. I'm kind of starving."

"Of course." She smiles cheerfully, her hair held up tightly in a bun. "I wrapped up a plate for you after Mr. uh…Smith ate this morning."

"Wait, he's up?"

"Oh, yes. He's in his study, and doesn't wish to be disturbed."

How the hell is he functioning?

She goes into the fridge, taking out a white plate wrapped in foil. "I've made some crepes since they're his favorite, as well as some sausage. Does that sound good?"

"I'm not picky. Whatever you have is fine. And your crepes are amazing. He gave me some when he, um—brought me breakfast in bed one day."

I have a feeling "while he held me hostage in his room" wouldn't go over very well.

"That's very sweet."

Ha! Lady, you have no idea.

I suppress an exaggerated laugh, skimming my hand past my lips.

She removes the foil, tossing it in the trash before placing the dish into the microwave. "Mr. Smith doesn't entertain women in the house. You must be someone special."

"Oh, I'm special all right," I mutter, more to myself.

Once it's warm, she hands me the plate and returns to her tomatoes.

"I was thinking a steak salad with some sweet potato fries for lunch," she says over her shoulder.

"That sounds…" The rest of the words are caught in my throat as an idea forms. A great idea if I can execute it properly.

"You know, I was thinking, how about you take the day off? I can make Brian lunch and dinner as a thank-you for everything he's done for me."

That rat bastard. Maybe I can poison him?

"What a wonderful idea!" she exclaims, turning to me as she wipes her hands on her white apron. "He's such a lovely man. It's so nice to see someone equally lovely in his life."

"Oh, yes. He's very lovely."

If by lovely, she means insane, sure.

"How about we don't tell him about this?" I throw in, a huge grin spreading from cheek to cheek. "I want it to be a nice surprise."

"He will love it!" She looks genuinely excited, and I now feel bad for being a liar.

"Could you maybe give me some directions? I'm not really the best cook." I twist my lips shyly as she laughs.

"Of course I can."

She proceeds to give me step-by-step instructions, and I hope I can remember all of it.

"Can you also show me where the plates and things are? Then you can go have a spa day or something."

"Me? Spa day? Oh, goodness, no." She dismisses the idea with a wave of her hand. "I'm going to go see my daughter and spend the day with my grandkids. She just had a baby a month ago, her third, and she could really use the help."

Suddenly, tears prickle at the edge of my eyes.

"Are you okay, dear?" Her brows hunch over as she places her hand on top of mine.

A burning ache crawls up my body, centering in my chest. My mom and I will never have these moments. She'll probably never meet my kids if I have any. She'll never be there for me at all.

"Chiara?" Sonia asks again. "You're crying."

A broken laugh falls out of me. "I'm sorry."

Wiping under my eyes, I try to fake it, but it's no use. The tears douse my fingers.

"Don't you be sorry." She pats my hand with concern written over her kind eyes. "If you ever need an ear, I'm here. I may be old, but they still work."

"I have no doubt," I add. "Well, you have fun with your family. We'll be fine here."

"Those kids keep me on my old-lady toes, that's for sure." She removes her apron. "Let me throw this into the hamper, then show you where everything is."

I follow her as she walks out to the laundry room, which I come to see is located behind a closed door in the same hallway where Brian had me up against the wall. She places the apron into an empty wicker basket, then closes the door. We tread back into the kitchen, and she shows me around before gathering her things to leave.

"Well, I'll be going now. My phone number is on the fridge in case you need me."

"Thank you," I say politely before she heads for the foyer.

Rushing back into the kitchen, I start on lunch, taking out the steak she had in the fridge and slicing it on one of the cutting boards she had out. Hopefully, I can manage without burning anything.

I figure if Brian and I share an intimate meal or two together, he'll warm up to me. There's this strong carnal connection between us, and I need to light the fire. I need to lead him into the flames.

Placing the seasoned chopped potatoes into a pan, I turn on the oven before putting them inside. After they're halfway done, I proceed to fry up some chopped-up steak and cut the tomatoes and cucumbers while it's cooking. Before I have a chance to finish, a heavy crash of footsteps comes nearer.

"Sonia, I'll be—" Brian's voice cuts off when his confused expression lands on me.

"What the hell are you doing?" he asks, irritation marking his words. "Where's Sonia?"

I grin through his unhappiness. "I sent her home. I wanted to cook us a meal as a thank-you for not killing me yet."

I turn off the stove, noticing the steak is already too black to be edible.

Why did I even bother? I don't know how to cook at all.
His jaw flexes as he pins me with an angry stare.

"Did I tell you to do that?" His tone splashes with frustration as he takes a single menacing step closer. "Did I ask you to send my staff home? Who the fuck do you think you are? This isn't a hotel or your home."

His body is closer now, and with a single step, he's in front of me. He grips my chin in between two fingers and lifts my face up to the fiery pits of hell within his gaze.

"You're nothing more than a helpless little girl I'm using to get what I need. So stop getting comfortable where you don't belong."

The back of my nose burns from the cruelty. And as his eyes continue to hold mine, I feel the ache of the tears filling my gaze.

Of course this was a stupid plan. Why did I think this man would ever like me enough to want me? He hates me as much as he hates my father. That much is clear now.

I grit my teeth, my rage-filled gaze sharper than the knife I was just using. "Fuck you, Brian. I'm so damn sorry for trying to make this tolerable for the both of us. I'm so fucking sorry eating a meal I made is so inconceivable to you."

He peers down blankly at me now, his Adam's apple vibrating as he swallows, his eyes never leaving mine. We are at a stalemate, both of us hotheaded and refusing to give in.

"You're going to make some poor woman miserable one day," I throw in. "I feel sorry for her already."

Gripping his wrist, I pull it away from my face, marching away from him to the other side of the counter. Lifting up a knife, I start unevenly slicing up cucumbers, taking out the anger on them instead.

"Easy there before you chop off your finger."

My hand goes still and my eyes slowly crawl up to his. Picking up a piece of cucumber, I throw it at his face, but he instantly catches it and pops it into his mouth as he smiles cruelly.

I grunt with disappointment, gritting my teeth harder, my jaw rattling with the force. I hate him so much. I can't believe I ever wanted to fuck him.

"You're so lucky that didn't end up on my work shirt, Chiara."

"Oh, yeah?" I snicker. "And what in the world would you have done if it did?"

He rushes around the counter so fast, his front pressing into my back with the knife still in my hand. I could flip it and cut him in an instant.

"Whatever you're thinking with that thing in your hand, I suggest you stop. Now." He leans his body over mine, pushing me into the counter, my body falling over it, the knife close to my chest. "I wouldn't want to dirty up my kitchen with your blood."

"You're not as scary as you think you are," I bite back with a hiss.

He fists my hair, pulling my head back so hard that I wince from the pain, laughing viciously despite the ache.

His eyes land on mine.

Cold.

Brutal.

Cutting through me with a single stroke.

Not an ounce of the man from last night behind his gaze.

"You're really testing me, Chiara, and I'm growing tired of it," he threatens in a calm, collected voice. "Maybe I should do something about it."

His other hand slides up and down my side and my eyes drift to a close from the hypnotizing touch. My mind is at war, fighting an attraction it can't seem to control. I'm lost to him, even when I wish I weren't.

He's lust in its cruelest form. I want to savor every inch of him and hurt him while I do it.

"There's nothing you can do that hasn't been done." I can't help fighting back. It's been built in me, like a brand I wear with honor.

"That's where you're wrong. There's so much I can do to you." His hand delves deeper into my hip, his fingers bleeding pain through me.

I don't mind the hurt. I rather enjoy it.

I push my ass further into him, dropping the knife before it finds itself embedded in his thigh.

His hand lets go of my hair, sliding to my front, right above my breasts. I control my breathing, not wanting him to see the effect he has on me, even though I bet he knows how much my body craves his.

The pads of his fingers climb up leisurely.

Slow. So slow.

My nipples harden of their own accord from the anticipation, the need for him twining up my body, setting me off with thoughts of him sinking inside me right up against this counter. I want him to take me right here, right now, without asking.

The desire is unfathomable and demonic. But I want him. The rational side of me is long gone. I'm taken over by euphoria.

His cock is hard against the small of my back as his fingers skim up the length of my neck, finding home around the base of my jaw. He cups it tightly, but it's more of a possession, showing me his power.

He tilts my head back once more, and my eyes are back on his. The inexplicable thirst, the need, spills from his gaze.

"You want it, don't you, baby?" He arches his hips roughly into me, erasing any confusion as to what he meant. His hand on my hip glides south until a finger slides up my wet slit. "I'll bet you taste real good when you come."

I whimper from the dirtiness, and he groans, pressing his finger harder on my clit, making the fabric of my panties rub against me.

"I bet you want to find out," I add.

"I'd lie if I said I don't picture you at my mercy," he drawls with a long, throaty rasp, his gaze still pinned to mine, his thumb brushing roughly over my lower lip. "There are so many things I could do to you, Chiara. So many ways I can punish you for…"

His brows furrow with an unexplained change of emotion, from lust to pain.

Before I can ask what he was going to punish me for, he's off of me so fast, it's as though he wasn't there at all, strolling away like I don't matter.

And I guess I don't. I'm no one.

A minute later, I hear what sounds like the front door closing. I press my fingers into my eyes, rubbing away the tension he put there.

The oven alarm for the potatoes I forgot about comes on. I shut it off and storm out of the kitchen, finding a guard in the living room, right by the door leading toward the pool. I get his attention with a polite wave.

"Ma'am." He nods.

"Hi. What's your name again?" I twirl a loose strand of hair, giving him my doe eyes.

"I'm Miles, ma'am."

"Nice to meet you, Miles," I tell the man, who looks maybe ten years older than me, a touch of a beard lining his tanned jaw. "Can you tell me if there are cameras by the pool area?"

He looks unsure of whether he should answer.

"I only want to show Mr. Smith how well I'll be enjoying this pool that he so kindly allowed me to use."

"I can call him for you and you can ask him yourself." He reaches into his pocket.

I raise a palm to stop him. "Oh, no, don't bother him. I'm sure he's working. I'll tell him all about it when he gets home."

"All right, ma'am." He opens the door for me, leading into acres of greenery and the bluest pool I've ever seen.

"Thank you." I smile triumphantly and walk right outside.

DOMINIC

TWENTY

I shouldn't have allowed her to get close to me last night, to help me with my wound. It made her think we're friends. We're not.

We never will be again.

The last time I allowed her to get close, she broke me. Shattered me into pieces. And I'll never let her break me again. Some wounds never close. They only fester, gnawing at the pain, reminding you they'll never forget what you wish you could. And I remember all of it.

The shit I did earlier in the kitchen…man, I don't know what I was thinking.

I wasn't. That's the fucking problem. I never am when she's that close to me, looking at me like she's about to claw at my clothes.

This attraction between us is on a whole other level. If I let her, she'll have the power to sink her venom into my flesh and spread her poison through me. I can't trust her. I can't afford to, and neither can my heart.

The girl I once thought I knew tore my heart while it still beat for a friendship I thought we had. And the woman now? She's no different.

I grip the back of my neck as my assistant, Camille, fills me in on my meetings today, her voice drifting in and out of my thoughts.

"You have a meeting today at four with Damian Prescott of JDG Global," I think she says. "It's regarding the security for the…hotels."

I roll my chair closer to my desk, looking up at her, pretending I heard whatever the fuck she said. She flips her blonde hair past her shoulder, her dark brown eyes waiting for me to respond.

"Okay," I throw out casually.

Enzo has a thing for her, even though she's about fifteen years older. But then again, he has a thing for any hot female. If it weren't for me putting a stop to him getting with her, he'd probably break her heart and make her quit. Not happening. She's good at her job and has been with me for the past two years. I'm not starting fresh with someone new.

She taps a few more buttons on the tablet I supply all my staff with and peers down at me from beneath her glasses.

"Let me know if there's anything else you need."

"Will do."

She walks out of the office, and I get back to work.

Hours later, my burner cell—the phone reserved for my enemy—goes off with a text. A surge of anger fills me as I take it out of my pocket, unlocking it.

Opening the text, I read his words, clenching the phone so hard it almost breaks in my palm.

> **Faro:** You don't know what you've done. I thought we had a deal. Now you'll die. I took one brother. I'll take them all. Then I'll kill you like I killed your father. On your knees. Begging.

My breathing comes out in a mangled strain. My heart pounds inside my chest. I squeeze the phone so tight, it digs into my palm with an ache before I throw it across the room. It crashes against the wall with a heavy thud.

The hatred for that man runs through my veins, filling me with savagery. There's nothing I want more than to watch him die. I crave it more than oxygen. It's the only thing I've lived for since he took them from me.

My office door flies open.

"What the fuck happened, man?" Dante asks, Enzo behind him.

Dante's office is right next to mine, and my other brother must've been with him when I lost it.

I grind my teeth, my breaths deep. Heavy.

They both take a seat on the black leather sofa, leg crossed over the knee.

"He texted," I spit out. "He threatened all of us."

Dante releases a low chuckle. "Good. It means we got to him."

I fist my palm, slamming on my desk. "We can't underestimate him."

Dante raises a palm, sitting back as he winces, the left arm probably still hurting from the wound. "All right, brother. I know. But we can't let him get to us, either. We'll get him. All of them.

For Dad and Matteo. They'll fucking pay."

"He has no idea we know where he is," Enzo adds. "I can't wait to see the look on his ugly face when he sees us pull up there, guns blazing."

I suck in a harsh breath, rubbing a hand down my face. They're right. I can't allow him to get a hold of my emotions. The worry for my brothers is crushing, and sometimes when I close my eyes, the fear that I'll watch them die too takes over me until it consumes my every thought.

As the older sibling, I've gotten used to being like a father figure in their life, and protecting what's left of my family is a job I take seriously.

Dante stands to retrieve the phone I threw, flipping it around. "Shit, it still works, minus the crack on the screen."

"Considering the impact it took, I'll take it."

I'm not getting another burner just to give that piece of shit the number. He'll not be hearing from me, unless it's with violence. Dante hands me the phone, and I slip it back into my pocket.

"You guys can't come to the charity event in a few days." I change the subject.

Enzo looks at me all pissed. "What the fuck, man? Why?"

"Chiara," Dante answers.

I nod. She'll definitely recognize Enzo with his green eyes. I can't risk it.

Every year, Tomás hosted a charity event to sponsor a different organization benefiting kids. This year, it's a children's hospital in the city. We bring in a lot of donors, and it's an event the rich look forward to.

"I was counting on bringing some fine-ass women home that night," Enzo grumbles.

"Don't you have a stripper who needs your attention?" Dante

asks, facing him with his arms folded against his chest.

"The woman doesn't even like me, and when she talks, it's to cuss me out." He smirks. "There's something going on, though." His eyes turn thoughtful, and he takes a brief pause before speaking again. "She told me I had to let her go, or Faro will hurt someone she loves."

"Who?" My forearms lean onto my desk.

"I have no idea. But I'll find out if she's lying, one way or another." There's a ferocious glint in his eyes, and I have no doubt my brother will.

Just then my cell rings—my real one—and I see Miles's name on the caller ID.

Chiara.

Concern for her grips at me and I answer immediately.

"What's wrong?" I ask him.

"Sir, we've got a situation at home that needs your immediate attention."

"What the fuck happened?" I'm already on my feet, grabbing the keys off the desk.

"It's best if you see it for yourself."

I clench my jaw. "Spit it out. Is she in danger?"

I register the puzzled looks on my brothers' faces as I head out of my office.

"She's not in danger. Not exactly."

"I don't speak in riddles—"

He starts to reply.

"Give me a second, Miles," I cut him off, then mute him and talk to Camille. "I have to go. Cancel the meeting with Damian. Send them my sincerest apologies and a bottle of the finest cognac."

JDG Global is the best security firm out there, and I need them working for me.

"Of course, sir. Not a problem."

This better be a good fucking reason to get me out of the office. The house better be on fire. And considering the live feed of the house on my phone shows it's not, he better have a damn good reason for disturbing me.

Heading for the elevator, I unmute the call with Miles. "On my way."

Then I end the call.

I swing the door open, finding Miles already there. "What the fuck is the big emergency?"

"Come with me, sir," he says, already marching toward the living room, with me beside him. "I wouldn't have called, but neither I nor any of the men knew how to handle this without offending you."

What the fuck is he going on about?

Miles practically towers over me, and I'm a pretty big motherfucker. He's about six-seven and three hundred pounds of muscle, but right now, he looks scared as hell.

Opening the door to the yard, he leads me toward the pool, where I first see the top of Chiara's head on a lounger. Four of my men are stationed there, all four trying hard not to stare at her. I know she's beautiful. I can't blame them for that, but that's all they'll fucking do, or I'll rip their goddamn hearts out.

But as I get closer, my pulse punches me right at the side of my throat.

"What the *fuck* do you think you're doing?" A disapproving growl thunders out of me.

Her shoulders jump as she yanks a pair of my Bluetooth headphones off her ears. She gazes up at me with a twist of her neck, her eyes squinting beneath the sunlight, but all I can see are her bare tits.

She's in a fucking pair of black lace panties. That's all. The matching bra is beside her on the ottoman.

Motherfucker. She let all these men see her like this?
I want to carve their eyes out.

"I'm sorry. What's the problem?" she asks, her brows bowing in defiance. "Am I not allowed to tan?"

"Not like *that*. Not when every man here can see your tits." My voice hovers above complete rage.

"Oh, *please*," she huffs, putting her headphones back in as her lashes flutter to a close.

With a touch, I yank that shit from her ears. "Pick up that fucking bra and put it on."

My patience is close to gone, my tone edging with ruthlessness.

"Are you fucking kidding me, asshole?"

"Chiara." I drag in a long breath. "I'm close to losing my damn patience."

"So scary," she taunts, her voice twisting with a laugh.

"Put it on. *Now*." I can't even enjoy the sight of her while knowing all these men are doing it too.

"Get the men out of here," I tell Miles. "And make sure you all scrub the image of her tits from your minds."

"Yes, sir." He gestures with a hand, and they all follow him out.

"You have on the count of three to put that fucking bra on, Chiara. I will not tell you again."

"You're insane," she hisses, her ass still planted on the lounger.

"Three," I count, my palm twitching with the shit it wants to do to her.

"I'm not a child." Her features crawl with disgust. "You don't get to tell me what to do."

"Two." I ignore her.

She spears me with a furious look, folding her arms under her breasts while I tame the wild need even as my cock grows.

"One."

"Oh, plea—hey!" she yells as I scoop her up, throwing her over my shoulder, holding her around the small of her back, her bare ass in the air.

She showed them that too? She's going to pay.

I may not be able to have her, but no one else will either.

"Put me down, you animal!"

"I warned you," I growl, as I open the door, heading inside. "You're not good at listening, are you?"

The guards are all gone from here too. Miles knows me well.

"I don't know who the hell you think you are, but you don't own me. I can walk around here butt-ass naked if I want to."

I tighten my hold around her, my other hand landing sharply over her bare ass cheek, my palm itching to turn her skin a bright shade of pink.

She lets out a small moan, so I let the rough pads of my fingers sink deeper, getting a wince out of her. I like knowing I have control over her body even when she isn't mine—not in the way I want her to be. But we're too far gone for that.

We're nothing but enemies who were once so close it'd have taken an army to tear us apart. Sometimes I want to go back to a time when she was the only person besides my family who mattered.

"Why do you care who sees me naked, huh?" Her voice comes out all hoarse.

My cock likes the sound, wanting to fill that mouth of hers.

"My body doesn't belong to you." The words fall over my back, her warm breath caressing me.

"Like hell it doesn't." I smack her ass harder, and she yelps, practically jumping off my shoulder. "You belong to me. Everything in this house does."

"I belong to *no one!*" she roars with fervor in her tone.

I let out a mirthless laugh as I climb up the stairs to my room. "Is that why you're working for the man you claim to hate?"

"Fuck you!" she fires back with more ammunition than should be allowed for a woman in her compromising position.

Forcing the door with my foot, I carry her inside. Once I have the door locked, I slide her down my body, her feet beside my black loafers.

She bores her eyes into mine, her cheeks flushed from the sun and from what I hope is me. The harshness of her breathing matches the fieriness in her gaze.

Her stare narrows, her arms crossed over her chest, denying me the sight in private that she was so willing to share in public.

"What do you want, Brian?"

I circle around her slowly, getting a nice view of her round ass. A single finger hooks into the side of her thong.

"Take it off," I demand as I pull the lace at her hip, before letting it go.

"No." She pops her brows as I face her again.

"Why not? You wanted all of them to see you. So let's see you." I tip her chin up with a finger. "All of you." I place my hand over her wrist. "Drop those arms, Chiara. Don't be shy now."

Her chest rises with every quick breath as her steady gaze draws into mine, and without a show of hesitation, she lets her arms fall.

My lips slither into a smile as I back away, staring at her heavy breasts, wanting my mouth, my hands all over them. Wanting to hear her say my name while I fuck her. My *real* name.

I creep closer, until her hardened nipples graze across the

buttons of my shirt. She whimpers as my mouth falls close to her lips. "You're not done yet, baby. Now lose those panties."

With her chin high, she hooks her fingers into the black lace and lowers them, and I step back.

"That's more like it," I say smoothly, drifting my gaze down her body, drinking in every curve.

My blood swells with need, wanting to touch, to taste. She's so beautiful with those full hips and an ass I want to watch bounce on my cock.

I once thought I'd marry her, even as a kid, but now that dream feels like it belongs to another person, living my life in some alternate reality. I don't recognize the woman before me. Then again, why would I? She's someone else now as much as I am.

"What are you going to do to me?" she asks with a shudder in her voice, her thighs clamped shut.

All I want is to tear them wide open. I reach a hand toward her face, and she doesn't even flinch, her breasts trembling with each weary breath.

"What do you think I should do?" I run my hard knuckles down the side of her cheek, my gaze slamming into hers. "Are you afraid I'll touch you?"

Instead of pushing away, she leans her face closer into my touch as she shakes her head, her brows creased. "I'm afraid you won't."

Fuck.

The sensuality beneath those words drowns out every thought that screams at me to stay away. Knowing she craves my touch, wants it this badly, makes it harder to refuse us both.

Would she still want me if she knew who I really am? Who I've become? I doubt it. Maybe that's the biggest reason why I haven't given her my real identity. She'll hate me for it. I've grown comfortable with my disdain for her, but I'm not ready for hers.

My hand drifts down the side of her smooth body, coming around her hip. "I'd be more than happy to show you just how much of your body I own."

She pants with a barely there groan.

I lean forward, my breath lingering over the shell of her ear before my teeth sink around her lobe, taking a little bite.

"Is this what you want, Chiara?" I ask harshly, my hand gliding down past her stomach until a finger lands on the heat between her thighs.

"Is that all you've got?" she spits out, finding my eyes again, making me want to see that fire burning within hers.

And it's there, coursing through her gaze, making my dick throb. I should force her onto her knees and feed her every inch of it, then fuck her like the animal she branded me as.

I take a few steps back and start undoing my tie, my eyes slowly lavishing the hills of her curves. She stands there, hungrily watching my hands work the tie, and I have the urge to use it over her mouth so she has nothing more to say. All I need are those gasps and moans.

Once the tie is off my neck, I approach her slowly. "You woke the beast, princess. Now you'll have to pay for it."

She fists the collar of my shirt, and I allow her to pull me close until her breath laces over my lips.

"What the hell did I tell you about calling me that?" she grits through clenched teeth.

I snarl as her long fingernail inadvertently scratches my neck, and without another thought, I flip her around so harshly that her hand falls off my shirt with a gasp.

Before she has a chance to figure out what's happening, I bring the tie over her neck from behind, clutching the ends tightly in my palm, pushing her forward with my body until her hands hit the wall in front.

She breathes in and out heavily, the tie allowing her some air.

"I hate you," she hisses with a tremor, the words sounding like a lie even when they shouldn't be.

She *should* hate me. I *am* the animal she claims I am. She'll never be the one for me, even if our past was different. Even if she hadn't ruined everything with her betrayal.

The boy she knew back then is gone. I'm soulless now. Depravity is my only friend. Revenge is my new name. And Chiara was always too beautiful for a world like that.

I know I shouldn't allow her to lower my inhibitions. I know I shouldn't be touching her at all. But I can't help myself. Not with her. She always had a piece of my heart even when she didn't know it, and still, that part will always be hers.

Before I have a chance to change my mind, I give her what she's too proud to ask for. I yank her neck back with the tie, wanting to see those eyes the moment she feels me touch her. Wanting to own that moment and make it mine.

Her head falls against my chest, her teeth tugging at her lower lip, the heat within her gaze simmering with desire. My hand crawls around her hip, my fingers gliding down to her slit. And once I'm there, once I feel the warmth of her pussy, I run two fingers over it, squeezing her lips.

"Fuck," she whimpers, her brows twisting as her gaze clasps to mine, her lips shuddering as I slip a finger inside, finding her soaked.

I circle a thumb over her swollen clit just as I pull the tie harder, causing her to wince and moan all at once.

My veins should be filled with contempt, but instead, my body wants to be filled with the sweet taste of her pussy.

"You like it this way, don't you, Chiara? You like it hard. You like to be controlled. Owned." I twist the tie around my wrist and jerk, ensuring she can't move away as I spread her wet slit with my fingers before slamming them hard inside her.

"Oh, God!" Her cry morphs into a frazzled pant, her nails piercing jaggedly into my thighs as I thrust roughly, curling my fingers as I do, hitting that spot inside her.

"God isn't going to help you, baby," I say. "Not with me."

Her gaze narrows, as though looking away would mean her losing.

I like the game, and I play to win.

Chiara may be used to ordering everyone around at work, commanding respect. But right here, right now, I'm the one in charge. And no matter how much her brain may deny it, her body knows it too.

I work her faster, adding a third finger, stretching her pussy. She moans, loud and unabashed, her eyes now hooded, her lips parted and trembling with every whimper.

My thumb runs over her clit, and once her walls clench around me and her moans come in waves, I know she's close.

"Harder," she groans, rubbing her ass over my stiff cock.

Fuck, I need inside her. But I can't.

Hard and fast, I sink my fingers, over and over, until her body jolts. Until her moans are so loud, I'm sure they're heard outside. When I feel the clenching of her pussy get tighter around my fingers, I slip out.

"No, no, no," she cries, her voice rippled with need, her eyes begging me for what I won't give her.

While holding her captive with my tie, I lift the hand that was just inside her and run the fingers over my lips, my tongue dipping for a taste.

"You don't get to decide what happens in my kingdom,

princess." I press the tips of my fingers into her mouth this time, fighting my way inside even with her teeth scraping along the way.

"This is how I want you. Mouth too full to talk." My eyes drift to a partial close as I lean my mouth to her ear. "You remember this feeling the next time you take off your clothes in front of another man in my home. You want to take them off? You take them off for *me*."

Pulling the tie away, I stroll toward the door.

She doesn't even move as I leave, her back to me, her body still as I shut the door behind me, wanting more than anything to walk back in and tell her I'm sorry.

CHIARA

TWENTY-ONE

I hate him. I hate him, yet I want him, and I despise feeling this way. When I decided to go topless yesterday, I knew what I was doing. I knew his men would call him. That he'd come.

When he looked at me without my clothes on, it was through the eyes of a man who wanted what he couldn't have, but wouldn't allow anyone else to have it either.

There was jealousy. Possession. Just like I knew there would be.

I'm usually good at reading people, and Brian Smith—which I don't believe for a second is his real name—is not hard to read.

He's running on bottled-up pain, an intimate part of himself he won't allow anyone to see. It's obvious from the way he lives that he doesn't let a soul get close enough to unearth the fortress he's built around himself.

He's strong.

Powerful.

But unclothe his armor, and I bet you'd find a scared little boy.

I don't feel sorry for him, though. My father may have taken people he loved, but that doesn't excuse him kidnapping me, nor denying the fucking orgasm he owes me. I'll be paying him back for that. I just haven't figured out how.

I thought seducing him would be easy. I thought finding a home in his bed would be simple. But he's proven me wrong.

Every time I think I've won, he's a step ahead. Now I'll probably never get out of here.

He's avoided me all day. I'm not even sure he came home last night. Not that I give a shit. I'm all alone in this giant house with nothing to do and no one to speak to. I could strike up another conversation with Miles, the giant statue of a man, but I have a feeling he'd rather not talk to me, so as to not upset his precious boss.

I wander around the house, finding spaces not occupied by Smith's obedient foot soldiers. Walking down a wide hallway on the other end of the kitchen, I find locked door after door, wondering what could be inside each one.

And just as I'm about to give up and go to my room, I find a library all the way at the end to the right. My heart's paralyzed with excitement as I stare through the glass door, finding a huge ceiling-to-floor bookshelf on each side, with a gray ladder next to the left.

In the middle lies a glossy black coffee table and four cushioned ivory armchairs. I step closer, wanting inside.

Would he care if I went in? Do I even care if he does? And what the hell is he doing with a library? Does he even read?

Fuck it.

I tiptoe another step, my hand on the door now, and I open it.

"Wow," I mutter when I discover that it's a two-story library, completely mesmerized.

The spiral staircase leads upstairs to shelf after shelf of more books than I've ever seen in a home.

I used to love books as a child, and that love hasn't died. Reading is my passion. A way to decompress. Romance, thrillers, I don't care. I read it all.

I gently glide the door back to a close and take tentative steps inside. Running nervous hands down the black spaghetti-strap jersey dress I have on, I walk over to the right, feathering my fingertips across the spine of the books there, wanting to consume every word.

I make it to the end, and that's when I realize there's another large area behind the bookshelf, one with an L-shaped ivory sofa and a bar full of liquor bottles behind it.

Books and booze? I think I've found my new room. I could use some strong alcohol in my life right about now. Other than red wine at home or a shot or two at work on occasion, I don't overindulge. But with the state of my life at the moment, I should probably chug a bottle of vodka.

Practically running toward the black leather bar, I pick up a shot glass and the closest bottle, reading the label:

BOWMORE ISLAY SCOTCH WHISKEY
1957

Great. Sounds expensive enough. I don't drink whiskey, but

there's a first time for everything. Unscrewing the sealed bottle, I pour a shot.

"Here's to one hell of a fucked-up life, Chiara Bianchi. May it only get more fucked up, because why the hell not?" I raise my glass to an invisible shadow and flip the honey-hued liquor down my throat.

Hell, it burns like acid. All I want is more, so I pour another. The liquor pools in my stomach, warmth and an instant buzz overtakes my senses, and I do what I probably shouldn't. I drink some more.

Three or four shots later, I'm a little woozy, but still managing to walk on my bare feet.

Sort of. Kind of.

I almost trip.

"Oops." A giggle falls out of me as I grip the edge of the bar to steady myself.

"Having fun?"

I gasp, startled by a voice I've come to rather enjoy hearing.

DOMINIC

She ignores my question, still giving me her back. All that ebony hair spills down her back, hitting that curvy ass of hers, one that I want to spread open with my tongue.

She runs a hand through her hair, flinging more past her shoulder, tempting me further. Ever since I felt her bare pussy, heard her cries of pleasure, all I've wanted was more of that.

More of her.

I spent all of last night at one of the clubs with my brothers, even though they're not my scene. We were all there for a business meeting with a new investor for the clubs. But once some of the women Enzo invited to our table started grinding on my lap, I had enough.

I was in no fucking mood for anyone else's cunt. I wanted inside only one, and it's right here in front of me. Only a short dress separating me and that warm slit.

My cock swells and jerks beneath my slacks, demanding to see every bit of what she's hiding under those clothes. If she weren't obviously drunk, I'd fuck her bare. I'd own her in those moments, fleeting as they would be. She'd still be mine, and she'd know it.

The past and the present are colliding into one, and I can't stop it.

"Do you know how expensive that bottle is?" I ask. "How rare?"

A laugh oozes out of her as she turns around, her back against the bar. "It's cute that you think I care."

I grin, uncuffing my baby-blue button-down, rolling up the sleeves over my forearms until they hit my elbows.

A small, barely there whimper makes it out of her lips. I lean against the other side of the bookshelf watching her watching me, her glassy eyes taking in my arms, my chest, my face.

She licks her lips, rubbing her inner thighs against one another.

I follow the movement. Knowing she's hungry for me has me wanting to devour every inch of her, body and soul.

I want everything.

When I'm alone with her—when my passion runs hotter than my despair—that's when the hurt is almost forgotten, as if it's not even there. And that's when she's the most dangerous.

"It took a lot of money to secure that bottle," I add. "Only twelve of its kind."

"Wow," she whispers, tightening her brows with a twitch of her lips. "I'm entirely too impressed."

"Really?" My voice grows low as my appetite gets ravenous.

"No." She shakes her head. "Not even a little."

She turns to the bar, giving me her ass, peeking from below the dress, the one I want to flip to her waist. Would she fight me?

Would she beg for my cock as I let my palm strike her flesh again and again, until she can't take any more.

"Is Mr. Smith upset?"

She whirls back to me with pouty, fuckable lips, the bottle of my Bowmore in hand. The one I bought for almost two hundred thousand.

"Well, I'll tell you what," she continues. "I'm in a very sharing kind of mood. So how about I give you a little taste?"

I fold my arms over my chest, my feet crossed at the ankles as I shoot up a brow, quite intrigued at what drunk Chiara is capable of.

She slithers across the floor, edging closer to where I stand, the bottle rattling in her grip as she rocks on her feet.

The black dress that's molded to her curves rides up to her upper thighs, making me want to rip it right off.

She takes another step and almost trips over her feet. Before she can fall and stab herself on the pieces of my whiskey bottle, I reach out a hand and wrap my arm around the small of her back, my fingers massaging her hip.

"My hero." Her lips tip up right before the bottle makes it to her mouth, and she takes a swig.

And with one hand on my shoulder, she leans in, her eyes delving into mine, and she kisses me. The liquor from her mouth courses into mine, and I swallow it down right before I take her tongue and suck, milking every drop.

I fist her hair, grabbing the bottle from her hand and taking a mouthful, kissing her back, giving her what she gave me while placing the bottle on an end table beside me.

Feeling her lips after all this time—tasting her like I was always meant to—it's better than any whiskey I've come to acquire. And though I try to fight the feeling of affection squeezing at my heart, grasping at my throat, I can't. Chiara always had a way of lighting my heart on fire.

I groan as her moans vibrate over my lips, the liquor from her tongue coursing down my throat, her nails sailing down my chest to find me hard as a rock. My fingers tangle wildly through her waves, pulling hard as her palm squeezes around the head of my cock.

Our kiss turns savage, the moans and groans piercing through the walls as hard and fast as our hands pierce our very skin.

Consuming.

Devouring.

Aching for more.

Her other hand moves to the buckle of my belt as she unfastens it, her lips still moving over mine, her whimpers growing more intoxicating.

I yank her head back, my fingers winding through her hair, needing to see her eyes, needing to see what lies within them.

"You need to stop," I warn. "You're drunk."

She eyes me defiantly, chin high in the air, as she continues to undo my pants, sliding the zipper down.

"What are you doing?" I hiss with a growl as her hand slips inside my boxers, sheathing me in her softness.

She gazes at me, hypnotizing me with her beauty.

"What does it look like I'm doing?" Her husky voice is dipped in raw determination. "I've wanted to know what you feel like. Taste like."

My jaw stiffens, my cock straining for what it shouldn't want. She moans as her teeth entrap her lower lip, her face straining as she jerks me up and down, nice and slow.

"You want my cock, huh?"

She nods with a glint in her eyes, sending a jolt down to where I need her with a desperation I'll never admit.

Placing the width of my palm on top of her head, I push her down to the floor. "Then go get it."

She pants as her knees hit the floor, her frantic hands on my pants and boxers, lowering both.

I peer down as she holds my cock in her fist, and without her eyes leaving mine, she sticks out her tongue, leans down, and takes a long swipe up from the base, all the way up to the tip.

"Fuck." My voice strains, my eyes drifting to a close from the sensation pouring down my entire body.

My hand is on the back of her head now, pushing her further into me, needing to fill her any way I can. She swallows me whole, gagging on the thickness as her hand squeezes my balls.

"Yeah, that's it." I drive in deeper, making her choke on every inch. "Show me how much you want it."

She whimpers over my dick as her lips move up and down, refusing to let even a little bit of me out of her talented mouth. My release grows, burning at the base, needing to give her every drop.

"I'm about to come, baby. Better move if you...fuck!" I groan as she stays where she is, sucking me harder, deeper. "Oh, damn. That mouth, Chiara. It's mine. You're *mine*."

My cock pops out of her mouth.

"Never," she fires back, stroking me with a sardonic smile.

Growling, I push her back down on my dick. "Did I say you could move?"

My grip on the back of her head is strong, keeping her there as she gags and moans in the most beautiful way. The sound music to my ears.

"That's right, baby. I want you so full of me you can't fucking talk."

Clutching her hair, I fuck her mouth with fierce brutality, the vibrations from her moans getting stronger, and with one more thrust, the burn from my release hits me harder than I've ever experienced from any woman before her.

I spill into the warmth of her mouth, never wanting to fill another one again, and hating that I feel this way. No matter how good this is, it's not real. It never will be.

Gripping her hair, I keep her lips pressed against the base of my cock while I burrow deeper into her mouth, twitching until every drop spills down her throat.

"Mmm," I groan, yanking her up by her hair and slamming her lips to mine, kissing her hard before pulling back. "You did good. So fucking good."

Her hand snaps to the back of my head, nails raking, breaths hastening. "And what do I get for my A-plus performance?"

She looks at me, and I look at her, our gazes caught in seduction and deceit. I lean into her mouth and nip her lower lip with my teeth.

"How about I show you?" My breath skims over her mouth as I wrap my arms around her lower back, walking us backward until we get to the ladder by the bookshelf.

Grabbing her around the jaw, I edge my lips closer.

"I want to feel how wet that pussy is for me, and you're gonna let me."

I don't give her a chance to respond. I flip her around by her hips, pushing her facedown onto a single ladder step with my palm. Her cheek is planted against the cold metal as she moans, her side-eye hungrily taking in my every move.

"Do you think about me, Chiara?" I ask as I lift up her dress with my other hand, exposing her sun-kissed ass. "Do you drip down from this sweet pussy when you touch it, imagining it's my big cock stretching you, filling you?"

I let a finger fall in between her slit, running it up and down, careful not to touch her clit.

"Fuck," she groans brokenly, unable to fight her desire for the villain I've become.

She arches her ass up, silently begging for more.

"What a bad girl, wanting her pussy fucked by the likes of me." My palm strikes one ass cheek while my other hand firmly holds her face where it is.

She yelps, followed by a moan, wiggling her ass from side to side.

"Tell me you want me, Chiara. Tell me how badly you need me to make you come."

"Fuck you," she spits out, gritting her teeth, her brows squeezing tight, her lips forming an O as my finger hooks into her black thong, slipping it to the side.

I slide it inside her, circling it into her G-spot, finding her soaked.

"So, fuck me. What are you waiting for?"

Another finger dips into her as I thrust in and out slowly, wanting to stretch her until it hurts.

"Oh, yes. Don't stop!" she cries as my pace increases, her hips pushing me deeper, her cries clinging to her throat as her need tightens around my fingers.

But I do. I stop.

Clutching her hair, I tug her head back as far as it will go. Falling over her, I take her lips in a searing kiss, my tongue diving inside like I wish my cock could.

She whimpers around my lips, and then I set her mouth free.

"Beg," I groan, our gazes tortured, daring one another. "You're not gonna come until you beg me to make that pussy spill."

I push her face back down onto the step.

"Don't move," I demand while my hands find her hips, fingering the tiny scrap of her thong. "I don't think we'll be needing these."

As she whimpers low, I tear the tiny scrap of material right off her body.

A raspy pant is her only response. I toss them to the side, returning my fingers to her slick entrance.

Lifting up one of her thighs, I place it on another step. "You're gonna stay nice and open for me while I take my time exploring every bit of you."

I slip two fingers inside, curling them as I roughly drive in, then out, hitting her G-spot until her desperate cries and hungry moans beg to end what she began.

"This feels so good," she whimpers, her body jerking violently against the stairs as I continue to move before slipping out and finding her clit.

"Still won't beg?" I ask, surrounding my fingers around each side of her clit. "I'll have to try a little harder."

And when I rub both fingers at the same time, she screams out my name. My fake one.

Her calling me that is a good thing, I convince myself. It keeps a safe distance between us.

I'm not the guy she once knew. I'm a monster born from the hell of my existence. It's best if the both of us don't cross that invisible line we're slowly teetering on.

But as she looks at me and I unearth the wave of emotions in her eyes pulling me in, I realize I haven't buried my feelings for her deep enough. They're there, threatening to imprison me.

I can't let them.

My hurt is still too raw, even after all this time. I can't let it go, no matter how much I want to. There's nothing I wouldn't do to go back in time and ask how she could ruin our friendship the way she did.

Did she ever care about me? About us? Was it all pretend? Is she just like her father?

I hate to think she is. Even back then, as I stared at the proof, it never made sense. But maybe I didn't know her as well as I thought.

I bend over her tight body, no longer wanting to see her brown eyes. They're like gazing into a pool of the past where things were once beautiful.

But they're a lie, just like she was.

My fingers sink back inside her, fucking her to a steady pace.

"Yes...oh, God. Just like that."

I lower my lips to her neck, working her faster as my tongue licks its way up to her ear. Taking her earlobe into my mouth, I flick and bite, loving her gasps and moans, never wanting to hear anything else.

"You feel so good, Chiara," I whisper as my lips land on the back of her head, my eyes falling to a close as the smell of her floral shampoo invades my senses. "I can only imagine what you'd feel like riding my cock."

Her walls clench around me, responding to my dirty talk.

"You think about it too, don't you, baby?"

She pants, refusing to answer. I thrust harder, adding another finger. She's close. I can feel it from the hastening of her breathing to the clasping of her walls and the tightening of her hands around the handrail.

"It's okay to admit you want me," I say. "It'll stay right here in this room."

I hit her G-spot with a deep thrust, and she pants harder.

And when I ease my movement to a slower pace, she growls in frustration.

"Yes, you bastard! I think about you all the time, even when I don't want to."

"Mmm," my voice hums in approval as I slide my fingers out of her, cupping her pussy. "Beg."

I knead her flesh, her clit rubbing over my palm before I spank her cunt.

"Beg me for something you don't even deserve."

She half-cries, half-moans, her voice no longer strong, carrying defeat, and I relish it.

I pinch her pussy lips, rubbing them against each other. "You're soaking my fingers, baby. Make it easier on yourself and ask for it."

"Fuck," she growls, her breaths uneven, her shoulders bouncing desperately. "Please, let me come. I need to stop hurting. I need you to make it stop."

As soon as the words fall from her lips, I ram three fingers inside her, filling her to capacity, wondering how well that tight little hole would take my cock. I bet she'd take it nice and hard and then ask for seconds.

"Oh, God. I'm close," she whispers with a series of weighty pants. "Harder. I need it harder."

"Shit." I grip a fistful of her hair, yanking her head back, needing to see her face as she comes.

Her gaze finds mine as I thrust as far as I can go, wanting her to feel me everywhere.

"You're dripping down my hand," I groan as I slam into her with a frenzied pace, never wanting this moment to end. Never wanting to stop making her feel this good.

"Oh, God, Brian. I'm...I'm... Fuck!" she screams as her

release hits, bolting through her body.

I milk every ounce of her pleasure, driving harder until her moans slow, then I slip out of her and find another hole to fill. I shove my fingers between her already-parted lips, opening them wider.

"This is what I do to you."

She moans, running her tongue over each finger.

"Yeah, that's it. Taste yourself, baby."

She sucks the flavor from my hand, whimpering, with her gaze still fastened to mine. Once I'm satisfied, I let her go, taking a step back while she's still grasping on to the ladder as though it's the only thing keeping her stable.

I glance at her one more time, wishing like hell I could kiss her again. That we could find the love we once thought was ours.

But instead, I walk away, the same way she once did.

CHIARA

TWENTY-TWO

I may have been a little drunk, but my memory was fine. I remember every tantalizing detail from yesterday. No one has ever turned me on the way he does, and it should make me all kinds of sad knowing I can't truly have that with him. Not beyond whatever we have right now.

Once I find a way to disappear, I'll be gone from his life for good. I should be thrilled, but a part of me—that little part I don't want anyone to see—wishes I could stay.

I release a silent sigh, tossing and turning in bed, unable to sleep. The clock reads midnight, but it might as well be noon.

I wonder where he is right now. He's avoided me since the incident yesterday. I haven't seen him since then. I ate alone, watched TV, sat out by the pool fully clothed, and read a book I took from his library.

It was a political thriller.

Kind of fitting, except no heroine was kidnapped in that story. But she also didn't get the most amazing orgasms from her kidnapper. Not sure who the lucky bitch between us is.

Last night, I only slept two hours when a dream—or maybe I should call it a nightmare—woke me up. In it, Brian held me in his arms, whispering adoration as I smiled with my back to him.

But then I woke up sweating, realizing my lust has now permeated my own sense of reality.

That man doesn't exist. He never will. He's a villain in my story, not a hero to crave.

If I were ever to marry anyone, it'd have to be someone as strong as him. Someone who's not afraid of my father. But he'd actually have to like me first. Kind of hard to fall in love with someone when you're so busy hating the person, and when they despise you in return.

What would I know about love anyway? I never even had a boyfriend when I was young. My father scared every last one away.

My hand inadvertently slips to my neck, where half of that friendship necklace I gave Dom used to sit. The day Brian took me, I forgot to put it on. It's still at home. I hope it's still there.

Dom, I miss you so much.

It hurts to think about him. Even saying his name is painful. Our friendship was once so real, I thought it would last forever. But then he disappeared, leaving me with a gaping hole. To this day, I wonder, are they alive? Or are they dead?

I think my father had something to do with their disappearance, the same way I know he was involved in my mother's too. He somehow has a hand in everything he claims to know nothing about. When I asked him about Dom, he swore to not know anything, claiming he heard Dom's dad owed lots of money to the bank for the bakery and probably fled.

I didn't buy it. Dom would've found a way to contact me, even years down the line. Often I wonder if he still thinks about me like I do him.

As soon as we met back in third grade, we gravitated toward one another like stars born from the same galaxy. It didn't matter that we came from very different tracks or that our families would never get along. All of that never stopped our friendship from only getting stronger.

From the day he sat next to me in the lunchroom—a lonely girl with no real friends and a boy who wore his heart in his eyes—we were inseparable. He was my Dom, and I loved him…as a friend at first.

But the night he disappeared was the night I planned to tell him that my feelings for him were blooming into more. We were only thirteen, but I guess as I matured, my feelings for him did too.

The unknown still eats at me. Even with fifteen years between us, I think about him all the time and the man he is today. I bet he's a good one. Someone who loves fiercely and protects his family. I'm sure he has kids and treats them as sweetly as he did his brother Matteo.

I miss that little boy so much. We had a special bond, he and I. They were all like my extended family.

It's better to think about Dom happy somewhere instead of dead. I've done all I can to find him, searching online for any breadcrumbs, but I've come up empty-handed. If they're alive, it's as though they've vanished.

I'm sure if Dom knew what Brian has done to me, he'd find a way to kill him. Dom was never athletic when I knew him. He was a skinny, short boy, but with his determination, he could've taken anyone on. I truly believe that.

And those eyes…he had the greenest ones you'd ever see. They were breathtaking.

When he looked at me, I felt like the most important person in the world. I wonder if he still looks the same.

He was always kind too. Not just to me, but to everyone he met. Dom was like his parents in that way. They were the sweetest couple.

I stare at the white ceiling, fighting the memories of my past. The good ones with Dom, the bittersweet ones with Mom, it's all there within my mind, tormenting me.

It's hard to think about those days when I'm trapped with a man who might kill me. With him, it's difficult to know. I think he's deceitful enough to make me think he won't hurt me, but at the same time, I don't think he'd hesitate to pull the trigger if he needed to. Wanting to fuck me isn't really a reason to keep me alive. He can do that and then dispose of me.

Closing my eyes, I will myself to sleep, but just when I'm about to get comfortable, the loud screeching of tires has me jolting to a sitting position, knees tucked to my chest.

What the hell?

Jumping out of bed, I head for the window. A woman's high-pitched laughter filters through as I part the curtains. Brian has her up against the hood of his car, her long black hair spilling to one side, and the micro-mini hot-pink dress leaves very little to the imagination.

My heart instantly squeezes, and a cold shudder runs down my spine. My stomach turns at the sight of him with someone else.

He isn't yours.

But I can't suppress the jealousy running foul within my heart.

She reaches a hand, her nails riding down his chest, and my pulse slams hard in my ears.

At first he seems uninterested, looking at his cell, completely ignoring her. But then, with a quick jerk of his head, his eyes find mine.

A menacing smile forms on his face. Without his eyes leaving mine, he slips his cell into his pocket and plants his palm on the top of her head, forcing her down onto her knees.

Just like he did me.

My vision blurs, my hands tremble. It's like a punch to the gut, nerves erupting there, sending a cold wave down my back. I don't want to watch, yet I'm doing it anyway.

She eagerly kneels down on the concrete as she unbuckles his belt, unzipping him. He pulls out his cock, his eyes still chained to mine as he fists the crown, easing it inside her mouth.

I gasp, shutting the curtains, but I can hear his masculine chuckle as the woman moans around his dick.

He wanted me to see. I bet he planned this to hurt me.

Asshole.

I pull the drapes apart a tiny bit, finding his eyes still at my window as though he knows I'm still watching.

I know it shouldn't, but my core pulses with desire, seeing him with someone else.

It makes me sick. *He* makes me sick.

I grind my thighs, watching her go faster, my pussy spasming from the emptiness.

This is just a normal reaction, I attempt to convince myself.

Then why the hell do I want to throw her across the goddamn street?! Why do I want him to do what he did to me in the library, but this time with his cock?

Getting on my knees for him wasn't just a drunken spell. I wanted it. Wanted him. The liquor only gave me the courage to admit what I wouldn't.

My hand slinks down under my shorts, discovering myself wet and hungry. The orgasm that's been building within me since I saw him with that woman roars to life.

Still looking, I rub my fingers around my achy clit, wanting him inside me. Wanting that powerful masculinity pushing down onto me.

His eyes are on the drapes, still only opened enough for me to see what's happening. He can't stop looking at the window, even as he grips the back of the woman's head.

Why the hell does that turn me on even more? I pretend it's me on my knees, making him grunt.

Does he want it to be me? Is that why he can't stop staring?

I separate the curtains just enough for him to know I'm still there.

"Fuck," he groans so loudly, I could have heard him from a mile away.

I work myself faster. Harder. The orgasm soars higher, the need for release so strong I almost can't make my finger work.

My hand clasps around the curtain, my fist tight as I fire out his name in between gritted teeth, unable to control how I feel, how much I want him. I shouldn't want the man who's holding me hostage. But I do. I want him, and I can't deny it, no matter how hard I've been trying.

My orgasm rises until there's nowhere to go but down. I fall, forcing myself into a release that has my body convulsing and my hand pulling on the curtain so hard I open it even more.

And when he sees me, when he sees where my hand is, the corners of his lips curl into a knowing smile. He saw what I was doing, and right now, I don't give a fuck.

DOMINIC

"Get up," I order the woman, not allowing her to finish me off, as soon as the curtain closes back up and my intuition tells me Chiara is really gone this time.

It feels like an unspoken betrayal to come in this woman's mouth. I don't even know her. Not so much as her name. I don't care to know it.

She was a random girl from one of my dance clubs. The reason I was even there was to meet with another investor to help expand the opening of more nightclubs. But I could've had my brothers handle it if I wanted to. The real reason I went was to try and get the smell and feel of Chiara's body out of my mind.

I needed to forget her.

But it didn't help. Knowing Chiara was watching this woman suck me off made me want her even more. Seeing her touch herself was the only reason I let it go on for as long as I did. It should've been her on her knees. That was what I wanted. What I was thinking about the whole damn time.

"I'll have my driver take you home," I tell the woman.

"I was hoping to come inside." She twirls a loose strand of hair, her pink lips sliding up at the corner.

"No." I stare firmly, my voice brisk like the temperature. "The car should be here any second. Have a good night. Thank you for coming to my club."

"Asshole," she whispers just as my driver pulls up.

I sit back inside my blue Lamborghini Aventador, driving it back into the garage. No one is allowed to touch it but me.

Unlocking the door from the garage leading into the house, I trudge inside, hoping to see Chiara all pissed. But I'm greeted with silence, and I hate it.

CHIARA

TWENTY-THREE

The next day, I glare at the chicken burrito bowl Sonia made, remembering the events of last night.

Why do I even care that some attractive woman was sucking his dick? He's not mine. He can have any woman he wants. But I can't help this jealousy still flitting through me, tainting my thoughts.

The only reason to sleep with him is to help me get out of here, not to fall for him. But of course, the first guy I've had a serious attraction to turns out to be a psycho.

"Is it not good?" Sonia asks, glancing up at me while mixing some rice in a pot, steam rolling in the surrounding air.

"Oh, no. It's amazing." I grin, poking at the chicken and popping a piece into my mouth. "I guess I'm just not as hungry as I thought."

She smiles warmly, going back to the rice. She definitely knows how to cook, but my stupid appetite has left the mansion.

Once again, I haven't seen him today. He must've never come home. I wonder if he's still with that woman, doing all kinds of dirty things to her. Does he use a tie on her too? My toes curl from the memory, and I bite down on the inside of my lower lip, suppressing a moan.

My fork clanks against the white porcelain plate, causing Sonia to whip her head up.

"Sorry," I murmur, stuffing some beans into my mouth.

"He said he'd be done with work by dinner." She suspends my dirty thoughts, carrying a plate for herself and sitting across from me.

"That's great," I mumble sullenly.

"Figured you'd want to know." She blows over her food, peering up at me coyly with a side smile.

"I don't care where he is or what he's doing," I respond with a bit too much defensiveness, avoiding her knowing gaze.

"Mm-hmm." She doesn't say much else.

Sonia is a very kind woman and why she works for such an asshole is beyond me. But whenever Brian is around her, he's someone else. Someone softer. And that's saying a lot, because there's nothing soft about that man. Except his eyes.

There's something there, something human, but it vanishes as quickly as it comes. I need to find that part of him and use it to escape. I'm not ready to die. Not for anyone, and especially not for my father.

It takes me a while to finish my food, but when I finally do, I get up and rinse my plate, then throw it into the dishwasher.

"Thank you for the lovely lunch," I tell Sonia, then excuse myself, heading up to watch TV.

Climbing the stairs, I head toward my room, and as I near the door, I keep walking until I get to his.

The door is ajar, sunlight darting through it. He isn't here, and he kept the door open? He always shuts it. I know because I have a habit of checking every time I go down the stairs. If he's seen me do it on one of his secret cameras, he hasn't said.

My fingers inch forward, my nails fledging over the handle, flirting with the thought of walking inside.

I shouldn't.

I push on the door just a little.

He'll find out and get mad. Really mad.

I push it open some more.

Maybe he'll get the kind of mad he was when he saw me drinking his liquor. Or if I'm lucky, a lot angrier. Angry enough to fuck me. And when he fucks me once, I know he'll want to do it again and again until his heart slices open, allowing my deceit right in.

I shove the screeching door open all the way, the sound echoing through the empty hall. My heartbeat pounds in my ears.

This is a bad idea.

But the fear only pushes me further into danger.

Quickly glancing down each side of the hall and not finding his guards anywhere, I dash inside. Gently closing the door behind me, I finally take in the room.

Holy shit.

His bedroom is straight out of a luxury magazine. I'm mesmerized by the space, big enough to be a penthouse in New York City. I never really got to see it the last time I was here, with the whole cleaning-his-bullet-wound thing. But now that I'm here, I intend to get to know this room very well.

To the left, I find a low-lying black king-sized bed with ceiling-high leather upholstery. Further down, there's a square black table with four white velvet armchairs around it, plus a matching bar with all kinds of liquor and glassware atop.

But the fireplace on the right is my favorite part. It's not on now, but it looks so cozy with the shaggy ivory carpet in front.

I wonder if I can find some evidence that holds the truth to his real identity. Would he keep anything worth finding in this room? I intend to find out. I skip the bathroom, heading for one of the rooms I haven't yet been in.

Opening it, I discover a huge walk-in closet.

Well, wow. This is nice...and organized.

His shoes are neatly lined on the floor, his suits on one side, casual shirts and pants on the other. I run my fingers up and down one of his suit jackets, leaning over to take a whiff and smelling a hint of his expensive cologne on it, the one he always wears.

I open some drawers, finding socks and neatly folded boxers, carefully looking under every item for anything that could help me know him. But every drawer I open contains nothing but clothes, no shred of evidence of the man behind the well-constructed mask.

Who are you, Brian Smith?

Closing the drawer containing dozens of belts, I march over to the other side, finding more ties than I can count hanging on a spinning rack.

I reach a hand for them, flinging my nails across the silk, remembering how it felt to have one wrapped around my neck while I clung to every breath.

Snaking my hand around a black tie, my eyes zero in on one that looks eerily familiar. Could it be the very same one he used on me? Nerves explode in my stomach, my pulse jolting in my ears, slamming down my throat.

I pull it off the rack, and as I do, an idea forms. A really dangerous idea. Yanking a powder-blue button-down shirt from the hanger, I wander back into the bedroom with both.

Sauntering toward his bed, I drop the items on top of it.

He did say I was boring, so I'll give him a show.

A cunning smile dresses my lips as I remove my black tank top, dropping it on the edge of the bed. My leggings and thong are next.

I slip on his shirt, leaving the buttons undone. Clutching the tie in the palm of my hand, I climb under his covers.

My fingertips skid up and down in between my breasts, and once I reach a nipple, I circle a fingernail around it, getting it nice and hard. I let the tie fall against my pussy, squeezing my thighs together, yanking one end while I ride the length of it, rubbing it over my aching clit.

Memories of me against the wall with his strong, hard body pressed into mine has my core throbbing with gaping need. The orgasm builds, flaming through my body like the fire of a blazing sun.

Once it comes—once my orgasm licks up his tie—I'll put it right back, hoping that the next time he wears it, he'll take a little piece of me with him.

DOMINIC

TWENTY-FOUR

I've done all I can to avoid her since the incident with that other woman, not because I'm ashamed of what happened, but because I want more than anything for that to be her. Thoughts of being more, giving her more, are consuming me, and I can't take it.

With my cell in my palm, I watch on my camera as she makes herself at home in my room, which I purposely left unlocked, wondering if she'd dare to go inside. I'm not one bit surprised she did.

I'm supposed to be finalizing arrangements for tomorrow's charity event while locked away in my office, yet I've found a better way to occupy my time. And currently, she's in my closet, probably looking for something on me. Too bad for her, I keep nothing of personal value in my bedroom.

As soon as the notification that someone entered my bedroom hit my cell, I immediately went to check the feed, concerned Faro or one of his men had broken in somehow, putting Chiara in danger. I know that fear is irrational. He wouldn't be able to get past my men outside. But I can't help worrying about her. I care for her more than I do myself. It's not something I'm able to turn off.

But when I took a look at my phone, I was happy to find Chiara there instead. I've been sitting here, kicking my feet out, crossed at the ankles, watching her, wanting to see what she planned to do. Unfortunately for me, there are no cameras in my closet. I'll be sure to remedy that very soon.

Minutes tick by, and I grow impatient.

What the fuck is she doing in there for so long?

Another moment later, she comes out with my shirt and tie in her hands. Now, I'm even more curious about what she's thinking. She reaches my bed and...

What the hell?

I sit straighter, the beats of my heart firing through my veins, my chest falling to a beastly rhythm.

I ball my hand into a tight fist as she strips off every inch of her clothes. Those gorgeous tits bounce out, calling for my hands and mouth to make them come alive. My cock swells and throbs at the sight of her.

All I want is off this seat, to be where she is, to punish her for invading my space without my direct permission.

But I wait.

What are you doing, Chiara Bianchi?

She drapes my shirt over her glorious curves, and goddamn, it never looked better. My breathing grows monstrous, the savage desire for the girl I once considered my best friend comes barraging to the surface. I want to grab her, to kiss her, to tell her who I am and how much I still fucking love her.

Damn it!

She slides up on my bed, and as soon as my tie slips in between those soft thighs, I'm off the chair before the first moan slides out of her lips.

If she's going to touch herself on my fucking bed, it sure as hell is going to be with me watching her do it.

I shouldn't be climbing up the steps to my bedroom. I shouldn't have my hand on the door as she moans. But here I am, taking something that doesn't belong to me.

Again.

She's like my favorite dessert, the one I can't deny, no matter how much willpower I think I have. With her, it all crumbles.

Her beauty is my temptation, her soul my downfall. She'll send me to the depths of my despair, and I won't do a thing to stop her.

Deep down, buried amongst the ruins, lies a heart that still beats for her. Even then, being just thirteen, I knew Chiara was someone I never wanted to let go of.

But one moment—one slice in time—changed everything, taking away my friend and my future. And now, she's no longer the girl I once knew and I'm no longer the boy who held her hand and swore to protect her from all the monsters.

I'm the monster now. And there's no one to protect her from me.

The cut in the doorway gives me a nice view of her spread thighs on my bed, the tie still rubbing on her pussy. Her breasts arch up as she shoves her fingers deep inside her.

Fuck, the imagery goes straight to my cock. I palm it roughly in my pants, gripping tight as I clench my jaw. I should be there, burying myself inside her wet cunt.

"Mmm...Brian...yes."

My name on her lips, those thighs trembling, has me pushing the door open harshly, my footsteps creaking over the floorboards.

She gasps, grabbing the other end of the comforter, draping it over herself.

"What the hell are you doing?!" she shrieks, her breaths running rampant.

I snicker, crossing my arms over my chest, my mouth twisting into a slow smirk as I stare down at her. "Shouldn't I be asking *you* that question? You're the one naked and in my bed with my tie on that sweet pussy."

She gapes up at me, completely speechless, her brows straining, her cheeks a soft pink.

"Don't stop now, baby." Reaching down, I yank the covers off of her body, exposing every gorgeous inch. "I was quite fond of the performance."

She crosses her legs at her knees, her palms cupping her tits while my eyes take a leisurely swipe up her body.

Her lips pout, her rough exhale a little too sexy.

"You're sick!" she pants.

"I'm not the one who watched me get my dick sucked." My tone is deep, hoarse, unable to control the hunger permeating through me.

My gaze drowns over her body, sweeping over every line, every curve, wanting my hands there instead.

"Did I tell you to stop?" I ask, my tongue darting out for a taste. "Show me how you touch yourself. And keep that tie exactly where it is."

She lets out a half pant, half moan, her brows curling downward.

"Come on, Chiara." The tone in my voice is rough, my cock throbbing. "Don't make me ask again."

I witness the momentary inner battle within her eyes. Finally, she drops one hand from her chest, giving me a view of her gorgeous tit, the nipple a deep pink. One I want to taste. To bite.

"Drop the other hand," I demand, taking her in.

Her hand slowly travels down, giving me what I want.

Her aroused gaze, those full parted lips, those tiny whimpers, I devour them all as she gradually drifts her hand even lower until her fingers are lost to her wet slit.

"That's it, baby. Rub that clit over my tie. I want it to smell like you."

"Oh, God!" She grinds her ass on the sheets, pinching a nipple with her free hand while she touches herself with the other.

"Yes, Brian! I'm gonna come all over your tie."

I groan, wanting so badly for her to call me by the name she once used.

I know what I told myself at the library, about her calling me by my alias being a good thing, but I hate hearing it now. I should always be Dom to her. To me, she'll always be my Chiara, no matter how many years and how many lies have been built to keep us apart.

She flips around onto her stomach, her ass in the air, her fingers still inside her. Her head's angled to the side as she holds my gaze, getting brasher while she fucks herself.

"Is that what you like?" she asks with boldness as she gyrates over my bed, holding me prisoner. "You like seeing me touching myself, thinking of your cock inside me?"

My nostrils flare, my jaw flexing so hard my teeth rattle.

Her toes curl as she rubs herself, upping the pace, her moans getting louder.

"I...I shouldn't want you. But I do," she cries. "You're all the things I should stay away from, but I can't. I don't want to."

"Fuck this," I growl before I'm on the bed beside her, lifting her in the air by her hips as she yelps.

I drape her over me, holding her on top as she stills in my embrace, and with one look into her eyes, the loud whispers telling me to run, quiet to a hum.

Her hooded gaze settles on mine, and whatever's left of my heart begins to beat.

"Chiara..." I whisper.

"Brian..." Her brows furrow and her palm softly flutters over my cheek.

I shut my eyes, savoring her touch, not knowing when this moment will end. And for the first time in years, I don't want it to.

I want her despite what she did. Despite her lies and all the hate I've carried through the years.

Underneath all that, I'm still the boy who loves her, who would've shattered the entire world to make her smile. I just got better at trying to forget him.

But if she knew who I was, would she want me then? Could she ever learn to care for the man I've become?

"I'm sorry my father hurt you," she says, grazing her knuckles over my jaw. "But I'm not him. I'd never hurt you. And I *know* you don't want to hurt me. Tell me I'm wrong."

I bury my face in her chest.

Of course I'd never hurt you. I still care so much about you.

My cock strains against my boxers, needing to find refuge inside her.

"What are you doing?" she asks, cupping my face, pulling me back into her softened gaze.

I search her eyes, my heartbeats unraveling inside my chest.

"Fighting," I confess with a whisper.

"Fighting what?" Her words are as soft as mine.

"Fighting wanting you."

She runs her thumb over my lips. "Stop fighting." Her lips fall closer to mine. "Because I have."

And before I realize what's happening, my palm is on the back of her head and her lips are on mine. I take and she gives, her sultry moans shooting down my body, the rhythm of our kiss both light and darkness.

I suck on her lower lip, taking her back down onto the bed, the heaviness of my body sinking over hers. She lifts up her hips to meet mine, draping her calf over my ass, pushing my hard-on deeper, groaning as my cock drives into her pussy.

The sound she makes sends a rush of electric power down the length of me. I've never wanted a woman right down to my bones. Never thought I could. That part of me was dead until she woke the beast and tamed his flaming heart.

My hand tumbles roughly in her hair, pulling her head back, giving me access to her neck.

"You're the only one I fear." I kiss the curve of her jaw. "There's no one who scares me more than you do."

"Don't be afraid." Her nails rake my back through the shirt. "Let me in."

My lips are back on hers, never wanting to stop kissing her. She reaches toward my pants, fumbling with my belt.

I groan, pulling away, rising to my knees, intending to take off my pants, but she reaches for them instead, and without taking her eyes off of mine, she unbuckles my belt.

I watch as she drags it out, her hungry eyes devouring mine while she pulls the zipper down. Reaching inside, she grabs my cock, tightening her hand around the tip.

"Chiara." I clutch her wrist, not allowing her hand to move. "I need to fuck you before I lose my damn mind."

She buries her teeth in her lower lip, groaning out my name.

"Please, Brian."

"Don't call me that," I implore. "Not today."

Yanking off my pants, I toss them to the side, grabbing a condom from the nightstand and rolling it down my length.

I lay my body over hers, my lips descending to the smooth skin of her neck, kissing her without a hurry as I take each of her wrists and pin them over her head.

"What's your real name? Tell me," she asks, searching my eyes for something I won't give her.

"Not yet." I slide my tongue up to the soft spot below the curve of her ear.

"But—" I swallow her words with my tongue.

And before she can ask me any more questions, I align my cock at her center and slam right where I want to be.

"Oh, fuck, yes!" she screams.

I can't seem to move inside her at first, consumed by her warmth, her skin on mine.

I thought about being with her when I was young, but I never thought this was how our first time would be. Our bodies seeped with deception, soaked in betrayal. But it's what we are and what we have. And I'm not about to give it up for anything.

"Mmm..." Her moans tremble into my mouth, her desire sheathing me, and I thrust deeper, erasing my thoughts, wanting to go as far as I can.

She claws at my biceps, whimpering—crying out for more. I lift one of her thighs, keeping my hand steady on the back of her knee, letting her hands roam.

The new position feels deeper.

"Harder. Fuck me harder," she begs, squeezing her tits together.

I grab her hips and flip her onto her stomach. Lifting her ass with a hand, I position myself at her pussy again and ram back inside.

"Shit! Yes...just like—oh, fuck!" She screams out a moan as I grab her hair, tugging while my cock finds a hurried pace, sinking in and out with rough strokes. She's flat on the bed now, my body over hers, and I take what's always been mine.

I find the tie she used on herself beside her head and pull it up to my nose, inhaling her. Then I ball it up in my fist.

"Open that sexy mouth," I demand.

"Wha—oh, shit," she cries, her voice trembling as I hit her G-spot harder.

I stuff the tie into her mouth, fitting most of it in. She continues to moan against it, turning her face to the side to find me staring at her.

"Fuck, look at you. Damn beautiful."

I clench my hand tighter in the softness of her hair, her walls clenching around me, causing my balls to burn with a release I know is coming.

She spreads her hand, touching herself while I continue impaling her.

"Yes, baby, rub your pussy for me. Let me feel you dripping down my cock."

She whimpers louder now, her walls squeezing tighter, and I know she's almost there. I remove the tie from her mouth, leaning down to take her lips in a brutal kiss.

I nip and suck every inch of them, fucking her like a man completely lost to a woman. And I am lost to her in every way that matters.

With another thrust, she comes, squeezing my cock with a tight grip. My hips continue colliding with her ass until my own release slams to the surface.

When the aftershocks of her orgasm still and my every drop is hers, I lean down to my side and hold her close against my chest, my palm sprawled over her stomach.

After we catch our breath, she's the first to speak.

"I still want to know your name." She runs lazy circles on the top of my hand.

"You'll know when I'm ready to tell you."

"When will that be?" she murmurs.

"I haven't decided yet."

She inhales, letting the breath fall harshly out of her lips. "Okay. Oh, and just so you know, if you let another woman touch you again, it won't end well for you. I'm pretty skilled with a gun in my hand."

I chuckle, kissing the back of her head. "Is that a promise, baby?"

"Mm-hmm."

She scoots closer to my body, and for the first time in a long time, I smile.

And I feel it in places where I've long been unable to feel anything.

CHIARA

TWENTY-FIVE

"**Y**ou're so beautiful," he whispers as he spoons me close, his lips kissing my temple.

I moan, encased in euphoria, tugging my body even closer to his, not realizing I'm doing it until it's already done. His calloused palm splays over my lower abdomen, his fingers sinking deliciously into my skin.

What am I doing? How can I let him make me feel so at ease?

I've welcomed him into my body, and if I'm not careful, he'll take my heart.

He's a man whose name I don't even know, who's taken me against my will. So how can the arms of my kidnapper feel so tender?

It's as though I'm not in the arms of the man who swore to hurt me when we first met, but rather like I'm being held by the same man I lusted over back in the club. Someone I once wanted to know better.

But all that doesn't erase my circumstance.

I was taken. By him.

I don't know what he has in store for me, but sleeping with him is nothing more than my getaway ticket.

He groans, kissing my neck, and I purr like a goddamn cat. I barely recognize myself. My mind has to stay sharp at all times to find a way to escape.

But what if...

No. I can't even finish the thought.

But as hard as I fight it, the thought finishes itself. It's scary to even consider that this could become something real after everything is over. But what if...what if he's finally showing me the real him? What if the world is giving me something I don't yet understand?

I'm being an idiot. The men in my life have only tried to chain me, not love me. It must be the sex making me crazy.

Of course we can't be together. We're two people who were never meant to find a home in each other's arms. And right now, feeling so at peace beside him, it's kind of making me sad.

He rustles beside me, a single finger skimming down my stomach, finding a neat path to my core. He slides it inside, rubbing my clit, drawing a low, throaty moan from me.

"Your ass should permanently stay glued to my cock." The deep-chested rasp of his voice only strokes me harder, goose bumps slithering up my arms and breasts as he continues to rub me slowly.

"You like my ass, huh?" I pant.

"It's the nicest ass I've ever seen, and I've seen a lot."

My pulse jumps to my neck, and my stomach hardens.

Why the hell did I become instantly jealous?

His hand stills, and suddenly, he flips on top of me, his eyes searching mine as my hands are pinned above my head with one of his. I never want his eyes to stop looking into mine. They consume me.

He's a monster with the eyes of the gods. Soulful and beautiful.

He wakes up the parts of me that I keep hidden. The parts that crave stability. Love.

"Didn't like me telling you about all the women I've seen naked?"

I ache from the lack of his fingers, from the way his cock rubs between my thighs.

Holding himself up with his other arm, he rocks his hips up and down, his eyes holding mine.

My mouth falls open, my eyelids drifting to a close, and before I can open them to tell him how much I don't care who he's fucked, he kisses me.

His tongue skirts around mine, his lips devouring my lower one. He pulls back, his gaze swimming with want. The fire in my heart, the flames deep in my soul, are ready to burn the lies from my tongue, the ones I'm about to give him.

"I don't care who you've been with in the past," I say defiantly. "I've had plenty of men who've enjoyed my ass too." I pop a brow with a curl of my lips. "You're not special."

He growls, thrusting the length of his cock against my throbbing clit, my hurried breaths causing a rapid rise and fall of my chest.

"Liar. I think I am. Just look how wet this pussy is for me."

His filthy words have me whimpering. I don't recognize myself when I'm in bed with him. And maybe that's not a bad thing. Maybe it's good to discover new parts of ourselves when we're with someone who makes us feel so alive, so craved. Even when it may not be real.

His lips are on my neck while his hips move slow, burrowing into me.

My hands are on his back, carving into his flesh, needing to mark him so he never forgets me, even when I'll be miles away.

My heart skips a beat at the thought of leaving him behind. The lust is taking a front seat, leading all my thoughts.

It's stupid. He means nothing. I'm using him for sex, which I need badly. That's all this is.

Liar.

You like him. You know you do. You're so fucked up, you like a man who took you as revenge.

The tears burn within my eyes at the glaring truth. I swallow away the pain, hiding it behind his shoulder.

"I have a charity ball at the house tomorrow night," he whispers, his breath tickling up my neck in between kisses. "I want you there."

He pulls back, peering up at me from beneath thick mahogany brows.

"As my date—of sorts."

I scoff, faking a smile. "I don't do parties with my kidnappers. It's not my thing."

"How do you know if you've never tried?" His voice turns serious before humor lines his face.

"Ha." I roll my eyes. "I don't even have anything to wear. I doubt you packed the only evening gown I own."

"I can get you a dress."

His cock grazes my clit, and my whole body buzzes with a high, my lips shuddering with a pant.

"Otherwise, you'll be here all alone," he adds in a gravelly tone.

"In your bed?" I bite the edge of my lower lip, rolling my hips over his hard-on, needing a release so bad, I'm about to beg for one.

He drops his face closer, his eyes delving into mine. "If you want."

"I want." I grind myself against him.

"Yes, you do," he groans, his palm landing hard on my jaw as he kisses me with a frenzy rivaling madness.

He bites and sucks, both of us in a state of ecstasy consuming everything but the both of us.

Right now, all I know is him, and all I want is the way he makes me feel. I never want it to end. The crown of his length eases inside me, while his mouth devours me to the same rhythm.

He does unspeakable things to my body, and if I'm not careful, he'll do unspeakable things to my heart.

CHIARA

TWENTY-SIX

Sleep calls to me, lulling me back into its abyss even as my eyes peer open, finding the morning light flitting through the gray curtains.

I yawn, stretching out my arms above me. It takes me a few seconds to realize that Brian let me sleep with him last night, and that he isn't here anymore.

I glance at the clock on his nightstand, reading ten a.m. He must be at work, wherever that is.

Then a thought hits me. The party tonight. That could be the perfect way to flee unnoticed amongst the throng of people.

Shit. Why didn't I think of that last night?

Maybe because he was fucking me in all sorts of insane positions and my brain was jumbled. I should've told him I wanted to go tonight. Maybe it's not too late.

THE DEVIL'S DEAL

I sit up, swinging my feet down, when I notice a small white folded paper sitting up against his silver lamp. Picking it up, I open it, finding a note from him.

I could get used to waking up with you curled up against my chest.

My heart squeezes tight in my rib cage, and my every breath stills as I clutch the paper against my chest. Taking a deep breath, I continue reading.

I left you something on the bed in your room. I'll see you tonight.

A smile spreads over my face. Grabbing my clothes from the floor, I hurriedly slip them back on, needing to see what he left me before I run into the shower. Exiting his room, I walk over to mine, practically running inside.

On my bed lies a long, white garment bag, and I instantly know what's inside.

A dress.

He wants you there.

There's a fluttering in my stomach that I don't recognize. It's so foreign, I almost think I made it up, but it's real, just like last night was.

But I have to get away. I have to leave him. I can't stay.

My fingertips tingle, my chest burning at the conflicting feelings crackling with my heart, relief clouded by desolation.

I push the thoughts far down where I don't have to feel them as I unzip the bag, finding two of the same bright red gowns. Though I don't like wearing color, I can make an exception for the exquisite work of a high-end designer I easily recognize.

Each dress is at least five grand. I lift one by the hanger, running my fingers over the soft, thick material, then lower until I hit the thin, sparkly belt sewn into the waist.

The deep V-neck will definitely put the girls on full display. Thank goodness for the mesh in the middle, or I'd be flashing everyone all night. He guessed on the sizes, giving me two options, one of which should fit like a glove.

Now, I'm a little excited for tonight.

I glance at my reflection in the full-length mirror, happy he had the sense to pack my makeup and hair supplies.

My long locks are sleek straight, parted in the middle, and my makeup is sultry, with a thick layer of black liner on the top lid with a mix of brown and gold shadows. Picking up a brush, I add some bronzer to my cheeks and the tip of my nose, then swipe a nude lipstick on my lips.

I've just put everything back into my makeup case when there's a knock on the door, and before I invite him in, Brian walks inside.

I can see him treading across the floor through the mirror, his black loafers and black trousers coming closer from behind, and my heart pounds in my throat with desire. His firm hands are on my shoulders, his face hidden behind my hair as he turns me around.

Facing him, I lift up my chin with a warm, inviting smile. He backs away, his eyes grazing over my body.

"You look…"

He sucks in a breath as his ravenous gaze traces every contour of my curves.

"Wow." His tone sways with a husky beat, the back of his hand stroking the underside of my jaw as he nears.

Without looking away, he reaches into his pocket and pulls out a black jewelry box. My eyes fling from him to the box as he opens it, staring at me as he does. When I see what's inside, my eyes widen in disbelief. Long chandelier-style earrings sparkle beneath the well-lit room.

My parents never lacked in money, but I was never this rich. Whatever money my father had, he was careful in how he spent it. We didn't live a life like Brian is clearly used to.

"Are those diamonds?"

The question is so stupid. What do I expect them to be, cubic zirconia?

"Of course." His voice sounds like velvet, smooth and tempting. I want to kiss him so badly. Fuck this lipstick.

"How rich are you, exactly?"

Dumb question number two. Keep them coming, Chiara.

He smirks, and it goes straight to my core. Damn this sexy creature of a man.

"Rich enough." He removes the earrings from the box. "I want to see them on you."

His fingers are on the side of my face and my breath hitches from the way his eyes connect with mine. He inhales sharply as he carefully slips my hair behind my ear, his gaze pinning me where I stand like a statue. His Adam's apple bops as he slips on one earring, then moves on to the next.

A shiver runs down my spine from the simple, yet intimate, way he touches me. The way he looks at me as though I'm the only woman on earth. My body hums with want, even when my mind's already out the door, running as far as it can go, away from a man it still thinks is a monster.

"Maybe I should keep you all to myself tonight?" he whispers against the shell of my ear, his voice inviting itself into my most intimate places. "I should tie you to my bed and enjoy you for dessert." He takes a bite of my lobe. "I know you taste good. I tasted you enough last night to remember."

I groan, grinding my pussy against the insides of my thighs as my hand lands on the back of his head, angling him closer.

"And allow every man at your party to miss out on seeing this?" My hand flows down my body for effect. "Maybe even touching it too."

He must catch the movement, because the next thing I know, his hand is gripping my wrist in a firm grasp.

"Fuck, baby," he growls. "If you let another man touch you…" He clutches the back of my neck, his gaze possessive. "You can't blame me for what I'll do."

I grow slick from his erotic tone dripped in envy.

"Why do you sound like a man who thinks he owns more than just my freedom?" I dig my nails into his scalp.

His fingers bite into my neck, his sharp inhale marks my lips as he rests his forehead against mine. "Even though it may not make sense, you're the one who owns me, Chiara."

There's a twinge of agony in his voice, and I want nothing more than to soothe it away.

And he's right. His words make no sense at all.

He withdraws from me with a bated breath, fixing the lapel of his tuxedo jacket, which looks way too good on him.

"Come on." He lifts his arm, waiting for me to hook mine through his.

Once I do, we make it out the door, and I realize this might be the last time I feel him against me, so I cling tighter to the strength of his arm.

DOMINIC

Every goddamn man in here can't keep his eyes to himself. Why the fuck did I think it was a good idea to have her here, amongst these smug, rich assholes who want nothing more than to use her body?

How the hell are you any different?

The question hangs in my head, suspended in time. I don't know if there can ever be a future for us, but I realize I want it.

I want her.

I can forgive her for the past. I'm sure she had a good reason for what she did. We were kids then. We aren't now. Maybe she's sorry. I'll tell myself anything just to give us a chance.

I watch her from across the room, her long legs hidden beneath the length of the dress. Sitting at a table, she sips on a blue cocktail, completely comfortable being alone as I talk to every man and woman with deep pockets.

"You've outdone yourself," Dr. Costanza says.

She and her husband are both prominent surgeons who donate a nice penny every year at my galas.

Last year, I managed to raise twenty-five million, and the hope is to up it this time to at least thirty. Between the auctions for expensive items, like my house in St. Tropez, and artwork that looks like it's been made by a child, I'm sure I'll reach that goal.

"Thank you very much," I say, shaking her hand, my eyes wandering between Chiara and her. "I hope you and Mike are having a good time."

"We are. Everything…so…" Her voice drifts in and out.

I've stopped paying attention to the blonde doctor. The only thing I'm focused on now is the back of a man, the one currently talking to Chiara. The one who shouldn't be here at all.

Chiara nods, looking past him as her face contorts with an uncomfortable smile. I can tell she's trying hard not to tell him to fuck off. The bastard either doesn't care or doesn't take the hint. Knowing him, it's the former. The muscles in my neck twitch, and I grit my teeth so hard, my jaw may crack in half.

Cain, my fucking gun supplier knows he's not allowed at my home. I can barely stand him, but I have no choice but to deal with him. He's the only one in a five-hundred-mile radius who doesn't suck Faro's dick. If I want weapons, he's the only one I can go to. His biggest competitor is loyal to the Palermo family.

He lowers himself to the empty chair beside her.

"I'm sorry. Excuse me," I tell Dr. Costanza, my feet moving, already steps away. "I have an urgent matter to take care of."

"Oh, of cour…"

I march toward Chiara just as Cain puts his hand on her fucking thigh. He's going to regret that. My eyes are on him, while his are on her. She sees me coming before he does, mouthing a *thank you*. The asshole doesn't even notice me until I rip his hand off of her, fisting the collar of his shirt.

"Get your damn hands off of her, Cain," I mouth low, every word stamped with venom.

"Relax!" He tries to get my hand off of him with a laugh, but it's not working out so well for him. "I'll leave the pretty lady alone, okay? I only came for a good time."

My grip intensifies.

"You weren't invited. Leave. *Now*," I threaten through gritted teeth.

"I can see you're mad. I'll go. No worries."

I don't attempt to remove my fist from his shirt. I tighten it instead, glaring into his soulless hazel eyes.

Cain has a good twenty years on me, and the grays on the side of his head are making their appearance. His biggest problem is that he thinks pussy is his for the taking, whenever and however he wants it. I've heard he's been brought up on at least two rape charges, but he's never gone away for it. Rumor is he paid the women off before the law could make a case against him. It's part of the reason I hate working with him. The fucker needs to be put through a grinder.

"Get your hand off of me so I can go," he throws casually.

I'm almost afraid he'll call me by my real name. That's not how I want her to find out. I plan to tell her who I am once I kill her father.

But I knew inviting her here would be a risk, and the twisted part of me didn't care. I want her to know. I want her to hate me. I don't deserve her or the happiness we could have.

I finally remove my fist from his shirt, and he gets to his feet, fucking off toward the exit.

"Are you okay?" I ask her, my hand on her cheek, concern punched in my voice.

"I'm fine, Brian. I've dealt with bigger idiots at the club than that guy." She tilts her head sideways with a deep smile. "You don't have to worry about me."

"Right."

I take the seat the asshole was just in, gazing at her.

"I forgot who you were for a second," I chuckle.

"And who's that?" Her lips curve up.

"The chick who punched a guy at the club."

She's so beautiful, I never want to stop staring.

Her brow whips up as she angles her body toward me some more, purposely rubbing her calf on mine. "That's right, and don't ever forget it again."

She pulls her chair closer and leans her luscious lips to my ear as I suck in a breath like a horny high school kid.

"You don't need to save me from anyone but yourself."

Her exhale runs over my skin, and I instantly harden. My palm lands on the back of her neck in a sign of ownership as I gaze at her, and she gazes just as relentlessly.

"I need you upstairs in my room."

"Maybe I don't want to go." The words spin out of her lips like a wicked game she likes to play.

"Oh, you *will* want to. If you don't…" I swallow her lower lip with my teeth, nipping hard as she moans. "I will flip you over my knee and fuck your pussy with my fingers."

She pants. "Maybe you should. I bet you'd get a lot more donations."

"Fuck," I groan, my fingers sinking deeper into her soft skin as I pull her face back. "Get upstairs and get on the bed. Keep your clothes on. I want to be the one to take them all off."

Her gaze is drunk with the same appetite I have growing, her body still on the chair.

"I hate asking twice," I tell her as she sucks on her lower lip, making me want to be the one to do it.

Not giving her a chance to respond, I go and shake some hands, needing to empty their pockets before I spend the rest of the night pleasing a woman I can no longer hate.

CHIARA

TWENTY-SEVEN

I practically run up the stairs, unable to wait for his hands all over my body, forgetting about my plan to run. I doubt I could, anyway. He has more security than he normally does tonight, and I'm sure he made it clear to all of them that I'm not to leave.

I'll basically make any excuse to be with him right now. This is starting to feel like more than just sex. There's something there. Something beginning to sprout from the ashes.

But even if we could have something more, does he want that? Can I accept him as he is? Whoever he is?

There are too many things unknown for me to make such a decision. For now, I'll enjoy the time we have. The rest will come into focus when I have more answers.

The music is only a soft whisper now as I land in the dark

hallway upstairs, my heels clacking against the wood floors. I'm only a few steps away from Brian's door when I almost trip, but strong hands catch me.

"How did you get here before me?" I ask Brian with a small, nervous laugh.

Someone snickers and a chill skitters from my face down to my legs when I realize that the man in the shadows isn't Brian at all.

I try to run, but it's too late. A hand twists my hair, yanking me backwards, pulling me as I stumble onto the floor, my heel caught in the hem of my dress.

"Help!" I scream with all my might until a fist lands across my jaw, silencing me.

My head whips back roughly, and flickering dots of light flash before my eyes. I taste the copper in my mouth and I hear my whimpers lodged in my ears.

"Shut your mouth, you whore, or I'll slice your throat."

I grumble from the pain, shivering from the harsh words.

I know that voice, I realize.

It belongs to the man from the party, the one who touched me after I rejected his advances.

"He seemed so possessive over you." The man's voice cuts into my chest. "Must be something special about that cunt for him to care whether I play with it or not. I'm going to find out what makes you so important."

No.

No, no, no. I can't let this happen.

Oh, God, what do I do? How do I get the hell out of here?

I swallow against the thick wave of nausea swirling up my throat.

My heart is racing, my pulse beating loudly in my ears.

I won't let him touch me. I'll go down fighting until the very end.

He drags me further down the hall, then swings to the right.

My knees hit the corner of a wall.

I yelp from the sharp pain, but he doesn't care. He just chuckles at my suffering.

We stop, and I hear a door open, then another.

I lose count as to how many he opens before we stop. He drags me inside a room and flips on a light.

My eyes sting as they adjust to the brightness, and I find myself inside a bathroom I've never been in. The click of the lock sends an ice-cold shudder down my body, submerging me in dread.

"Brian," I call with a voice so small I don't recognize it, knowing he can't hear me at all.

DOMINIC

I've shaken enough hands and smiled in enough pictures to be done with this party. I let Miles know I'll be heading upstairs now. I have more important things to do.

I take out my cell from my pocket, checking the feed upstairs, wanting to see her waiting for me on my bed. But when I open the app, I don't see her there. I check the cameras in the hall, but they're all off. Like they've been disconnected.

What the fuck?

I check the camera in Chiara's bedroom and don't find her there either.

Something's wrong.

"Miles!" I shout over to him. "Kill the party quietly. Say I've had a family emergency."

"Done."

He gets on the walkie-talkie, informing all the men.

"What's wrong, boss?" he asks with obvious concern.
"Someone may be upstairs with Chiara. I'm going up."
"Shit."

He radios the rest of the team, giving them the additional information, but I don't wait for him as I run up.

If Faro's men are here—if any of them so much as lays a finger on her—I'll kill them all with my bare hands in front of every one of my guests, my reputation be damned.

The music stops when I reach upstairs, finding the hallway quiet. The silence swallows me as I open my bedroom, finding it empty. I don't want to call her name and let whoever has her know I'm on to them.

Heading for her door, I gently push it open, finding no one inside. I go from room to room, finding nothing.

The panic sets in when I reach the end of the hall, and when I hear a muffled cry from one of the guest bathrooms, the panic turns into full-blown terror.

Removing the gun from my ankle, I tiptoe toward her strained voice, knowing whoever has hurt her is already dead. Once beside the door, I kick it open, almost taking it off the hinges.

My men are suddenly behind me, guns pointed at…

I see Cain's face as he spins around, hands raised in the air, the knife in his hand falling to the ground.

My chest heaves, my face vibrating with rage as I see what he's done to her.

Chiara's on the floor, her dress ripped, tattered at her waist, her palms cupping her breasts as streaks of mascara run down her face whirled with tears. And that blood on her lip and jaw…

Fuck!

I rush for him with a growl. No one could stop me even if they wanted to.

Chiara whimpers as I pick him up off the floor, bashing the back of his head against the hard porcelain wall.

Letting go, I let him crumble to the floor as I land kick after kick across his stomach and then his face before I land two more to his balls.

He moans like a dying animal.

I crouch down.

"You fucking hurt her?!" I say loud enough for all to hear. "You *touched* her?!"

He mutters something unintelligible in response.

"You're dead, Cain. This is just a preview of what I'll do to you."

I pick up the knife I suspect he used on her dress. I'm too far gone, lost to the raging bloodshed coursing through me, needing the taste of vengeance to satiate the beast. It's one thing I know how to do well.

Lifting my foot for another kick, I pause when Chiara cries, and suddenly all I care about is taking care of her. I tuck my gun into my waistband, giving one of my men the knife.

Removing my suit jacket, I move slowly toward her, draping it over her shivering body before lifting her into my arms. I will finish with this piece of shit in a minute.

"Shh, baby. I've got you."

She circles her arms around my neck, sniffling on my shoulder.

"I'm so sorry, Chiara. God, I'm sorry." An ache lodges in my throat, and I grind my teeth, stilling the desire to burn that son of a bitch to the ground.

Miles comes for Cain next, a gun pointing toward his head. "If I didn't think my boss would kill you himself, I would've done it already."

Cain has only one good eye to see through. The other is

completely shut. Blood drips like a fountain from his nose as he holds his hands up, covering his face from the bullet he fears.

The only bullet he'll be getting is the one coming from me. He's mine.

"Bring him into the guest bedroom. The one with no rugs."

Miles drags him across the floor by his feet, purposely bumping him into the door as he moves him out of the bathroom.

I carry Chiara out, heading for my bedroom, wanting to leave her there while I take care of business.

"Where are you taking me?" she asks, her voice pierced with a cry.

"My room, baby. I'll join you once I'm done with him."

"No," she says harshly. "I need to be with you."

"Chiara, you don't want to see what I'll do to him." I lean in and kiss the tip of her nose. "Believe me."

"I don't care." She shakes her head. "I'm coming with you."

"Okay, baby." I won't fight her, not when she's in this state.

I fucking pray she doesn't see me differently after tonight. I don't want her to think I'm more of a monster than she already does. I already feel like absolute shit for fucking her while she thinks I'm someone else. Once she finds out, she'll probably never forgive me.

I enter the room where four of my men stand around the floor with Cain in the middle. I place Chiara down on the bed and kiss her forehead, noting that the blood on her mouth has slowed.

"I'll be done soon. Promise. Then we'll get cleaned up together." I kiss her forehead again, closing my eyes.

Before I can walk away, she grabs my forearm. There's vulnerability in her gaze, but also so much strength. She lifts up on her knees, palming each side of my face.

"Thank you," she whispers, her eyes streaked with red, tears still shining in her eyes.

My body fills with more rage than I can handle. I don't want those gorgeous eyes to look as sad as they do right now.

"For what?" I ask.

"For hurting him. No one has ever protected me that way."

I steel my jaw, remembering what she looked like when I found her. "You never have to thank me for slaying the ones who hurt you. I'll always do that, no matter what."

She doesn't realize how true that is.

I lift each one of her hands and kiss her palms before heading for Cain.

My men part, allowing me to get close to the trash on the floor. One of them hands me the knife back.

Cain tries to pick himself up to a sitting position, but falls before trying again successfully.

"Did I tell you to get the fuck up?" I ask, lowering my shoe over his stomach. "Stay down where you belong."

He tumbles back down, and I dig my shoe in deeper.

"Co-come...come on, man," he cries. "I thought we were friends." He coughs violently. "I...I thought you sha-shared your playthings."

I circle around him, the knife pointing at his throat.

One eye follows my every move as he continues. "Remember those whores at your club?" He swallows, coughing again, blood dripping from his nose as he wipes it away. "You didn't care then."

I stop, rushing up toward his face. Lifting him until he sits, I stick the pointy tip of the knife under his jaw, drawing just enough blood for him to watch his fucking mouth.

"Does she look like a whore? Did I give you any indication that you were welcome to her body?"

I move the knife a centimeter away, nicking him again.

"Did I?!" I shout, the words burning with something sinister like brandy poured into an open wound.

"I...I thought she wanted it. I didn't even fuck her."

"Does she *look* like she wanted it?!" I ask with a barely steady voice. "Answer me!"

I turn his face sharply toward her with the side of the knife, almost slicing his cheek.

"Look at her!"

Chiara eyes him with a deadly glare, drops of blood still spilling from her busted lip.

"All right, I fu-fucked up." I hear the fear. "Won't happen again. You have my word."

"Your word means nothing to me. Not anymore." I spin his head back to face me. "Do you have no shame? No honor? Taking a woman against her will? I should've killed you as soon as I heard the rumors."

He laughs, finding an ounce of courage. "Where the fuck will you get your supply then? I'm all you've got."

"You don't have to worry about that."

"You can't kill me." The full pound of fear is back.

"Apologize. To her."

He coughs with a chuckle. "I'm not apologizing to no bitch."

He's making his inevitable death that much easier on me.

Kicking him on his jaw, I stomp on his face with my shoe as he collapses, and something cracks.

"My nose!" Blood sputters from it.

I should try again until he can't speak at all.

"You're going to wish I'd killed you quickly." I flip the knife in my hand, once, twice until I plunge it into the top of his hand.

"Ahhh!" His screams echo through the room.

"If I had more time..." I remove the knife and slam it into his other hand as he wails in agony, begging for mercy. "I'd make you suffer even more. But I have a woman I care for who needs me."

Retrieving the gun from my waist, I aim it at his chest.

"They'll never find your body."

Bang.

The sound of a bullet punctures through the air, hitting him right in the temple.

Chiara gasps.

"Call the cleanup crew," I tell Miles as I drop the gun next to the body and go to Chiara, who can't stop staring at the dead body on the floor.

"No problem, sir," he responds.

I've never needed my cleaners at the house before, but there's a first time for everything. They're the best out there, and know how to dispose of a body and all the evidence.

My clothes are covered with his blood. I need them off so they can get rid of them too, along with hers. They're usually quick to show up, especially for the amount I pay.

"Come on, baby. Let's get cleaned up." I pick her up off the bed and carry her out.

She remains silent, her head on my shoulder, my jacket still around her.

"Don't be scared of me," I say. "I'd never hurt you."

My heart thunders in my chest at the thought of her fearing me like she did the bastard who dared to put his hands on her.

"I'm...I'm not scared."

She gazes up at me with eyes drowning in sorrow, and I want to dry her ocean of tears.

"I just need a shower and..."

Her trembling hand lands over her mouth as I kick the door of my room open.

"I don't know." Her voice cracks a little, and her brows knit tightly with waves of emotion.

"It's okay. You're safe now. I'll always protect you."

She nods, tears leaking from the corners of her eyes.

"I didn't think you'd get there in time. I thought he'd..." She sucks in a harsh breath as the tears continue to fall.

My own damn heart cracks right along with hers.

How could I have let this happen?!

"I'm so sorry I wasn't there to begin with, baby." I hold her tighter. "I should've never sent you up here alone. I swear to you, no man will ever hurt you again. You hear me?"

"It's not your fault." A battered breath leaves her as she looks up at me.

Of course it is.

If she hadn't been in my home to begin with, this wouldn't have happened. But I had no choice. She had to be here.

I slowly place her feet down on the floor. "Let's get you showered, okay?"

She nods as her trembling hands slip my jacket off her body. Grabbing it, I try hard not to stare at her breasts, making sure I look at her face instead.

But then I see her bruised lip and I rage again, clenching a fist against my thigh.

How could you let this happen under your damn watch?! What good are all these men and these fucking cameras when you can't keep the woman you care about safe?

"Brian? Did you hear me?" she asks, her soft hand slipping into mine.

"What?" I pause, finding her eyes full of worry. "I didn't. I'm sorry."

"I was asking if you could help me with the zipper. I think

it broke when he tried to..." She doesn't finish the sentence, swallowing away the words.

I cage the fury racing through me. I need to control it. She needs me to take care of her right now, even when she isn't asking for it.

Years may have passed, but I still know who she is at the core. Chiara has always been strong, but if you know her well enough, you'll see little glimpses of the scared little girl she's always been good at hiding.

But I'm not blind. I saw her then, and I'll see her always.

She turns, giving me her back. My fingers move to her hair, swiping it past her shoulder before shifting back to her dress. I yank the zipper with a little force as it resists, but finally it moves down slowly. When it's free, I reach down and pull the dress up. She lifts her arms, giving me the permission I need to take it off.

My dick instantly hardens at the sight of her in a black lace thong and thigh-high stockings held up by a garter belt. I wouldn't be able control my reaction even if I tried.

She faces me, and I suck in a breath, the muscles of my neck tightening from the protectiveness and want surging through me.

"Promise you'll stay in the room?"

I caress her chin in between two fingers. "I'd never leave you."

A small smile crosses her face before she slips out of her beige heels and heads inside the bathroom, shutting the door.

I release a long exhale, finding a seat on one of the armchairs. Slipping my cell out of my pocket, I text my brothers about what happened.

> **Dante:** Why the fuck didn't you call us? I would've at least cut off some of his important parts before you shot him.

Enzo: I would've enjoyed getting my suit bloody. I never liked his ass.

Dante: No one did.

Dominic: It happened fast.

Dante: Is she okay?

Dominic: She will be.

Dante: Tell us what you need.

Dominic: I need you both to look into finding a new gun supplier out of state. Our current stash is still good, but we'll need more soon.

Enzo: On it.

Dominic: I have to go.

I end the conversation, sliding my phone back when I hear a bang, like something fell. I jump to my feet. The sudden throb of my pulse in my neck knocks through me.

"Ow, shit!" she yelps.

"Chiara?"

I rush into the bathroom, steam greeting me.

"What's wrong?" I ask through the glass door of the stand-up shower. I can't see much inside.

"Can you help? I think I twisted my ankle."

I immediately open the door, finding her palms flat against the white tile to my right, her long black hair soaked, draping down to her ass. Her right foot is slightly raised as she eyes me, pain etched in her gaze.

"I was getting the shampoo," she explains. "And somehow, I managed to turn my foot the wrong way."

"I'll help you get out."

"I still have shampoo in my hair and I didn't even wash my body." She grimaces. "Do you think you can help?"

The pulse beats savagely in my ears, my chest heavy. How the fuck am I supposed to do that and not get rock hard? I'm not built for this. I want to fuck her like an animal, even in the state she's in. How can I be in there with those tight curves and not do anything about it?

I hate myself for even thinking about that after what happened to her.

"Please? It'll be too difficult for me to do it on one foot."

"Okay." Before I change my mind, I remove my shoes and socks and step under the warm spray of water.

She lifts a hand off the tiles and turns her face to the side, looking puzzled. "Aren't you going to take off your clothes?"

"No, that's not necessary," I say with my front to her back.

"But you're soaked."

"It's okay." I pick up a bar of soap, my clothes sticking to my skin.

Before I have a chance to wash her, she uses the wall to turn all the way around. Her fingers are on the buttons of my shirt. She undoes one, avoiding my gaze, then moves to another.

"Chiara." My hand lands on hers, stopping the movement. "Don't." The word comes out strained, like I don't mean it.

She finally looks up at me. "You need to get clean too."

I drop my hand, letting her do what she wants. If she's comfortable with this, then I'll have to be too.

"You have blood on your neck," she points out as she undoes

the last button.

I slip it off, rolling it up and tossing in on the other side of the shower floor.

She unbuttons my pants next, then lowers the zipper before I pull them down with my boxers, and my cock jumps out.

"I can't do much about that," I groan with shame.

"It's okay." She takes a glimpse of my hard-on before her eyes climb back up to my face. "I'd be a little offended if you weren't."

I sigh. "I'm sorry. For everything."

"You should be." She tries to smile, but winches from the pain in her lip.

"Shit." I gently rub her swollen mouth.

"Mmm." She closes her eyes, relaxing a bit. "Can you massage my head?"

"Sure, baby." My fingers land in her wet hair, bending them as I work the shampoo in.

"Thanks." She drives herself further into my touch.

After a few minutes, I finally begin cleansing her body, using the soap as a barrier between my hands and her skin. I keep it as mechanical as possible, even when I slip the soap in between her legs. My balls contract from the throbbing in my cock.

I should have kept my clothes on.

CHIARA

TWENTY-EIGHT

It's been a week since the charity ball, and I'm slowly getting over what happened thanks to Brian, who's made sure I'm never without him.

He's been with me night and day, skipping work and whatever else he has to do. He's made sure I eat, sleep, and have whatever I need. This man, my father's biggest enemy, has taken care of me more than my own flesh and blood.

Luckily, my ankle no longer hurts and my lip is nicely healed.

I'm curled around the softness of Brian's comforter with his strong body holding me firmly within his grasp.

It sounds insane even to me, but slowly, when I wasn't looking, I've started to care for the man I'm supposed to fear. There's nothing frightening about him anymore. He's just a man with a painful past who swore to protect me, even when that must've been difficult for him to do.

I feel the way he cares for me. Wants me. And I want him too.

I'd like to see where this could go. And when his fight with my father is all over, I plan to tell him how I feel and hope he feels it too.

The wounds of our past gave way to scars we can build a new life on, but only if we let it.

I cling to the hard muscle of his forearm, remembering what happened with Cain.

The way he glared at me as he cut into my dress…it was like a man who enjoyed rape and slaughter. I don't think I've ever been that afraid of dying. Not even when Brian first took me.

"Do you want to go to the pool?" Brian asks, grazing his fingers up and down my bare stomach, his lips on my neck, peppering me with soft kisses.

"Probably not." My tone is raspy, intoxicated by his touch. "The last time I was there, someone got all grabby and ruined all the fun."

I pull my lips into a smile as I slowly turn to face him.

His brow shoots up as his lips slant up at the corner. "That's because you were showing off something that belonged to me."

"Really?" I drape a leg over his hip. "You think my body belongs to you?"

His eyes turn hooded. "Doesn't it?"

"Not even a little."

He chuckles for a mere second before he flips over me, his muscular body pushing into the softness of mine. His hand cruises down my torso, dropping to my hip.

"I know you don't like to admit defeat, but, baby…" His fingers slip under my shorts. "Your body's mine now."

"I know when I've lost," I murmur with a moan as two fingers rub over my achy clit.

It's been a week since he so much as touched me this way, and fuck, I've missed him.

His eyes gaze into mine so tenderly, my heart clenches.

"Sometimes we gain even when we've lost." His voice is raw and unbridled.

"And what have I gained?" I ask with a sigh.

His fingers stilling on my core makes me delirious. "Not you, Chiara. I'm the one who gained something, baby, and I'm *never* gonna let her go."

And this time, when his lips fall to mine, for once in my life, I feel free, even when the cage is still all around me.

I sit across from him, staring at his perfectly carved jaw as he picks up a fork, popping a piece of steak into his mouth. After he fucked me with more than just his fingers, he had lunch brought up for us.

Sonia was more than happy to see us together. There's been a knowing smile on her face every time she brings us food.

"Brian," I call out as he continues to eat.

He peers up at me with a beaming smile. "Yes, baby?"

"How long are you going to keep me here?" I ask, needing answers.

The smile vanishes. "Until your father and uncles are dead."

"You're killing all of them?"

He nods once. "Every one of them had a hand in the death of people I care about. So yes. The Palermo name will be no more, if I have anything to do with it."

I feel a twinge of pain for my uncles. I know they're awful people, but a part of me is sad at the thought of them all dying. Even my father, as awful as he is...the finality of his death is deafening. We could've had a good relationship. He could've been the father I needed. But instead, he was nothing more than my warden.

"I'm sorry about what they did." I peer down at my plate, memories of my mom pulling me in. "No one should lose someone they love at the hands of another human being."

He takes a deep sigh, running a hand down his face as I look back at him. "I hate that you're in the middle."

"I've always been put in the middle. Nothing is new. Why do you think he has me working at his club?"

He stares, waiting for me to continue.

"I'm a pawn in his wild kingdom." I laugh bitterly. "That's all I've ever been. He wanted me to run the club to help keep the heat from the feds away from him. He thought I could run the place better, which would make the feds less likely to pull the trigger, so to speak."

"He doesn't deserve you," he says, his tone clipped. "He deserves nothing."

"I know. He's not a good person. Never has been." I pull an exasperated inhale. "I've wanted nothing more than to disappear from his life, but he won't let me go."

"You have an out now, Chiara. I promise. Once this shit with him is done, you're free to go, or..."

"Or, what?" My pulse jumps to my throat, my knee bouncing under the table.

"Stay. I want you to stay here with me." His brows draw closer, his face tightening. "I'd never hold you against your will, but if you want me, then I'm yours."

"I—"

"You don't have to tell me now," he cuts me off. "Take your time."

But I know what I want already. He was never part of my plans, but we never know what we'll find when we accept our life the way it was meant to be lived.

He grins, that dimple deepening with the glint in his eyes. "You're not so bad for the devil's daughter."

"Funny," I laugh. "That's what I call him too."

Then we're laughing together. The kind of laugh that rocks your heart, leaving it fuller than before.

Once we've composed our emotions, I take a sip of my ginger ale. "Can I ask for a favor?"

He lifts a brow. "Depends on what it is."

"I want my phone back."

He shakes his head immediately.

I raise a palm, stopping him before he says something. "I only want to check up on my cousin and my aunt."

"Your cousin is fine."

I jerk my head back. "What do you mean? Do you know her?"

"Chiara, don't—"

I instantly get to my feet, coming around and standing over him. "You'd better tell me what the fuck you know!" I cross my arms over my chest. "And do *not* lie to me."

He smirks. "You're insanely sexy when you're all angry like this."

"I swear, Brian, if you hurt my cousin—"

He grabs me around my hips and pulls me on top of his lap. "She's safe." He lays a palm over my neck. "She's with my brother. He's taking care of her as well as I'm taking care of you." He smiles devilishly.

"What?!" I place both palms against his chest, pushing at him. "Speak. Now."

He cups my chin and pulls me down for a slow kiss. I surrender to that all-consuming power he holds over me.

"We knew about her father arranging a marriage she didn't want," he says against my lips.

I pull back, my jaw slackening, eyes popping wide.

"Now, with my brother's help, she doesn't have to get married."

"I don't understand." My fingers land on each side of my temple. "How's he helping?"

"Let's just say they came up with a mutually beneficial arrangement. She's happy not to get married to that asshole. That's all you need to know."

I glance skeptically at him. None of this makes sense. I know my cousin was desperate to get out of the marriage, but still, I don't understand what deal she could've made. And I can't even ask her. But if being with Brian's brother gives her the escape she needed, then so be it.

"I don't know what the hell you guys have planned for my uncles, but I swear, you'd better be telling the truth when you say she isn't hurt."

"I am, Chiara. We're not in the business of hurting women. I promise you that. She's in no danger with him."

"Fine, but I'll want to speak with her soon." I try to get off his lap, but the steel cage of his arms has me staying in place.

"Okay. You will." He thrusts his hips up. "Are you still mad, baby?"

"Mm-hmm," I fire back with a glare, trying hard not to moan.

"Even better." He stands, flipping me over his shoulder. "I like angry Chiara when I'm inside her."

"If you don't put me down, Brian, you're about to get a lot more than me angry."

He smacks my ass. "Bring it, baby."

DOMINIC

We spent a long, hot shower together with her on her knees sucking my cock like she was punishing me for everything wrong in her life, after which I fucked her bent over, giving it to her just as rough.

I have her draped over my chest, her slick, naked body sinking into mine. My arm curls over her back protectively, wanting to keep her beside me every waking moment.

After what happened with Cain, it's hard to leave her, but tomorrow, I won't have a choice.

"Chiara, we have to talk."

She lifts up her head, worry etched in her gaze. "What's wrong?"

"It's happening tomorrow."

At first she doesn't understand, but as soon as the realization hits, her eyes widen. "Oh."

Tomorrow, I leave her to go and finish the war with her father. One I know we will win. I'm so grateful she gave up his location.

"When?"

"We're getting to the house at midnight."

She hides her face in my shoulder. My hand lands on the back of her head, wanting to stay there permanently.

If I don't make it back alive, I've instructed my lawyer to give her a letter I wrote, explaining who I am and why I never came for her after I ran off when we were kids.

If I do make it out alive, we'll have that talk we never got to have fifteen years ago. I want her to finally look me in the eye when she explains how she could've hurt me the way she did. How she could've betrayed my family, who loved her like she was their own.

I hope like hell she has a good fucking reason. If she doesn't, I don't know what I'll do.

That's assuming she forgives me for all the lies I've told. We're a damn mess. But then again, we always were.

Every day I lie beside her, I fight hard not to think about the past. Because if I do, if I allow myself to go back, I won't want to be anywhere near her. I hate feeling that way.

I've always loved her in one way or another. Now that she's back, that love that's been sitting dormant has festered, except it's deeper now, as only a man can love a woman.

Love doesn't always make sense. It weakens the heart and deepens the soul. And no matter what I do, I can't shut out these feelings.

I want her love in return, even when it makes no sense to want it after every ugly thing standing in our way.

CHIARA

TWENTY-NINE

He left an hour ago, leaving me alone with the darkness and even darker thoughts. I should be comfortable in the embrace of the shadowy void that's been a constant in my life, but I don't feel at home right now. Instead, I'm filled with worry for Brian.

My father has many at his disposal who wouldn't hesitate to kill for him, even when it means their own untimely death.

Every person in his life is nothing but a stepping-stone to his next plan. He cares for no one, and killing Brian, his enemy, would be something he'd take great pleasure in.

Unable to sleep, I slip out of Brian's bed and head for the door. Maybe I can find a late-night snack and watch some TV until he returns. I'll wait all night if I have to.

Opening the door, I find Miles there, guarding me. Brian

insisted.

"Hey. Any word?" I ask, knowing he'd have information if there was any.

"None at this time, ma'am." He shakes his head, his body towering over me. "If I hear anything, I will let you know."

"Thanks. I'm getting something to eat. I'll be back."

He nods as I head for the stairs. When I reach down, I flip the light on, walking aimlessly around the house, passing guard after guard. When I walk by a room that looks like an office, I freeze in place, wondering if it's Brian's office.

Finding no guards in this hallway, I march inside, quietly closing the door behind me before heading for his desk. There's still so much to know about him, so much he won't tell me. I need to know everything before I decide whether I'll stay or go. I open the first drawer, finding nothing but office supplies.

Next, I pull open the larger one below, finding manila folders neatly aligned inside. I take one out, scanning some financial documents for a company called Vendetta Corp. I don't see his name on anything here, but I'll be looking up that company as soon as I have access to the Internet.

I open another file and the same shit. More stuff on the same company.

Come on! Give me your true identity.

I'm running out of time before Miles comes looking for me, knowing Brian will have his head if something happens on his watch.

I check another file, and my heart immediately races. My father's name is written on the side. Opening it with a shaky hand, my skin crawls with tiny ants when I find surveillance photos of not only him, but me too.

There are a ton of photos of me coming out of my house, going to and leaving work, even some of me and my cousin out to lunch. He's the one that's been following me all this time.

Oh my God.

A tremor runs down my spine.

I scan photo after photo, still not having many answers about who this man I've let into my heart is. Closing the file, I start to slip it back, but it won't go in all the way.

"What the hell?" I pull it out, reaching inside to see what's blocking it.

That's when I feel it: something hard and rectangular. And as I take it out, I find a small tape recorder.

A sinking feeling hits my stomach, and I swallow against the thread of anxiety rushing up my throat. I know there's something bad on that tape. I know it has something to do with me. Brian put it all the way on the bottom for a reason. He didn't want anyone to find it.

Clenching it tightly within my palm, I give my furious heartbeats a few moments to calm, but it's no use. The nerves have completely taken over and they won't be going anywhere.

I shut my eyes, pulling in a long, weighty inhale, and press play.

"My, my how far you've come." My father's voice rips through the silence. "I admire that you made yourself into what you are now. A real made man."

"Why the fuck are you calling me, Faro?" Brian asks, his anger evident in the sharp tone.

"You and your brothers have done one hell of a job hiding from me all those years. I couldn't even find you. I gave up looking after three years, and I'm not the type to give up easily. Bravo."

Brian remains silent. If it weren't for the recording, I'd think he hung up.

"I've called to discuss a business proposition," my father continues. "We're both businessmen now, are we not?"

He waits seconds for an answer that never comes.

"I get it. You're still angry over the past, but I think we can come to a mutually beneficial agreement to end all this bloodshed."

"Get to the point, Faro."

"You've destroyed two of my places of business. Killed men I needed. But I'm willing to let it all go, and even throw in something I know you'll want."

My skin crawls. My breathing turns erratic, my heart beating so fast, it may rip through my chest. I don't want to listen anymore. But I do anyway, needing to know everything I can.

"What's that?" Brian asks with complete disinterest.

It takes him only a second to answer. "My daughter. Take her. I know you want to."

My mouth falls open and I stop the recording, tears slamming behind my eyes, some slipping past my defenses.

My father did this to me?

The man who should protect me had me taken by his enemy?

Bile curls in my stomach. I'm going to be sick. A palm falls across my mouth as I continue to listen, tears dripping down my cheeks like a steady rainfall.

"Do whatever you want with her." My father digs my wound in deeper.

"Anything I want?"

"Yes, why not? She'll be your property, but only if you agree to end this battle before it turns into a full-blown war. I don't want you to lose any more of your brothers, Dominic."

"What?" I gasp, the recorder slipping from my fingers, rattling onto the floor with a loud bang.

I hold on to my chest with trembling hands. My lungs explode

with my heavy breathing, disbelief clouding my teary vision.
It can't be. I don't believe it.
It must be a coincidence. The eye color isn't Dom's.
But that can be changed.
He wouldn't. He couldn't.
My body shivers from the icy cold blanket wrapping around the length of me, my pulse pummeling in my ears.

A whimper climbs from the depths of my despair as I lower to the ground to retrieve the recorder. It wobbles in my shaky hands, burning through the pads of my fingers.

I hit rewind, then press play, needing to hear his name again. Wanting to make sure I didn't make it up.

"I don't want you to lose any more of your brothers, Dominic."

I play that part again and again. I play it so many times, I lose count. My chest tightens, my stomach pounding with its own pulse, knotting into the most unbearable pain.

But my heart, it bleeds.

Raw.

Agony.

I hurt everywhere.

If the man who's been with me this entire time is the same boy I once trusted above anyone in the universe, I won't survive the betrayal.

How could he do this? How could he not tell me who he is? How could he accept my father's deal? The same man he knew would hurt me and my mother.

I continue playing the rest of the recording as I openly sob, unable to take two betrayals in one night. At least I always expected one man to hurt me, but I never expected Dom to be the one to break my heart.

"I'm sure you can find lots of things to do with her," my father adds. "But if you don't want her, kill her. Whatever you need to do to get over it."

I sob louder now, the drumming in my tears like battering raindrops on a windowsill.

"You'd let me kill your daughter?" Brian—no, *Dom*—asks.

I don't fucking know who he is anymore.

"I want this over with as soon as possible, so yeah. I can even sweeten the deal."

"How?" Dom asks, the undercurrent of his tone as sharp as the blade he used on Cain.

"If you don't want to kill her yourself, I'm willing to do it for you. My own kid. I'd do that as long as you promise to end it once and for all."

My chin trembles with a heavy onslaught of tears, the back of my nose stinging, unable to take any more of this.

Nausea swirls in my stomach and the need to throw up hits me like an iron fist. I grab a garbage pail beside the chair and hurl into it for a few seconds before I realize nothing is coming out. Snatching a tissue from the box on the desk, I wipe my mouth and toss it into the pail just as Dom continues.

"Give me a day."

Click.

There's nothing else after that.

With a trembling hand, I stuff the recorder back inside and place the file where it was. My entire body shivers, like I'm flailing through freezing waters of hell.

I can't stay in this house another minute. I have to find a way out, but none of these men will let me go. Not unless I find a weapon of my own. They won't want to hurt me. Brian—I mean Dom—would kill them if they dared. I know that much to be true.

Just the thought of him being Dom rips a new hole in my

already bleeding heart.

I fall onto the floor, my body rocking from the heaviness of my sobs, not caring who hears.

A few minutes pass before I'm calm enough to rise, scouring his desk, looking through the other drawers for a weapon. He has to have one here. I open the lower one on the other side, lifting up a stack of files, and before I've given up hope, I find what I've been looking for.

I take out a black handgun, checking the chamber to make sure there are bullets in case I need them. Slipping the weapon into the waistband of my leggings, I conceal it with the oversized t-shirt I have on.

I turn the light off, my pulse still ravaging in my ears, and head back up. When I get there, I head toward my room instead of back to Dom's, needing to pack just a few items for the road.

"Still no word, ma'am," Miles says, anticipating my question.

I nod curtly with a small smile, my heart twisting within my chest. "Thanks for letting me know."

I bet he can tell I've been crying, but I'm sure he'll assume it's because of my worry for Dom.

"I'll be right out. I need to get something."

"I'll be here, ma'am."

I enter the room in a hurry and lock the door.

Dashing toward the closet, I find the duffle Dom used to pack my things. Ripping off some of my clothes from the hangers, I hurriedly stuff them inside, followed by some water bottles and snacks from the fridge.

My heart aches from having found the man I loved as a boy, only to lose him again. A man I've pictured so many times in my head, wondering if he was still alive. Never did I imagine he'd turn into this. Someone who'd strike a deal to harm me. Someone who'd deceive me.

I head for the nightstand, finding a random piece of paper and pen inside. I shouldn't leave a note, but I want to let him know I know. I want him to feel the same way I'm feeling, except it'd never come close.

All this time, I wished for you to call, to write, to find me and take me with you like you promised me long ago. But you've been right here, living a life without me. I can't believe you could hurt me this way, Dom. Your betrayal hurts even worse than my father's.

Did I ever matter? Do you hate me this much? So much so you'd make a deal with him and pretend you're someone I don't know? Why? How could you want to cause me so much pain? I loved you. Don't you know that? Whoever you are now, I don't want to know you. Don't look for me. I never want to see your face again.

I drop the note on my bed, slip into my sneakers, and head for the door. The duffle's hoisted over my shoulder as I take a deep breath, stepping out into the hall, immediately rushing for the stairs.

"Ma'am, where are you going?" Miles asks.

I remove the weapon, pointing it at him.

"Whoa." He raises his hands in the air. "What's going on?"

"Tell him I know. Tell him I'm leaving. Make sure no one here stops me. I am my father's daughter, after all, and I'm not afraid to shoot."

"Okay, let me get my radio from my waistband." He points a finger down. "And I'll let them know. No one will stand in your way. I promise."

"Great. You do that while I head down."

He nods, picking up his radio, giving whoever it is on the other end instructions to allow me to leave the premises.

Rushing down the steps, I make it to the entry door, finding two guards standing on each side.

With my gun pointing at one of them, they stare me down, a grim look on both of their faces before they part and allow me the exit I need.

I don't waste a second, opening the door and running out to freedom. I don't know where I'll go, and I have zero dollars to my name, but I'll figure it out once I'm long gone.

My aunt would be my best bet, but first I'd have to get to her. She lives an hour and a half from here. Maybe I can hitchhike.

Running down his block, the gun once again hidden, I make it to a gate with a security booth, and walk out onto the main road, hoping I can find someone to take me far away from here.

DOMINIC

"Are you sure Faro and his brothers are still at the house?" I ask Miles over the phone as we drive up to Chiara's mother's home, the one Faro is hiding in.

"They were half an hour ago. With the radar, our man was able to detect four people inside."

"Okay. Keep an eye on Chiara. Call me if there's a problem."

"Of course, sir."

I hang up, needing to be done with this once and for all. Being head of security, Miles ran point on logistics, including leading a team to stake out the place. If he says they're there, then I have no doubt bodies will fall tonight.

When we kill Faro and his brothers, whoever is left in their organization will be easy to dispose of. Not that there are many left to destroy.

"After we kill them, we've gotta celebrate at Volt and take a few shots in honor of Pops and Matteo," Enzo says, pulling up his black hoodie. "We've been waiting for this for too long not to get shit-faced properly."

"I don't think Dad would want us remembering him with liquor," Dante adds with a chuckle.

Then we all join in, remembering how much our father hated any and all types of alcohol. We never even saw beer at the house.

All alcohol does is make you weak, Dom. You remember that.

I hear his words clear as day, as though he's right here, but I don't see his face as well anymore. I try hard to remember every detail of my parents, but it's not as loud these days. Their image is fading, and I hate thinking that one day, I may not see them at all. Sometimes, I want to go back in time and find them again, hear their voices, but I'll never get that.

"You assholes watch your back tonight," I tell my brothers.

"We'll be fine," Dante adds. "I have a pretty little thing named Raquel to get back to." He wags his brows.

I shake my head. "You tell her you don't ever plan on divorcing her yet, or are you saving that for the honeymoon?"

"Nah." He grins. "She's going to fall in love with me way before I give her the cold, hard truth. I can't wait to invite her daddy to the wedding tonight before I kill him." He laughs methodically.

"And how's the stripper?" I ask Enzo.

"Difficult." He clenches his jaw. "Feisty as hell too." A smile spreads on his face. "Just the way I like 'em."

Dante grips his shoulder and snickers. "You're so used to them falling at your feet. Poor boy, found himself a real hard one to crack."

"She'll crack, don't worry. And if not, I'll make her."

"Sir," Roger calls out from the driver's seat. "We're going to be there in one minute."

I nod, turning back to my brothers, our expressions now serious. "We're going to kill fast, then burn down the fucking place. No one get creative. Got it?"

"You've gotta let me have a little fun," Dante throws in as the van stops.

I glare at him with a warning, and he laughs in response. Dante likes to find sadistic ways to hurt our enemy. As much as I admire that, I don't want the risk. I don't plan on losing any more of my brothers.

A spasm shoots right into my rib cage as I remember Matteo, the bronze-skinned, brown-haired boy with eyes as big as saucers. He was a beautiful kid with the sweetest demeanor. He'd never hurt a soul. He once found an ant in the house and begged my father to let it go. That's who he was, and who he would've been if Faro hadn't killed him.

The rage fuels my depravity, feeding my blood with adrenaline, powerful enough to break the neck of every man inside that house.

"All right. Let's do this," I say, opening the door, jumping out once we arrive at our spot, with my brothers and Roger following.

We've got one of our SUVs behind us, carrying six of our men, ten of us in total. We shouldn't need more than that to kill the four of them and anyone else they have there.

Collectively, we march toward the house, shrouded in darkness, sitting on probably two acres of property. There is not a home in sight within a two-mile radius. We have that to our advantage.

I have some of my men positioned in the front while the rest are following me to the back.

Once we're there, I peer through the window, not seeing a

thing. The inside is pitch black. Roger scans the first floor of the two-story colonial home with the motion detection radar.

He shakes his head, indicated no movement on the first floor. But they may be upstairs.

I gesture with a hand, indicating that we're moving in.

Roger pulls out a small, thin screwdriver and begins to pick the lock. Five seconds later, I'm opening the door, gun in hand, walking inside with the rest of the team behind me.

They all take their positions, two at the front, my brothers and Roger going up the stairs with me.

Our boots thud against the wooden steps, and once we reach the hallway, we find it quiet.

Too quiet.

They aren't here, Dante mouths behind me.

And I have an eerie suspicion that he's right. How is that possible if they were here only thirty minutes ago? How did they know we'd be here? Someone had to have tipped them off.

"Check in every room," I demand.

They do as they're told, running into every room in the house.

"Not a damn person here, Dom," Enzo shouts from across the hall. "They fucking knew. Who the hell told them?"

I push open the door to another room, finding it empty too. As I rush inside, I notice a note on the bed, written in red. Lifting it up, I read it.

I know she told you I'd be here, but it was a test my darling daughter failed. You'll always be a step behind, Cavaleri. Tell Chiara she's as good as dead. I have no use for her now.

I ball the paper in my hand, clutching it as I growl, tossing it against the wall. Getting out my cell, I call Miles.

We have a mole. One of my men is compromised, that's how Faro knew we'd be here. Miles is going to help me find out who the hell it is, and when I find do, I'll string him up by his balls.

I dial Miles, but all it does is ring. I call again. No answer.

What the hell is going on?

Then it hits me.

Faro could be at the house right now.

I run out of the room, my heart pounding. He won't take her from me. I can't let that happen.

"We've gotta go!" I yell. "Now! They're probably at the house."

"Shit," Enzo mutters as he and Dante take two steps down at a time, urging the men below to return to the van.

Once we're all inside, Roger guns the engine, taking us on the road. It's only a twenty-minute drive for normal people but I have no time to worry about cops. I make Roger drive as fast as he can.

I take out my cell and dial Leo's number, who's also stationed at the house. If he doesn't pick up either, I know we're in trouble.

"Boss." His voice is calm, not like that of a man who's busy battling.

"Is everything okay there? Did Faro or his men show up?"

"No, but we have a serious issue, and you don't sound like you're aware."

My pulse slows to almost nothing.

"Aware of what?" I hiss.

"Chiara left, sir." I instantly grow cold. "Miles said he called you."

An invisible fist slams into my chest, my breaths stilling in my lungs.

It can't be.

"Who let her out?" I ask, my voice a calm before the storm.

"She found a gun in your office, sir, and threatened Miles with it. She told him something about knowing everything and took off. Miles said you wouldn't want us putting our hands on her and told us to let her go."

"Fuck!" I scream as all eyes turn to me. "Where is Miles now?"

"He went after her a few minutes after she left."

"If he calls you, tell him to call me. You got it?"

"What's going on?"

I can't tell him I suspect a mole, or that I think the mole is the man I trusted most.

"Keep your eyes open. And call me if you hear anything about Chiara or Miles."

"Of co—"

I kill the line before he finishes.

Miles was right. I probably would've told them to let her go so there was no risk to her well-being from an accidental bullet.

But now that I know her father means to kill her for snitching, I would've told them to fucking pepper-spray her if that was what I needed to do to keep her alive.

But if Miles is the mole, if he went after her, what the hell does that mean?

Dread poisons my thoughts. Maybe he couldn't reach me. Maybe he wanted to get her back. I can't assume the worst. He's never done shit to lose my trust until now.

Then another realization hits.

She knows who I am now. That has to be what she meant. If she was in my office, she must've found the tape I kept hidden.

I never wanted her to find out who I am this way. Does she realize that the only reason I took her was to protect her from her father? I had to take her so he couldn't kill her, and I know he would've.

I was going to set her free once they were all dead, but all that went to shit the moment we spoke at the club. I know that now. The attraction, the pull…it was all there taunting me, and I took the bait.

Now, I might lose her for good before I can tell her how much she means to me. How much I love her. How much I never stopped.

CHIARA

THIRTY

My pulse is trapped in my throat, anger and fear fighting for first place inside my heart.

I don't know how long I've walked down the dimly lit two-way road, but it's been at least a mile and I've yet to see a single car. Not surprising, since it's probably past one a.m. already.

I need someone to show up before Dom comes after me. I can't stand the thought of being anywhere near him.

He's worse than my father. At least I knew where my father stood with me. Sure, maybe I didn't know he was planning on offing me, but I did know he never loved me.

But Dom was different, or at least he used to be. I guess things have changed. I guess some things aren't meant to last. He managed to ruin every good memory I had of him, and instead of finding me and making new ones, he ripped our future from the ground and watched it shrivel up and die.

Holding on to the strap of my duffle, I continue on my path, about to give up hope of ever finding a ride, when a pair of bright headlights appears behind me, illuminating the entire street.

I stop, frantically waving my hands and jumping up and down from the side of the road.

The car slows while it's still yards away, the lights blinding me.

"Hey! Please stop!" I shout, my pulse quickening.

Finally, the lights flicker off, and thanks to the nearest lamppost, I make out the black sedan.

My heart lurches in my chest. My stomach tightens with knots. *What if whoever is inside isn't here to help me at all?*

I'm no longer excited, my legs held down by cement. My heart races so fast, I can no longer catch my breath. I grip the gun still at my waistband, getting ready to shoot.

The window starts to roll down.

"Hey, miss," says a woman's voice. "Do you need help?"

A whoosh of a breath pours from my lungs, and I crouch a little, dropping my palms to my knees with relief.

After I compose myself, I run toward the passenger side, finding a blonde-haired woman, probably in her early fifties.

"Yes, please," I beg.

"Sure thing. Where are you going?"

"Anywhere but here."

"You're not gonna kill me, are you?" she asks with a lighthearted laugh.

"I don't think so?" I giggle nervously.

"All right, young lady. I'm Laura. Hop in."

"I'm Chiara. Thank you!" I open the door and rush inside, and then we're off as I fasten the seat belt.

"You running from someone?" she asks, passing side-long

glances at me while juggling to keep her eyes on the road.

"Kind of." I don't want to tell her too much in case she gets afraid and kicks me out of the car.

"Well, I'm heading to the city, so hopefully that's far enough," she says, the sides of her eyes crinkling as she gets the words out. "I had my son's engagement party tonight, lucky for you. It's usually dead here at this time of night."

"I know," I scoff. "I was walking a while before you found me."

"Good thing, too." She exhales loudly. "Lord knows what kind of creep you could've met at this ungodly hour."

I nod in agreement. "Would it be okay if I used your cell to call my aunt?"

"Of course you can." She gestures with her head toward the cup holder. "Grab it. The code is seven five seven five."

"You're an angel. Thank you."

"My pleasure."

I quickly pick up the phone, unlock the code, and dial my aunt's number.

She doesn't answer.

"Fuck!" I spit out, then am immediately embarrassed to curse in front of a stranger who probably already thinks I'm insane. "Sorry."

"Shit, honey. I say way worse things than that." She chuckles, her shoulders bopping up and down a little. "Did she not answer?"

I shake my head with disappointment.

"Why not text her and say it's you? Worth a try."

"You're right."

I do as she suggested and wait a minute before calling back, and this time, I hear my aunt's voice.

"Chiara? Oh my God! I've been worried sick after I couldn't

reach you at work!"

"I'm okay. Kind of. Can I come to you? I don't have anywhere else to go. I'll explain everything when I get there."

"I'm home, waiting. You don't know how scared I've been. I thought your father hurt you. I was ready to call the police."

"I'm glad you didn't. He'd definitely come after you." I release a burdened sigh.

"Let that bastard come." Her tone is as rough as sandpaper.

"I'm about an hour or so away," I explain. "If you need to reach me, call this phone."

"I love you, sweetheart. We'll run together if we have to." Her voice breaks. "I won't lose you too."

"You won't. I love you. I'll see you soon."

"Okay." She sounds more composed now.

I hang up, placing the phone back where I took it from.

"You two sound close," Laura remarks.

"We are. We only have each other." There's pain riddled in my words.

She nods in understanding. "It's good to have that one person you can count on. Sounds like she's that for you."

"She's the best."

I love my aunt, but I'd do anything to have my mother back. To feel her arms around me. To hear her voice. Without her, there'll always be a piece of me missing.

We continue on the road at a comfortable speed when suddenly headlights jump behind us, a car speeding its way closer. Laura looks in her review mirror while I turn my head, wondering where the hell this car came from.

"That person sure is in a hurry, ain't he?"

"Yeah," I laugh nervously, my pulse back to a frantic pace.

The tires of the car screech as it makes its way closer until maybe a car's length separates us. I find it hard to breathe, my chest tingling, stomach rolling inward.

"I'm going to move out of the way so this idiot can go past us."

"Okay," I mumble, my throat going dry. My wild heartbeats thrash in my ears, my fingers trembling.

Could it be Dominic? My dad? Maybe it's a crazy driver? Let's hope that's it.

But my gut's screaming that we're in danger.

They're here for you. To kill you. You're dead already. You were dead from the moment you were born.

Laura signals and moves to the right, and the car follows.

Fuck!

"Let me out," I quickly tell her, my voice a shrill. "You don't need to be in the middle of this."

"This about you?" Her brows knit tight, her eyes still on the road.

"I think so, but I don't want to wait to find out." I grip the handle of the door, yanking it. "Stop and let me out right now."

She only increases her speed. "Absolutely not. I'm not leaving you for some psycho. I'd never be able to live with myself."

"Please! You don't understand the people I'm running from." Tears well up in my eyes. "They'll kill you."

She frowns as she glances at me, the battle weighing heavy in her gaze. This stranger owes me nothing. Why should she pay for my problems?

The car gets closer now, driving at a higher speed.

"No." She shakes her head, her lips in a tight line. "I won't do it."

My vision dims, my head spinning. I don't want to be the reason she's taken from her family.

The car zooms closer as Laura peers up at the mirror again. I can see the worry on her face. Why is she doing this?

"It's not too late!" I urge her. "Let me out!"

But before she has a chance to respond, the vehicle is beside me. I turn to stare at the passenger, and relief washes over me.

It's Miles.

I roll down my window. "What are you doing, Miles? Tell Dominic I don't want to see him. Go! You scared the shit out of me."

His eyes hold mine as he continues to drive, and there's nothing friendly within them.

They're empty.

Cold.

He must be pissed about my pointing the gun at him. His dark blue sedan continues to keep pace with us.

"What the hell is wrong with that guy?" Laura asks, and when I turn to her, I find her eyes staring at my window, gaze widened in horror. "Look out, Chia—"

Boom.

Her words die with the scream ripping out from her or maybe from me.

There's pain on the right side of my body from the force of our car being hit, causing the vehicle to roll over multiple times at high velocity, our screams piercing through the night until the car stops abruptly with a bang on its hood.

I tremble, my entire body shuddering.

"La-Laura? You okay?" I stammer with a cry, finding her still in her seat, groaning in pain.

There's blood coming out from her forehead, but it doesn't seem deep.

"It's going to be okay. I—I'll get us help." My shaky hand lands on the seat belt as I press to release it, but the damn thing doesn't budge. "Come on. Don't do this to me. Please work."

I press the button repeatedly, until it finally gives way and slides out.

My hand lands on the door, adrenaline filling me as I push it with all my might. Heavy pants roll out of my chest as it flies open.

Yes! I think to myself

But it's short-lived. Rough hands grab me, and the next thing I know, I'm being dragged out roughly by my legs. I glance up to find Miles, his eyes evading mine. My head wobbles against the hard concrete as he continues to pull.

"What the hell are you doing?! You almost killed us!"

"Shut up," he growls, no kindness in his brown eyes as he finally looks at me. He picks me up by my armpits. "Walk."

He pushes me between my shoulder blades as terror fills me. He isn't the guy he appeared to be back at the mansion.

Why is he doing this? Did Dominic order him to hurt me?

I keep moving toward his sedan, my hip aching from the car accident he caused. "Why are you doing this? Where are you taking me?"

He ignores my questions, opening the door to the back and shoving me inside. Instead of getting into the driver's side, he locks all the doors and moves to the trunk. I follow his every movement, my pulse beating loudly in my ears. The trunk opens, then a few seconds later he slams it shut, holding a red canister.

What the hell?

He marches back to Laura's car, and part of me hopes he'll get her out too, but instead he's opening the cap of the canister and pouring the liquid all around.

"No!" I shout, gripping the handle, pushing, pulling, hitting the window with my other hand, desperate to get to Laura. "Don't hurt her, you son of a bitch!"

I bang on the window, my palm stinging from the repeated blows. But I'm too late. He's walking back to his car just as the flames start, slow at first, and then, as though out of nowhere, they light up the sky with angry orange and red sparks.

"*Nooo!*" I shriek, sobbing, my palm planted against the cool window. "I'm sorry! I'm so sorry!"

He gets inside, turns on the ignition, sending the car rolling back down the road. Laura's burning car gets smaller as he drives away. A stabbing pain hits the center of my chest.

"How could you do this?" I scream out with tears etched in my voice. "She was an innocent person! A mother!"

His eyes meet mine through the rearview mirror.

"Call Dom right now," I demand. "I want to hear him tell me he ordered this."

He laughs, frosty and sinister. "Dominic? You're not going to see him anymore."

My entire body's swallowed up by fear. "What the hell are you talking about? Where—where are you taking me?"

But even before I ask, even before those words leave my mouth, I know the answer.

"Your father. He's demanded your presence. And he doesn't like to wait. Now shut up and go to sleep."

Then he stops the car momentarily, takes out his handgun, and whips it hard on the side of my head until everything goes dark.

CHIARA

THIRTY-ONE

My eyes pry awake, and my body tries to follow suit, but the headache at my left temple makes it harder. Confusion settles in the depths of my cluttered mind, and as I try to lift a hand to rub my eyes, I can't move my arm.

What the…?

I pull my wrist, then the other, causing my shoulders to ache. When I yank again, something cuts into my wrists and the realization hits: I'm tied up.

Again.

Fighting through the heaviness in my eyelids, I come to find myself sitting on a chair in a large, slightly darkened room, my arms twisted backward, bound behind me.

I can't tell where I am, but it's eerily cold, devoid of life. It doesn't feel like I'm in someone's house.

"Hello?" I whisper, my voice scratchy. "Where the hell are you, *Daddy*? What is this?"

Pounding footsteps crash against the floor.

Looming closer...and closer.

A chill runs up my arms, dread filling the crevice of my mind, taunting me with awful thoughts.

The fact that my father could do this to me should not shock me, yet it does. On some subconscious level, I'm still a girl who wants her daddy's love.

"So nice to see you again, my darling daughter." My father's tone drips in bitterness.

My vision is a little blurry, but I can make out his figure in the shadowy darkness, marching over to where I helplessly sit.

"What the hell are you doing?" I spit out. "What kind of father does this to his child?"

His laugh is cold and conniving, crawling over my skin like a snake readying itself for a bite.

"Ah, I'm your father now, am I?" In the hollowness of the room, he sounds like he's talking through a speaker. "Was I your father when you betrayed me by giving that scum my location, or at the least the location you assumed I'd be at?"

How the hell did he know it was me? Dom promised he'd never say anything. It had to be Miles.

Regardless of who he pretended to be, I refuse to believe Dom would purposely put me in harm's way by telling my father something he swore he wouldn't. The man I slept with truly cared for me. I felt it when he touched me, when his lips worshiped me. It was real.

"Yes, Chiara. I know everything." He takes a few more steps forward and turns on a light above me, shining brightly over my eyes. I see him better now, his loafers almost touching my feet. "You're no daughter of mine. You showed your loyalty."

My brows twist with vile disdain.

He snickers. "I knew you were listening to my conversation when you came by the house. I intended for you to hear every word, wanting to see what you'd do with it once Dom took you like I suspected he would."

"You don't deserve my loyalty. You never did." Balling my fists, I contain the anger wasting away my very heart. "I heard what you said. He recorded you when you told him to kill me, promising to do it yourself if you had to."

I spit at his shoes. Before I can say another word, his palm connects harshly against my cheek, my skin flaming with searing pain.

"You're a fucking whore, like your mother was. Betraying me like she did." He lowers his face to mine, his hand snaking up, his fingers squeezing my neck until I can't breathe.

My eyes bulge. My chest tightens with agonizing pain, my fingers scraping at nothing but air. "Do you know how much worse it is that you betrayed me to *that* family?"

He drops his hand and my chest heaves with hurried breaths, clawing for every ounce of air I can draw into my lungs.

"My mother wasn't..."

Inhale. Exhale. Breathe.

"She wasn't a whore, you asshole!" I say, my words marred with vitriol.

"She *was* a fucking whore. That's why I killed her."

My eyes bulge as violent tremors rock my entire body, tears swelling, collapsing down my face.

"No," I cry with a shaky voice, squeezing my eyes shut for a moment from the room now spinning, my tone betraying all the confidence I had moments before. "Why? How could you take her from me?"

He pulls a chair and places it before me, sitting down.

"She never told you what she was planning with *him*, did she?"

"What the hell are you talking about?" I sniffle.

He laughs, and it's one of those purely evil ones.

"You may have been sneaking around with the baker's son, but your mother was all about the baker."

My head tips to the side, a fluttery, heavy feeling filling the pit of my stomach.

"Don't look so surprised." He leans back in the chair, all smug. "I knew everything she was doing, what *you* were doing, going to that bakery to see that boy. I only let you continue because I knew soon enough he'd be gone from your life."

"What the hell do you mean, gone?"

"You see, when I found out your mother was telling Dominic's father our personal business and getting his help to run away, I set out a plan to kill her and kill Francesco's entire family."

I suck in a rough breath, my body breaking out in a tremor, tingles forming over every inch of my skin.

"How could you want to kill innocent children? Wha-what is wrong with you?" I stammer with shattered words.

"Blame your slut mother!" he bellows. "It wasn't good enough to spill our secrets, but she decided to fuck him too. Placing a bug in her handbag was the best thing I did. I'd hear every word, every time they were together in the back of his bakery. The whore couldn't fuck him anywhere else." His chuckle slithers up my arms like a creepy snake. "Can you imagine going from me to that lowlife?"

His features bend with revulsion, as though he really thinks he's better than Francesco.

"You didn't let her do anything! She was a prisoner! I'm glad she had someone to spend her time with instead of the likes of you."

"You little bitch!" His palm hits me harder than the undercurrent of his tone.

"I feel sorry for you." I grit my teeth. "You're not even human. Hell, you're not even an animal. You're something worse."

And then it hits me... He must've killed someone from Dominic's family. This is what this whole thing is about. Oh, my God...

"What have you done?" I whisper. "Who did you kill other than..."

It's hard to get the word out, too painful to say out loud.

"Other than your slut mother? None other than Francesco himself, but not before I put a bullet into his little Matteo."

A heavy pounding of tears wells into my eyes.

"No!" I scream, my heart squeezing tight under the imaginary weight of his fist. "No, no, no." The heavy sobs wreck me, my shoulders shaking. "You didn't. Not that sweet baby."

"Don't worry. I made it quick." A callous smile crosses his face.

Nausea churns in my stomach and I try hard to keep it down. No wonder Dominic is so desperate to kill them all. The urge to do it myself rises from the depths of my grief.

"Your uncle Agnelo was more than willing to off them both, but I needed to be the one to pull the trigger. I needed Francesco to know I, Faro Bianchi, was the one who took his son away, and if it weren't for Dominic and the other boys running away, I would've killed them too."

I cry violently, not caring how weak it makes me in front of this demon.

"But at least before his death..." he continues, ignoring my tears. "Francesco thought all his sons would die. He had no reason to doubt me, considering one of his sons was bleeding before his eyes."

My uncle Agnelo is as evil as my father. They all are, really, but he lacks the same humanity my father lacks. The older I got, the more I saw it. His daughter, Aida, might as well be a stranger to Raquel and me. We never saw her growing up, except at family functions. She didn't even go to school with us. He had her homeschooled. I often wanted to find a way to speak to her in private, but I never did. I was afraid her father would find out and get angry at her because of me.

"There's something not right with you," I tell my father with a shaky breath.

"Shut your damn mouth!" He rises to his feet. "You don't speak to me that way!"

His jaw clenches, teeth baring before he reaches into his pocket and takes out his cell. He moves back a step and starts typing.

He glances up at me through narrowed slits of his eyes. "You, my daughter, are as good as dead. Your betrayal is the final nail on your coffin. And Dominic will watch you fall before I kill him, just like your mother did, seeing her lover dead." His mouth curls into a sneer. "It's kind of poetic, isn't it?"

"No! I won't let you hurt him!" I pull on my binds, rattling the chair, trying to find a way to loosen my hands, but it's too tight.

He reaches his other hand behind him and pulls out a handgun, pointing it right at me, his glare as deadly as the weapon.

"What do you think you're gonna do about it?"

DOMINIC

"Find her!"

I slam my fist against the desk, shattering the decanter full of whiskey in the process. I watch as the honey-colored liquid drips onto the floor, the glass scattered across my desk in large fragments.

"We looked everywhere for both Chiara and Miles, but—"

"There's no *but*!" I explode at Enzo. "You find them."

He stands from the leather armchair in my office, clasping me on the shoulder.

When I look up, the icy glare I know that's smeared on my face has him sitting back down.

It's been hours, and there's not even a hint of where she could be. Miles would've found a way to call by now. He's either dead or he's been working for Faro all along. The mere thought has me seething, the rage twisting in my gut like a blade.

If he hurt Chiara, I will end him myself. I'll enjoy hearing his screams right along with Faro's as I burn both of their bodies to the very ground.

And if she's dead, if *I* did this to her, I'll put a bullet in my own brain. If it wasn't for my lies, she'd still be here with me, under my fucking protection.

When I found her note, I read it so many times, the words blurred into one another.

Her pain oozed through each letter. I feel it in my heart still. My pulse grips around my throat, the sharp pain radiating down my arm.

Picking up a large piece of glass with my other hand, I run the pads of my fingers across the sharp edges, staring at the note still beside me. My body turns rigid, and I grit my teeth so hard my jaw throbs. I ignore my brothers. I ignore all the noise in my head, focusing on every sentence she wrote.

"Fuck, he's bleeding!" Dante shouts. "Get a towel from the

bathroom."

Glancing down at my hand, I find a clenched fist with the same piece of glass within it, droplets of blood leaking down like a faucet.

Shit, I got blood on her letter.

I open a drawer and place the note inside so I never forget how much pain I caused her.

"I'm fine," I mutter as Enzo throws a towel at me.

"You're not. Get the fuck up. Raquel is gonna stitch you up."

"I said I'm fine!" I unclench my fist, removing the red-stained shard and placing it on the desk.

It's definitely a deep wound, but I feel no pain. If it's there, I'm immune. The worry for Chiara is too great to let something like a cut bother me. I wrap the towel around my hand to appease my brothers.

"Listen, asshole, you may be older by nanoseconds—"

"A year," I correct Dante.

He chuckles. "Whatever you say, old man. I don't care how much older you are, you're going. Now, get up, or I'm bringing her here."

I release an exasperated breath, not wanting the back-and-forth I know is coming. He's as stubborn as me.

"Fine, make it quick. I can't sit here and not try to find her myself. After Raquel is done, I'm gone."

At first, I wanted to wait at home in case she showed up, but that hope has died.

I rise to my feet with Dante behind me, both of us heading out the front door.

"This is ridiculous. You know that, right?" I tell him.

We cross the street to his place and he takes out his keys as we get to the door.

"Stop crying and get your hand fixed, dumbass. You want that shit spilling blood while you take care of Faro and that fucker Miles? You know he's involved, right?"

I hate when he makes sense. But I highly doubt a bunch of stitches will hold my hand together with the brutal force I'll enact on everyone who hurt my girl.

He unlocks the door. "Honey, I'm home."

"I'm not your damn honey," says a feisty black-haired woman, who resembles Chiara.

They might as well be sisters, especially with those attitudes. Her face curls with a grimace as Dante grins, draping an arm around her shoulders from the side.

"Are you sure about that? Because you taste so sweet, especially when—ouch!" he chuckles as her elbow lands square into his ribs.

She steels her glare, huffing in response.

"My wife has a mean streak," Dante adds without taking his eyes off her. "And I like it."

The humor is gone, and from the way he looks at her, I feel like I'm interfering.

"I told you not to call me that," she whispers, her eyes glued to his.

"But you *are* my wife, whether you like it or not, until the papers say otherwise. And I don't remember agreeing to your demand anyway..." He leans into her ear, but I can hear every damn word. "...while I had my tongue deep inside that pretty pussy."

Her cheeks flush as her eyes land to mine, clearly embarrassed, but unable to handle my brother's charm.

"Sorry to cut this short," I say. "But can she fix this shit so I can go?"

She finally sees my hand, slipping out of Dante's arm.

"Oh, that's my older brother," Dante explains. "He's a dumbass who cut his hand and won't go to the doctor."

"What happened?" she asks, her brows pinching tight. The concerned doctor mode is clearly on as she picks up my hand, removing the towel to examine the cut.

"Had too much fun with a piece of glass," I grumble, hating being taken care of.

I'm not used to it. I've been alone for so long, taking care of my brothers, that this type of shit irritates the fuck out of me.

She scoffs. "Remind me not to engage in your version of fun."

"Last time I checked…" Dante cuts in. "You like a little pain with a little pleasure."

"Shut up, Dante," she and I say in unison.

He chuckles, arms raised in defeat. Unlike me with Chiara, he had no reason to lie to her about his name. She doesn't know who the hell he is.

She turns to him. "I need all my supplies and a room to work in." Her tone's professionally demanding.

"Yes, ma'am." He salutes her. "The kitchen has good lighting."

"Okay, let's go."

We move there, and Dante brings a black leather bag from upstairs.

She gets right to work, taking out all kinds of crap from inside it, opening a bottle of saline.

"This might hurt," she warns before pouring it over my wound above the sink basin.

"It's fine. Do what you have to do as fast as you can."

"In a hurry?" She peers up in between cleaning the cut.

She doesn't know anything about Chiara. As far as she's concerned, Chiara is still working at the club, safe in her home every night.

"Yeah. Have some business to take care of, and I need to do it now."

"All right. Well, you definitely need stitches, so I'm going to shoot you up with some lidocaine. The pain shouldn't be bad at all after that."

She removes a long, thin syringe and sticks me with it. Once it's all in, she gives it a few minutes to take effect, then flicks my palm.

"Do you feel that?"

"No."

"Great." She removes a curved needle-looking thing, but I glance away, staring at the wall, my mind on Chiara.

She could be lying somewhere half-dead, crying for help, and I'm over here getting a cut closed like a pussy.

"How long will this take?" I tap my foot against the black stool.

"One more stitch, and…there."

"Can I go now?" I yank my hand away.

"Geez, you're really impatient." She slides her brows up, lines etching her forehead. "I need to wrap the wound first, or you may find yourself bleeding again."

I begrudgingly lay the top of my hand on the cold granite.

She sneers, her lips tight. "You're not doing me a favor here. You know that, right?"

Raquel begins wrapping my hand with gauze.

"Yeah, yeah. Thanks and all that shit." My lips turn up into a sort-of smile.

"I see your language is just as bad as your brother's." She grins.

Dante laughs. "Isn't she the best?"

He comes around to her side and kisses her temple.

"Stop distracting me, you idiot." She continues to cover my gash, adding medical tape once she's done.

"I especially love when she calls me names. Payback is always that much sweeter, isn't it, wifey?"

"You're done," she says, ignoring him. "You can go now."

I practically jump out of the seat. "I'm out of here."

"Obviously, I'm coming with you," Dante says.

"So let's go."

"I will, just have one thing to do before we leave."

"What's that?" I give him a death stare, growing impatient.

"This." He grabs her face, a palm landing on the back of her neck before his mouth falls over hers.

I shake my head at the display. He's really making a show of this.

"I'm leaving," I tell him, turning away and heading out the kitchen.

I hear him mutter something to her, but I'm too far now to hear it. Seconds later, his sneakers are trudging behind me.

"Are you finally done?" I ask, pulling the door open.

"My woman needs a lot of convincing where I'm concerned. A man's gotta do what a man's gotta do. She isn't leaving me, and I'd rather her stay willingly instead of hearing me demand it. I don't want her to hate me."

"And she won't hate you once she realizes you're going to kill her father?"

"She'll understand."

"Sure, she will." I'm being a dick, I know that, but I'm in a bad headspace right now.

As I reach my house, my burner vibrates in my pocket. I stop short, pulling it out, causing Dante to stop short.

"Is it him?" he asks as I retrieve my phone, finding a number I don't recognize.

I stare at him, anxiety shooting up my neck before I press a button. "Who's this?"

"Is that how you treat your friends?" Faro's vile voice wraps around my throat, my pulse quickening to an unnatural pace.

"Where the fuck is she? I swear, if you killed her—"

"What will you do, hmm?"

He waits for my answer as my exhales turn wildly ferocious.

"Yeah, that's right." He chuckles. "You'll do nothing."

"Tell me where she is." My voice is low, every syllable punctured with a threat.

"Dom!" she screams. "Don't come for me! He'll kill you. He has people all—"

A loud thud erupts through the phone, and then I hear her cry.

"Faro, you fucking coward!" My voice thunders, my palms tingling, my heartbeats slamming in my temples. "I'll slice off every limb on your body and feed it to your fucking dogs. You're already dead."

"Really? Because I'm still alive. And always a step ahead, aren't I? You didn't even know I had my man with you the entire time, playing you like a fool." He takes a deep, casual breath. "It's pathetic how easily I deceived you. But I've waited for this very moment. Waited for the look on your face when I took her from you like I took your father and brother."

Rage pulses to a beat of its own, my hand squeezing the phone until my palm stings, reminding me of the gash. But I only squeeze harder, wishing it were Miles's neck.

"You want her?" Faro asks, carving through the wrath filling the marrow of my bones. "Then come and get her. I'll even let you say goodbye before I put a bullet in her brain."

Chiara sobs, and my heart clenches.

I'm coming, baby.

"Tell me where, you son of a bitch," I spit out, my hand rattling around the cell.

I hear a ding come through the line. Lifting the phone away from my ear, I find an address.

"I'm coming for you. You're a dead man."

"Good lu —"

I cut the line, stuffing the phone back into my pocket.

"Let's get the men ready. All of them. We're going to war."

DOMINIC

THIRTY - TWO

My men and I arrive at a warehouse. The white, unassuming building stands high, covering a lot of ground. There is not a single window present. Just one blue door.

One fucking door is what's keeping me from tearing his fucking head off. I hope Miles is with him so I can kill them both.

If his brothers aren't with him, I'll find them next, and I'll give them the same fate. After all, they stood and watched my father and brother die. That was the very last time I ran from the Bianchis. It's ironic that now, they're running from me.

Leading the team, I gesture for them to move in, all thirty of them, with more waiting in the van. All of us strapped with vests and more firepower than we could ever need.

One, I mouth, lifting a finger.

Two.

Three.

My other hand is on the door handle, turning it slow, before I swing it open into a barely lit room, weapon at the ready.

Pop.

A bullet whizzes past my head as soon as I march in, hitting the metal wall at the back of me.

My men all storm inside. Then all hell breaks loose.

Bullets fly from all around. I can no longer tell which one belongs to which person. His men are everywhere, on the first level and the second.

From the corner of my eye, I see Dante smashing the butt of his gun on the head of one man before firing shots above at some others.

Carnage spills onto the floor, body after body of Faro's men fall like poorly orchestrated domino pieces.

Someone hits me on the back of my head, not strong enough to cause me to fall, but enough to piss me off. I veer, kicking the man on his kneecap.

A scream rips out of him, and I stomp on his ankle.

"You chose to work for the devil on earth. Now meet the one in Hell."

Pop.

The fight in him is gone as blood oozes from the center of his chest.

Another one comes at me, hitting me right in my vest, but I brush it off. When he realizes he hasn't hurt me, his eyes widen as I lift the gun, firing twice into the chest.

I find Enzo rolling on the ground, shooting bullets at two men as they fire back. They don't even see me coming, my pulse pounding in my ears, not with fear, but with the need for vengeance filling my veins.

Pop. Pop.

One dead.

Pop. The other one hits the floor.

Enzo stands, shock riddling his face. "Shit, man. You're on a fucking roll."

The sound of bullets seems to have stopped, and I look around, finding over twenty of his men lying on the floor.

"How we doing?" I ask my guys.

"Good, boss," Roger says, appearing beside me. "Considering."

"Who's hurt?"

"Dwayne has a wound on his arm, and Vinny has one on his calf. One of the guys brought them out to the van. They've been replaced by two others and are being taken to Ricky."

"Good. That's good."

I'm glad Roger got them out of here. They've got kids. I'm sure Ricky will patch them up nicely. He's a vet we use for shit like this, someone Tomás knew. Ricky was once a surgeon resident who gave it up after his wife was killed. Decided to be a vet instead. I'm sorry about his wife, but I'm not sorry he chose a different path. His hands are gifted. He helps us as a favor to Tomás.

I gaze up at the second level railing. "Faro, you motherfucker, show your face. Let's end this once and for all. Just you and me."

There's quiet at first...until a rattling sound jumps at the silence.

"I know you're there, you piece of shit. What happened? Too scared of me now, old man?"

Deep, maddening laughter resonates through the space.

Beside me, my brothers point their weapons up, waiting for a man who destroyed our family. I hold out a hand, telling them to stand down.

"He's mine."

I know Faro won't shoot right now. He likes to toy with people before he kills them.

I see a shadow approach above us, footsteps stomping across the bare floor.

"Dominic. So nice of you to come. Tea? Coffee? Blood?"

I see his face: older, yet still carrying the same cruelty it did then.

He scans our faces. "And you got your band of brothers beside you." His brows rise. "It brings a tear to my eye to know Matteo will never join you."

Dante sucks in a breath. Enzo grunts, his tone sinister.

I take a step forward.

"Don't mention his name again!" I warn with a roar, my chest rising and falling from the weight of my immense fury.

"Still sensitive, I see."

I take another step, wanting to run up there and throw him off the ledge and watch his neck crack in half.

"Where is she?" I demand.

"You know what your problem is?" he asks, lifting a hand with his own gun in his palm. "You care too much."

"This is getting boring," Dante cuts in. "Let's kill him and be done with it."

"Which one are you?" Faro asks with a sneer. "The dummy or the smaller dummy?"

"Dom, you gotta let me shoot him," Enzo says behind me, loud enough for Faro to hear. "You can kill him. But I need to make that cocksucker scream before you end him."

"You'll get your turn. We all will." I glare at Faro's smug face. "We deserve that much."

"You never deserved a goddamn thing! Filth, all of you, especially that father of yours."

Dante growls, rushing for the stairs, but I run faster, gripping his body with an arm around his chest, keeping him restrained.

"You don't talk about my father," Dante snaps. "I'm going to fucking kill you!"

Faro snickers. "Keep your dog on a leash, would you?"

I gesture for Enzo and Roger to hold Dante back, and they take over for me. "You all stay here. No one goes upstairs until I tell you."

"Okay," Enzo says as I climb up the steps.

"Where do you think you're going?" Faro asks.

"Talking is now over. Where is she?" Two more steps and then I'm in front of him.

Now that I'm taller, more powerful, he seems like a roach I can step on. Short, round, grays on both sides of his head.

He's nothing.

"Come. She's waiting eagerly for your attendance."

I keep my gun pointed to the floor, not wanting to shoot until I see Chiara with my own eyes. If I take him out now and he's hidden her somewhere, I may never find her.

Footsteps echoing, I stomp down a semi-dark narrow path, him leading the way. We keep moving until the space widens, opening into a larger, well-lit area. As my eyes adjust, that's when I see her. Chiara.

But she isn't alone. Miles is there too, with a gun pointing to the back of her head, her hands hidden behind a chair, blood trickling down her lip.

My heart urges me to run, to get to her—to kill them all—but my mind stabilizes my irrational thoughts. I have to be smart about this.

"Nice to see you, *boss*." Miles smirks, planting the barrel against her head, and I catch the sight of the swelling around her temple.

It reminds me of when Cain hurt her. Anger fills my heart to capacity, battering from within my rib cage like an imprisoned animal finding its prey.

"I'm gonna get you out of this, baby," I assure her. "I swear to you."

Her chin trembles, fresh tears leaking down her cheeks, weaving with the blood on her mouth.

"Kill him." She grits her teeth at Faro.

"Shut up, bitch," Miles says from behind her, pushing the gun harder into her scalp, her head bending forward.

My breathing barrels through me with force.

"I'm gonna kill you nice and slow," I warn Miles, but he only looks amused.

We'll see how amused he is when I put a bullet in his face.

"You're done, Faro." I point the weapon at him. "Tonight, you die, and after I'm done with you and your puppet there…" I gesture toward Miles with my head. "I'm going to kill every last man in your family until there's no one left."

Faro sighs facetiously. "You Cavaleris think you can take everything from me. I made you an honest deal." His feet plod loudly as he takes a step closer to me, a few feet between us. "But instead of being an honest man, you took her without agreeing to our deal, like I figured you would. You're exactly like your father."

His face turns hard, and as he looks at me with a dead look in his eyes, he points a gun at Chiara. "That day I killed that scumbag you called a father, I not only took his youngest son, but the woman he came to fall in love with. *My* woman."

"What the fuck are you talking about?" I ask, lifting my own weapon, pointing it at his chest.

"Your father and my wife, they were having an affair almost

three years after your ma died. I guess you didn't know. Why would you?" he scoffs. "You were just a stupid kid chasing after my daughter."

I growl; if Chiara wasn't in harm's way, I'd use the knife at my ankle and slice both of their necks.

"She wasn't even supposed to be there," he continues. "But she found out what I planned to do and thought she could beg for their life, but..." His mouth curls up at the corners, the deadpan laugh filling the room. "She was too late. They were already dead. But I planned to kill her anyway, so she did me a favor showing up. I shot her in the back of the head as she cried looking at your dead brother and father."

My body grows cold at the memory of what I saw that day.

I don't believe anything he's saying. My father was never the type of man to fall for a married woman, no matter how bad her marriage was. I never even saw him with anyone after Mom died. I mean, yeah, he was friends with Chiara's mother, but that was all it was.

At least I thought so.

"After I shot them all, we dumped them together into the dirty harbor where they belong. If you look, you might still find their bones." His weapon remains aimed at a tearful Chiara.

I squeeze my hand around the gun in my hand, pain stretching over my fingers. "Your death will be the best thing I'll do as a man. I only wish I'd done it as a boy."

From the corner of my eye, I see Miles's gun lift up toward me. Before I can think, I point at my target and pull the trigger.

Miles falls to the floor with a loud thud just as Faro's lips curl upward and a bullet from his weapon bursts through the air, straight for Chiara.

"No!" I scream, my pulse pummeling in my ears, my feet

taking over.

Everything moves in slow motion, yet too quickly at the same time.

Running forward, I go as fast as I can to shield her as she falls—her body rocking sideways before the chair hits the ground hard. But as I make it to her, I find no traces of blood.

She glares past me, her body curved to the side, the chair missing one of its legs, and picks up the gun Miles left behind. She must've found a way to free one of her hands.

"Nice try, Daddy," she coughs on a laugh.

And this time, she's the one pulling the trigger.

Faro screams, holding out his hand, a bullet hole right through his palm.

The crunching of multiple footsteps is behind me as I turn, finding my brothers and my men there surrounding Faro with their weapons drawn.

Once I know we're safe, I undo the rope he used on her, freeing her other arm from the chair.

My hands are on her, checking for wounds, but she brushes me away, her eyes still on her father.

Crawling away at first, she gets up with the gun in her hand, a look of seeping rage on her face as she moves toward him.

Her hand slowly crawls up, the barrel pointing at Faro.

"No, Chiara!" I yell. "Don't do it!"

I know she wants to kill him—I get that more than anyone—but taking a life…it changes a person. I don't want that for her. That burden is mine. Finding out someone they love was murdered can make someone irrational enough to do something before they've had a chance to consider the consequences.

Her gaze flickers to mine, a flash of anger filling the emptiness in her eyes.

"You're not the only one who lost someone at his hand." Her exhales pulse with frantic indignation, and all I want is to hold her and tell her everything will be okay.

"All this time...I knew he killed her." Brushing away the errant tears filling her eyes, her lower lip trembles. "But a small part of me hoped I was wrong That she really did run away. And though that would've hurt, I'd have understood. I'd have found her and forgiven her. But..." Silent whimpers flow steadily from the heartbreak residing inside her heart. "He killed her. She's really gone, Dom."

My heart fills with agonizing grief, her pain and my own blended together into one. I wish I could take hers away and make them mine.

Testing the waters, I tread lightly, until I'm close enough to cup her cheek. My palm lands with a light touch over her damp skin, attempting to pull her away from the darkness I've been at peace with for so long.

"I know you're hurting, Chiara. But killing him might change you. Think about this before you do what you think is right at the moment."

The narrowed slits of her eyes crinkle with a new slice of ire.

"You, of all people, have no right to tell me what to do. After all the things you've done in the name of revenge, you're what now?!" she roars, the words emphasized with a sharp bite of truth. "My friend again? No. You're nothing, just like he is."

"Chiara..." I warn as she levels the gun at her father's chest, her eyes glued to mine. "Let's talk about all of that and forget him. I know I fucked up. Plea—"

"Do it!" Faro hisses like a cornered serpent.

Her gaze zaps to his as she makes her way to her father, her long hair now tattered and caked with blood on the ends. My men let her pass, refusing to stand in her way.

"Goodbye, *Daddy*," she grits out, her hand aiming at his head from a few feet away, her tone even. "You'll never hurt another innocent child again."

"You fucking who—"

A bullet splits the air, drowning out all else as it hits him right in between his eyes. She doesn't even flinch as his body falls, unblinkingly staring down at him.

Then suddenly her hand trembles, and the rest of her body follows. I rush over as a sob breaks from the chained wounds of her heart, and I'm there, doing what I can to hold her together, never wanting to let go.

CHIARA

THIRTY-THREE

"**G**ive me your phone," I demand, my tone clipped with reserved anger while we still stand inside the warehouse after my tears stopped.

I can't believe I let myself cry on him. How could I have been so weak in front of him?

After I killed my father, the shock held me in its ugly grip, refusing to let me go until I sacrificed my tears. But I didn't cry because I missed him or regretted what I'd done. It was cathartic.

After all these years of being his prisoner, I was free. And though I still hold his blood in my body, it doesn't own me or define me. I don't have to be his daughter beyond the ties of familial lines. I will no longer be controlled. Manipulated. Abused.

"Are you okay, baby?" Dom asks, concern plastered on his face like he gives a shit.

My jaw tightens and my eyes turn to two daggers about to take him out as beautifully as I did my own father.

"You don't fucking have the right to call me that ever again, you fucking bastard."

"Please, let me explain," he begs, but I don't want to hear any of it.

I extend my palm. "Give me your damn cell. I have to call my aunt, who's probably called the cops by now."

He slips a hand in his black sweats and removes his phone, handing it to me.

I immediately call her.

"Hello?" her voice trembles.

"It's me. I'm so sor—"

"Oh my God, Chiara," she sobs. "I thought you were dead. When you didn't show up, I was certain he hurt you."

Of course she means my father.

"He will never hurt anyone again. I made sure of it."

"What?" Shock weaves around her question.

"It's a lot to explain, but I'll be there soon."

"Okay. Please hurry."

"I will. Bye. Love you."

"Me too. So much. See you soon."

I disconnect the call and hold the phone out for Dom, refusing to even look at him, and as he takes the cell, his fingers caress my palm.

Yanking away my hand, I steel my gaze, not allowing any of his kindness to seep through the tough wall I built around my heart as soon as I found out who he was.

"Chiara, we have to talk."

"No, we don't. I'm leaving. Drive me into town, and I'll get an Uber from there."

But as I start to give him my back, his hand lands on my wrist, his fingers curling around me in a tight embrace. He pulls me toward him and I land against the hardness of his chest, my lips hovering over his, his sharp, penetrating gaze holding me in place.

His brothers and the rest of the men must notice the intense moment, because they scatter away.

"I know you're pissed." His breath flirts over my lips, irritation slinking in his voice. "But you will *not* be going anywhere by yourself."

His other hand captures my chin, and my body instantly grows warm.

"Who the *hell* do you think you are telling me what to do?" I grate through a tight jaw, my nostrils flaring, my pulse slamming in my neck.

"You're goddamn irritating, you know that? And even still…" he grunts, his gaze dancing to my lips, his tongue caressing his lower one. "It makes me want you more."

The whip of warmth courses through my every cell, melting the icy chill of my heart. But as I remember everything that transpired between us, I shake my head, willing it away.

"I'm leaving." I push out of his grip with all my might, and for a second, I think he's going to let me go.

"Like hell you are."

The next thing I know, I'm in the air, flipped over his shoulder, his forearm wrapped tightly around my ass.

"What the fuck do you think you're doing?! I need to go to my aunt's, you asshole!"

"And you'll go," he throws out casually. "In my car. While I drive."

"I'm not sitting in the car with you for a minute, let alone over an hour!"

"I guess you have no choice, baby." His hand squeezes the inside of my thigh, and I can't control the rush of desire pouncing over me. "I'd never let you go alone, knowing your father's men are out there. Once they hear about this, they'll come for you. Are you trying to die?"

"Would you even care?" I retort.

"Are you fucking kidding me?"

He flips me back to my feet as we make it to a black SUV. He stares down into my eyes, a painful look marring the green pools of his gaze, stopping me dead in my tracks, and all I want to do is kiss him—not as Brian, but as Dom.

My Dom.

"How could you think I wouldn't care?" He takes a step forward, forcing me back against the door of his car. "I loved you."

"Loved," I add with melancholy stringing up the word, choking the life out of it.

Peering down, I avoid looking at him anymore. It's too much. I'm barely holding on.

He pushes up my face with a finger, and I have no choice but to meet his probing gaze. "*Love*, Chiara. I *love* you. I always will. Through the years, my love changed. It was different then. I was a boy, and you were my friend. I had feelings for you that I didn't quite understand. But I do now. You have to know I do."

"You don't do what you did to someone you claim to love," I remark, swallowing away the tears I prefer to hide.

He sighs. "I'm sorry. I only took you for your own safety. I know I should've told you who I was, talked to you about it all, but I couldn't risk the plan I spent years constructing. I waited too long to watch it all fall apart."

"If you would've told me who you were that day at the club, I would've been there to help you, but you chose not to trust me."

"I had my reasons, Chiara. Or did you forget what you said to me?"

My head jerks back. "What the hell are you talking about? When?"

A sharp exhale rolls out of him. "Let's get out of here before his men come. We'll talk then and get it all out in the open."

"Looking forward to it," I fire as he backs away, opening the door for me.

And once we're both inside, I welcome the silence I've been missing.

We pull up to my aunt's colonial, a large white wraparound fence surrounding it. She's already out front, sitting on her porch steps, hands clasped around a mug, a burgundy sweater clinging to her shoulders.

As soon as she sees the car and me getting out of it, she drops the cup so harshly on the step, it tips over, spilling black liquid down onto the grass.

She practically runs to me, and when I'm beside her, she clutches my cheeks in her palms, tears running down her face. Without saying another word, she holds me tight.

"You don't know how happy I am to see you." Her voice shatters with a gasping sob. "I was going insane with worry, thinking he killed you like…"

"Like Mom?" I pull back, searching her eyes. "What do you know, Aunt Kirsten? Please, if you know anything at all, you have to tell me."

We never talked about what happened to my mom. I brought it up when we first started talking, but she found ways to avoid the question, only telling me Mom would never leave without me. As

I got older, I stopped asking.

Her eyes close briefly as she pulls in a rough breath. "How about we go inside and talk?"

Her eyes wander to Dom, her brows pinching in question. I turn, seeing him standing against the passenger side, his arms crossed over his massive chest.

"Who is he? Your bodyguard?"

I scoff. "That's Dom."

"Wait a minute?" Her eyes widen and her mouth goes slack. "Francesco's son?"

I nod slowly, my heart growing heavy, a fluttery feeling hitting my stomach as my skin tingles from the cold shiver sliding down my arms.

I've mentioned Dom's name before, but never his father's.

"Oh my God!"

Her palm falls over her lips.

"I thought they were all dead," she whispers, her hand falling back down.

As though knowing we're talking about him, Dom strides over to us.

He reaches out a hand for my aunt's. "Hi. I'm—"

"I know who you are." She takes his hand, staring at him as though seeing a ghost. "I knew of your father. He was good to my sister. Her mom."

She gestures toward me with a flick of her head. My brows furrow. All this time, my aunt knew so much and never said a thing.

"Let's head in," she says, opening the door into a large foyer with a cathedral ceiling and a small crystal chandelier overhead.

We remove our shoes, following her into the den.

"Have a seat. Let me make you both some coffee."

"I don't want coffee," I say, frustration lacing in my voice. "I want to know what you know."

She purses her lips, glancing between Dom and me.

"All right." She takes a seat on the brown leather sofa.

Dom and I sit across, and he knows better than to sit beside me, taking the opposite end of the couch. My aunt crosses her legs at her knees, gripping her cardigan with a jittery hand.

"Was Mom having an affair with Francesco?" I ask, ending the silence, knowing she's probably too afraid to say what she knows without knowing what I know first.

Her eyelids fall to a close for the briefest of seconds before they soften, a wrinkle appearing between her brows. "Chiara..."

"I don't give a shit about the damn affair. Okay? Just tell me what happened."

She sighs, her fingers laced together. "Your mom was planning on taking you and running away. Francesco found her a man who could create fake passports and gave her money to help her wherever she'd be going. He didn't know where, and neither did I." She slouches a little, peering down at her lap. "He didn't want to know in case you father tortured him. They started out as friends." She glances up at me. "But the closer their friendship got, the closer they got. And she fell in love with him, and he fell in love with her."

Her gaze drifts to Dom, who's listening intently.

"He was a good man," she tells him. "He was willing to give her up just so she could be saved."

From the corner of my eye, Dom's jaw rattles.

"She called me in the morning, the day she disappeared," Aunt Kirsten continues. "She left a voicemail, saying she thought your father knew about her plan to disappear. She sounded afraid, and when I found out she was gone, I just knew he killed her."

"He did," Dom grates with a tremor in his breath. "He killed her, my father, and my baby brother, who was only eight."

She gasps, her eyes bathed with tears, her fingers falling over her lips. "I knew she was dead but hearing it…it's hard." Wiping under her eyes, she shuffles in her seat. "I'm sorry for your loss, Dom."

He leans back, ankle bopping over his knee.

"I'm sorry I never said anything before, Chiara. Your mother didn't want you to know anything about Francesco until you really had to."

She gets up, kneeling beside me, clutching my hand.

"Please, forgive me," she begs, tears shining brightly in her eyes.

"I understand." I nod, my tone cut with so much turmoil.

Clearing her throat, she rises to her feet. "She left you a letter."

"What?" My pulse quickens. "Why didn't you ever give it to me?"

She purses her lips. "She asked me to only give it to you when you came looking for answers. I wanted to respect her wishes."

"Where is it?" I stand up instantly.

"I'll get it." She pats my hand. "Sit. I'll be right back."

A moment later, she returns, handing me a white business envelope. I quickly remove the paper inside, unfolding it, unable to wait another second without reading my mother's words.

Dear Chiara,

If you're reading this, it means I'm gone. I'm sorry, baby. That was never my plan. You were my whole world. Are my whole world. No matter where I am, you'll always be my everything. You're the only good thing

I did in my life.

When I met your father, we were both young and fell in love so fast. My parents were old-fashioned, wanting me to marry young. They liked the sort of family your father belonged to, so they had no objections when he asked my father for my hand. Back then, all I saw were hearts, even when he was possessive over what boy spoke to me or looked at me. I brushed it off as him loving me. I was a fool. I know that now.

Your father was awful to me, to us. It's my fault. You should've never been on the receiving end of it, but by that point, all I could do was run away. And I tried, but I think he knows and that's probably why I'm dead now.

Plop.
Plop.

Tears drip down onto the black ink, smudging over her words.

I hadn't even noticed I was crying. I swipe under my eyes, ignoring them, and continue to read.

With Francesco's help, I planned to take us to France, so we could eat our crepes and wear our fancy dresses like we'd always pretend to when you were younger. Do you remember that? I'm sorry we never got that chance. I wish I didn't have to leave you, especially knowing who you're left with. It kills to even write this letter. My heart's breaking with every sentence.

Please, don't be mad at your aunt. This wasn't her story to tell. I asked her to only give you this letter when she felt the time was right.

I love you forever. I'll always be with you.

Hold on to your aunt, and to Dom. It's okay to hold on to the strength of others when we need it.

Love,
Mom

Clutching the paper against my chest, I pull in a breath so shallow, it clenches my chest, my heartbeats stuck in my throat.

I let the tears cleanse my soul, my eyes falling to a close for mere seconds before I'm standing up, running outside. The air feels good on my lungs as I force myself to inhale, exhale, and then repeat.

I hear the heavy thud of his footsteps.

"Chiara, wait!" Dom calls, as I round the house, heading for the yard.

I try to shut the door in his face, but he plants a palm, stopping me. Marching inside as he closes the gate, I turn to him, hand on my hip, tears leaking from the corners of my eyes.

"What the hell do you want from me?!"

"Baby, I'm sorry. That must've been a hard letter to read."

He stands where he is, a few feet between us. When I don't respond, he continues with a sigh.

"I care for you, Chiara. So much. Can we talk? If you want me to go after that, I will. I promise."

Biting the inside of my cheek, I glare at his softened features. "Fine. Say what you want to say and then get the fuck out of here."

"The day we ran away, the day your father killed mine…I got a text from you. A cruel fucking text. Do you remember what you said?"

My every muscle goes rigid, cold dread washing over me, prickling at my skin. "Wha—what text, Dom? I never wrote you one. It wasn't me."

"Yeah, you did. You told me you never liked me, that you felt sorry for me, that my family and I are all losers like your father always said." He moves up a step toward me. "Can you imagine how broken I felt, just seeing Matteo and Dad shot in front of me, then reading those fucking words from you, of all people?"

He palms the back of his neck, his triceps flexing through his clothes from the force of it.

I clutch my chest, gasping. "You saw them die?"

"Yeah, Chiara, I did."

The color drains from my face. I can feel it just as much as I can feel my heart squeezing, as though shrinking into nothing.

"I'm so sorry." My voice splits with a cry, my hands wanting to reach for him, to hold him.

Something trickles down my cheek, and I realize it's my tears. I swipe at the remnants of my pain, hurting for the both of us.

"You need to know I never sent you those texts, Dom. I promise you. I would never say that to you. Not ever." I shake my head, my brows huddled close. "You were my best friend. You meant everything to me. So did your family."

Dom's expression pales. "Then how did—"

My heartbeats thunder in my ears, the shock of it all drowning me in icy waters. My father always knew how to destroy lives. He did it flawlessly, especially to me.

"My father took my phone the day my mom di-died." I flinch, taking a deep breath. "I never got it back until days later when he changed my number. I kept texting you to tell you I had a new one, to find out where you were, but you never replied."

"Oh, fuck! If only I had my damn phone! I tossed it after I read your texts."

He clenches a fist and slams it into his palm, pacing back and forth. When his eyes are finally on mine, he takes an unsure step toward me, and then another.

"If I'd known you didn't send them...if I'd known it was him... My God, Chiara!" he roars, his features tortured.

"I can't believe you thought so little of me and our friendship." I shake my head in disbelief.

"I didn't know what to think!" he shouts, not with anger, but with complete grief. "I swear, at the time, I was broken. I thought I'd lost you too, that you hated me and my family like your father did. I thought you took his side, that our friendship was over. Then as I watched you years down the line, seeing you working at the club. At *his* club. I thought your alliance was with him."

This is too much to handle right now. I struggle to breathe, unable to pull air into my burning lungs.

Moving even closer, he destroys all the space between us, taking my hands in his. But no matter how close he gets to my body, I won't let him get close enough to my heart.

Not again.

He broke all the trust I used to have in the boy who'd slay dragons for me. I never thought that one day, he'd be the dragon I'd need to slay.

"Why were you following me?" I ask. "All this time that was you, wasn't it?"

"Yeah, it was. I told myself it was because of your father, but that was a lie. I wanted to know you, to be close to you somehow. I missed you, Chiara. Don't you get it? Even when I was at my lowest, thinking you hated me, I still missed you. I still cared about you." His fingers tighten around my hands, his gaze delving into mine. "Please forgive me. Forgive how I did what I did. I wanted to protect you from him, but I went about it all wrong."

My heart coils with the beauty of his words, but instead of letting it consume me, letting it take me to a place where I can sympathize with his decisions, I clench my jaw and yank my hands away.

"It's too late for all of that," I whisper-shout, not wanting my aunt to hear. "We're not the friends we once were." I pin him with a glare. "All this time, you thought I was this awful person who could say those awful things after everything we've shared?"

I look to him with disbelief, a cry falling from my lips.

"I know I fucked up," he whispers, "I should've—"

"You should've what, huh?!" I shout. "Should've come to me years ago? Confronted me?" I poke him with my finger. "You should've!"

My brows bend with agonizing pain. "You could've come to me." My voice drops. "You could've told me what was going on. I would've helped you. I would've done whatever you wanted." An ache builds behind my nose, tears stinging my eyes.

He grips my shoulder while his other hand feathers under my jaw, sending a jolt down my spine.

"I couldn't take the risk," he tries to explain. "I couldn't tell you my plans, because I wasn't sure who you were loyal to, and I couldn't let anything get in the way of what we had in store. I waited so long for it, Chiara. We all did."

He grips my jaw within the large span of his palm, his own eyes glazing with his own hurt.

"I knew that the only way to destroy your father was to grow my kingdom so I could watch his burn. But even through it all, I wanted you. I always did. I just thought you didn't want me, so I let my heart die the moment I read those texts. But, baby…" His voice softens with the beat of my heart. "Since I got you back, I can feel my heart beating again. I never thought I'd be capable of loving anyone, but now I've realized that the only person I *want* to love is you."

My hand closes around his wrist, a silent whimper falling out of me, wanting to hold on while at the same time knowing I should let go. Of him, of us, of any chance we could've had. How can I ever trust him after what he's done? How can we build a future on top of the ruins of us?

His eyes search mine for the forgiveness I can't seem to give.

"In my mind, you had wronged me," he continues. "I couldn't see anything beyond that."

His tone's swimming with wave after wave of regret. It's drowning us both with his mistakes.

"Why was it so easy for you to believe that? I know we were kids, but how could you not see how much I loved you? How much I loved Matteo?"

A sob rips from my very soul as I remember that little boy who'd sit on my lap at the bakery and feed me cupcakes his father made. Or the times his face would light up when I came in with my mom. He'd run to me, grabbing my waist and hugging me with all his might.

"I'm sorry," is all he manages to say, his voice growing huskier, his forehead falling against mine.

I let it stay, letting every part of him stay beside me knowing it won't last for long. Knowing that after he goes, I won't see him again.

He eases his head back, and then his lips land on my forehead, so velvety soft. I drown in intoxicating longing for a future we could've had.

"I don't want a life without you." Pain stitches up his voice. "All this time, I could've had you, and instead I fucked it all away. Baby, I lo—"

"No!" I push him off of me, my hands on his chest. "Don't you *dare* say those words to me again."

I move a step away.

"Don't say that." His eyes plead. "I don't expect your forgiveness or understanding today or tomorrow, but please, baby, forgive me."

My vision drowns with tears as I look back at him, both of us consumed by so many years of anguish, both at my father's hand, destroying the Dom I once knew. The Dom who'd never lie or hurt me. The one who I thought knew me more than anyone else did.

"Forget me," I tell him. "Pretend I'm that girl who deceived you and let her go. Forever."

He releases a bitter laugh, his hand landing sharply on the top of his head, his fingers biting through as though wanting to make it hurt. "I couldn't do that then, and I sure as hell can't do that now."

He nears me but I move away, shaking my head, the back of my eyes aching, my soul breaking off into pieces.

"We didn't know each other for fifteen years," I cry, swiping under my eyes. "We...we don't have to know each other now."

"Chiara, I'm begging you."

The shimmer in his eyes slices through me. Everything hurts. My heart, my head, every piece of me is lost to the pain.

"Bye, *Brian*." My voice shatters right along with his heart.

"*Don't* call me that." His words are coated in turmoil. "I'm still Dom."

"Not to me. My Dom would never hurt me. He only ever wanted to protect me."

"Why the hell do you think I took you after what I thought you did?!" he shouts. "I didn't want him to kill you or find someone else to do it."

"That doesn't change anything! You still lied about who you were. You had so many chances to tell me, to test my true allegiance, but you didn't. You settled on believing a lie he created." My chest falls harshly. "After I confessed to you about how he locked me in a room, after I gave you his location, you could've told me. But you stayed silent. How do you expect me to forgive that?"

He drops his head into his palm. "I wasn't sure what to believe."

"That's too bad, because whatever I thought we could've had when I thought you were Brian is now gone."

He laughs dolefully. "So you could've forgiven him, but you can't forgive me?"

I shrug. "He was nothing to me. But *you*? You were *everything*."

My throat dries, fresh tears streaming down my cheeks.

"It's as though in one single moment, you forgot all that. I once thought I could trust you above everyone. And now..." A sob wrecks all of my defenses. "It's as though I'm losing you all over again."

His arms are around me now, steadying my cries even while he's the one who let me fall into despair. "Shhh."

The soothing sway of his voice is like a lullaby for my shattered heart, and I wish more than anything it was enough to piece it back together.

But it's not.

I shove at his shoulders, needing him far away.

Needing him gone.

"Don't call me. Don't come here. I don't want to see you ever again."

A weighty exhale breaks from his lips as he stuffs his hands into his sweats.

"I'll never stop trying to earn your trust," he promises, his eyes searing an oath into mine. "I'll give you space, time, whatever you need, but I won't let you go. You opened my heart to something I never thought would be mine. And I want that, and I only want it with you."

"Dom...don't." I close my eyes, letting the tears drift down my face, unable to take any more of his heartfelt words. "I once loved a boy who made me feel the beauty of the sun, but now you're nothing but his shadow, swallowing me into the dark."

His eyes go downcast. "I'm sorry. I'm *so* sorry. But I'm not giving up on us. And those three words you wouldn't let me say..." He plants a palm over the center of his chest. "I feel them *here*. They're not going anywhere. They'll be waiting for you when you're ready."

As he walks away out of the gate, a sob wrecks my body, my knees hitting the grass, and then I hurt all over again.

# DOMINIC
ONE WEEK LATER

THIRTY-FOUR

Every day in the past week has been hell. I miss her. I want her. Not just her body, but her smile, the way she cared for me when I was hurt, the way I know she could love me if she gave us a chance.

I know I messed up, and maybe she won't forgive me, but I have to get us to a place where she has a chance to try.

Knowing where she is and being unable to see her and talk face-to-face is breaking me down. But forcing her will only drive her further away from me. I have to give her time. I have to do what's right for *her*, not for me.

I haven't been sitting around doing nothing, though. I've left a voicemail telling her I missed her. I've texted multiple times, groveling like a motherfucker, but it hasn't worked.

I wrote her a letter too, and mailed it to her aunt's. I couldn't say everything I wanted to say with a text. Writing to her, putting the time in to get the words right, felt like the better move. But who knows if she even read it?

I hate that I hurt her. I'd undo it all for a moment where she didn't look at me the way she did back at her aunt's. I can't get that wounded look out of my head. I relive it on a loop like a brutal punishment.

I've been barely able to focus on anything besides Chiara, but finding the other Bianchi brothers is still ongoing. For now, we haven't located them, but we're close.

Word got out immediately about Faro's death, making Benvolio the new don. My brothers had also found out some more about what the Bianchis have been up to.

Once Chiara was saved, they filled me in on the other vile things the Bianchis were up to. Things I can't stop thinking about. Things that sheath my heart in too much rage.

All I smell is the blood of my enemies.

We've captured another one of their men, hoping he can give up their location, so I can give them a taste of what they've done to us and so many others.

"Come on, Vincenzo," I say. "I know you know where they are. If you tell me, I promise I won't make it slow. I'll end you nice and quick."

By the looks of his round face, my brothers had their fun before I showed up. They knew the angry state I've been in and saved the best for last.

He rocks in his chair, tied in the basement of a building we own, blood dripping from his cheek, his lip. He'll tell me what I need to know, and if he doesn't, I'll break him until he does.

Uncuffing my white button-down, I lift up a sleeve to my elbow, doing the same to the other, taking my time as my loafers hit the concrete, the sound deafening in the stillness, making him squirm.

He eyes me, fear trickling from his gaze, but he tries to hide it.

I pick up a chair from the side, dragging it purposefully loudly, and place it in front of him, sitting backwards as I smirk.

He huffs, his chest climbing hard with force, and then he spits in my face.

The motherfucker spat at me.

"Oh, shit," Enzo says from behind as I wipe it off with the back of my hand. "You shouldn't have done that. You just wrote your own *very* painful death sentence."

"Fuck you *all*!" Vincenzo bellows, bloody sweat dripping down his face.

I get to my feet, walking off to the corner, kneeling down to open a black briefcase full of fun toys we use to motivate the unmotivated.

Grabbing my favorite one, I stand, kicking away the chair I was in. It connects to the floor with a bang, the menacing sound resonating across the walls.

I tower in front of him, glancing between him and this beauty in my hand, knowing he's about to not only tell me their location, but to do it with a smile.

Sort of.

I flip a button, revealing blue-yellow flames shooting up from the torch in my hand.

His eyes bulge. "You gonna burn me, you pussy? Do it, then! Do whatever the fuck you want. I ain't talkin'."

I switch the torch off, then on again. "We'll see."

Circling around him, I keep flipping it on and off.

"You have one more chance to tell me. Then the fun begins."

I ease the fire closer to the back of his neck, letting him feel the heat that's about to become his most intimate partner.

"I don't know where the hell they are!"

I come face-to-face with him. "The captains know everything. They wouldn't neglect to tell you. I know how much they all trust you. You're their cousin, after all."

He narrows a stare, probably surprised at how much I know. But we've learned everything there is to know about their major players.

"Do whatever you've gotta do. I won't betray my family."

"You're right. Family is everything."

And this time, when the flames shoot up, they leave a stench of burning flesh. The skin of his upper arm, right at the bicep, ignites as he screams.

I grab his throat, my fingers tightening as I stare at his face, no longer smug.

He struggles to breathe and cry at the same time.

"I'm this close to burning off your dick," I continue. "So now's your time to choose. Your cock or your family?"

He wails, his exhales ragged with every inhale.

"For me," I say. "It'd definitely be my dick. I mean, I love my brothers, but a man only has one dick. Don't make me take yours."

"That's cold," Dante cuts in. "You'd do us dirty?"

Enzo snickers. "No way would I let someone make a shish kebab out of my wiener. I'm with Dom."

"Listen to my brother," I tell Vincenzo. "He's not always right, but this time, I'd take his advice."

Vincenzo grits his teeth, the whimpers fading.

I can't wait to kill him.

I flip the switch on again, roasting his upper thigh, closer to the place he really doesn't want me to hurt him.

The room cuts in with another one of his screams.

"Not spitting at me now, are you, motherfucker?" The torch

blazes to life. "Last chance. Then I'm taking your balls."

He sobs, his crying drowning out the room.

I light up the torch once again.

"Wait!" he begs with a pant, putting out his hand. "I'll tell you, okay? Just stop."

"Keep talking." The fire nears his other thigh.

"I got a ca...ca...cabin upstate. Secluded. No neighbor for miles."

No doubt they're planning how to get us before we get them.

"I hope you're telling the truth."

"I am, I swear."

He gives up the address and Enzo texts it to one of our men so he can start surveillance.

"Let me go," Vincenzo implores. "I won't breathe a word of this. I'll be your inside man."

"I wouldn't trust you with dog shit," I chuckle. "Let alone our lives."

"I can hel—"

Dante pulls the trigger, silencing him as the bullet carves into his brain.

I turn to my brothers' solemn faces, all of us determined to end the war once and for all.

CHIARA

THIRTY-FIVE

Shivering from the crisp, chilly air stirring around me, I wrap a knitted yellow blanket around myself, my legs pulled up to my chest on my aunt's outdoor sofa. A warm mug is safely tucked between my palms, my hair whipping wildly past my face.

For the past week, I haven't been able to get Dom out of my mind. I might not know the man he is today, but the boy he once was—the boy I loved—he's still there, trapped somewhere within his heart. I have to believe that. The alternative is too painful to bear. Someone as beautiful, as kind, can't be gone for good.

I'm torn between wanting to find out if he's still there and not being sure if I can forgive him enough to try. For once, I've found someone to have a future with, something I never thought I'd have, but it's slipped from my fingers.

Relationships shouldn't start out the way we did. Love shouldn't knock on deception's door. But for us, it did, before we had a chance to feel what we could be.

He's tried to get in touch, but I haven't responded to any of his attempts. As soon as I got my new cell a few days ago, I received multiple messages from him, begging to talk to me, to forgive him, but all I've done is ignore them.

But today, there was a letter.

One I haven't opened.

One I'm afraid to.

What if it breaks me? Breaks this cage I've built around my weary heart? What if I'm not strong enough to keep him out of it? What if I don't want to?

For so long, I've imagined being with him, creating a whole future out of thin air, and now that he's here...

It's so unfair.

It may seem silly because we were nothing but kids back then, but he was my person. The one I could count on to hold me up when life tried so hard to push me down.

Picking up my phone, I read his texts again, as though enjoying the torture.

> **Dom:** I can't stand being away from you. Not when I just got you back. Give me another chance to prove to you that I've always been the man you thought I would become. I'll spend every day of my life making it up to you. But first, you have to let me.

Placing my mug down on the end table beside me, my hand jumps to my eyes, wiping away some tears, reading the next text.

Dom: Do you remember when you told me that football player from school asked you out? That was when I realized I liked you. I planned on telling you the day everything went to hell, but I never got the chance. Even at thirteen, I knew you were special, Chiara. And to me, you still are. Always will be.

"Asshole," I murmur, the tears cascading down my face like raindrops spelling heartbreak.

Suddenly, I realize we were both going to tell each other about our feelings on the very same day.

We could've had a life together, something that could've been more than we ever thought possible. But the mirror containing our future cracked into darkness, turning into the nightmare that became our life.

I set the phone next to my coffee and close my eyes, taking in a long breath, embracing the bitter memories and sweet recollections between a boy and a girl who were never meant to be anything more than what they are.

∞

"*Do you know Rocco, the football player?*" *I ask Dom, who sits beside me at lunch, stuffing an orange slice into his mouth.*

"*Yeah,*" *he mumbles, swallowing it down. "What about him?*"

"*So, get this. Yesterday, right before I went home, he came up to me and asked if I'd go to the dance with him.*"

"*Oh,*" *he says casually, peering down at his red tray. "What'd you say?*"

The question comes off indifferent, like he doesn't care that the most popular boy in school just asked me out to the end-of-the-year dance. To be honest, I don't care either. The only boy I want to go with is the one beside me, but I don't think he likes me that way. That's assuming my stupid father would even let me go.

It'd be weird to ask Dom to go with me, because girls don't really ask guys and he'll probably say no, even if we go as friends. Dances and stuff aren't his thing.

"What did you tell him?" he asks.

I glance at my cup of water, circling my finger around the straw.

"I didn't say anything. Yet." I side-eye him, biting the corner of my bottom lip. "What do you think I should say?"

"I don't know," he grumbles, his eyes on the tray. "Do you want to go with him?"

No! I want to go with you, you buffoon.

"No, not really." I sigh. "I want to go with someone else."

I look right at him this time. Well, more like his cheek, because he won't look at me.

"But I don't think he wants to go with me."

"That sucks. Sorry, Chiara."

Oh, now you look at me? It's you! Should I spell it out for you?

"He must be an idiot."

I giggle. "Yeah, he is sometimes. But I still like him."

His cheeks grow red, and he doesn't say anything after that. Neither of us do.

That memory eats away at my heart until nothing is left but a tiny spark, keeping me afloat. And though I try my hardest to bury the rest of our past, it storms in with a vengeance, reminding me of the lost, forgotten dreams of those lost, forgotten souls.

"Do you think your dad will let you go away to college?" Dom

asks as we swing side by side at recess.

I kick the sand with my sneakers. "Probably not."

I shrug with disappointment. I'd do anything to leave as long as Dom is with me.

"That sucks. I had this plan for us to go to the same school. Somewhere close, but not so close that you'd have to live at home."

"I wish." I frown, turning my head to find disappointment on his face.

"Me too. I don't want us not to be friends when we're done with high school."

My brows shoot up. "Why wouldn't we be friends?"

"I don't know," he laughs shyly. "You'll probably forget me with all those football players asking you out."

"Shut up." I giggle, kicking my foot, sand shooting up toward his leg.

"I'm serious." He gazes at me with a genuine expression. "Don't forget me, okay?"

My heart skips a beat, and my belly scatters with butterflies.

"Never," I say with complete affection. Complete truth. "You're my best friend. A girl never forgets her best friend. Even with all those cute football players around."

His laughter howls out of him as he jumps off the swing, rushing over to me. "You think you're funny?"

He pushes my knees, causing me to swing backward sharply as my own laugh falls out of me. I hold on tightly to the handles, kicking out my feet, causing him to stumble for a brief second.

We continue to giggle, in our own little bubble while he grabs the handles, spinning me around until he stops, keeping our gazes locked.

"I'd miss you if I didn't see you all the time."

"I'd miss you too," I whisper, not sure why. "I never want us to *be apart, Dom. I don't know what I'd do without you."*

"Ditto." His lips tip upward into a tentative smile.

Though his smile may mean nothing to anyone here, to me, it's everything.

Clutching my chest, I swallow the hurt building in my throat. It wasn't enough for my father to destroy a future with my mother, but he took Dom away too.

I'm so glad he's dead. I'm at peace with what I've done. There are no nightmares, no lingering regrets.

He's gone.

Finally.

I turn my face to the sun, my eyelids drifting shut, the rays radiating through my skin.

"It's okay, you know," my aunt says from behind.

I hadn't even realized she came out of the house.

"It's okay what?" I ask, squinting.

She takes a seat beside me, placing her warm palm over the top of my hand. "To forgive him. You don't have to, but if there's a part of you that does, that's okay too. You don't owe anyone an explanation."

My aunt knows everything. I've laid out every detail to her.

"What he did. Taking me, lying about his identity…all of it. It's hard." I purse my lips, my brows furrowing.

"Of course it is." Her features turn with a grimace. "Believe me, I want to kill him every time I think about you being in that house. I don't care what he thought. He went about it all wrong. But at the same time, he wanted to protect you, even while thinking you took your father's side."

I nod, conflicted in the same way. What he did wasn't all light or dark. It's blended in numerous shades of gray.

My aunt is right. I do feel a sense of shame for even considering forgiving him. I should hate him and be done with it. I should close our book and burn every last page. But I can't seem to light the match. Instead, I hold it tighter against my chest, wanting so badly to know what happens next.

Aunt Kirsten leans in closer, wrapping an arm around my shoulders. "Take it one day at a time, honey. Give yourself grace to figure out what you want without all the background noise."

"I want to read the letter," I confess. "But I can't seem to open it."

I lean my head against her chest as she strokes my arm.

"To your heart, he isn't a stranger. It knows him well. And the heart doesn't let people go that easily, even when we may want it to. Is there anything left fighting for? Only you know the answer to that. And I know you'll find it." She squeezes me to her side. "But whatever you decide, I'll be here. No matter what."

Finding newfound courage, I pick up the letter, peering at my aunt. "Will you stay here while I read this? I don't want to be alone."

"Of course," she promises. "You take all the time you need. I have nowhere else I'd rather be."

Tearing open the envelope, I remove the neatly folded letter and begin to read.

Dear Chiara,

I know I don't deserve your time or understanding, but I hope you can give me both. I hope that the past we once had can somehow make up for the present mistakes I've made. And I've made a lot of them when it comes to you.

When your father proposed killing you, I lost it. The thought of you being harmed in any way tore me up inside. So instead, I took you. Not in the best of ways, but I wanted to keep you out of danger. Yet, at the same time, I held on to the anger I was afraid of losing, as though it would make me weak. I'm sorry for that. I'm sorry for all of it. I didn't know you never sent those texts. I swear.

Try to understand where I was coming from. Where my pain was coming from. After I read your messages, I thought I no longer had my best friend.

I've lived all these years with a piece of my heart missing. The part that was always yours. I spent years hating the thought of you, or at least I thought I did. But as I saw you for the first time, years ago when I followed you, I realized I didn't hate you, even when I believed I should. And that made me hate myself.

I'd do anything to go back in time and change it all. But we can't go back. We only have today. I don't know if we'll even have tomorrow. But I want them all with you.

Just you.

My heart is yours, whether you want it or not. There's no one else for me but you. There never was, no matter how many times I told myself to forget you.

Remember our promise of together forever? I do. I'm sorry we never got to keep that promise for all these years, but we're here now, and I want that again, even if it takes a lifetime to get it.

If you give me a chance, if you let me earn back your trust, your friendship—and maybe someday your love—I promise you, I won't take any of it for granted. I'll keep it safe, just like I kept my necklace.

My eyes water over, my lips shuddering beneath my fingers as I continue to pore over his words.

If you want to see what we can be together, meet me at Vixen, one of my clubs, tomorrow at seven. Let me know if you come. I'll send a car. They're still out there, and I don't want you in danger.

I hope you decide to show. If you don't, I'll understand. But I won't stop trying.

Dom

When the letter falls to my lap, my heart opens like a dam, and sob after sob bursts through me. Before I fall into disarray, my aunt's arms loop around me, soothing me while I shatter.

CHIARA

THIRTY-SIX

The following morning, I decide to try my cousin again. I have been calling her line for the past week, but it's been going straight to voicemail.

But today, it's finally ringing.

On the third ring, a voice comes through. "Raquel Cavaleri's phone. This is Dante, her very handsome husband, speaking. How may I help you?"

I flip my head back, my brows shooting up to my hairline.

"Husband?!" I practically shout. "What the hell are you talking about?"

She *married* Dante? Oh my fucking God. He was a funny kid growing up, always cracking jokes. I don't know who this Dante is now, though, and I especially don't know why he married my friggin' cousin!

Growing up, I didn't tell her about Dom or his family. I was scared she'd tell her dad, who'd tell mine. So obviously, when she met Dante, she had no clue who he was.

"Ah, Chiara. How very pleasant to hear from you on such a fine day." He sounds obnoxious. "It's been way too long. We must catch up."

"Shut up, Dante. What have you done to my cousin?"

"Oh, I've done a lot of things to your very sexy cousin. After we were legally married, of course. I am nothing but a gentleman."

"You're an asshole," I fire back.

"I apologize. We really wanted to send you an invitation, but we eloped rather quickly."

"Can you stop sounding like a moron and tell me what the hell is going on?"

"Nothing. *Much*. We came to a very mutually beneficial arrangement. She's happy. I'm happy. Be happy, Chiara."

"We haven't spoken in fifteen years, jerkface. I don't know you enough to be happy you married my cousin. And for what? Another form of revenge against my demented family?"

"You and your cousin are anything but demented, and I have done nothing she didn't want me to. Believe me." I can just see him smiling all arrogantly.

"You're not keeping her locked away like he did me, are you? Because I swear—"

"I've not hurt a beautiful hair on her body. She's doing just fine. Free as a bird…of sorts."

"Let me speak to her. Now. Or I'll show up at your house with a blowtorch, and I'll start with those nice cars I'm sure you drive."

His voice grows silent, and I look down at my phone to make sure he didn't hang up. He's still there.

"Dante. Where is she?"

He pulls in a heavy sigh. "She's here at the house, lying out by the pool. I haven't hurt her. I don't intend to."

"Great." I roll my eyes, completely irritated. "Let me talk to her and confirm that. Your word means very little."

"Only if you promise me one thing."

"Depends on what it is."

"Don't tell her about who we are and how we know your family."

I sneer. "Excuse me?"

"If she finds out from you, she'll never forgive me."

"Good!" A snicker rolls off my chest. "She shouldn't."

"I get that you're pissed." There's shuffling on the other end, like he's sitting down or standing up. "You have every right to be, but during all this shit, I've started to care for her, and I think she cares for me too. Let this play out until we get Sal and the rest of them, and then I'll tell her. Give me some time."

I don't say anything, my words trapped in my throat. The genuineness with which he speaks of my cousin melts my heart.

"We could be something, Chiara. I've never felt like this before."

Geez. He really does care about her.

"Why did you even do this? How does this serve your purpose?"

He sighs. "You know more than anyone how much the Bianchis hated us. Imagine how they'd feel if one of their daughters married one of us. Sal won't be happy, will he?"

I laugh humorlessly. "Not even a little. Does he know yet?"

"Not yet. I don't want to use her that way. I'll tell him right before I put a bullet in his brain, though."

"You're so romantic."

"I try." He chuckles.

"Heads will roll, and not just Sal's," I add. "Carlito's too."

"I can't fucking wait. I hate that bastard."

"How do you kno—?"

"Long story for another day. Just promise me you won't say anything to her. Please, Chiara."

I consider it, but how can I lie to my cousin?

Yet, at the same time, who am I to take away her chance at escaping the constant threat of arranged marriage? Maybe this is what she really wants, even though she's not getting the entire story. I have to know how she feels about Dante.

"I won't say anything right now. Not if I see she cares for you like you clearly do her. But if she's afraid, if she wants to leave, I'm telling her everything."

He inhales deeply. "Okay. I'll go get her."

"Wait," I say. "Don't take too long to tell her. Look at what happened with Dom and me. The truth always finds a way to slither out from the dirt and bite you when you least expect it. I don't know how long all this with my uncles will play out, but she has a right to know that you're going to kill her father. That you're not who you say you are."

"You were always such a pain in the ass."

"I was so not!"

I hear the opening of a door as he chuckles.

"For what it's worth," he continues. "Dom is a fucking mess. And he's never a mess."

I remain silent as he goes on.

"I remember him crying one night after we ran, after we ended up in one of those dirty shelters."

They were in shelters? Oh my God.

"I'm sure he didn't want me to hear, but I did, and it was your name he spoke as he cried. It was like he was mourning you too. You were the one person outside of all of us he could count on, and he thought your friendship was over."

My jaw stiffens, an ache building behind my throat. "Why didn't he try to contact me? To ask me about those texts?"

"I know. You're right. But he was a kid who was thrust into having to be a man. It was an awful time for us. Being on our own, losing our parents and our brother…it fucked us up. He'd believe anything at that time. Then the years just flew by. I'm asking you to be a little sympathetic. Not a lot." He laughs. "A little, all right?"

"Shut up, Dante." My mouth curls into a warm smile, my fingers wiping away stray tears lingering within my eyelashes.

"I missed you, dumbass," he throws in.

"Whatever, dweeb."

His laugh bellows through the line. "Raquel, Chiara's on the phone."

"Really?" She sounds excited. "It's safe to talk to her?"

"Yeah, but make it fast, baby. Just in case."

"Okay," she replies to him. "Chiara? Is that really you?"

I breathe in a sigh of relief. "It's me. Oh my God, I missed you! Are you okay?"

"I'm fine. I swear! I'm sure you have a million questions. But I met this guy, and he agreed to marry me to help me avoid marrying Carlito, and he needed a wife for business purposes. So here we are." She finally takes a breath. "It all happened so fast, and then I couldn't call you in case my family or Carlito could track us."

"Yeah, he told me the happy news. Is he treating you okay?"

That's all that matters to me. She can tell me the rest another time, when this is all over.

"He's wonderful. At first, I was nervous." Her voice drops to a whisper. "He's so hot, and he was technically my husband. I couldn't stop myself from resisting him anymore."

"You didn't!" I feign a gasp.

It feels like we're normal, gossiping about men like women do, but our situations are anything but normal.

"I did. A lot. And, yeah…" Her voice drifts off with a sigh. "He's so good at that."

"Well, okay, then. Glad you're…ah…having fun."

She giggles low. "I love you, and I can't wait to see you soon. If my family contacts you, don't tell them anything."

"Are you kidding? I'd never." I pause. "You sound happy." My lips pinch with a smile.

"I am. I only miss my job, but they're fine with me taking some extended time off. I told them I had a family emergency. I'd say being forced into a life I didn't want is an emergency." She lets out a dreary sigh. "I thought my life was over, Chiara. I really thought I'd have to marry that asshole or die. Now, I'm married to someone else. I know it's not supposed to last beyond our arrangement of three months, but…"

"But what?"

"What if it did? What if we stayed married? I mean, he's nice to me, and it feels like he genuinely cares." A heavy breath rushes out of her. "I sound insane, I know. I barely know him. It's only been just short of a month."

Wait, a month? Around the same time I was taken? Shit. I had no idea.

"You're not insane. You've been with him all this time, alone in that house. Things happen."

"I guess, yeah. I don't know what's going to happen with us, but I like it so far. Anyway, I should go in case they have the phones tapped, but we'll speak again soon. I love you."

"I love you too."

She hangs up, and I drop the phone on my bed. She's really okay. Dante wasn't lying.

I'm glad one of us may get their happiness. I don't think that's ever in the cards for me. But even still, with everything Dom has done, I want to hear him out. I think I need that closure, even if forgiving him might not be something I can do.

I arrive at Vixen promptly at seven, but I can't seem to make myself get out of the rental car. Remaining in the parking lot seems safer than what awaits inside.

It's not that I'm afraid of him. It's more that I fear for my heart and what he can do to it.

There's so much hidden beneath our wounds, so much shrouded by agony, yet still it's hard not to stare at it, to feel it in my bones.

The old Dom and Chiara are within the walls of our demise, waiting to find their freedom, waiting for what could've been.

Running my fingers through my pin-straight hair, I flip open the car mirror and look at my face. The dark brown shadows do a great job at concealing the puffy eyelids, but I still don't look like myself.

Closing the mirror, I exit the car and shut the door. My black stilettos click against the pavement as I near the club entrance. The parking area is near empty, except for a few cars. I doubt the place is even open at this time. Most dance clubs don't start until at least nine.

As I approach, a tall, fit man with a shaved head and black t-shirt greets me with a smile.

"Are you Chiara?" he asks as he palms the door handle, pushing it open.

"Yes, I am."

"Go right in, ma'am."

The entryway greets me, and I thank him before stepping inside.

The door shuts as my eyes adjust to the narrow, empty hallway. There's a window to my left with a sign that reads "coat check," but no one is there.

I keep walking, not sure where he is.

"Hey," he greets me from behind.

I gasp, my body hyperaware to the undercurrent of his power. His energy is all around me, his deep, raspy voice flipping my stomach erratically.

My heart races as I remain still, unable to look back, afraid I'll want to jump into his arms and feel them around me, keeping all the bad away.

But he was the one who was bad. He's the one who hurt me when I never thought he could.

"Why am I here?" I ask, my voice surer than my heart.

I whirl, gradually facing him, and my eyes widen just as my heart beats faster. It feels like I'm looking at him for the first time.

He's all grown up. Hard muscle and sharp, masculine edges have replaced the lanky boy I once knew. He's all man now.

My body grows warm as I take in his black shirt, the buttons practically popping off at the chest. I know what lies beneath his clothes, but at the time, I didn't know who it belonged to. Now that I do, I want to taste him as though for the very first time. And for me, I guess it would be.

He moves a step until only a slice of a hand separates our beating hearts. His eyes turn hooded, and his Adam's apple bobs as he gazes down at me, his tongue darting out, licking between his lips. It's as though we're thinking similar dirty thoughts.

"You're here because I missed you." His brows bend so hard, I can feel his anguish vibrating through my body. "And you being here tells me you missed me too."

He takes my hand, and I let him hold it. Let him feel my tingly skin, even if he can't feel the way he makes it come alive.

"I need you, Chiara." His eyes deepen into mine. "Please stay. Not just right now, but forever."

He lowers his mouth to my forehead, his lips leaving a kiss. My skin prickles in the wake of his affection, my heart hammering for a man it wants.

"I know we may not know each other anymore. Not like we used to." His soft words glide over my lips as his nose feathers over mine. "But I still feel you everywhere. Your laughter, our inside jokes, the way you'd lay your head on my shoulder when you were sad. Those memories...they're ours, Chiara."

Blinking back tears, I pull away enough to find his eyes staring back at me.

"I wish you would've talked to me." My voice seeps with emotion, the words tearing me apart.

His hands cup each side of my face. "I'm sorry, baby. For all of it." His eyes turn hazy, my words tearing him up too. "Forgive me."

"Dom." The word is a plea. For something I hope we can find, keep, and treasure for infinity.

"Chiara..." His gaze swims between my eyes and my lips.

My breaths fall faster, my chest falling in and out with the fastened beats of my heart. My eyes find his mouth, and as they do, his lips collide with mine. The feel of them, now knowing they belong to the boy I loved, makes this kiss different than any others we've shared.

This kiss, it's gripped from the ashes of our past and from the roots of our future.

My hand clutches the back of his neck, his clasped to my face, his thumbs rubbing over my damp cheeks. His lips move slowly, passionately, over mine, as though he wants to memorize every motion, every breath.

And knowing all the wild things his mouth can do, it's nice to know he can do this too: show me what I mean to him.

He drags his face away, his forehead slanting over mine, both of us panting.

"I didn't mean to do that," he says, swallowing harshly, his arms circling around the small of my back.

"That's too bad, because I wanted you to," I confess in a whisper as I move an inch.

My hands come around his neck, and as I stare at Dom, I realize I can't allow my father to take another thing away from me. My future is mine to create, and I want that future with this man right here.

"Does this mean you forgive me?" he asks, the depthless pools of his eyes searching mine.

My lips part as I gaze back at him, my heart swelling with so much of everything, it's hard to contain it all.

"I think I can try."

A heavy exhale slips out of his chest before reaching into his pocket, removing a black wallet.

I look at him, confused, and before I have a chance to ask him what he's doing, he removes something from inside. My eyes widen, and I let out a gasp as I see what's in his hand.

"You really kept it?" I ask through the blanket of tears now covering my vision.

"Of course I did." Half of the friendship necklace I gave him the day of his mom's funeral dangles from his hand. "I kept everything about us right here." He palms his chest. "I've never forgotten a single thing, even when it hurt to remember."

I reach a hand for the necklace, running a finger over the soft angles.

"I really can't believe you still have that. I know you said you did in the letter, but seeing it…" My voice cracks with a raw edge, tears drifting like the years we lost.

"I swore I'd never take it off," he says, his arm curving over my back, pulling me in. "It's with me everywhere I go. Reminding me of you."

"I wish I had mine," I confess.

He smiles, and it catches my breath. "You do."

"What? No." I shake my head, my brows bowing. "It's still at my house, in the—"

"Bowl by the picture of you and me," he finishes.

He drops his hand from around me, reaching into his pocket for the second time, pulling out the other half of my heart.

My trembling hand slowly nears my mouth. "You took it?"

"Yeah." He smirks. "Your panties weren't the only thing I stole."

I let out a laugh, remembering how pissed I was.

"I didn't want anything to happen to it in case your father went to the house," he explains.

"Put it on me," I tell him tenderly, smiling with happiness for the first time in a long time.

"I have a better idea." His face lights up, his dimple deepening with the curve of his lips. "Turn around."

When he fastens the necklace around my neck, I notice it isn't mine. It's his. *Dom* is written on the back of the pendant. As I face him again, I find him placing my half around his neck.

"Now you have a piece of my heart and I have yours," he says, his knuckles rolling down my cheek.

My heart lurches with a beat, waves of emotions settling into the center of my chest.

I reach for my pendant, running my fingers over it as his gaze captures mine. "I'll never take it off."

"Me neither," he swears.

"We probably look so childish," I laugh, biting the edge of my lower lip.

His palm fits over my cheek, the intensity in his gaze—gentle, yet hungry—pulling me in, owning my every breath.

"We probably do," he rasps, so deep I can practically feel it.

My pulse yanks at my heart; my stomach drops.

"Do you care, baby? Because I sure as fuck don't."

Then his lips crash to mine, taking me with a searing kiss. It's harsher, more demanding, this time. As though he wants to devour my lips, taking my body with them.

I'm lost to everything but the feel of his mouth moving with the flow of mine. His hand slides into my hair, the pads of his fingers rough against my scalp, his other hand grabbing my hip sharply into its palm.

Angling his face, he circles his tongue over mine, kissing me until it consumes us, while pushing me up against the wall with the strength of his body.

With his fingers woven through my hair, he pulls my head back, tracing his lips over my jaw, his teeth raking my skin before his tongue glides down my neck. His mouth skims past my shoulder, his finger slipping into the thin strap of my blue tank top, dragging it past my arm.

"Dom," I groan, unable to control the lust-induced ache between my legs.

"Fuck," he growls, his eyes pinning me with a fiery gaze. "I've been waiting for you to call me that. And now, hearing it…"

He tips up my chin with his thumb, his lips landing slowly over mine. Once. Twice. He grunts as he backs away, as though fighting the same desire I feel.

"I want you, Chiara. I want it all. But I don't want to fuck this up. I think we should go slow, even if it's the last thing I want."

His palm reaches for the back of my neck, holding on to me as he dips his mouth close to mine, making me crazy for another taste of him.

"I want to know you," he says, his breath flirting with mine. "All of you."

"I want to know you too." My reply comes with a hush, softly resonating between us.

"Then let's start right now." He moves back, giving me his hand, asking for mine. "This moment can be our new beginning."

"New beginnings," I say, twining my fingers with his as he leads me deeper into the club.

DOMINIC

THIRTY-SEVEN

When I told her to come, I never thought she would. We shared a private dinner with a chef I always use for private parties, and after that, I asked her to come back to my place. She accepted without hesitation, and I can't believe she's in my arms.

I don't remember the last time I was afraid of rejection. But with her, it messed me up.

But after I kissed her, it was like we formed a bond. I know I have a lot to make up for, and I plan on doing that every day I'm alive. I have my best friend back, the girl I loved more than anything, and I won't take our second chance for granted.

Closing my eyes, I roll my fingers up and down the smoothness of her arm, her head tucked against my chest. I never want this moment to end.

"I'm sorry I couldn't take you out on a proper date," I tell her. "My clubs are secure, and I couldn't risk your safety."

"I don't care where you take me, Dom. I don't need fancy restaurants. That's not what I'm about."

"I know that. But I want to give you everything. I want us to make up for all the dates we missed."

"We will." She grabs my hand, squeezing it in reassurance. "When the time's right."

"You're right, baby."

We're silent for a moment before I speak again.

"I'm almost sure I told you I'd have a driver pick you up. I don't want you driving around by yourself."

I knew Chiara well enough to know she wouldn't have accepted my offer to have a driver pick her up, but I had to try.

"I'm not afraid of them." She lifts up her head, peering into my eyes.

Shaking my head in frustration, I exhale a sharp sigh. "I know you're not, but I am. If anything happens to you..."

I can't even think of that shit.

"So take care of yourself for me, would you?"

"Nothing will happen to me." She places a palm against my cheek.

My mouth twitches with a smile. "Stubborn woman. But that's what makes you even more mine."

"Mmm, say that again," she moans, circling her arms around my neck as she lifts her hips off the sofa, straddling me, her pussy rubbing against my hard cock.

"Say what?" I groan, arching my pelvis up to make her feel what she does to me.

"You know what." Her voice quivers.

"You're making it so difficult to keep my promise of going

slow." I fist her hair, gripping it tight, peppering kisses down her neck.

"I can't wait to be with you, Dom." Her words stumble with a whimper. "My Dom."

"Fuck, baby. Say that again." I continue to devour her skin, her hips running circles over me.

"Say what?" she teases.

I pull her face close to mine, caught in her sultry gaze, and as she looks at me that way, I'm left wondering if she sees me as a monster for all the lives I've taken and all the lives I still have left to take. And though I don't want to hear the truth, terrified of it, I ask anyway.

"You know I'll have to kill them all, right?"

The question hangs in the air between us as she peers down at me.

"I do."

"Do you hate what I've become? A killer? Can you really handle who I am now, Chiara? It's okay if you can't."

That's a fucking lie. I won't be okay.

Her brows draw tight, her knuckles caressing my cheek. "I could never hate you, especially for that."

Relief hits me, and I clench my jaw to steady my emotions.

"I loved your family with all my heart," she confesses. "And knowing what my family did to Matteo..." Her eyes go dark, even as the tears drown them. "You do *whatever* needs to be done. And you make sure it hurts."

My eyes slam shut, grateful she gets it. We'll be hitting them again very soon. My men are working out the details.

"I love you, Chiara. More than anything in this world."

"I love you too, Dom," she breathes out. "I always have."

A sense of peace overcomes me.

Finally, I have her, not only as the love of my life, but a true partner in my plan for revenge. My plan that's only just beginning.

CHIARA
THREE DAYS LATER

THIRTY-EIGHT

"**H**ow the hell do you not know how to cook?" he asks as he takes out a pan, placing it on the stove. "I don't know." I cross my arms over my chest and narrow my eyes. "I just don't. Deal with it."

"How have you managed to survive on your own?" he teases, unscrewing a bottle of olive oil, adding a little to the now sizzling pan.

He throws in some minced garlic and ginger, the wooden spoon in his hand as he mixes.

"Takeout. Duh." I roll my eyes. "Sorry we don't all have a Sonia in our back pocket."

He chuckles. "I *do* cook. As you can see, she's off today." He winks.

"Oh, my. Your personal chef is off? Poor little you."

"Well, she's your chef now too, considering you live here."

I did basically move in. He purchased me a whole new wardrobe, a new car, and everything else I might ever need.

A smile curls over my lips while I skim over his muscular arms, calling for my hands. "Lucky me."

He pops a brow. "Don't look at me like that."

"Oh, yeah? What are you gonna do about it?"

His hand stills, his gaze drinking me into the emeralds of his eyes.

"If you knew all the things I want to do to your body right here on this floor…" His jaw stiffens, making the hollows beneath his cheekbones more pronounced.

My lips turn up along with my brow. "You should probably do it, then."

"Fuck, Chiara. I was trying to take things slow, but that's the last thing I want to do right now."

His words tease the space in between my thighs, giving me a little of what I crave.

He hasn't touched me, not in that way I want him to, and three days is long enough. I need him inside me. I want to connect with him in the way only we can.

For these past few days, we've been holed up in his house, talking, getting to know one another, revealing everything from our past.

When he described his experiences at the homeless shelters, I was sick to my stomach. I never imagined what he endured on top of losing the people closest to him.

I don't care what he does to my uncles. They deserve it. The blood we share no longer matters. All three of them are dead to me. I meant what I said to Dom. I hope he hurts them just as badly as they hurt him and his family.

Laura's death still haunts me. I can't get rid of the image of her burning alive in that car. My family has no mercy for anyone, so why should they get any in return?

Dom made a large contribution to the children's charity her family set up in her memory. She sounded like a beautiful person, always helping others. She ran a women's shelter for ten years. It's no wonder she wouldn't let me out of the car.

"Get your pretty ass over here." He stumbles through my thoughts. "We're cooking together."

"Okay," I agree, rising from the chair, strutting over to him. "But if I burn the shrimp, don't blame me."

He grabs my hips, pulling me flush into his solid body, his lips drifting over mine, the smell of his woodsy cologne permeating my senses.

"Don't worry..." He leans his lips even closer, until they skim over mine. "You'll make it up to me."

And just when I think he's going to kiss me, he draws back, smirking devilishly. He flips my body toward the stove, slapping my ass.

"Let's see what you've got, baby."

"Asshole," I mutter playfully.

"Mmm, keep talking," he groans, the hardness of his cock rocking over the small of my back.

"If you don't stop," I say, lifting the wooden spoon from the counter. "You may find me on my knees with your cock in my mouth."

He pulls in a sharp breath, and suddenly his fist is in my hair, pulling my head back.

"I'm done waiting," he promises with a hardened, hungry gaze.

I let out a moan, rubbing my ass on his hard-on.

His other hand grips my ass cheek, hidden beneath a pair of

thin black yoga shorts. He kneads my flesh, his eyes boring into mine.

"You want my cock inside you, baby?" His finger dips in between my ass cheeks, eliciting another moan. "You want me there too, don't you?"

"Yes. Fuck me, Dom," I beg.

"Pick up the bowl of shrimp and add it to the pan."

"Wha…?"

He lets go of my hair, and both hands are now on my hips.

"Turn the shrimp over until they start to get pink." His thumbs slip under my shorts, and he starts to pull them down past my ass. "After that, add the tomatoes."

"What are you—?"

"Do what I said."

His voice is an explosive cocktail, making my core throb for more.

"Don't burn it," he cautions, his lips dipping into the crook of my neck as he kisses and sucks.

My thighs press together as I lift the bowl full of shrimp. All the while, his hand creeps down my ass, cupping my pussy.

"Pull your thighs apart before I do it for you," he warns as I let out a whimper.

I flip the bowl into the pan just as my thighs do what he's commanded. I don't know how the hell I'm going to cook with him doing whatever he's about to do to me. I'm afraid I'll not only burn the food, but probably the both of us.

Just as I'm about to mix the shrimp, one finger glides between my slit, and I cry out in pleasure as he rubs a little, giving me only a taste of what he has in store.

He pinches my pussy lips, and I groan, needing more.

"I didn't tell you to stop. Keep stirring."

My legs grow weak, my heartbeats falling faster, even as I do what he says.

"Good girl." His hand leaves my core, and the next thing I know, his arm is lifting my leg and draping it over his shoulder.

I pant as I glance down, finding him on his knees, his eyes on mine. But his lips, his tongue, are where his fingers have just been. He takes a swipe, outlining the shape of my lips, and I gasp, my knees trembling, my hand almost about to drop the spoon.

"If you stop, I stop," he threatens, his gaze daring me to disobey.

That only makes me grow wetter. I like this side of him. The dominating side. I need it. I want it.

His mouth is on me, feasting on every inch, his tongue entering me while his thumb plays with my clit. I keep mixing with stuttered motions, moaning while my eyes roll back to my head.

I want to feel him enter me, stretching me fully, completely. The more he works me, the more I'm pushed over the edge.

He stops, and I moan in frustration.

"Dom, damn it. I need to come."

"Are the shrimp done yet?" he asks casually, not like a man who smells and tastes like me.

"I...ah...um...I think so."

"Add the tomatoes."

I do it immediately, tossing them right in just as his tongue flicks my clit, two fingers inside me, curling into my G-spot.

"Oh, fuck. Yesss..." I gasp, my hand grabbing the edge of the counter, the spoon whipping in my other hand.

He pumps harder, his fingers driving into the most sensitive part of me, his tongue picking up pace to the rhythm of my hand stirring the food, unable to sustain speed.

I'm falling, aching for release.

One more touch of his tongue, and my orgasm explodes.

"Yes!" I cry as the overflowing wave of passion hits me like a grenade, the spoon falling onto the floor. My hands clutch the cold granite, lucky I didn't accidentally reach for the stove.

He takes his time, devouring me until every ounce of pleasure is on his tongue. Standing up, he curls a hand around my front, gripping my arms tight, my body molded into his. He reaches over, shutting off the stove, and yanks me backward until we hit the table behind us.

He spins me around to face him, his fierce gaze searching mine. "You taste so damn good."

"That was...wow," I pant, my chest falling frantically with uneven breaths. "I need you. Right now. I can't wait another moment to feel you."

He groans, his hand gripping the back of my head, his eyes dipping wildly from my eyes down to my mouth before his arms come around my hips and I'm lifted off the floor.

He kisses my stomach, inhaling my scent as he sets me on the floor, my back over the cold porcelain tiles.

"Do I need a condom?" he asks, his voice deep and gravelly as he stands over me.

And the sight of him—the flexing of his muscles, the dominating way he looks at me like I'm a meal he's about to devour—is so erotic, my hand brushes in between my breasts. It slinks lower, falling in between my thighs, touching myself, watching him watching me.

"No." I shake my head, my hips circling the floor, needing him inside me.

"Good girl," he growls with approval, undoing his belt buckle.

It clinks, the sound reverberating through the room, arousing me even more.

"You're so damn gorgeous." His words are an echo of worship, his eyes a silent praise.

I smile, his compliment giving me the courage to sit up and lift the black tank top off my body.

"Fuck," he mutters as he pulls the zipper down, his gaze feasting on my breasts, then his pants and boxers fall to the ground. He steps out of them, taking off his shirt.

I lick my lips, my heart pounding as I take in his chiseled abs flexing beneath his tanned skin.

Holy hell, he's really mine.

With our eyes locked, he lowers down onto the floor, grabbing my knees and pulling me closer. His body falls on top of mine, and the feel of his strength pushing into me drives me wild.

My hand wraps around the back of his head, and his gaze keeps me warm. I can practically feel the love pouring over me.

"It's you and me from now on, baby," he promises. "No one will come between us. I won't let them."

"Never." I shake my head, the moan slipping from my mouth, the raspy tone of his voice lighting a fire in my belly, spreading into every space in my body.

He kisses me softly, then comes back up onto his knees, spreading my thighs before positioning the tip of his cock against my wet entrance.

"I love you," he swears. "I love you more than I can say. More than you can understand."

"Show me." I rock my hips around his bulging erection. "Let me feel it."

And without taking his eyes off of mine, he thrusts inside me, filling me completely.

We both groan, slick with desire, as he picks up the pace, his body working me harder.

Faster.

Deeper.

My body comes alive, my core clenching, aching around him, another orgasm catching flight.

"Yes, that's it, baby. Pull my cock deeper into that pussy."

He lifts both of my thighs, bending them until my knees touch my chest.

"Oh, fuck, you feel so good," he growls, hitting me with punishing strokes.

My nails claw at the floor, the need building until my entire body trembles, until I can't hold on.

He pulls out, and I scream in protest, but suddenly his fingers are inside me, three of them, curling into me, fucking me so hard, it's like an out-of-body experience.

"Yeah, that's it, baby. I want it pouring out of you."

"Wha...t? I never..."

He pumps my pussy harder, gritting his teeth. "Yeah, you can. I know you can."

He puts in another finger, thrusting against my spot, and before I realize what's happening, I come.

"Oh...my...yesss!"

It all rushes out of me, raining over my body, over him. I want to feel self-conscious, embarrassed, but I don't. He stares at me as though he's staring down at his most prized possession.

He smirks. "I told you, you can fuckin' do it. And you're gonna do it again."

Before I have a chance to protest, his cock slides back inside, fucking me until his orgasm builds, until mine crests to a new high.

And when he comes, so do I, more powerfully than the last time.

"Goddamn, baby. I could watch you do that all day."

When the tremors in my body still, I lie there, naked, unable to speak, and he scoops me up on top of him.

"I should probably get us to a bed, or at least a carpet."

"Mm-hmm," I mutter, the pleasure still coursing through me.

"See, you didn't burn anything." I hear the laughter in his words.

"No, but I think I burned my ass from how hard you fucked me."

"Turn around. Let me make sure that sexy ass is in one piece."

As his hand slides down to my core, his phone vibrates on the counter. He ignores it, playing me like his favorite toy. But then the cell buzzes immediately after.

"Go get it," I tell him.

"I'm busy." He sinks a finger inside me, and I whimper.

It vibrates again.

"Just get the damn thing," I groan in frustration, lifting up my head.

"I'll be two seconds." He kisses me on the tip of my nose before jumping to his feet.

"What is it, Dante?"

At his brother's name, I sit up. After all, my cousin is living with him.

Dom's eyes land on me, but there's something there. Something off.

"Mm-hmm. When?"

A second passes.

"Okay. Get the team ready. I'm coming."

I put my shirt back on as I stand. "What's going on?"

He gestures with a finger, indicating he needs a minute. "We'll find her. Don't worry. He'll pay."

An icy shudder runs down my arms, a knot forming in my stomach, growing larger, overtaking my thoughts.

Something bad happened to Raquel. I know it.
He hangs up, and the look in his eyes is troubled.
"Tell me," I demand. "What happened to her?"
He inhales sharply, picking up his clothes and getting dressed. "I don't want you to worry."
"Tell me, God damn it!" Anger clouds my vision. "Who has her?"
"Carlito," he says softly, reaching for my hand, rubbing a thumb over mine.
"Oh, God!"
My breath hitches, gasping with a shallow breath.
"If he knows she married another man, he's going to kill her," I sob. "If he hasn't already."
"She's still alive," he explains. "That's what Dante said."
"You have to save her. Please!"
"I will do *everything*, baby. I swear it."
"How did he get to her?" I ask.
He glances down onto the floor before peering up again. "She stepped out of the house, and a van took her."
"I fucking told him to tell her everything! She must've run. This is all my fault!" I yank my hand away, covering my eyes.
"No, it's not," he says softly. "We don't even know what happened. Dante didn't tell me much else."
I sob, wiping away tears. "When are we going after him?"
There's no way I won't be there.
"Chiara..." He tilts his head to the side, his gaze tender.
"What?" My tone turns sharp.
"Baby, you have to stay here."
"Absolutely not! I'm coming with you."
"You're not."
"I'm not going to stand around worried for her. For you, all of

you. No!"

"Baby, I will use every resource at my disposal to bring her back safely." He tucks the back of his hand under my chin, his eyes level with mine. "But I can't do that when I'm worrying about you."

My eyes water over.

"My men will be here. You'll be safe."

I hate this. I should be there, but I refuse to put the man I love in any more danger.

"Find her. Bring her back," I say, my voice an anguished whisper.

"I will. I swear."

But what if he can't?

"I love you, Chiara. Remember that."

I draw back.

"No!" I shake my head desperately. "Don't make it sound like you're saying goodbye."

He remains silent for only a moment, taking in the pain written in my eyes.

"I've never cared about coming back alive. But for once, I do." He leans down, rubbing his mouth over mine, kissing me desperately. "I'm not done loving you."

I reach for the necklace still around his neck, gripping the half of the heart in my palm.

"You'd better not be." My voice lodges with a heavy wave of emotion.

He reaches for the heart dangling from my neck and holds it tight. "I have to go, baby. Dante's waiting."

I nod, tears tripping over one another. "Go."

He backs away, but his eyes can't seem to part from mine.

"When I come back, we're making macaroons together." A

smile flits over his lips.

I try to return one. "I'd love to see that happen."

He winks, mouthing *I love you* before he turns, jogging for the door.

And as I hear it shut, I miss him already.

I've welcomed him into my body and let him take my heart. And now, I'm left wondering what the future holds.

For all of us.

THANKS FOR READING!

If you can spare an honest review, I'd appreciate it. They help a lot!

ALSO BY LILIAN HARRIS

Fragile Hearts Series

1. *Fragile Scars*
2. *Fragile Lies*
3. *Fragile Truths*
4. *Fragile Pieces*

Cavaleri Brothers Series

1. *The Devil's Deal*
2. *The Devil's Pawn*
3. *The Devil's Secret*
4. *The Devil's Den*
5. *The Devil's Demise*

PLAYLIST

- "The Beginning of the End" by Klergy and Valerie Broussard
- "Play With Fire" by Sam Tinnesz feat. Yacht Money
- "Madness" by Ruelle
- "War of Hearts (Acoustic Version)" by Ruelle
- "Here Come the Monsters" by Adona
- "Revolution" by Unsecret and Ruelle
- "Get Free" by Whissell
- "Devil's Playground" by The Rigs
- "Saving All My Love" by Empara Mi
- "Scorpio" by Pour Vous
- "Pay" by Ramsey
- "Where We Rise" by Neoni
- "Warfare" by Katie Garfield
- "Wild" by John Legend feat. Gary Clark Jr.
- "Minefields" by Faouzia feat. John Legend
- "Daddy" by Ramsey
- "Vices" by Mothica
- "Kiss Me, Kill Me" by Ari Hicks
- "Cinderella" by Wens
- "Forest Fire" by Wens
- "Bite" by Troye Sivan
- "How Villains Are Made" by Madalen Duke
- "Nightmares" by Ellise
- "You Better Run" by Unions
- "Walk Through Fire" by Zayde Wølf feat. Ruelle
- "Sinners and Saints" by Andrea Wasse

- "In the Shadows" by Amy Stroup
- "Never Surrender" by Liv Ash
- "I Do" by Aloe Blacc
- "Vendetta" by Unsecret feat. Krigaré
- "Easy on Me" by Adele
- "Still Into You" by Hannah Trigwell
- "Death of Me" by Julien Kelland

ACKNOWLEDGEMENTS

As I write this, it's my two-year publishing anniversary. I'm beyond ecstatic to be a part of this community. Thank you to the readers who've stuck by me, even when I decided to write something a little different. Thank you to the new readers who've given me a shot. I'll always give you stories that speak to me, and the Cavaleri brothers haven't stopped talking for years now.

Thanks Carmen for being an awesome editor! I'm so happy we connected back in 2019! Also, thank you to Judy, my proofreader, and Dee of Black Widow Designs for my gorgeous cover! You brought my vision to life.

To my beta readers and bloggers, thanks for your support and continued help. I value your time so much, you have no idea!

And Ainsley, I loved your name suggestion for the heroine's aunt! Aunt Kirsten it is. Thank you!

Lastly, to my husband and my kids, thanks for not throwing my laptop out the window yet.

Lilian Harris

For Lilian, a love of writing began with a love of books. From *Goosebumps* to romance novels with sexy men on the cover, she loved them all. It's no surprise that at the age of eight she started writing poetry and lyrics and hasn't stopped writing since.

She was born in Azerbaijan, and currently resides in Long Island, N.Y. with her husband, three kids, and a dog named Gatorade. Even though she has a law degree, she isn't currently practicing. When she isn't writing or reading, Lilian is baking or cooking up a storm. And once the kids are in bed, there's usually a glass of red in her hand. Can't just survive on coffee alone!

Lilian would love to connect with you!

Email: lilanharrisauthor@gmail.com
Website: www.lilanharris.com
Newsletter: https://bit.ly/LilianHarrisNews
Signed Paperbacks: https://bit.ly/LHSignedPB
Facebook: www.facebook.com/LilianHarrisBooks
Reader Group: www.facebook.com/groups/lilianslovlies
Instagram: www.instagram.com/lilianharrisauthor
TikTok: www.tiktok.com/@lilianharrisauthor
Twitter: www.twitter.com/authorlilian
Goodreads: https://bit.ly/LilianHarrisGR
Amazon: www.amazon.com/author/lilianharris

Printed in Great Britain
by Amazon